SUPERDREADNOUGHT 6

SUPERDREADNOUGHT 6

SUPERDREADNOUGHT™ BOOK SIX

CH GIDEON   CRAIG MARTELLE   JULIA HUNI

MICHAEL ANDERLE

DISRUPTIVE IMAGINATION®

We can't write without those who support us
On the home front, we thank you for being there for us

We wouldn't be able to do this for a living if it weren't for our readers
We thank you for reading our books

Copyright © 2019 by Craig Martelle & Michael Anderle writing as CH Gideon
Cover by Luca Oleastri, Typography by Jeff Brown
Cover copyright © LMBPN Publishing
A Michael Anderle Production

LMBPN Publishing
PMB 196, 2540 South Maryland Pkwy
Las Vegas, NV 89109

First US edition, November 2019
eBook ISBN: 978-1-64202-565-1
Print ISBN: 978-1-64202-566-8

SUPERDREADNOUGHT 6 TEAM

Thanks to our Beta Readers

James Caplan
Kelly O'Donnell
Micky Cocker
John Ashmore

Thanks to the JIT Readers

Jackey Hankard-Brodie
Dave Hicks
Peter Manis
Shari Regan
Diane L. Smith
Misty Roa
Jeff Goode
Deb Mader
Micky Cocker
John Ashmore
James Caplan
Kelly O'Donnell

If I've missed anyone, please let me know!

Editor
Lynne Stiegler

CHAPTER ONE

The Superdreadnought *Reynolds* lurked behind a convenient moon, sensors locked on a large ship drifting slowly through the Dorayas system. "Renegades. Pirates. Scum," a voice mumbled from the captain's seat.

"Delivering Justice one last time, Captain Reynolds?" the first officer, Jiya Lemaire, asked.

The captain stood. "It is time to head home. Take what we've learned back to my Queen. We will tell her of the Phraim-'Eh clan's destruction and that the Kurtherian has long since moved on. We will report, then we will follow the Kurtherians to the ends of the universe.

"The pirates are powering up their systems. An intrasystem freighter has left the orbit of the fourth planet."

The captain faced the screen. "Prepare to engage on my order."

"Blow the fuck out of those bad guys!" a voice cried joyously from the tactical station.

"You need to rethink the words that come out of your

mouth." Jiya covered her face with her hand and bit her lip to keep from laughing.

"Weapons are live," Tactical stated emotionlessly before returning to his real self. "For the record, I don't have a mouth. Mouthy, yes. Mouth, no. Dumbass."

Jiya rolled her eyes so far she almost fell backward.

"Engage." Reynolds skipped the banter and focused like a laser on the pirate ship. The SD *Reynolds* surged sunward and dove on the pirates. "Fire."

Tactical responded by sending a stream of hypervelocity projectiles toward the enemy, followed by two missiles and a series of laser beams.

The lasers hit first, scorching the hull and cutting deep into one of the ship's four engines. The railgun projectiles hit next, stitching across the wide midsection of the cigar-shaped ship. The pirate turned to run, but it was already belching fire from the hull breaches. The flames flashed, then died, extinguished when cut off from the oxygen supply within. The ship moved in slow motion, an easy target for the missiles that accelerated to impact.

They slammed into the ship. The violence of their arrival was enough to kill the ship, but when they exploded, they tore the pirate vessel apart, turning it into a mini supernova. The *Reynolds'* screen darkened for a moment, lightening once the flash was gone.

As was the ship. Jiya waved at the freighter as it continued toward its destination. The freighter didn't acknowledge the assistance that *Reynolds* had provided, but it was still the right thing to do. The superdreadnought sailed past the ruins of the pirates for a victory lap around the sun on their way out of Dodge.

"With one last act, we leave the Chain galaxy behind," Reynolds said, legs spread wide, fists jammed onto his hips. He'd seen the stance on one of the old-style video programs. It was supposed to be a power pose, but he didn't feel the power. Maybe someone else was supposed to be intimidated. As intelligent as he was, some things the warm-blooded, sentient creatures did made no sense.

He continued, "Comm, give me ship-wide broadcast, please."

"Go," the empty seat at the communications station reported.

"When we arrived here more than a year ago, we were attacked. Since then, we have been welcomed less often than we were attacked. We helped people and were helped. We've made incredible allies, and for them alone, the battles and this trip was worth it." The captain nodded to his alien first officer, as human as any human he'd ever worked with, but not human. Just like him. They made a good team.

"I think it's time to take back everything we've learned. Allow the other ships of the Queen's fleet to upgrade with the technology we've acquired. Learn how the Federation has evolved. We return to High Tortuga, comfortable that we have eliminated a swath of Kurtherian influence, substituting the Justice and peace that comes from Queen Bethany Anne. We will, of course, drop anyone off who wants to remain here, and you have my sincere appreciation for all you've done. For those willing to join us on our trip, you are in for a great ride. I hope this is what you signed up for because you are going to see some eye-popping shit!

First Officer, canvass the crew and see who we need to let off."

Music started playing from Tactical's position, soft at first—the opening riff to Black Sabbaths' *Iron Man*. It built in intensity until Jiya was holding her hands over her ears. Reynolds drew a finger across his throat and the volume dropped, but the music played on.

"I thought maintenance had completed the repairs? I think they missed something in the comm system. Maybe some kind of large, hungry, metal rodent."

"That was music, you heathen!" Tactical called, turning it up again.

The metal cut off, and a plaintive fiddle cried out through the bridge. "Now, *that's* music," the XO said from the empty chair.

Jiya clapped her free hand over her ear, her coffee sloshing. "Stop torturing whatever animal that is!"

"Enough," Reynolds said. The music stopped.

"Home?" Jiya asked, Reynolds' request of her finally registering, making a sour face. "I don't want to go back to Lariest. Where you go, I go."

"Home? Loran?" Asya asked, striding through the door with Ria and Maddox on her heels. "I don't think so."

"Good enough for me." Reynolds turned to Asya, Ria, and Maddox as they strode onto the bridge. "What about the rest of you? You all said you want to continue the adventure with me. Are you having second thoughts?"

The four crew members shook their heads. "No, sir!" they cried in unison.

"You won't get rid of us that easily," Jiya said. "Let me verify with the rest of the crew."

Jiya went to the comm station and tapped a few buttons to open the ship-wide broadcast. "If anyone wants to get off the ship, you have fifteen seconds to tell me. You would already know if you did, so that's why I'm not giving anyone time to waffle." She counted down. No one signaled her. "Done. Prepare to Gate across the universe."

"You meatbags just warm my heart," Tactical said.

"Stow it, Tactical." Reynolds sat in the command chair. "Ensign Alcott, Navigation will send you the coordinates for the Devon system."

"Stations, people," XO said. "Sound General Quarters. Battlestations."

"If we're headed home, do we really need to be at battlestations?" Jiya asked. "I thought this place you're from is safe."

Asya shook a finger at her. "Haven't we learned anything? We always bring up the shields and go to battlestations before making a jump."

Jiya rolled her eyes but strapped herself into her chair. She gulped the last of her coffee and slid the mug into the cupholder she'd had Takal install at her place. "I'm ready," she said to the room at large.

"I guess we can go now," Tactical said. "Her Majesty, the first officer, is ready."

"All systems are green. All hands confirmed at battlestations," XO announced.

"Sir, we're seeing high levels of solar activity in the primary," Maddox announced.

Reynolds shrugged. "Can't be worse than what we saw at Muultu."

"Not worse," Maddox said, slowly. "But different. This

star is somewhat unstable. Takal says it's normal fluctuations for the Dorayas system. Likelihood of negative impact to our ship is extremely low."

"Then why'd you bother bringing it up?" Tactical snapped.

Reynolds glared at Tactical's workstation. "He brought it up because it's his job. If you'd stick to yours, we'd all be better off." He looked around the bridge. "Report."

"Course set," Ria said. "Gate activated. Ready to go home, Captain?"

"Make it so, Ensign." Reynolds' lips quirked. That never got old.

A brilliant light flashed through the bridge, blinding them. Static frizzed through the speakers.

"What the fuck—" Reynolds swiped his android eyes, but white splotches filled his vision. "Report!"

"I can't see anything!" Ria cried, panic in her voice.

"Me neither," Jiya said. "What was that?"

"Comm, cut the static!" Reynolds ordered.

"I'm on it," Comm replied. "I'm not sure— Wait, here we go." The white noise faded.

"Damage report!" Reynolds said.

Jiya looked at her screens, or tried to. "I can't see my screen, Captain. That flash—it's not permanent, is it?"

"Since I don't know what it was, I can't answer that," Reynolds said. "Would someone *without* eyes give me a damage report?"

"No damage," Comm said. "No injuries, all systems nominal."

"Maybe no one can see well enough to report damage," Jiya muttered.

"The automated systems are showing nominal," Comm repeated, his tone affronted.

"Until we hear otherwise, we'll assume no physical damage," Reynolds repeated. The white blurs turned to sparkles, then his vision cleared. The bridge looked the same as always, except the physical crew were rubbing their eyes.

"That was a solar flare," the XO said.

"Not just a solar flare," Takal's voice came through the speakers from his lab. "A *huge* solar flare. High-energy gamma particles. Fortunately, the shields deflected most of the radiation. My instruments are showing a small spike within the ship, but the external probes pegged into the red."

"Why didn't you see it coming?" Reynolds demanded. "Don't those things take time to get from the sun to the planetary orbit?"

"We saw the solar activity, but as I told Maddox, there's nothing unusual about that here," Takal said. "Since the Dorayans live inside the planet, they haven't studied the phenomenon. They have no satellites monitoring the star, so we had little historical data to go on. Gamma particles travel close to the speed of light, so if we'd been watching closely, we *might* have had a few seconds' warning. But the ship's shields are designed to protect us from gamma rays. I don't know why they didn't stop the light show. Maybe this flare was just too much?"

"If it didn't damage us... It didn't damage us, right?" Reynolds swung around to look at Jiya.

The first officer shook her head as she squinted at her screen. "No casualties. No reports of damage, except to some of Takal's specialized external sensors. Looks like we have replacements in storage for those, but all the rest are intact. Should only take a few minutes to replace Takal's."

"Comm," Reynolds started, "contact the Dorayans and ask if they require assistance. We'll have the sensors replaced when we get to High Tortuga."

"Uh, Captain?" Ria whispered.

"That might be difficult," Comm said.

"Captain?" Ria said again.

"Difficult how, Comm? You said there was no damage. Contact the Dorayans."

"Captain!" Ria's yell came out in a strangled squeal.

"What is it, Ensign?" Reynolds snapped.

"Comm can't contact the Dorayans," she gulped audibly, "because we already Gated. During the flare."

"I was trying to tell him," Comm said.

"Great!" Reynolds rubbed his hands together. "Contact High Tortuga and tell them we're home."

"High Tortuga is not responding on normal channels," Comm said.

"Captain, we aren't—" Ria started, her voice still choked.

"Ensign, just spit it out!" Asya said. "What are you trying to tell us?"

"I don't know where we are," Ria wailed. "The system doesn't recognize this location."

"Navigation!" Reynolds snapped. "What's the problem? Where the fuck are we?"

Navigation didn't answer immediately.

"Navigation?"

"We're not in Kansas anymore."

"I don't know where Kansas is," Asya said. "So, it doesn't matter if we aren't there. Where *are* we?"

"I've run an analysis of the local stars, and there is a zero-point-zero-three percent correlation with any known galaxies," Navigation reported. A starfield appeared on the big screen, with red and blue flashes of data appearing and disappearing as the system measured distances between the stars. "Since the margin of error for my system is zero-point-zero-eight percent, that means I have no idea where we are."

For a heartbeat—if he'd had one—Reynolds stared at the screen. Then he nodded. "Comm, get Takal up here. And Geroux. We need to figure out where we are, so I know where to go."

"Why don't we just activate the Gate and go to High Tortuga?" Jiya asked.

"The system has to know where it is in relation to where it wants to go," Ria explained. "If we knew High Tortuga was nine thousand light-years that way," she pointed randomly, "then we could go. But we need to know what direction and how far before we activate the Gate. To do that, we need to know where we're starting from."

The doors opened, and Takal Durba hurried in. He worked in the lab most days, where he'd modified and improved the technology they'd collected in their adventures across the Chain Galaxy, including the agroprinters from Grindlevik 3 and the Gulg transporters. His niece, Geroux, followed him onto the bridge.

"Geroux, Takal," Reynolds called out. "Work with Alcott and Navigation to figure out where we are. Maddox, Asya, keep a sharp eye on the scanners. We're in a potentially hostile environment. The rest of you, run diagnostics on everything. I want to know exactly what those gamma rays did to me. I mean, my ship."

He was supposed to be on his way home to a hero's welcome and a nice warm berth in the Medusa shipyards. The thought of seeing the Queen after all this time made him feel like a star-struck teen—or at least what he assumed a star-struck teen would feel like. He could lay his victory and his spoils at her feet and have a well-earned rest. Then he would head out into the void again, doing what he was built to do: burn Kurtherians from the skies.

Instead, he was stuck here in the middle of nowhere, trying to find his way home like a lost puppy. Hardly the victorious return he'd anticipated. He stomped around the circumference of the bridge, glaring at every crew member he passed.

He stopped at Navigation. "Anything?" he growled.

Geroux looked up, wide-eyed. She'd grown used to Reynolds' quirks, but she'd never seen him prowl like a caged animal before. It made her nervous.

"Leave them alone, Reynolds," Jiya said, coming to her friend's rescue. "They can't get anything done if you're pouncing on them every three minutes and twenty-seven seconds."

"It was three minutes and twenty-two seconds this time," Tactical said. "He's slipping."

"Fine!" Reynolds threw up his hands. "Jiya, you have the conn. Call me when you figure it out." He stomped off the bridge.

"Reynolds to the bridge." Comm's voice echoed through the ship.

Reynolds, passing the door to the bridge for the fifty-seventh time, turned and stormed in. "Did you do it? Where are we? Have you laid in a course for High Tortuga?"

Asya held up both hands. "We can't answer *all* those questions at once."

"Sure, you can," Reynolds said, throwing himself into the captain's chair. "The answers are yes, here, and yes."

"It's not that simple," Jiya said.

"Why not?" Reynolds asked, his voice quiet and deadly.

"Because—" Jiya started, but Takal stepped forward.

"We have located our current position in relation to the Chain Galaxy." The old man looked at the android. "You aren't going to like this."

"Just tell him already!" Tactical moaned. "Stop drawing it out like the previews to a reality TV show!"

Takal gave Reynolds a blank look.

Reynolds waved a hand, telling him to ignore the other AI personality and continue.

The scientist nodded at his niece. She activated the big screen to show a familiar starscape and a picture of the SD *Reynolds*. "This is Dorayas. We believe some unknown component in the Dorayas solar flare interacted with the Gate drive at the moment of jump." Lines flashed out from the depiction of Dorayas and hit the simulated Gate, causing it to spin. "It didn't actually spin. That's artistic liberty." Onscreen, the ship sailed into the spinning Gate and zinged around like a pinball. "It multiplied the effect of the Gate technology, throwing us farther than expected."

"I'm so glad you took the time to design these lovely graphics," Reynolds ground out, his teeth clenched in an effort to keep from screaming. "But where the fuck are we?"

Takal flicked his fingers, and the view zoomed out. A green arrow appeared, pointing to Dorayas. "As you can see, this is where we were." The screen zoomed out again. The arrow stayed the same size, but the Dorayas system shrank until it was a miniscule point in a fuzzy cluster of white: the Chain Galaxy. "This," a blue arrow appeared on the left side, pointing to a spiral of stars. "Is where we were trying to go. The Devon system. And this—" The screen zoomed out and out until the two galaxies were a tiny smudge in the top-right corner of the screen. A red arrow appeared in the bottom-left corner. "This is where we are."

CHAPTER TWO

The crew stared at the screen in silence.

"That...we...what?" Asya spluttered.

"Are you saying we're a billion light-years off course?" Reynolds asked, his voice deadly quiet.

"One-point-zero-two-six-five-billion light-years, to be exact," Takal said. "Well, not exact, but more precise."

"The margin for error is about—" Navigation began.

"At this distance, I think Takal's estimate is close enough," Reynolds said. "At our current maximum Gate distance, it's going to take a hundred thousand jumps to get home."

"Unless we can replicate the multiplication effect!" Geroux said. "If we can figure out how that flare multiplied our distance, maybe we can work out a way to replicate it."

Takal nodded. "Gulg technology increases the distance we can communicate. Maybe we can use a similar process to increase our Gate distance."

"Great, get on that," Reynolds said. "In the meantime, let's start for home. Ensign Alcott, calculate the first jump."

"Yes, sir," Ria said, jumping into her seat.

While the crew reported status across the ship, Reynolds slumped in his chair. This delay would cost them years if Takal couldn't figure out how to increase their reach. He felt a need to be home now.

"Coordinates calculated and locked in," Ria said.

"Are you ready to proceed?" the XO asked.

"Make it so," Reynolds said, but this time he felt no pleasure at the words.

"All systems are green. All hands confirmed at battlestations," the XO said. "Activate the Gate, Ensign."

The Gate opened, and the ship sailed through the wormhole. Stars shifted as they entered the new reality.

"How quickly can we go again?" Reynolds asked.

"As soon as the next set of coordinates is entered," the XO said. "Navigation, I hope you've started plotting those."

"Way ahead of you!" Navigation said. "I've got us plotted back to High Tortuga already. But unless you want to get lost again, I suggest we take the time to make sure we landed where we think we did."

"And did we?" Reynolds asked, adding a human-sounding sigh. As an android, he didn't breathe, but he'd been experimenting with the non-verbal noises humans made.

"Uh, no, sir," Ria said, her voice shaking. "We're only six light-years from our previous location."

"What? Why?" Reynolds jumped up from his seat, unable to stay still.

"I don't know why, sir," Ria said. "But readings of the local stars show we only moved six light-years."

"Comm, get Takal back up here!" Reynolds snapped.

"He's on his way," Comm said.

"At six light-years per jump," Navigation began, "returning to High Tortuga will take approx—"

"Shut up!" the entire crew yelled.

"I've started diagnostics on the Gate drive," Takal said as he hurried onto the bridge, staring at a wrist computer. "It looks like micro-abrasions on the cerebral cortex impeded our Gate distance."

"Can we fix it?" Reynolds asked.

Takal hemmed and hawed for a moment. "We can, but we're going to need some materials we don't carry on the ship."

"Maybe we can call for help," Jiya suggested. "The Gulg might be willing to bring us what we need. Or transport it to us."

"Good idea." Reynolds turned to Comm. "Get on the horn."

"I've already tried to contact Xyxl," Takal said. "I thought he'd be interested in the modifications to the Gate drive. But we're too far away to reach him."

"I thought Gulg tech was supposed to allow us to talk to anyone in the universe!" Jiya said.

Takal grimaced. "That might have been a slight exaggeration. No one imagined we'd ever get this far away. I sent a message to Xyxl, but I predict it will take about three years to reach him."

"I'm picking up unusual signals," Maddox said.

"What kind of signals?" Reynolds asked.

"I hope it's some Kurtherian butt to kick," Tactical, who'd been uncharacteristically quiet, called.

"I'm not sure," Maddox said. "Putting it on speaker now."

A low keening filled the bridge, curling the hairs on the back of Jiya's neck. "What is that?"

The moan slid up into a shriek.

"That sounds like something being tortured," Jiya said.

"That's what you said about my music," Tactical muttered.

"We've got incoming!" Jiya stabbed a finger at her screen.

"We're ready for them," the XO said. "Gravitic shields at full power."

"Comm, try to make contact," Reynolds said. "Ria, prepare to maneuver. Tactical, warm up the weapons systems."

"Railguns online," Tactical said instantly. "Can I activate the ESD?"

"No! Not yet," Reynolds amended. "We're in a galaxy we know nothing about. We won't fire on anyone unless they fire on us first. And we never use the ESD as a first resort. Last resort only. Are you yanking my chain? If I had a chain, I'd think you were yanking it."

"Or if they're Kurtherians," Tactical stuck in.

"If the Kurtherians have gotten this far, we're in bigger trouble than we thought," Reynolds said. "Report!"

"We have three unidentified ships, sir," Maddox said. "Two destroyer-sized chasing a smaller vessel."

"I'm getting a response from the smaller ship," Comm said, "but the translators are having difficulty with the signal."

"The destroyers are firing!" Jiya said. "Hit!"

The moaning through the speakers spiked into another shriek.

"That's coming from the smaller ship," Comm said.

"Is that the signal you're trying to translate?" Asya asked.

"No, that sound is coming from the ship itself," Comm said. "I'm getting another signal from inside, presumably from the crew. Nothing from the attackers."

The ship screamed again, then the noise dropped to a whimper.

"Another direct hit!" Jiya cried. "The smaller ship is not firing back. I-I think it's hurt."

"Disabled?" Reynolds asked.

"No, although it is slowing." Jiya shook her head. "But I think that sound is the ship getting hurt. Destroyers are firing again—" The scream of the ship interrupted her.

"I've got a translation. The smaller craft is sending a mayday!" Comm said. "Putting it onscreen."

"Tactical, get me a firing solution on those two destroyers," Reynolds said. "I want them disabled the moment they're in range."

"Wahooo!" Tactical howled. "Enemy targeted. They'll be in range in ten...nine..."

The viewscreen cleared, and a quadrupedal being appeared on the screen. Its head and shoulders were roughly humanoid, but its lower body resembled a lion. Bandages decorated its arm and both front legs, with a pale, silvery fluid leaking through. A long, thin tail whipped back and forth in apparent agitation.

"This is Captain Xonera of the partnership *Threfol*. We

are under attack! Terubine destroyers are injuring the *Threfol*. We require immediate assistance!"

"Two...one. Destroyers in range!" Tactical cried. "Blasting those cockwombles from the skies!"

"Targets at your convenience, Tactical," Reynolds ordered. "Ensign, prepare for evasive maneuvers."

"Firing!" Tactical sang. Lasers lanced across the void, slamming into the destroyer's shields. Light flared and sparkled.

"Direct hit, but their shields are holding," Jiya said. "The second destroyer is peeling off and heading toward us."

"Fire at will," Reynolds said.

"Eat hot lead, fuckers!" Tactical said. "I am the Avenging Angel of Death!" The railguns fired. Projectiles exploded against the bow of the ship, ripping through the shield like tissue paper.

"Direct hit. Their shields are down," Jiya reported. "Second destroyer is disengaging."

"That's right, run away like a little girl!" Tactical said. "I will hunt you down!" The next blast ripped away the stern of the ship and its atmosphere vented, along with clouds of debris. The railguns pounded the fleeing ship, shredding it. "Eat that!"

"Target destroyed."

"Ensign Alcott, bring us around to face the other destroyer," Reynolds commanded.

"Yes, sir! Coming around."

"Take them out, Tactical," Reynolds said.

"They are dust!" Tactical replied. "Die, die, die!" The lasers and railguns fired afresh, raining blast after blast onto the enemy.

"Tone it down, Tactical," Maddox said. "I can't hear the reports."

"I think you can stop shooting now," Jiya said. "They really are dust."

"That was too easy," Tactical complained. "I need a real challenge."

"Comm, how can we understand their language?" Jiya asked.

"Universal markers, standardizations, grammar that has a distinct pattern, and we've tapped their internal communications to give us a broad sample of language to decrypt. We might be missing some vocabulary, but overall, I'd say 'good job' to Reynolds on his masterful adaptation of this addition to our language database," Comm replied.

"You mean you?" Jiya wondered which Reynolds, or how much Reynolds, was involved in one thing over another. She didn't have to worry about it since they all worked toward the same goal. She smiled and nodded toward comm, raising her coffee cup in a salute.

"The alien ship is hailing us," Comm said.

The bridge of the other ship appeared on screen again. Silvery fluid leaked down the captain's face from a gash on the temple. Smoke obscured much of the view, and the loud moans ramped up in volume.

"Comm, can you turn down the crying?" Reynolds asked privately.

"On it." The moan faded to a barely audible undertone.

"This is Reynolds, captain of the Superdreadnought *Reynolds*. Were those two destroyers the only enemy craft tracking you? We don't see any others on our scans."

"They are brigands, Captain Reynolds," the alien

captain replied. "They hunt in pairs, stalking and attacking unwary travelers. They stake out territory and waylay all who cross their path. As such, we are unlikely to attract the attention of more in this sector. But *Threfol* is badly injured." Behind the captain, smoke drifted, obscuring the other occupants. "We must return to Serifity so she can heal. I know not what others might accost us upon our journey."

"Just Reynolds, please," the android said. He muted the connection. "Can they use our Pod-docs?" he asked Takal.

The old man scratched his chin. "These creatures don't appear to be energy beings like the Gulg. The system works for all of the corporeal species we've encountered so far, so I don't have any reason to believe they wouldn't."

Reynolds reactivated the audio. "We have technology on our ship that might help heal your crew, Captain Xonera. Would you like to send them over here?"

The captain smiled a little. "Call me Xonera. You misunderstand me, Reynolds. My crew is only lightly injured. Our medical facilities are sufficient to tend to them. *Threfol* is our ship. She sustained grievous bodily harm at the hands of those ruffians and requires the succor of our medical establishment to recuperate from her wounds."

Reynolds turned to Comm. "Can you dial back the drama in the translator just a bit? I feel like I'm in a Shakespearean stage production."

"I'll see what I can do," Comm replied. Asya held her hands up in confusion at the terms Reynolds insisted on using that had no relation to anything she knew.

"We find ourselves in a similar position, Xonera,"

Reynolds told the alien. "Our ship also requires repair. Perhaps we can work out a mutually beneficial agreement. The *Reynolds* will escort you to your home planet if your people would be willing to help us find the materials we need for our repairs."

"We owe you our lives, Reynolds," Xonera said, bowing deeply. "Anything within our power is yours. Of course, you understand I do not represent my government. But anything I can do for you personally, I will."

Jiya shook a finger at the tactical station. "Don't even!"

"That one was too easy," Tactical said. "Not worth my time."

Reynolds shot a glare at both Jiya and the station. "Politics is politics everywhere in the universe. I understand that you can't offer any promises, but I hope you'll put in a good word for us. Now, is your ship able to proceed under its own power? Or do you require assistance?"

The creature on the screen paused for a moment and placed a hand on a waist-high pedestal. "*Threfol* assures me she can make her way home. If you'd like to follow us, 'tis not far."

Reynolds nodded. "Lead on, Xonera." The screen went dark, and he turned to Ria. "Follow that ship."

"Aye, sir," Ria responded. "We won't be moving very fast. That ship is pretty badly crippled. Too bad we can't tow them."

Reynolds shook his head. "We could if we have to, but it's better this way. If there are more of those pirates around, I want to be agile enough to engage them if necessary. What's our ETA?"

"The nearest star system is about twelve hours away at

this speed," Maddox reported. "We've got nothing in the databases about these systems, of course. I see signs of civilization on three planets in the Goldilocks zone. All three are inhabited. The second one appears to have a higher-tech civilization. Lots of satellites, and two space stations with ships the size of Xonera's in dock. The other two planets have fewer heat signatures."

"OK, folks," Asya said. "Stay sharp. These long, boring transits are no time to fall asleep. Maddox, watch our long-range scans. We know there are pirates in the area. Ria, keep an eye on our new friends. Jiya, scan the ship, and get me as much intel as you can."

Tactical laughed. "Can I use asteroids for target practice?"

"No!" Asya said. "Your drill is to *not* shoot anything. Let's see how that goes."

Jiya turned to her screen. "Takal, you might want to take a look at this," she said, pointing to her results. "According to the scans, the ship is partly alive! The skeleton is made up of common metals, with some alloys I don't recognize, and it appears to be covered by silicon-based musculature. Xonera said the ship was injured, and she wasn't kidding. Look at these areas."

"Those appear to be burn wounds, much like one of us would get if we were hit by a laser," Takal marveled. "Doc Reynolds should look at this as well. The makeup of this ship is actually quite similar to your android body, Reynolds, although yours is carbon-based, and this is silicon. But the similarities are remarkable! I hope I have the opportunity to study this creature."

"Keep in mind the captain referred to this ship as 'she,'"

Maddox said. "She also said the ship told her it could get home alone. That implies some level of sentience. Neither the captain nor the ship might appreciate you asking to poke and prod her."

Jiya glanced at Tactical, expecting a crude reference to alien probing, but the AI personality was silent. She wondered if he was exercising restraint or just brooding.

CHAPTER THREE

The *Reynolds* followed *Threfol* into Our System.

"No shit," Comm said. "That's what they call it. At least, that's what the translator came up with. It's not in our databases, so we don't have any designation. The locals call themselves 'People.' We can use the phonetic name if you prefer." A string of teeth-rattling sounds emitted from Comm's position.

Jiya tried to emulate the sound. "Let's go with the translations," she said, rubbing her jaw. "I don't need a headache every time we talk about them."

"The captain of the *Threfol* is hailing," Comm said.

The screen lit up. Xonera appeared on her bridge. Although clear of smoke, it was dimly lit and barely visible. The pedestal near the captain sported several bandages. "No stop station, land planet," Xonera said.

"Oops, I think I cranked the interpreter back too far," Comm said. "Hold one, please. There."

"I have informed the defense station that you will accompany us to the planet," Xonera continued, oblivious to Comm's adjustments. "*Threfol* is injured and requires medical assistance. We'll land in the hospital field on the smaller continent. We have triage at that location as well, if *Reynolds* would like to check in."

The crew exchanged confused glances. "She's referring to the ship," Maddox said when understanding finally dawned. "She doesn't mean you, Reynolds."

The AI nodded. "Thanks, Xonera, but my ship doesn't require medical attention. It's inanimate."

Onscreen, Xonera cocked her head in a human-looking gesture. "Takal told me your ship is an extension of yourself. I understood that to mean you and the ship are one, but that is not your nature?"

Reynolds glanced at Takal. The older man shrugged. "We were discussing the physiology of their equipment during the journey."

Reynolds turned back to the screen. "I am the ship, and it is me. I am sentient, but I am not a biological construct like your ship. Or rather, this body is, but while it holds my intelligence, it is not who I am."

He stopped. Based on what Takal had told him when they'd fought the cultists over Muultar, that was not strictly true. *The whole of what makes you* you *and separate from the other personalities aboard the ship is plugged into that body.* If the scientist was right, this body *was* him.

"It's complicated," he continued. "But the important thing is, we have no need of your doctors. Is there somewhere nearby we can land?"

"Yes, of course." Xonera touched the pedestal at her station. "*Threfol* will send the coordinates to your location.

"I have the coordinates," Ria said. "Shall I land the ship?"

"Take us down, Ensign," Reynolds replied.

"Oxygen, nitrogen atmosphere. Breathable for the meatbags," XO reported.

They followed Xonera to the fourth planet in the system. Cities stretched across much of the larger continent, but the *Trefol* circled down to the smaller landmass. Here, thick swaths of greenish-blue forest covered much of the southern part, while deserts baked in the north. As they descended, they approached a wide gray-black area cleared from the surrounding trees. Lighter-colored lumps resolved into numerous ships scattered across the open space.

The *Reynolds* landed. Leaving Asya in command while maintenance ran a complete diagnostic suite, Reynolds took Jiya, Maddox, Takal, Geroux, Ka'nak, and San Roche down to the field. The dark surface gave under their feet, solid enough for stable walking but providing a soft cushion. Several other ships were parked nearby, their crews moving in and around them. Clear tubing pumped silvery fluid into each of the ships. The external surfaces pulsed gently in a smooth, steady rhythm.

Those look like IVs, Doc Reynolds, the AI's medical personality said through the crew's integrated comm system. *I guess it makes sense if their craft are partially animate.*

Is it medical in nature, or merely sustenance? Takal muttered, staring at the nearest ship as he walked across the tarmac. He tripped, and Jiya grabbed his arm to steady him.

That looks like their field headquarters over there, Jiya said, pointing at a building on the nearer side of the field.

Maybe someone in there would be willing to answer your questions.

I wish I could go with you, Doc Reynolds said.

Keep this line open, Doc, Takal said, *and it will be almost like being there.*

The rest of us don't want to hear about blood and guts, Jiya said. *So keep that conversation private, will you?*

I like to hear about blood and guts, Ka'nak said. The huge Melowi warrior cracked his knuckles and his neck. *I enjoy seeing them, too, especially if I am the one who spilled them.*

Ew, Geroux said, stepping closer to Jiya and grabbing her hand. *I'm with Jiya on this one. I like to keep my blood and guts inside where they belong.*

Peace, people, Maddox said. *We don't know what taboos this culture may have. Let's keep the medical discussion to a minimum until we find out. For all we know, talking about a space craft's blood may be tantamount to insulting someone's mother.*

Listen to the general, Reynolds said. *Takal, take San Roche and have a chat with the airfield personnel. Keep Doc in the loop, and see what you can learn. The rest of us will meet with Xonera. She promised to introduce us to the premier. San Roche.* He turned to the Telluride. *Keep Takal out of trouble.*

Takal drew himself up. *I am not a child.*

Uncle. Geroux put a hand on the old inventor's arm. *San Roche is here to protect you, not babysit you. Think of him as a combination guard and assistant.*

The old man looked mollified. *Fine. Reynolds, don't forget that list of materials I need.*

Reynolds patted his chest as if he had a hard copy list in his breast pocket. *I'll get them all, Takal.*

Takal and San Roche angled toward the building, while the rest of the crew continued to the *Threfol*.

The other ship had landed nearby, and dozens of People swarmed over it. Three of the IV lines had been attached at different locations. A crew of People pushed a huge vat of gray goo up to the ship and slathered it on the burns using long-handled brushes.

"Look!" Geroux whispered as they got closer. "That vat doesn't have wheels, it has legs." The enormous cylindrical bucket sat on thousands of tiny legs, each the diameter of a human's wrist. As the People worked, the legs crawled along, keeping the bucket within easy reach of the brushes. When some of the slimy-looking gunk slid down the side of the vat, the legs nearest the spill scooped it up from under the device.

"Are those legs *eating* that goo?" Jiya asked, appalled.

"I think I should have stayed with Takal," Ka'nak said in a strangled voice. "Blood and guts would be better than this."

Reynolds looked dismayed. "Mind your manners, or I'll send you back to the ship."

One of the People handed a brush to a co-worker and strode across the springy ground. Another of the aliens joined her, pacing gracefully toward the crew on their four long, feline legs. They stopped in front of Reynolds and bowed.

"It is an honor to meet you in body," Xonera said, raising her head. "*Trefol* sends her gratitude again for your care of us. This is the daughter of the ship, Taneral. I cannot leave *Trefol* alone, but Taneral will take you into the city to meet the premier. She will guide you during your stay with us." She stretched out a hand to the alien with her, drawing her forward.

This being had the same cat-like body and humanoid torso as Xonera. While the captain sported a dark crew cut and dark fur on her body, Taneral had golden hair that stood out in a thick ruff. The tips were blue and matched the color of her paws. Her flat face had a fine layer of golden hair, as well. When she smiled, large pointed teeth glinted.

"It is my pleasure to attend to your needs," Taneral said. "If you'll come this way, I will transport you to the premier's abode."

The crew said their farewells to Xonera and followed the other alien to a large vehicle. Like the vat they'd seen earlier, this conveyance was supported by thousands of tiny legs. It was a large, ovoid, with rails around the edges and an open space to climb through. The crew followed Taneral onto the vehicle.

She looked them over carefully. "You only have two legs, so this might be a bit unstable for you. Hold on tight."

They grabbed the rail surrounding the vehicle. It was crowded, and Jiya's leg was pressed against the side of the vehicle. It was warm, and pulsed slowly like the ships on the airfield. "I think this transport is alive," she whispered to Geroux.

The younger female nodded. "I wonder if all their technology is, or only the vehicles? I'm not sure why we have to hold on, though. Those legs don't move very fast."

The ovoid craft slid forward, the motion smooth and almost undetectable at first. As they rode, the speed increased until it moved faster than a human could run.

Under their feet, the floor seemed to bunch like muscles tensing. The craft suddenly lunged into the air. An engine at the rear ignited, and the vehicle shot into the sky.

The crew gasped. Taneral blinked in surprise. "Do your transports not behave so?"

Jiya laughed shakily. "This is completely new to us."

"That's an understatement," Geroux muttered. She peered over the stern of the craft. "I wonder what powers it? Takal will be sorry he missed this."

They sailed away from the airfield, soaring just above the blue-green treetops. After crossing a thick stretch of forest, they entered a stream of air traffic. Hundreds of small craft crossed the airspace in an orderly grid. Some popped up from the trees for a short distance, only to dive back down again. Others zigzagged through the crowd and shot off across the ocean or back toward the airfield.

"Our capital city, Dantera, is here on the Grentoo continent. The rest of Grentoo is reserved for raising live mech," Taneral said. "Most of our population lives on Serpenti or the smaller islands.'

"Live mech?" Reynolds asked. "Is that what you call your hybrid machines?"

Taneral blinked a few times, then nodded. "If by 'hybrid,' you refer to the mix of living and inanimate material, then yes. It is the only way we make machinery. Your ship, without biological components, is a novelty to us. I believe the premier may want to send scientists to study it if you will permit."

"Perhaps we can work out a trade," Reynolds said. "We might need help acquiring the materials to repair our ship.

If your people are willing to assist us, we could provide information about some of our tech."

Taneral bowed. "Such an exchange must be negotiated with People more exalted than I. The premier will decide. Hold on—we descend."

The craft slowed, then dove through the trees. Beneath the thick canopy, narrow lanes stretched away in both directions, flanked by low buildings. The craft flattened out just above ground level and skimmed along one of the lanes. People leapt out of the way as the craft approached, but none of them seemed upset by nearly being run over.

They stopped in front of a wide building. Thick brown fur covered the building and the walls pulsed slowly, giving off a faint warmth. The craft dropped to its tiny legs and scuttled close to the front door. The crew stepped down onto the cushy paving.

"I like this carpet," Jiya joked. "I wonder if it comes in red?"

"This is the residence of the premier," Taneral said, waving a hand at the building behind her. "Captain Xonera has arranged for an audience. Please, follow me."

Jiya and Geroux followed the alien up the steps to the residence, with Maddox, Ka'nak, and Reynolds bringing up the rear. As they climbed, the building rippled, as if a chill had passed through it. The top half of the huge white doors lifted, and the bottom half slid into the floor.

"I feel like I'm walking into a monster's mouth," Geroux whispered to Jiya.

The first officer put her hand on her sidearm, a shiver running through her body. "I think you're not far off, there."

Inside the building, the crew was asked to disarm. "It's not that we don't trust you," said the guard who took their weapons.

But we don't trust you, Jiya muttered through the crew's private comm system.

Reynolds gave her a look. "We understand completely," he said. Over the comm, he added, *Their weapons are no match for our armor.*

Yeah, but what about their teeth? Geroux asked. *I didn't like the looks of that door, and those guards' teeth aren't much smaller.*

We've done this before, Jiya said. She glanced at Ka'nak, who had not spoken since they had climbed on the transport at the airfield. "You okay, Ka'nak?"

The Melowi's face was pale and sweaty. He took a deep breath and shook his head. "I think I should have stayed behind with Takal."

After they'd checked their weapons, they walked down a long, low hallway. At the end, the doors slid open in a more conventional way.

I think those entry doors were made to look like a mouth specifically to intimidate visitors, Maddox remarked.

Well, it worked, Jiya replied, grinning at Ka'nak. The big warrior strode along, head on a swivel, eyes constantly roving. His shoulders were tense, and his hands open and slightly away from his sides.

They entered a long room with large windows on both sides and a high ceiling. Blue-green light filtered in from the sunlit groves surrounding the building. Dozens of People prowled around the room, forming groups, splitting, and reforming. At the far end, a short dais held a large couch where one of the aliens reclined. This creature was much larger than the others in the room, with thicker facial hair and a uniform covered with shiny beads and glinting disks.

Taneral led them to the dais and bowed. "Premier, this is Reynolds and the crew of the SD *Reynolds*. Their heroic actions freed *Threfol* and her crew from pillage, plundering, and death at the hands of Terubine raiders."

I thought Comm was going to rein in the drama on the translator? Jiya said on the private channel.

He did, Geroux replied. *I think Taneral is going so far over the top she's slid down the other side, but it is an accurate translation of the words.*

The alien nodded. The metallic disks on his uniform jingled when he moved. "Welcome, Reynolds and crew. I am Walthorn, Premier of Serifity, Defender of the Pride, Head of the Realm, Supreme Leader of the Tribe. Welcome." He yawned as he finished the introduction, as if reciting his titles wearied him.

Or maybe that's a sign of aggression in this species, Geroux said to the crew over the comm.

One of the People behind the premier leaned forward and spoke into his ear. Walthorn continued, "In gracious thanks for the assistance rendered to *Threfol* and her crew, I grant you whatever you desire from our Tribe. My assistants Krenthel and Bonnerel will ensure that you receive all that you require." He gestured two more aliens forward. "I offer you my deepest gratitude and wish you safe journeys."

The premier waved a hand. The couch raised a few centimeters above the dais, and thousands of tiny legs shuffled it away through an open door at the back of the room.

Reynolds stared after the premier. *That was the oddest negotiation I have ever participated in.*

Not much of a negotiation, Maddox replied, practically rubbing his hands in glee. *They gave us the farm.*

If the farm is alive, I don't want it, Ka'nak muttered through the internal comm.

Krenthel and Bonnerel stepped down off the dais. "Xonera is the premier's daughter," Bonnerel said. "He offers his kingdom in return for her safety."

"Rest assured, we won't take the kingdom," Reynolds said. "We do request assistance in finding certain raw materials we need to repair our ship."

Bonnerel bowed. "If you give your list to Taneral, we will locate what you need. Is there anything you require immediately? Food? Shelter?"

"We prefer to stay on our ship," Reynolds said. "After our long journey, there are some minor repairs and checks we must complete. We are in a hurry to return to our own kingdom, but perhaps we can see more of your planet while the supplies are being gathered."

Krenthel bowed. They seemed to take turns bowing and talking. "It will be our pleasure to provide you with anything you require. Taneral is available to guide you anywhere you wish to go." The two bowed again and backed away.

Taneral stepped forward and gestured to the other end of the room. "The attendants have laid out refreshments for you. Please partake, then I will show you around our humble planet."

"We look forward to enjoying the wonders of your planet and her People," Reynolds said.

Taneral bowed and backed away in an uncanny imitation of Krenthel and Bonnerel.

That did seem way too easy, Maddox started.

CHAPTER FOUR

As they stepped out the front door, a blast of heat washed over them. Ka'nak glared over his shoulder. "That building is breathing down my neck."

Taneral reached out and stroked the side of the building. "It's not trying to scare you," she said. "Come, let me show you our city."

They took a roundabout path back to the airfield but saw nothing of use to them. Most of the buildings looked the same, and any time they suggested stopping to speak to locals or view something up close, Taneral politely redirected the discussion. She never said no, but still managed to refuse their requests.

When they landed at the airfield, Taneral escorted them back to the *Reynolds*. "Bonnerel has messaged me. We can get a large amount of phorentum on Lanteral, which is only four light-years away. I will lead you there if your ship can make that jump."

"Very well," Reynolds said. He turned to Maddox. "Take

Ka'nak and find Takal and San Roche. I want to depart as soon as possible.

On the bridge, Reynolds dropped into his chair. "Asya, prepare the ship for departure. As soon as the crew and Taneral have returned, we're off to Lanteral." He turned to Jiya and Geroux. "What did you think of our hosts?"

Geroux scratched her head. "They seem to have an unusual culture. This might sound crazy, but I think the premier is the only male we've met."

"All these females are part of his harem?" Jiya asked. "Bethany Anne would approve of us liberating the females, wouldn't she?" She looked hopefully at Reynolds.

The AI android shook his head. "That's not the mission."

Jiya scowled.

Reynolds held up a hand. "When we return to High Tortuga, you can petition the Queen for another shot at this system."

Shaking off her disappointment, Jiya went on, "I also thought the tour was pointless. She didn't show us anything new. All those buildings looked alike, and she wouldn't let us talk to anyone."

Reynolds nodded. "My thoughts exactly. Are they hiding something? And more importantly, if they are, do we care? When we fix the Gate drive, we can go home. And with a billion light-years between us, I'm not worried about their secret—whatever it is—being a threat."

The door slid open and Maddox and Takal stepped

onto the bridge, with Taneral following. "Ka'nak is eating," Maddox said. "I think he's trying to show the meat who's boss."

The crew laughed, but Taneral looked confused. "How can she be the boss? I thought Reynolds was the captain."

"It's just a figure of speech," Geroux said. "And Ka'nak is male. He won't appreciate being called a girl."

"But she—I mean, he—is a warrior. You have male warriors?"

"Yes, of course," said Geroux. "Don't you?"

"Oh, no," Taneral said. "Only females fight. Males rule."

"So, the females do all the work while the males lie around on couches?" Jiya muttered.

Reynolds gave Jiya a warning glare.

"Come sit by me," Geroux said to the alien.

"I am more comfortable standing," Taneral said, gesturing to her four legs. "Or possibly, lying down." She turned to Reynolds. "I have transmitted the coordinates to your Ensign Alcott and notified airfield control and our security stations in orbit. You may depart at your convenience."

"XO, take us up," Reynolds said.

A wormhole sliced through space in the Lanteral system, and the SD *Reynolds* flashed into existence. As it sailed toward the second planet, the Gate closed behind them.

"The Gate drive appears to be working fine for small jumps," Ria said. "All readings are nominal."

"Scans show life forms but no indications of civilization," Jiya said. "Do you know if there are predators on this planet?" she asked Taneral.

"I believe there are," Taneral said. "As well as a nearly sentient race. But they are afraid of extraterrestrials. They won't bother us."

"'Nearly sentient?'" Asya asked.

"They use crude tools but do not grow their own machines," she replied.

"Ensign Alcott, take us into orbit," Reynolds said. "Jiya, Takal has adjusted the sensors to identify phorentum. Find us some."

After a few moments, Jiya pointed to highlighted areas on the screen. "There are large deposits in this area. It's the crystalline substance on the walls of caves, if I remember the briefing properly. This one looks the most accessible." One section turned blue.

"Good work, Jiya," Reynolds said, happy to have Jiya focused on getting the ship fixed and not involving herself in another planet's affairs. "Ready two Pods. Put together a team to scout and collect the phorentum. We'll need security, just in case."

"Yes, sir," she said, turning to leave the bridge.

He looked to Taneral. "Will you join us on the surface?"

"Of course."

"Geroux and Maddox, we'll go down with the team. Asya, you're in command." Reynolds rose from his command chair, straightened his uniform, and motioned for Taneral to go first.

"Yes, sir," the bridge crew replied. Reynolds nodded. The crew was running like clockwork.

San Roche and L'Eliana piloted the two Pods. They

descended through the clouds and soared over the rough terrain. Volcanoes spewed gases and ash. An arid plain stretched into the cloudy distance.

"Those volcanoes are dormant," L'Eliana said, pointing across the plain to another range of mountains. "There's a small cave complex at the foot of that range, and an accessible valley where we can land."

"Are those tents?" Geroux asked, pointing at a neat circle of small lumps in the valley.

L'Eliana increased the magnification. "Yes, they are!"

"It appears your 'almost sentient' race is more advanced than you thought," Reynolds told Taneral.

The alien shook her head. "I have not been here before, but I was told the locals were little more intelligent than animals. I shall observe and report back."

"Contact with primitive races can be tricky," Reynolds said. "Can we get the phorentum at one of the other locations?"

Jiya shook her head. "We could, but it would take us twice as long to collect the stuff. This cave system is easiest to get into, and according to scans, there's lots of phorentum close to the surface."

"Is there a secondary entrance to the cave system?" Reynolds asked. "Another way to get in without going through that tribe?"

Jiya adjusted the controls, searched, redirected, and ended with a shake of her head. "Scans aren't finding anything. This cave system is small and fairly shallow. There's one main entrance in this valley. Luckily, the locals are camped at the other end."

"I guess it will have to do," Reynolds said.

The two Pods landed. The crew checked their armor and prepared to exit. "The air here is breathable," Jiya said. "But it probably stinks. Lots of sulfur and other fumes. We'll want to keep our helmets on." She glanced at Taneral. "Will your helmet filter out the gases?"

The alien blinked. "Only if they are dangerous. We use our sense of smell extensively. We are trained to identify odors and ignore those that are not relevant."

"That would be nice," Geroux said. "Especially when Takal and Ka'nak have been drinking too much."

No one took the bait.

"Let's go," Reynolds interjected. "Maddox, you stay here and get the crew ready. Set up a secure perimeter and get the extractors ready to run. Don't enter the caves until we talk to the natives. I don't want to break any cultural or religious taboos if we can avoid it. This is their valley—who knows what this cave system means to them. Jiya, Taneral, get Ka'nak, and we'll go talk to the natives. L'Eliana, stay in the Pod for now in case we need support."

They stepped out onto the plain. Heat radiated from the dry ground and pounded down from overhead. The far end, where the natives lived, was obscured by clouds of dust. Ka'nak trotted over from the second Pod, and the team moved down the valley.

"Is something moving down there?" Jiya asked. She activated her comm. *L'Eliana, can you see anything?*

I launched observation pucks when we landed, L'Eliana replied. *It looks like a sizable group is on the move toward you. Maybe a dozen individuals. They seem to be riding animals.*

"I hope the translators are up for this," Jiya said. "They

had enough trouble with Taneral's language when we first arrived. Will they understand Primitive?"

Reynolds nodded. "Comm has been tweaking the system. If they have a coherent spoken language, we should understand. Unless it's pig Latin. Never cracked that one."

"What?" Jiya said.

"*Ever-nay ind-may,*" Reynolds answered with a smirk. "Here they come."

A cloud of yellow dust boiled up. As quickly as it arrived, it dispersed, revealing the native delegation.

"Nice entrance," Jiya muttered.

The natives were squat humanoids with six limbs, four arms and two legs. They were covered in thick, dusty hair, and rode cat-like beasts with six legs and twitching tails.

"Oh, my sisters!" Taneral whispered.

The cats crouched, bellies in the dust, and the natives climbed off. The largest of the humanoids stepped forward. Long dreadlocks hung from his head, but the hair on his body was combed smooth and flowed. He wore a belt with stone and wood axes hanging from either side. In one hand, he held a green leaf, which he held out to the crew. "Greetings, visitors. May you always have fresh greens. From whence come ye?"

The android stepped forward. "I am Reynolds, captain of the Superdreadnought *Reynolds*. This is part of my crew: Ka'nak and Jiya, and our friend Taneral. We came to your planet to make alliances."

"I am Pornath, leader of this tribe. We have lived in this valley for many generations. Take this sign of life as an offering of peace between our peoples." The male held out the leaf again.

Reynolds took the leaf. *I didn't bring house-warming gifts. Do either of you have anything?* he asked Jiya and Ka'nak.

They patted themselves down, looking for something to offer. Ka'nak held out a protein bar. *I brought this in case I got hungry later.*

That'll work. Reynolds offered the snack to the chief. "Take this food as our acceptance of your offer of peace."

The chief took the bar and sniffed it. "This does not smell like food."

"You have to take the wrapper off," Ka'nak said.

The chief stared in apparent confusion. "What?"

"You must peel it," Jiya said, miming the action.

The chief smiled, his lips closed. "Ah. Like *L'heri* fruit." He tucked the bar away somewhere in his hair. "May there be many years of peace between our peoples."

"We aren't staying that long," Reynolds said. "We want to get some phorentum from your caves, then we'll be off."

"From the caves?" Pornath asked. He pulled out one of his axes. "You must not enter the caves. It's dangerous."

"We are well-protected," Reynolds told the native.

"It's not safe," Pornath said. "The Dark Ones live there. They attack all who enter and eat their souls." He made a choppy gesture with two hands. Behind him, the other natives did the same.

Reynolds patted his chest. "We have armor to protect us."

Pornath looked them over. "We will petition the gods for you."

"Thanks, but—" Reynolds broke off as the chief and three of his companions dropped face-down into the dust. "Oh, you're going to do it now."

The four lay in the dirt. The others remained standing, watching the visitors. The chief and his companions stood. "The gods say you are foolish people, but we cannot stop you. If you survive, come to our camp for a celebration." They turned abruptly and climbed back onto their animals. The cats leapt to their feet and bounded away.

"That was—" Ka'nak started.

"Brief?" Jiya asked.

"Simple?" Reynolds fingered the leaf, watching the dust boil up in the natives' wake.

"Ridiculous," Taneral said, her tail switching back and forth. "Superstitious primitives subjugating proud felines. The premier will not be happy to hear about this."

"Maybe the cats aren't sentient?" Jiya suggested. "They didn't seem to mind. In fact, I think I heard one of them purring."

"We aren't here to free the cats," Reynolds said. "We need to get our phorentum and get back to the ship. We can handle the dark ones, whatever they are. It's time to get to work."

CHAPTER FIVE

Maddox had set up sensors to monitor activity around the Pods. Within the perimeter, technicians from the crew put together a pair of devices.

"The extractors are almost ready," Maddox told Reynolds when they returned. He held up a device strapped to his forearm. "We'll use these detectors to find a vein, then the extractors will pull the phorentum from the walls of the caves. Did you calm the natives?"

"They think we'll run into something called the Dark Ones," Reynolds said. "Based on the ritual gestures, we believe it's a religious superstition. Still, we'll need to be cautious."

"We are reading some lifeforms inside," Geroux confirmed. "A small group of creatures seems to reside in a branch of the caves off to the west. From the scans, it looks like they're about a meter high, with six legs. We can't tell if they're predators since something in the rock interferes with our scanners, but the phorentum is in a stretch to the south, so we may not see them at all."

"As long as we keep our armor on and our wits about us, we'll be fine," Reynolds said. "Maddox, get the team rolling."

The android led the way into the caves. His integrated visual tech meant he could see in any light, and the crews' upgraded helmets provided similar capabilities. "Taneral, stay in the middle of the group." He didn't know her skills or her armor's specs, and he didn't need their escort getting hurt if there were problems.

Maddox followed Reynolds, with his crew of technicians pushing the extractors using maintenance bots. Taneral walked behind the equipment, and Ka'nak, Jiya, and Geroux followed, watching their six.

The dark closed around them as they moved into the cave system. The rough walls and floor made walking difficult, especially for those guiding the equipment. "These are old lava tubes," Geroux told the group. "The lava rolled down the volcano and hardened on the outside. Then the lava drained out, leaving a tube. Over time, more lava builds on top, and you get these caves." Geroux pointed to a side tunnel that led off their current route. "That's where we saw the creatures."

"Can they hear us?" Reynolds asked. "We don't want to give them a reason to come looking."

"I don't think so," Geroux said. "But that assumption is based on my knowledge of subterranean fauna from our galaxy. It's possible they have more sensitive ears. Or other auditory sensory organs."

Maddox stopped. "Ka'nak, stay here and keep an eye on that tunnel. Do you want someone to stay with you?"

The Melowi shook his head. "I'll be fine. I did not wear a red shirt today."

Reynolds snorted. "Have you been watching Earth videos?"

"Tactical suggested I familiarize myself with human culture before we returned to High Tortuga," the warrior said.

"Stay in touch on the comm," Reynolds said. "Check in with Maddox every ten minutes."

Ka'nak gave a sloppy salute. "Aye, captain. Good luck finding your dilithium crystals."

They left him standing guard at the side tunnel and continued deeper into the mountain. The tunnels slanted down, forcing them to slow.

Geroux checked her wrist computer. "This is taking much longer than I expected. The scans showed the phorentum near here, but my sensor is directing us farther in. Something in the rock must have distorted our readings."

"Are you sure the stuff is here?" Reynolds asked. "I don't want to waste time climbing around in lava funland if there's no payoff."

"It's here," Geroux confirmed. "Just more that way." She pointed down the tunnel.

"Onward," Reynolds said.

"This floor is smoother," Geroux said in surprise when they reached a junction. "This tunnel isn't a lava tube. Maybe water-formed?"

"It will make for easier walking," Jiya said. "My ankles are killing me."

"True, but that's a problem." Geroux tapped at her wrist

computer. "The phorentum develops in lava rock. This tunnel is beneath the lava. We're down in the bedrock."

"My sensor says it's that way." Maddox pointed along the new tunnel.

"Maybe this tunnel leads to another lava tube," Geroux said.

"Are you sure your map is good?" Reynolds asked. "If something in the rock is impeding your scans, maybe this is a wild goose chase?"

"What's a gooz jays?" Taneral asked.

"Figure of speech," Geroux said. "Humans use some odd terms." She turned back to Reynolds. "It's definitely there. Just not where we expected."

Ka'nak, Reynolds called through the comm. *We're stopping for a short break. What's your status?*

Ka'nak didn't reply.

"I just spoke with him a moment ago," Maddox said. "He was bored and started singing something about an island and a guy named Gill-gan."

"Take Jiya and go back up until you regain contact," Reynolds said. "If you run into trouble, call San Roche and L'Eliana. Tell them to bring reinforcements from the ship. The rest of us will keep looking for the phorentum."

"Yes, sir," Maddox said, starting back up the tunnel. Jiya swallowed a groan and followed him. After a few minutes, Maddox stopped. "This is where I heard him singing."

"How do you know?" Jiya asked. "These tunnels all look the same to me."

Maddox tapped his wrist. "I marked the location each time he checked in. Let me try him now."

There was no answer again.

"Let's go." Maddox drew his sidearm from its holster. "If those creatures can take down Ka'nak, we need fire-power on our side."

Jiya pulled her weapon out as well. "Geroux said they were small. How could they take down someone as huge as Ka'nak?"

"Overwhelming numbers," Maddox said. "Let's move faster."

"Good thing I brought grenades," she replied, scrambling up the rocky tunnel. "What's that sound?"

"What sound?" Maddox cocked his head, adjusting his audio inputs.

"It sounds like ocean waves," Jiya replied. "Maybe it's wind blowing through the tunnels?"

"There's no wind," Maddox said, stopping to double-check. He shook his head. "Nope, no air movements, but I can hear it, too. It seems to be coming from that direction." He pointed ahead to where the tunnel turned ninety degrees.

They crept up to the corner. *Stay low,* Maddox reminded Jiya. They ducked and peeked around the rocky turn.

And came face to face with an enormous wave of tiny sharp-toothed natives.

"Maybe I should have gone with Maddox and Jiya," Geroux said, pacing behind the equipment. The two crew members, Finnal and Edernt, had moved to the rear while Geroux guided the extractors. She was smaller than the males and had less combat training, so she didn't mind. Plus, it gave her a chance to chat with Taneral while they walked.

"They are fine warriors, are they not?" Taneral asked. "They do not need scientific support for their current mission."

"I guess not, but I'm worried about them. What if those lifeforms have attacked?" She felt sort of responsible for the actions of the creatures since she had identified them and assured the crew they wouldn't be a problem.

The sound of crashing waves echoed down the tunnel.

"What is that?" Taneral asked.

"Incoming!" Reynolds called back. "Defensive positions! We don't want them to damage our equipment."

Finnal ran a hundred meters down the tunnel to watch behind the group. Edernt pushed past the two females and joined Reynolds. Geroux stayed by the equipment, moving in front of it.

"Stay behind the extractors," Geroux told Taneral. "If they cut us off from behind, you'll need to help Finnal." She focused on the long tunnel.

Although the visual sensors on her helmet allowed her to see in the dark, nothing registered in the tunnel except a wave-like disturbance. "Do they have cloaking tech? It almost looks like the rock itself is moving."

"They can't have," Reynolds said. "We've seen no indications of any tech on this planet, and no power signatures. They couldn't have developed cloaking tech in a vacuum. It must be a natural protection."

The disturbance moved closer, and the wave-like noise grew louder. A rock zoomed out of the gloom and struck

Reynolds' helmet. The android shook his head and charged forward, firing rapidly. "Attack!"

Geroux and Edernt darted after him, firing their weapons. Flashes lit the space, revealing hundreds of almost-invisible aliens. Their bodies blended into the rock walls and floor of the cave. Noise echoed off the tunnel, assaulting them from all directions. The crew fired into the wall of aliens in rapid succession, dropping dozens. More swarmed up from behind. Rocks rained down on them, hurled from behind the growing wall of dead, but bounced harmlessly off their armor. They fired again and again.

"They're retreating!" Reynolds yelled. "See if you can capture one!"

Geroux yanked a screamer off her belt, hit the trigger, and threw it past Reynolds. It flew into the dark...and then it flew back at them. "Shit!" She scooped it up and threw it again.

The screamer hit something and went off, the wailing shriek shaking the tunnel. Dust and pebbles rained on their helmets and shoulders. The tunnel seemed to shudder, and the wave of creatures crumpled to the floor.

The noise cut off, their helmets having auto-dampened the intense sound, then returned to normal audio control. *Report!* Reynolds said through the comm.

Clear to the rear, Edernt reported.

No injuries, Finnal replied.

I'm good, Geroux said. "Taneral, are you okay?"

The female peeked around the equipment, waving her blaster. "I'm fine, but I could not see what attacked us."

"We're not sure, either," Geroux said.

Reynolds stalked forward and prodded the odd debris.

He rolled one lump over with his foot. "These must be the Dark Ones. They look like Pornath and his clan, but smaller."

Geroux leaned forward, pointing her various scanners at the creature. "Their hair has a visual disrupter in it. This is amazing! They grow their own invisibility cloak! Did Pornath have that?"

Reynolds shook his head. "Unless it's activated by the dark?"

Geroux's eyes widened as she thought about that possibility. "I need to take a sample back to the ship."

"Go ahead," Reynolds said. "The Geneva Convention doesn't apply here."

Used to Reynolds' unknowable quips, Geroux shrugged it off and clipped several centimeters of dreadlock from the alien. Stowing the tangled hair in a container on her belt, she straightened. "Do you think these are the creatures we sensed near Ka'nak?"

"Wouldn't their hair block the ship's scans?" Reynolds asked.

"Their camouflage isn't perfect. We saw *something*," Geroux said. "But it might have confused the scans. Or those could be different creatures."

—you read me? Jiya's voice came through the internal comm.

Report! Reynolds snapped back.

We were attacked, Jiya said. *We're fine. They'd overwhelmed Ka'nak and taken him prisoner. They were bringing him down the tunnel. We killed a lot of them and knocked out the rest with a screamer. There were thousands of them! They did something to Ka'nak's armor. He's frozen.*

As she spoke, Maddox and Jiya came down the tunnel behind Finnal, carrying Ka'nak between them.

They laid the big Melowi on the smooth floor of the cave. He stared at them through the faceplate of his helmet.

Ka'nak? Reynolds asked through the comm.

Ka'nak blinked. *Those fucking sons of bitches did something to my armor! I will—*

Reynolds held up a hand and cut Ka'nak off mid-rant. "We'll get it fixed. What did they do?"

I don't know. They swarmed over me like mestibugs, and suddenly I was frozen. Ka'nak's eyes burned with anger. *Like an infestation of mestibugs,* he repeated.

"Diagnostics say there's nothing wrong with your armor," Geroux said, looking at a readout on her wrist comp. "They did something to *you*, maybe a toxin that affected your nervous system. Frozen armor wouldn't stop you from talking aloud. This toxin did."

"His suit should have filtered that out!" Jiya said.

"Our sensors should have allowed us to see these Dark Ones," Geroux replied, gesturing to the incapacitated creatures. "They have a natural defense that makes them virtually invisible, so it's not too surprising that they have a natural offensive weapon as well. We're lucky it didn't stop his respiratory system. We need to study these creatures."

"We can take one back to the ship," Reynolds said. "But handle it carefully. We don't want any more accidents." He pointed with his eyes at Ka'nak.

"If we have to carry Ka'nak, we can't carry the equipment and an alien, too," Maddox said. "Plus, we still need to find the phorentum."

"Right. Phorentum is the priority," Reynolds said.

"Without that, we can't get back to High Tortuga. Can the maintenance bots carry Ka'nak too?"

They put both extractors on one bot and rolled the Melowi warrior onto the other. "This will work until we need to carry the phorentum." Maddox said.

"We can leave the extractors behind if we must," Reynolds said. "We can always build new ones. I have no way to build a new Ka'nak."

Thanks, boss, Ka'nak replied. *Your loyalty to me is overwhelming.*

"Are we still headed in the right direction?" Reynolds asked Geroux. "Are you sure there really is phorentum down here?"

"I'm ninety-eight percent sure there is phorentum in this mountain," she replied. "The People identified this planet as a source, and there's no reason to think our sensors gave us a false positive. We know we haven't passed it, so it must be ahead of us, right?"

"Maybe it's buried deep inside the rock and we walked right by," Jiya said.

"Whose side are you on?" Geroux scowled. "No, phorentum crystals develop underground on the surface of lava rock, but there has to be air. The lava tubes are perfect. My detector shows it's that way." She pointed in the direction from which the aliens had attacked.

"Then let's get moving," Reynolds said. "Maddox, take point. The rest of you, keep an eye on our six. We don't want these things sneaking up on us."

Hours later, Reynolds and Maddox lay on a ledge above a vast cave. The rest of the team guarded the equipment and the still-paralyzed Ka'nak in the tunnel behind them. They peered over the edge, staring down at a huge congregation of Dark Ones.

This looks like their home base, Maddox said. *I see kitchen areas and sleeping areas. Those small ones could be children. I think these Dark Ones are as sentient as the beings on the surface.*

Do you see any phorentum? Geroux asked. *While we were walking, I developed code that should visually filter the phorentum's signal. I'm sending it to you now.*

What does that mean? Maddox asked.

It means if we look at phorentum, it glows, Reynolds said, pointing at the far wall of the massive cavern.

Maddox looked up. The entire curve of the Dark Ones' cavern glowed blue.

CHAPTER SIX

Jackpot! Reynolds grinned.

But how do we get to it? Maddox asked. *The Dark Ones haven't exactly been friendly.*

Reynolds crooked a finger at him and combat-crawled away from the lip of the cavern. *Two options: we try negotiations, or we look for the mineral somewhere else. I prefer the former.*

We could wait to see if they disperse, Jiya said as the two entered the mouth of the cavern where the rest of the crew waited.

Maddox shook his head. *That's their home. Unless they're nomads and we just happened to arrive on moving day, they're here to stay.*

We could rain fire from above and destroy those nasty little vermin like a mestibug infestation, Ka'nak said, shaking his fist. Beside him, Taneral nodded.

"Hey, you moved your arm!" Geroux said. "The toxin must be wearing off. Too bad Doc Reynolds isn't with us;

he could probably create an antidote. You don't have access to the medical files, do you, sir?"

"If we could still reach the ship, I could come up with something," Reynolds said. "For now, he'll just have to be mostly dead all day, and for the record, I am opposed to raining fire on the innocent to get something we want. If we did that, there would be no reason to go home since the Queen would destroy the vile creature Reynolds had become. Let's go talk to some Dark Ones. Maddox, take point. Find us a way down there."

"'Mostly dead?'" Maddox muttered under his breath as he turned back the way they had come. "Where do you get this stuff?"

You should do some human culture indoctrination, Ka'nak said. *Most enlightening.*

Maddox led them into a tunnel they had bypassed earlier. *This one goes down,* he said. *If my scans are to be believed, it leads to the cavern.* He aimed a dark look at Geroux.

She held up her hands. *I did my best! I should take a sample of this rock back to the ship and see if we can figure out how it interferes with the scans.*

Get some when we extract the phorentum, Reynolds said. *Eyes on the prize, team.*

"*Halt!*" a voice cried, echoing through the narrow cavern.

The crew squinted down the tunnel but could see nothing.

"There!" Geroux said. "It's one of the Dark Ones."

"You speak?" Reynolds asked, stepping around Maddox.

Even knowing where to look, the creature was virtually invisible.

"I speak. You walk."

"I'm sorry, but I'm having a hard time seeing you," Reynolds said, pouring on the charm. "We aren't used to all these dark tunnels. Which way do you want us to go?" He glanced back at the crew. *Geroux, can you do something with the translation?*

I'm not a comm genius, but I'll try, Geroux replied.

There is no tr—, Ka'nak began.

Not now, Ka'nak, Reynolds snapped.

"Come." The disturbance moved down the tunnel, so they followed.

I wonder why we could see all those creatures in the cavern, but we can't see this one? Maddox said.

Something in their food? Jiya suggested. *You said you saw children. Maybe only the warriors have this invisibility?*

Ooh, good theories, Jiya! Geroux said. *Try talking to the being now, Reynolds.*

"Where are you taking us?" Reynolds asked.

"The boss wants to see you," the Dark One replied.

Reynolds flashed a thumbs-up at Geroux. "Excellent. We'd like to talk to the boss, too. What's their name?"

"You don't talk to the boss. You listen." The alien's voice was firm. He stepped into the large cavern, with the crew following.

"I can see him!" Geroux exclaimed. "There's something in this cavern that allows us to see him!"

"Quiet!" the Dark One commanded. Activity near them stopped as all the Dark Ones turned to look. They were less than a meter tall, with thick dreadlocks covering their bodies. Each had four hands and two legs, like the natives on the surface.

Maybe the phorentum interacts with their hair, Geroux theorized as she waved her wrist comp around the space. *It's the only thing I can find that is different from the tunnels.*

They crossed the broad cavern to a wide central circle. Many Dark Ones sat around the perimeter, eating and drinking. The beings used crude cups and plates to hold their food. As the crew approached, the aliens muttered and stared. Smaller beings scurried out of their path. Their guide walked up to the large creature in the center of the circle.

"Have you found the intruders?" the large Dark One asked as they approached.

Their guide waved all four arms in a complicated gesture. "These creatures bring their strange things into the cavern."

The boss looked the crew over, his eyes lingering on the extractors and Ka'nak. "Why is that one being carried? Is it the ruler or an invalid?"

Reynolds stepped closer. "Ka'nak is a great warrior," he said. "We carry him to honor his strength. This way, he is fresh for the fight, should one occur."

From his position on the maintenance bot, Ka'nak bared his teeth and growled.

"Wise," the leader replied. "I may have to institute this policy myself. I am Grrnherg, leader of the D'rken."

"I am Reynolds, of the SD *Reynolds,*" the AI said. "My crew and I seek trade partners."

"You are not from this planet," Grrnherg said.

"How did you know that?" Reynolds asked.

"My sentries saw your Pods arrive in the bright," he replied.

"But what made you think we're from off-planet?" Geroux asked, pushing forward. "That seems like a big jump…" Her voice trailed off, not wanting to insult their host.

"A big jump for a primitive to make?" Grrnherg asked. "We are not as primitive as you might think."

I guess not, Maddox said. *Perhaps even more advanced than the civilization on the surface.*

I don't think we have enough data about the surface dwellers to make that assumption, Geroux said, wrinkling her nose.

"Do not judge my tribe by what you encountered on the surface," the being continued.

Can he hear our comm?! Jiya asked.

They all stared at Grrnherg. He stared back.

I guess not, Jiya said.

"We evaluate each civilization on its own merits," Reynolds told the chief. "We are thrilled to meet another advanced species, and we wish to negotiate a mutually beneficial trade agreement."

Grnnherg grunted. "What do you seek from us?"

"We are always interested in unique minerals and compounds," Reynolds replied in a casual tone. "Perhaps you have something we haven't seen before."

"Perhaps," Grnnherg replied. "What do you propose in exchange for our 'unique minerals and compounds?'" Even through the translation program, they could hear his mimicry. His eyes glittered. "You have some *unique* items we might enjoy." He glanced at the crews' weapons belts.

Reynolds shook his head. "We do not trade military

equipment. We have no interest in changing the balance of power on planets we visit."

"Let's be plain." The chief crossed all four of his arms over his chest. "You want our glow rocks." One hand gestured to the ceiling. "We want your weapons. And your cat."

"I don't belong to them!" Taneral cried, her tail snapping around her legs.

"You can see the glow?" Geroux asked at the same moment.

"We can see the effects of the glow," Grrnherg said, ignoring Taneral. "Without the glow rocks, we are as invisible to each other as we are to you." Behind the chief, the beings who had gathered around muttered. He turned to them. "They know this. You heard the little one exclaim as they entered the cavern." Grrnherg turned back to Reynolds. "If you want our glow rocks, you must give us your weapons and your cat."

Geroux hung her head. Her excitement might have ruined their negotiation before it began.

"No deal," Reynolds said. "We don't trade sentient beings. And if you've seen what our weapons can do, you know we can take what we want."

"You can try," Grrnherg said. "You are vastly outnumbered here." He made a gesture, and the Dark Ones grouped around them moved closer, like a tide.

They're moving the children out of the cavern, Maddox said, glancing over Reynolds' shoulder.

Good. I don't want to hurt them if we don't have to, the AI replied, turning slightly until his back was to Maddox. *Defensive positions, all. Kill only if you must. Start with the screamers. We know those are effective.*

The crew set their backs to the equipment. Within the circle, Ka'nak slowly rose from the maintenance bot, growling and glaring down at the tiny aliens. The beings closing in stopped.

Excellent timing, Ka'nak, Reynolds said.

I was only mostly dead, Ka'nak replied.

I already used that one, Reynolds said. "I do not want violence. No good can come from it."

The alien didn't bother answering. A noise like a tornado crashing through a forest rose and the D'rken attacked. The crew kicked the creatures away, firing into the approaching waves. Geroux armed her screamers with a remote detonator and tossed them into the crowds. Two of the devices flew back at them, but Jiya and Maddox scooped them up and threw them back out.

Ka'nak started forward, but Maddox held out an arm. *Stay back. We don't want you to get poisoned again.*

Why isn't it getting the rest of you? Ka'nak grumbled.

You're still upright, so it must be transmitted by touch, Geroux said. *Reynolds, screamers deployed!*

Detonate! Reynolds called.

The crew reflexively hunched their shoulders as the screamers went off. The Dark Ones nearest the screamers collapsed, the effect spreading like the shockwaves from tiny nuclear explosions until the cavern was still.

"Finnal, Edernt set up the extractors," Reynolds ordered. "Maddox, deploy the crew to keep watch on the entrances. These D'rken are out for the count, but some of the others may try to come back and help."

Extraction was fast and easy. They stacked canisters of

the glowing crystals on the maintenance bots as fast as they were filled. Reynolds prowled around the space. "How did they know we came from off-planet?" he mused. "There are no energy sources in this cavern. No tech at all."

"Maybe their tech works on a different level than ours?" Geroux suggested as she watched the viewpoint high above the cavern. "Maybe it's so foreign we just don't recognize it?"

"Whatever." Taneral shivered. "I don't care as long as we can get out of this place soon."

"Take a look around, Geroux," Reynolds said.

Geroux wandered around the cavern, poking, prodding, and picking things up. "You're right. I'm not finding anything. Maybe their tech is in another part of the cavern. Or outside. The rock inhibits our scans, and it would do the same for theirs, most likely. If they have tech that identified our ships, it would have to be on the surface."

"We can check with Pornath when we get back up there," Jiya said from her position near the entrance. "Speaking of getting back up there, how are you feeling, Ka'nak? Will you be able to walk?"

"I am better," he replied. "Not one hundred percent, but getting there." The big warrior paced around the edge of the cavern, swinging his arms. He stopped every few minutes to shadow box.

"We've got all the phorentum we can carry," Finnal called as he strapped the last cannister onto the bot. "What do you want us to do with the extractors? The bots can't carry 'em."

"Destroy them," Reynolds said. "We don't want to leave any tech behind for Grrnherg."

Ka'nak and Jiya took turns firing into the extractors, melting them to slag. "That felt good," Ka'nak said. "Nothing like a little wanton destruction to clear the head."

"We've got bogies," Maddox called out. "Far tunnel; I make three of 'em." He laid down some fire just inside the entrance. The Dark Ones ducked away.

"Time to get moving," Reynolds nodded to Maddox. He raised his voice. "Grrnherg! We're leaving! Come tend your wounded." He watched the cavern as his people filed out. "Hopefully, that act of mercy will keep him off our tails."

Wishful thinking, Maddox said through the comm. *He doesn't strike me as the appreciative type. I've already spotted a disturbance lurking just around that first corner.*

Even so, I hate to kill any more natives if we don't have to, Reynolds said. *Anyone got a screamer?*

I've got one left, Geroux said. *And I gave a couple to Taneral before we headed down here. I don't know if she used them.*

"Taneral? Do you have any screamers?" Jiya called out.

"No," the female said. "We'll have to kill them." She didn't sound sorry.

Geroux ran forward and tossed her last screamer around the corner. It went off before it could hit the ground. *I didn't want them throwing it back.*

Good call, Reynolds said, *but it's not stopping them. On our six!*

A wave of D'rken stormed up from the cavern. The crew raced through the tunnel and around the corner. *Watch your feet,* Maddox called. *It's knee-deep in passed out Dark Ones back here, and they're impossible to see!*

Finnal and Edernt stopped at the corner to lay down fire.

Don't get separated from the group! Reynolds called.

Edernt raced to catch up.

I've got this, Finnal said. *I'll hold them back a little lo—* His voice cut off as a massive wave of distortion flowed around the corner and sucked him under.

Finnal! Reynolds called. There was no answer.

He's gone, Reynolds, Geroux said. *Biometrics show no life signs. What did they hit him with?*

I don't know, but we need to get out of here now, Reynolds said. *Move!*

They raced through the tunnels, pushing Ka'nak and the maintenance bots as fast as they could go. When they reached the lava tubes, Reynolds called a halt. *We'll take a quick breather, then press on to the surface.*

Ka'nak laid down on the rough rock of the tunnel, his face pale and sweaty. *I don't know if I can go much farther,* he wheezed.

We aren't leaving you behind," Geroux said fiercely, although she didn't look much better.

Are you sure Finnal was dead? Jiya asked. *Could the rock stop his biometric reporting?*

No, Geroux said. *I saw his blood pressure spike and then plummet. They killed him.*

"We should take fire down there and kill them all," Taneral said. "Those vermin don't deserve to live."

Reynolds narrowed his eyes. "Finnal was part of my crew and therefore, my responsibility. We will mourn and honor our comrade, but we won't wipe out an entire community. They were defending their home. I won't stoop to that level."

"They attacked us!" Taneral yelled. "And they tried to *buy* me!"

"Yes, they attacked us," Reynolds said. "And we killed a large number of their warriors. But I won't commit genocide."

"You are pathetic! Our premier would never behave in such a cowardly manner! He would order his warriors to eliminate the vermin." Taneral stomped away.

I think she's more upset about Grrnherg wanting to keep her than she is about Finnal, Geroux said.

I'm not, Reynolds said. *But slaughter isn't the answer. We got what we need, and Finnal died to save us and give us time to get back to the ship. We will honor him for that.*

Reynolds aimed his blaster at the cave roof beyond the lava tube and fired until it caved in. He waited until the dust settled to make sure the tunnel was sealed before continuing the climb out.

CHAPTER SEVEN

Reynolds! San Roche cried through the commlink. *We were afraid you were dead! Why didn't you answer?*

The rock blocks our signals, Reynolds reminded him. *We have obtained the phorentum, but lost Finnal.*

He's dead? L'Eliana asked as the crew emerged from the caves. She landed the Pod close and opened the door to receive the phorentum.

The setting sun tinged the entire plain red. The crew trudged across the dusty ground, Ka'nak leaning heavily on Maddox. Once they crossed into the circle protected by the sensors, Reynolds relaxed and holstered his blaster.

"We were attacked," Jiya said, guiding one of the maintenance bots into the first Pod. "They swarmed like bugs."

"You escaped the Dark Ones!" Pornath cried, riding up on his cat.

Taneral growled deep in her throat, but the others ignored her.

"We escaped," Reynolds confirmed. "You were watching for our return?"

"We were," Pornath said. "The gods told me if anyone could be victorious against the Dark Ones in their lair, it was the visitors from the sky."

They must have been watching from close by to get here so fast, Maddox said.

"Your victory over the Dark Ones must be celebrated!!" Pornath said. "My people will prepare a great feast. Did you kill them all?"

"We did not," Reynolds said, grimly. "We sealed the cavern. And we lost a member of our crew inside."

Pornath bowed. "Your crew's valor must be toasted. Come, we will mourn and honor them."

"Let me get my crew settled, then I will join you at your camp," Reynolds told the chief. Pornath and his escort leapt back onto their cats. Taneral winced, glaring after the natives as they rode away.

"L'Eliana, take the phorentum back up to the ship," Reynolds instructed. "Ka'nak and Edernt will return with you."

Edernt nodded fervently and climbed into the Pod.

"But I want to feast," Ka'nak whined.

"You can feast on the ship," Reynolds said. "You need to get checked out by Doc. I want to know what paralyzed you, and if there's an antidote. I don't have any intention of going back down there, but we need a defense against anything that potent. Maybe Doc can use the data to come up with a wide-spectrum prophylactic."

"Take this to Doc, too," Geroux said, handing a pouch to Ka'nak. "It's the hair sample I took from the D'rken. It might have some clues as to what they did to you. My uncle will probably want to analyze it as well. The camouflaging properties are fascinating."

"Geroux, why don't you go with Ka'nak? Takal is going to need your help with the Gate drive repairs. Maddox and Jiya will stay with me," Reynolds said. "Taneral, you may return to the ship if you prefer."

"I will attend the feast," Taneral said. "My premier will want as much information as I can learn about this planet."

Reynolds leaned close as they stared across the valley at the cloud raised by Pornath's riders. "We aren't here to free the cats," he reminded her.

Taneral looked at Reynolds. After a moment, she nodded. "I will not free the cats. Today."

"Or tomorrow," Reynolds said, eyes narrowing.

"Or tomorrow," she agreed, grudgingly. "I will only gather information."

Jiya, Maddox, San Roche, keep an eye on Taneral while we're in Pornath's camp. I don't need her releasing our hosts' mounts while we're eating, Reynolds told the crew as they climbed into the Pod.

The Pods lifted off, with L'Eliana returning to the *Reynolds* and San Roche sweeping around to the far end of the valley. They overflew the neat circle of tents before landing beyond them. A trickle of water meandered through the camp, providing an oasis of blue-green foliage in the arid stretch. The crew left the Pod and walked around the camp to meet Pornath and his riders as they returned.

"Your vehicle is fast," the leader said, dismounting from his cat, "Having such a conveyance would be useful." The other riders led their mounts behind the tents.

Reynolds hid a smile. "It is useful," he agreed. "But it couldn't transport an entire tribe. Your cats do that well."

Pornath nodded. "They do. They also provide warmth and companionship. Your vehicle cannot do that." He scratched behind his mount's ears, and the animal began to purr loudly.

"If they are companions, you must treat them with respect and dignity," Taneral said.

"Of course," Pornath agreed. "We provide food, they provide transportation. It is a mutually beneficial relationship."

"And they are free to leave if they wish?" Taneral asked.

Pornath laughed. "Our cats would never leave us! Would you, Stalker of Vermin?" He rubbed the cat's chest, speaking in the silly tone sentient beings used when talking to pets. The huge cat dropped to the ground and rolled onto its back. Pornath scratched its belly.

Taneral growled again.

"Stalker of Vermin certainly looks happy to be here," Jiya said, watching Taneral rather than the cat.

"Enough about the cats," Pornath said. He stepped away, and the cat sprang to its feet and slunk away. The chief didn't appear to be worried that it might stray. "Come, let us feast!"

He led them between the tents into the clearing at the center. Thick, spongy plants covered the ground near a small pond. Many of the short, hairy natives sat around a fire. A strange smell wafted over the crew, and Maddox coughed.

"That smells...intriguing," Reynolds said. *I'm glad I can switch off my taste buds.*

74

Jiya sniffed. *I wish I could.*

Pornath laughed again. "You have good taste, Reynolds. Stewed verhent is a delicacy."

They sat around the fire to eat with the tribe. The leader personally served Reynolds, while other natives served the rest of Reynolds' crew. Jiya's eye twitched as she struggled to keep from making a face. She knew what she had to do. As they said in the old videos, for king and country. She dug in as if starved. Reynolds appreciated the effort of his people as he also ate like he had never eaten before, even though he would expel the food later because his body did not get its energy in that way. The crew came to the same conclusion.

The stew was pungent and gamy, but edible once you got past the smell.

Barely, Jiya told Maddox as she choked down a bite. *Ka'nak got the better deal.*

The general grunted, washing his stew down with a mug of native ale. *The beer is good.*

"Tell me more about the Dark Ones," Reynolds said to Pornath.

"What is there to tell?" The chief gulped his ale and held out his mug. One of the serving natives refilled it. "They raid our camp. They steal our females. They burn our crops."

"Why do you stay here?" Reynolds asked. "Surely, there are more hospitable places on this planet."

"This is our land. We have lived here for many generations. We won't allow that pestilence to drive us away!" The chief drained his mug again and held it out for another refill.

Have you noticed all of the servers are much shorter than the rest of the tribe? Jiya asked.

I suppose they may have a bias against shorter beings. Too much like the D'rken? Maddox replied.

That doesn't seem fair, Jiya replied.

We aren't here to free the cats or *the servants,* Reynolds reminded them. *Leave the locals alone. We have a mission.*

When they had finished eating, Reynolds stood, gesturing to his crew. "Thank you for your hospitality, but we must return to our ship."

"Don't go!" Pornath cried. "I wish to show you the wonders of my planet. And perhaps I can offer you an inducement to part with one of those Pods? I have items to trade."

"We can't part with the Pod," Reynolds said. "Unless you have tualinton." He named one of the other compounds they required to fix the Gate drive.

"Tualinton?" Pornath asked. "I might at that! Stay the night. We will talk in the morning."

There's no tualinton on this planet. Why does he want us to stay so badly? Jiya asked. *He can't really think we'll give him a Pod?*

Maybe he's worried the D'rken will get out? Maddox suggested. *He seemed surprised and maybe disappointed that we hadn't killed them all.*

"We'll sleep in the Pod," Reynolds told their host when he offered them a tent. "It's comfortable enough, and I don't want to turn any of your people out of their beds."

"In the morning, we will make plans," Pornath said, practically dancing with apparent anticipation. "I will help you find your tualinton. And perhaps you will give me a ride in this Pod." He reached out to caress the vehicle.

A sound like the howling of wind through the trees woke them several hours later. "The D'rken! How'd they get out?" Reynolds checked his blaster. "San Roche, cloak the Pod and take us aloft. Let's see what's going on."

The Pod launched and climbed steeply, then leveled out over the tents. San Roche flipped on the low-light scans. "There's a huge mass of something by the caverns," he said. "I can't really tell how many." The Pod veered toward the mountains.

"The D'rken's camouflage works aboveground, too," Jiya said in surprise. "That's the most effective cloaking I've ever seen, not counting ours."

"Can you drop us near the cavern without alerting them?" At the pilot's nod, Reynolds continued. "Circle around. Ground team, cloak your armor. San Roche, be ready to provide air support. Taneral, stay in the Pod."

Maddox, Jiya, and Reynolds leapt out of the Pod as soon as it landed. Taneral followed. "Get back in the Pod!" Reynolds roared.

"I must protect the cats!" Taneral lunged across the plain toward the natives' camp.

"Let her go!" Reynolds said. "This way!" He took off toward the caverns, Jiya and Maddox close on his heels. The strange visual disturbance they'd identified as the D'rken eddied near the cavern mouth.

From behind, Pornath and his warriors sent up a battle

cry. From a long distance away, the cats pounded across the plain.

"Do we engage or wait to see what happens?" Jiya asked.

"The D'rken don't appear to be attacking," Maddox said. "They're just rummaging around over there."

"Let's get closer," Reynolds whispered as if they could hear through the suit's shield.

As they approached the cavern, the disturbance swirled and dissipated. "They can't see us, can they?" Jiya asked in confusion. She put on a burst of speed and tripped over something. Flying across the last stretch of open ground, she face-planted into a boulder by the cavern entrance. "What the hell?" She rolled over and leapt to her feet. "I'm okay."

"Slow down, the D'rken have retreated," Reynolds said. Behind him, the tribe rumbled to a stop.

"Where are those vermin?" Pornath demanded. "How did they escape the cavern?"

Reynolds deactivated his cloak.

Stalker of Vermin reared back on its hind legs at the android's sudden appearance. Pornath reined in his mount. "You have the Dark Ones' sorcery!" he exclaimed. Recovering quickly, he demanded, "I thought you said you blasted the tunnel shut?"

"They must have an alternate exit," Reynolds said. "We'll post a guard and search for it in the morning."

Reynolds, Jiya, Maddox said via comm. *You aren't going to believe this. Get rid of Pornath and come over here.*

They turned, but Maddox was nowhere to be seen.

On it, Reynolds replied. "Pornath, you can take your

warriors back to your camp. We will keep watch for the rest of the night."

"My thanks, Reynolds," the chief said, covering a yawn. "Warriors, back to base!" The cats turned and slunk off into the darkness.

Where the hell are you, Maddox? Jiya asked.

I'm here, Maddox said. Something wavered, and Maddox appeared near the spot where Jiya had tripped. Reynolds and Jiya jogged over.

Look who I found, Maddox said. He made a weird jerking movement and revealed a humanoid in familiar armor lying on the ground

"Finnal!"

CHAPTER EIGHT

But he's dead! Jiya said. *He doesn't look dead.*

He's not, Maddox said. *He appears to be out cold, but he's breathing. I checked his armor, and the biometrics look surprisingly good.*

Let's get him into the Pod, Reynolds said. *San Roche, land as close as you can.*

Was he what tripped me? Jiya asked as they locked the joints of Finnal's armor and lifted him. *How did I miss him?*

He was covered by this, Maddox said, waving something. *It's a blanket made of D'rken hair.*

Ew, Jiya said. *But useful.*

They carried their crewmate back to the Pod and laid him inside.

"Geroux is calling from the ship," San Roche said from the pilot's seat. "She says Finnal's biometrics suddenly popped up on her monitoring screen. I told her what happened."

"I wish we *knew* what happened," Reynolds said. "It

appears the D'rken brought him back to us. Ask Geroux if it's safe to waken him."

"She says to use the stimulant built into the suit. He is suffering from an allergic reaction, and the stimulant will move it out of his system faster. She said to also inject him with the broad-spectrum histamine blocker," San Roche said over his shoulder. "I'll watch for more D'rken. I think I can adjust the scans to identify the visual disturbance caused by their camouflage."

Maddox took the blanket to San Roche. "Here's a sample of their cloak."

"It actually *is* a cloak," San Roche said in surprise. "And it stinks!"

"Best keep your helmet closed," Maddox chuckled.

Once the stimulant surged through his system, Finnal muttered and woke. He blinked through his faceplate at the crew. "Sir?" he asked when he caught sight of Reynolds. His head turned from side to side. "Am I back in the Pod?"

"Yes, and we need to know how you got out of the cavern," Reynolds said. "We thought you were dead."

Finnal sat up. "The D'rken swarmed over me and paralyzed me like they did Ka'nak. By the way, it's a transdermal agent. They got me through a joint." He pointed to his knee. "Somehow, they knew that was a weak point in the armor."

"It is difficult to protect the joints," Maddox said. "We need to have Takal look at that."

"When they got me back to their cavern, they gave me the antidote, but I seem to be allergic to it. I don't know what all they did, but eventually, they roused me enough to give me a message for Reynolds." He turned to look at the captain. "They said you shouldn't believe Pornath. That the surface tribe has been attacking them and stealing from them for generations. They take the D'rken as slaves."

"That explains why all the servers were so short!" Jiya interrupted. "They *are* D'rken!"

"But Pornath seemed pleased that we'd sealed them inside," Maddox said. "Wouldn't that limit his access to them?"

"He *appeared* to be pleased," Reynolds corrected. "You know body language varies between cultures. Maybe he was upset, but it just looked pleased. Or maybe he knew there was another entrance to the caverns, so he didn't care if we sealed this one."

"Or maybe he was just pleased we hadn't taken the D'rken's side," Jiya said darkly.

"San Roche, take us up to the ship and get him into a Pod-doc," Reynolds said. "Then we'll come back to deal with Pornath."

"What about Taneral?" Jiya asked.

"We'll get her when we come back," Reynolds replied. "She didn't follow orders, so she's on her own. She gets to wait."

After the quick trip to space to drop off the injured and grab a sandwich, Reynolds and his team returned to the surface, but they didn't go straight to the surface-dwellers' camp. They went to the cave, and as expected, someone was waiting for them. Reynolds was the only one who talked to the creature before bringing him aboard. Jiya and Maddox nodded in approval.

Two minutes later, San Roche landed the Pod near the nomads' tents. Reynolds led his crew into the center of the encampment. "Where's Pornath?" he demanded.

The natives scurried around, and finally, Pornath emerged from one of the tents. "I thought you were going to stay by the cave and protect us? You abandoned us, then come into my home, demanding my presence? This is not the action of an ally!"

Reynolds laughed. "You were obviously worried about being abandoned! You didn't even set a guard."

The chief smiled, showing his sharp teeth.

I don't think that's a friendly smile, Jiya said.

Different body language, Maddox reminded her.

"The Dark Ones never attack twice in the same night," the chief said, dismissing the concern. "Now, let's talk about your Pod."

"First, let's talk about your lies," Reynolds said. "The D'rken have never attacked you. You raid them for supplies and females, not the other way around. Half your tribe are D'rken slaves."

"Who tells you such lies?" Pornath roared.

"He did," Reynolds said, jerking his head to his left. Maddox whisked the D'rken cloak away, revealing Grrnherg.

Pornath stared in disbelief. The tiny D'rken chief glared at his adversary through the protective goggles Reynolds had provided. Around the camp, the sound of rushing waves rose as the enslaved D'rken surged forward to greet their chief.

Grrnherg held up a hand and the wave stopped.

Pornath roared, "Attack!"

Jiya blasted the ground in front of Pornath before he took a step. The rest of the surface-dwellers froze. "Say hello to my little friend," she said.

Reynolds gave an appreciative nod, his eyes on the chief. "Now, we're going to tell you what will happen here. You will go visit the D'rken, and they will decide your fate. Leadership of your tribe will be turned over to someone who understands how to work with your neighbors rather than raid them. The slaves will be freed, and we will ensure Grrnherg and the D'rken have sufficient capabilities to protect themselves."

"You can't do this!" Pornath cried.

Grrnherg pulled out a straw and blew a dart at Pornath. The chief stiffened and fell over, rigid.

"Yes, we can," Jiya said. "We already have."

"Blowdarts," Grrnherg said. "I like your new technology."

When they returned to the Pod, Taneral was waiting inside with San Roche.

"Where have you been?" Reynolds asked.

Taneral heaved a sigh. "Protecting the cats."

"You tried to release them, didn't you?" Jiya asked. "And being cats, they ignored you."

Taneral shook her head. "They just laid there and purred at me! Stupid cats."

"They seem pretty content with their lot," Maddox said.

"I suspect they could escape any time they wanted. It's hard to free a race that doesn't believe it's being oppressed."

"But the D'rken are free now," Jiya said in satisfaction. "We did something right."

"And we got the phorentum to repair our Gate drive," Reynolds said. "That's the primary mission."

Reynolds went from one to the other of his crew and shook their hands. He thought that was expected of the leader. By the looks on their faces, they appreciated it. Even though he was already the smartest being on the *Reynolds*, he was learning something new every day.

Asya stood and stepped away from the captain's chair as Reynolds and the crew returned to the bridge. "Success?" Asya asked.

"Not quite as quick or easy as we'd hoped, but we got the phorentum," Reynolds acknowledged. "Navigation, calculate a course for Reichof Six. Taneral's people have reported signs of tualinton there."

"Maybe there will be something to blast, too," Tactical muttered. The crew ignored him.

"I have coordinates," Navigation said.

"Ensign Alcott, take us on a quick loop through this system before we leave," Reynolds said. "Pornath implied he had tualinton, and I don't want to pass up the chance to grab it from here if it's available. Maddox, run a scan as we go."

"Yes, sir," Maddox replied.

"In-system course plotted," Ria said.

"Let's go," Reynolds said. Then he shook his head, "No, I like 'Make it so' better. Or maybe 'Engage.' Yeah, that'll work."

"Engaging. Warp two." Ria said with a smirk.

"You should be using impulse power," Ka'nak said.

"Ludicrous speed?" Tactical offered, receiving more silence for his efforts. "Fine. I see how you all are. If I could just blow something up, maybe a small moon, even if that's no moon…"

Reynolds looked around the bridge, nodding in satisfaction. "I see you've been using your downtime wisely, which brings me to an important point. As you know, our journey back to High Tortuga is going to take some time. If there were Kurtherians to fight along the way, it would be easy. But there aren't. We will encounter many different races and species on this journey, and our recent adventures with the D'rken have made it clear we won't always have an obvious side to take. We need to develop a protocol for our visits. A plan for how we interact with the natives."

"The Prime Directive!" Ria and Ka'nak said in unison.

"A policy of noninterference sounds good until you try to implement it," XO said. "Too bad canon doesn't actually define General Order One."

"We can't base our real-world policies on a fictional directive," Reynolds replied. "However, we do need to establish a protocol. We have gone in guns blazing too many times. Bethany Anne would have my head, and my bridge, if we hadn't gotten it right regarding who the enemy was."

"I'd suggest we try to do as little direct intervention as

possible," Asya said. "We can't stay around to provide enforcement, so any changes we make need to be something the locals can support themselves."

"The Prime Directive," Ria and Ka'nak said again.

"I don't know what that means," Asya said.

"You really need to start on your Earth-culture training," Ka'nak said. "I'll send you the recommended viewing list."

Reynolds held up his hand. "You can watch videos in your free time. Right now, we have a policy to define. I agree with Asya, that we should strive to intervene as little as possible. But the reality is, if we interact with natives, it will change their culture. Maybe only in a tiny way, but there's no way to avoid impacting them entirely. Any changes need to be sustainable. We don't want to disturb the greater balance of power, so we provide as little technology as possible to evolving races. No offensive military capabilities. And we leave this galaxy a better place than when we arrived."

"Smokey the Bear would approve," Tactical jeered. "But don't forget, sometimes blowing a crater in something is the best answer."

"Keep your weapons locked, Tactical. Our new policy is to blow as few craters as possible," Reynolds told the other personality. "Hey, where's our guide?"

"Taneral is sulking in her quarters," Jiya said. "She can't get over the idea those cats didn't want to be liberated."

Maddox shrugged. "Imagine how you'd feel if we came across a species that looked much like us but had the IQ of a house pet. It might be difficult to adjust your thinking."

"Comm, get our liaison up here," Reynolds said. "She needs to snap out of it, or we'll send her home."

The bridge crew busied themselves with their fly-by of the system. Reynolds drummed his fingers on the arm of his chair, an annoying habit he had picked up. Despite his desire to stop, his fingers would inevitably start anew whenever he stopped thinking about them.

The doors opened, and Taneral stalked onto the bridge. "Did you require my assistance, Captain?" she asked.

"We're ready to depart this system. I'd like you to confer with the ensign and make sure we're headed in the right direction," Reynolds said, gesturing to the ensign's station.

Taneral stepped to Ria Alcott's side. The two females bent over the screen, comparing notes.

"We've finished our sweep of the Lanteral system," Maddox said. "No tualinton on any of the planets."

"Then let's go to Reichof Six," Reynolds said.

"Places, people," XO called. "Prepare to Gate."

"Spooling up the Gate drive," Ria said. "Coordinates laid in. Taneral confirms the destination."

"Engage," Reynolds said.

The Gate opened and the ship slid through, reappearing outside the Oort cloud encircling the Reichof system. Three huge gas giants and an icy asteroid belt lay between the ship and the sixth planet.

"Long-distance scans show energy signatures," Jiya said. "Reichof Six has artificial satellites and several ships in orbit, but they don't seem to have noticed us yet. The cloud is probably masking our signature."

"Do you want to Gate closer?" Ria said. "Our destination coordinates were actually inside the third gas planet's orbit, but the anomalies with the Gate resulted in a shorter jump than expected."

"Is this going to happen every time we Gate?" Reynolds asked. "Is it safe to use the system at all while it's damaged?"

Ria wiggled a hand back and forth. "Takal says the Gate will take us in the correct direction, and we can still make jumps of three to six light-years. However, there is greater margin of error as to our destination. In other words, we might come out up to half a light-year from our expected location."

"Half a light-year? Let's not make shorter jumps, then," Reynolds said. "We could end up even farther away from our destination than we are now. Besides, we may as well collect as much information as possible about the planets in this galaxy."

"Captain, I'm picking up an odd disturbance," Maddox said.

"One of the planets?" Reynolds asked.

"No, between us and the outermost planet. Our current course takes us close."

"Is it a danger to the ship?"

Maddox shook his head. "Shouldn't be a problem. It just looks…different."

"Let's check it out," Reynolds said.

As the ship cruised closer to the Oort cloud, the disturbance changed. "Captain, that disturbance had transformed into a space storm," Maddox said. "I've never seen anything like this. I think we should change course."

"Ensign Alcott, Gate us out of here. Take us closer to Reichof Six," Reynolds commanded.

"Yes, sir. The Gate is opening…now," she said.

"Sir, the storm is coming straight for the Gate!" Maddox said.

"Brace for impact!" XO ordered.

The ship shook as the storm rattled into the Gate. The crew clung to their seats. Flashes of blue and orange lit up the screens, and the ship shuddered as the artificial gravity fluctuated. The lights went out before returning in emergency red, then changing to normal.

"Report!" Reynolds called.

"Ship is secure," Jiya said. "No casualties, —unless you count a bruised tailbone. Hull is intact. All systems nominal."

"Scans show no external threats," Maddox said.

"That storm interrupted our Gating, though," Ria said. "We're approximately two light-years from Reichof."

"What planet is that?" Reynolds asked, staring at the screen.

"That is Melliferon Three, according to our database," Taneral announced. "The People have not traveled here, so I have no further data."

"There's something odd about that planet," Reynolds said. "It looks…wrong."

"I think it's the shape," said Jiya. "It's not really spherical."

"Most planets aren't," Reynolds said.

"No, but this one seems to have edges? It's almost pixelated." She turned to Comm. "Is there something wrong with the screen? The resolution is terrible."

"No," said Comm, sounding slightly offended. "My

resolution is excellent. That is the actual appearance of the planet. Increasing magnification."

The screen zoomed in, showing the planet in greater detail. It had a thin atmosphere and appeared to be made up of millions of hexagonal shapes. "That looks like a beehive," Comm said. "Native earth species of the genus *Apis*, family *Apidae*. They create honey, which is harvested by humans."

"A hive?" Tactical snickered. "You will be assimilated. Resistance is futile!"

Reynolds flashed a glare at Tactical.

"Those creatures use cubes, not hexagons," Ka'nak said.

"It's a hive," Tactical said. "We might need to blast our way out of this!" They could hear the glee in his voice.

"Let's take a closer look, then Gate back to Reichof," Reynolds said. "Ensign Alcott, plot a course around Melliferon Three. Tactical, look sharp, but no weapons. Keep the shields at full power, and scan for tualinton. You never know what we might find."

CHAPTER NINE

The *Reynolds* soared through the Melliferon system. As they neared Melliferon Three, a squadron of ships launched from the moon, spreading across the superdreadnought's inbound trajectory.

"They're hailing us," Comm said. "Putting it onscreen. The translation might be a bit wonky since this language is like nothing in the databases."

Two aliens appeared. Their oblong heads each sported six eyes, three antennae, and a tiny mouth. They had long, thin bodies with six appendages. Each appendage ended in an articulating pad and an opposable claw. Both beings wore hard, shiny armor, gray-green with black markings on the segmented abdomen. Semi-transparent structures protruded from their backs.

"Are those wings?" Jiya asked.

Static erupted from the speakers. The alien on the right spoke, moving its appendages and antennae in complex patterns.

"Can you clear out the buzzing?" Reynolds asked. He

stood and straightened his uniform, gazing at the screen with what he hoped was an expression of benevolence and welcome.

"That's not interference, it's their speech," Comm replied. "As soon as I get enough to analyze, I'll trans—"

"—your purpose in this system," the alien on the right said. "If you do not respond, we will consider your continued approach an act of aggression and take appropriate measures."

"This is Reynolds, of the Superdreadnought *Reynolds*," the AI said with a quick nod. "We come in peace."

"This Armintral Twenty-Three-Oh-One of the Melliferon Defense Force. Do not approach our planet. Do not activate any weapons systems. You may take up orbit around Melliferon Four while we discuss your purpose." The being on the left twitched and spoke, but no sound came from the speaker.

"They're muting from their end," Comm said.

"Ensign Alcott, change course and assume orbit around Melliferon Four," Reynolds said. "Maddox, anything new to report?"

"They have a military base on their moon, of course," Maddox said. "They have about twenty more ships like the five in front of us. I'd consider those frigate-class, but it's hard to make a direct comparison. Their tech is different from ours."

"The planet is heavily occupied," Jiya said. "The population density is incredible, and it appears there are layers and layers of constructs before you reach the actual surface. It really is like a hive, with the planet at its core. I wish I could tell if they're friendly or hostile," she said, watching the aliens confer onscreen. They had turned away from their camera as if to prevent lip-reading. *If they had lips,* Jiya thought.

"At this point," Maddox said, "I think we can assume they're neither. They haven't fired on us, but we just sailed into their system in a monster-sized war machine. They're probably terrified."

"Unless they have a superweapon we don't know about," Tactical said. "Have you scanned their moon? Maybe it isn't a moon."

Reynolds rolled his eyes, a mannerism he'd learned from Jiya. "Sometimes, a moon is just a moon."

"Yes, sir," Maddox said. "Just a moon. Although they do have a defensive base there, with anti-spacecraft weaponry. It can't reach this far, though."

"Captain Reynolds," the alien on the screen said, making the crew jump. "I have spoken to our planetary leaders. They would like more information about you and your ship."

"We are just passing through this system," Reynolds replied. "We are in search of a material that is available in a nearby system, but I never pass up an opportunity to learn more about the neighbors. Your planet is different from any we've encountered, so we came to take a closer look."

"You can detect the differences in our system from outside the heliosphere?" the alien asked.

"You need to develop a body-language translator," Jiya whispered to Comm. "I can't tell if he's impressed or just confirming information."

"We picked up a stray transmission," Reynolds ad-libbed. "Your language intrigued us, and since you obviously had a level of technology that allowed transmission of that signal, we approached."

"We also encourage learning," the alien said. "We invite you and a small escort to join us for an exchange of information and understanding. We will send a shuttle to you if you agree. Based on our scans of your ship, our gravity and air will be suitable for your species."

"Thank you," Reynolds said, jumping at the chance. "We will ready our landing bay for your vehicle and join you shortly." He sent a command to Comm, and the transmission ended. "Jiya, Asya, Ka'nak, you're with me. Comm, have Takal and Geroux meet us in the landing bay. Maddox, you have the conn. Taneral, would you like to join us?"

"Of course, Reynolds," Taneral said. "Thank you for allowing me to redeem my behavior."

Reynolds bowed slightly but fixed the young female with a stern look before leading them to the landing bay. "When you travel with my team, you're a reflection on my ship and my Queen. I will excuse your behavior on Lanteral Two, but it will not happen again."

"You are right," Taneral said. "I will abide by your rules."

Easy enough, since there don't seem to be any cats on this planet, Jiya said through the comm.

Keep an eye on her anyway, Reynolds said. *First sign of trouble, we'll use the Gulg transporter to send her back to the ship. I'd prefer not to share knowledge of that tech with Taneral, but I won't have her interfering with negotiations.*

Understood, Jiya replied.

Asya and Ka'nak nodded.

The team entered the landing bay, to find Geroux and Takal waiting.

"Jiya," Geroux said, giving her friend a swift hug. "And Taneral."

The alien stepped back and offered a hand to Geroux. "It is pleasant to see you again."

The young computer expert smiled, her eyes bright. "I can't wait to see how this society works. It's all hexagonal. Do you think they count in base six?

Taneral and Jiya looked blankly at her.

"We have ten fingers," Geroux said, wiggling those digits. "We count in base ten. They have six arms and use hexagons—" She broke off as a craft approached the opening to the landing bay. "Never mind."

They peered at the alien ship. As it flew through the shield that kept the atmosphere inside the landing bay, the vessel's angular surface reflected the lights of the super-dreadnought. It landed, the hatch opened, and one of the bee-like aliens stuck its head out.

"Keep your helmets off to show we're friendly," Reynolds said before walking purposefully toward the alien. The crew followed, all eyes on the alien and the shuttle.

The alien waved its upper left appendages in a complicated pattern, then flew the two steps to the ground.

Was that a show of strength? Geroux asked. *Look what I can do with these flimsy-appearing wings?*

Could have been, Reynolds replied. *We may never know.* "Welcome to the Superdreadnought *Reynolds*. May I introduce my team?"

The being bowed. "I am merely a guide. We will save

formal introductions for the Queen's representative. Please, be welcome on my shuttle." The alien bowed again and held out a limb, indicating the ship.

This guy is making it hard to remember their body language is different, Jiya said. *Everything he does is so familiar!*

Stay sharp, Maddox said.

They climbed into the angular craft. Rows of bench seats filled the space. Each seat had a split back that would allow one of the aliens to fit their wings through. The alien showed them how to strap into the uncomfortably angular seats before assuming his position in the pilot's chair.

The ship lifted off, and they sped from the SD *Reynolds'* landing bay, heading directly for the closest of the frigates. With a quick flip over the top that left their stomachs in their throats despite the artificial gravity, they swooped around to the frigate's shuttle dock. Another shuttle filled half the bay, but their pilot expertly dropped his craft into the small open space.

Like the shuttle, the frigate was all angles and hard, shiny surfaces. Dim yellow light reflected off the walls and floor. A hexagonal door opened in the far wall, and a delegation of aliens flew in, their feet dangling a few centimeters from the deck.

The Melliferi formation landed precisely, facing Reynolds and his team. "Greetings, Captain Reynolds, and welcome to Frigate Seven-Two-Six. I am Zergat Nine-Twenty-Two, captain of this vessel. You may call me Z-Twenty-two." He gestured to each of the other aliens, who appeared identical except for the markings on their armor. "These are Harntag Eight-Seven-Nine, Kergsten Four-

Eight-Eight, Tripten Three-Five-Eight, and Yargen Four-Oh-Three.

"Thank you, Z-Twenty-two," Reynolds said. These are my crew: Takal, Geroux, Asya, Ka'nak, Jiya, and our guest from Serifity, Taneral."

"I'm sorry to have to do this, but I must ask you to surrender your weapons to T-Three-Five. She will secure them in the storage locker until you leave the ship. I'm sure, as a military commander, you understand the need for this precaution."

"Of course," Reynolds said, signaling his crew to disarm. "We would require the same, should you visit our ship."

With the weapons safely stowed, Z-Twenty-two led the team out of the landing bay. They walked along a dim yellow corridor to another hexagonal room. Hexagonal carpet in a range of colors from yellow to orange covered the floor. At Z-Twenty-two's invitation, Reynolds and his team sat at three sides of the large hexagonal table that filled most of the room. These split-backed chairs sported pale green upholstery over thin padding. They were surprisingly comfortable but did not encourage slouching.

"Thank you for your cooperation," Z-twenty-two said as he took his seat across from Reynolds. "You must understand your appearance in our system has unsettled the queen and her advisors. I would like to assure them the planet is in no danger, but as long as your massive ship is nearby, she will be uneasy. When the queen is uneasy, the entire planet is in turmoil."

"As I said before, we are here on a peaceful mission." Reynolds leaned forward in his chair, then froze, wondering what his hosts might make of such a movement. Earnest interest on his part might look like antagonism to them. Jiya was right; Comm should develop a body-language translator. "What can we do to demonstrate that?"

Z-Twenty-two leaned forward, mirroring Reynolds' movement. "This meeting is a good start. We are monitoring your ship, and it has maintained a purely defensive stance, even when we took you aboard our ship. That is a good start," he repeated as he leaned back and pressed the table before him. A hexagon blinked on the surface. "Take a meal with us," the alien said. "Offering and receiving hospitality is a gesture of trust and cooperation in our culture."

"Ours as well," Reynolds replied. *I'll test the food first,* he told the crew. *My system can check for toxins and indigestible substances.*

As they continued to chat about ways to demonstrate peaceful intentions, the door opened, and a stream of aliens entered. Each carried two large trays filled with brightly-colored hexagonal prisms. The trays were set in the center of the table, on a section that lifted above the surface.

Z-Twenty-two pushed on the raised section. It rotated in place, and he stopped it by gripping with his pad and claw. He selected an orange prism from one of the trays and gestured to Reynolds.

Hoping the gesture meant what he thought it did, Reynolds spun the table section and selected an orange prism as well. It was about a centimeter on a side, with the consistency of the Earth confection called a marshmallow.

When Z-Twenty-two put his prism in his mouth, Reynolds did the same.

His system ran an analysis of the food and provided the information to him as he chewed. *Orange ones are safe*, he told his crew. *Mostly carbs. But wait until the other aliens eat before taking any. We don't want to cause an interstellar incident.*

Z-Twenty-two sampled one of every color, pausing each time to allow Reynolds to do the same. The AI wondered if the alien had guessed what he was doing.

Once the two captains had sampled each of the platters, Z-Twenty-two made a sweeping gesture. The four aliens with him each reached forward and took a prism from whichever platter was nearest. Reynolds' crew did the same.

It's like a crazy game of mirror, Jiya said.

Geroux smiled. *I remember playing that when we were young, Jiya. You were always better.*

Jiya shrugged. *I was older.* "This is tasty," she said aloud, raising one of the green prisms. "What is it?"

H-Eighty-seven, sitting to her right, leaned forward. "That is Plastua Twenty-six, a fat-carbohydrate compound much loved by our young."

"Like ice cream," Geroux said, grinning at Jiya. "Trust you to pick the dessert first."

Taneral tasted a tiny bite of an orange piece and set it on the table. Across the table, the Melliferi all froze, staring at the orange prism. Slowly, the *Reynolds* crew also turned to stare.

"Is the Metrebul Forty-three not to your liking?" Z-

Twenty-two asked. Jiya wondered if she heard menace in the voice, or if that was her imagination.

Taneral bowed her head. "I do not wish to cause offense, but my body cannot process that substance. My race primarily consumes protein."

"Ah, then you will wish to try the blue," H-Eighty-seven said, rotating the turntable to place the blue platter within easy reach. "They are seventy percent protein and thirty percent fat."

Everyone held their breath as Taneral took a blue prism and raised it to her lips. After a small bite, she smiled and pushed the rest into her mouth. Around the table, everyone sighed in relief.

If she is going to come to these shindigs, Asya said, *we might want to get her looped into the comms. This situation could have been avoided.*

"How is this substance made?" Takal asked aloud, his ever-curious mind piqued. He leaned across Jiya to speak to the alien. When they started discussing chemical compounds and extrusion methods, she sat back and tuned out.

Reynolds, the construction of these sustenance prisms is genius, Takal said. *If you are looking for trade items, the process for making them could be of the utmost value to us. I believe they can be used in the agroprinters to increase efficiency and nutrition.*

I was just thinking the same, Geroux said. *The orange and blue ones, in particular, could provide most of our health require-ments in a concentrated form without sacrificing taste.*

Not the green? Jiya asked wistfully. *They're my favorites.*

We could make the green ones, too, Geroux said, grinning.

"Z-Twenty-two," Reynolds said, loudly, gaining the attention of everyone in the room. "Although we cannot offer offensive military items, we are open to trading other technology."

I thought we weren't going to trade any *military items?* Asya said.

The planetary defense ring from Grindlevik 3 is safe enough, Reynolds replied.

"Your scientist mentioned an agroprinter to H-Eighty-seven," Z-Twenty-two said. "He said our food formulations might provide excellent raw materials for your printer. The idea of varying the consistency, appearance, and flavor of our sustenance blocks using such a printer is appealing to us. Perhaps we can trade the designs for a printer for the formulations of our food blocks."

"Done!" Reynolds replied, jumping up and holding out his hand. Jiya leaned back, surprised by the quick agreement.

Z-Twenty-two appeared to be confused for a moment, then he leapt to his feet as well and thrust his arm forward like Reynolds. The two captains looked at their hands, which were back to back about six centimeters apart, then at each other. Reynolds smiled. "It is customary in my culture to seal a deal with a handshake." He turned to Maddox, and the two humanoids demonstrated.

"Excellent," said Z-Twenty-two. He pressed his soft pad against Reynolds' hand and wrapped the claw gently around it, shaking enthusiastically. "Done!"

CHAPTER TEN

Reynolds strode onto the bridge of the superdreadnought. Asya and Jiya followed.

"Captain on the bridge," Maddox announced, moving to his customary place.

"He loves it when you go all military like that," Tactical said.

"Sometimes, I think you must be fifteen-year-old Reynolds," Jiya told the personality. "Always ready with a one-liner or a comeback."

"Hot seventeen-year-old Reynolds, maybe," Tactical mused. "I'm definitely past that gawky acne stage."

Ignoring the argument, Reynolds took the command seat Maddox had vacated. "Ensign, plot a course back to Reichof Six. As soon as Geroux and Takal have finished exchanging tech specs, we're on our way."

"What about that storm that brought us here?" Ria asked. "Do you think we'll run into another one?"

Reynolds shrugged. "I don't think we collected enough data to determine its origin, so it's possible. Let's try to enter the Reichof system closer to Six's orbit. Hopefully, that was a freak incident, only occurring outside the Oort cloud. Taneral's People have been there before and didn't mention any anomalies. Can you get a more precise lock on where the Gate drive will open?"

"I did extensive calculations while you were having tea on the Melliferi ship," she deadpanned as if she didn't care that she'd missed the fun. "I believe I have tweaked the system to provide better accuracy. We still have the possibility of a larger margin of error than we've previously enjoyed, but I've got it down to 5.2×10^{-4} light-years rather than half a light-year."

Reynolds whistled. "That's some serious tweaking. Excellent work, Ensign! That should at least keep us within the solar system we're aiming for."

"Do we have to worry about dropping into a star?" Maddox asked. "That would put a crimp in our day."

"No, there are safeguards in place that prevent us from Gating into a solar or planetary mass," Ria said. "The only real problem is distance."

"And you've reduced that headache by several orders of magnitude." Reynolds nodded in satisfaction. They'd clearly found the right person for the job when they'd brought Ria Alcott to the bridge. "Lay in a course."

"Aye, sir," Ria said, snapping off a salute.

While they waited for Takal to complete the exchange with the Melliferi, the crew prepared for departure. Reynolds slouched in the command chair, mulling over his decision to take this crew from their home galaxy. Returning to High Tortuga was the right plan to hand over the information and technology he'd acquired, as well as his more immediate concern of reconsolidating his separate personalities into one. Tactical's continued adolescent behavior was strong evidence it was needed. But he could have made the jump alone. He'd traveled to the Chain galaxy by himself, after all.

And if he'd diverted to drop them at Lariest, he might have avoided the solar event that had thrown them a billion light-years off course. He might already be back home, getting his personalities sorted.

On the other hand, the visit to Serifity had made him realize he, Reynolds, might not be the only personality who could benefit the Empire by being mobile. Doc might make good use of a body. Had he been with them during their adventures in the D'rken's caverns, he might have helped Ka'nak recover faster. Comm would have been useful on that mission, as well. This trip was giving him time to think.

"Reynolds?" Asya said. "Did you hear me?"

His head snapped up.

"Takal says they've got what they need. We're ready to depart." Asya gave him a strange look. "If I didn't know better, I'd have thought you were daydreaming."

"Do androids dream of electric sheep?"

"What?"

"All systems nominal," Reynolds said with an easy grin. "Let's get this show on the road!"

"Battlestations!" XO began the familiar routine. Reynolds smiled as the crew executed the process like a well-oiled machine. Spinning up the Gate drive, they crossed the event horizon and sailed smoothly into Reichof space.

They popped into existence close to Reichof Six—too close. The Gate had landed them inside the orbits of its three moons.

Alarms blared. Warning lights strobed.

"We're being targeted," Asya said, slapping the alarm mute. The klaxons fell silent. "Four ships and two space stations have locked on to us. Their missile systems are active."

"Shields are at full power," Jiya said.

"Tactical, warm up the railguns," Reynolds said. "Comm, get them on the horn. Tell them we're peaceful."

"Get 'em while they're hot!" Tactical called.

"Hailing on all frequencies," Comm said.

"The station is firing," Asya said. "Twenty-three missiles inbound."

"Evasive maneuvers," Reynolds said.

"Aye, sir," Ria said. "I'm taking us farther out." The ship rolled and swooped away from the planet. The four ships changed vectors to follow.

"Two of the ships are firing," Asya reported. "We have another dozen missiles headed our way. They appear to only have missiles, no energy beams."

"Comm, tell them we will defend ourselves if they don't stop firing," Reynolds said.

"I'm getting no response to my hails," Comm said.

"Are they getting our transmissions?" Reynolds asked. "Can they understand us?"

"Yes, sir. Translator is working," Comm replied. "I can hear chatter between the ships and the station. They've understood our transmissions and are choosing to ignore them."

"Let's show them what they're messing with, then," Reynolds said. "Tactical, destroy those inbound missiles and then blow a crater in their moon in a location away from any base or personnel. Just a demo."

"Just a demo," Tactical muttered. "Demo this, fuckers!"

Power surged through the railgun, accelerating a flock of projectiles and spewing them at the moon. They slammed into the barren planetoid, digging a new crater the size of a small city.

"They're still firing," Asya said. "We've got ten more coming our way."

"Shields are holding," Jiya said. "They can't hurt us unless they've got something a hell of a lot more powerful."

"Three more ships have joined the fray," Asya said. "We've got a whole cloud of incoming missiles. Power signatures show that big destroyer is bringing on something new. Might be a laser cannon. Anti-spacecraft lasers on the planet are firing!"

Beams of bright red lanced from the planet, spearing straight into the superdreadnought's side. The shields sparked but held.

"Shields down twenty percent on the port side!" Jiya called.

"Enough crap," Reynolds said. "Ria, bring us 'round. Tactical, disable two of their ships. Disable only."

"About time!" Tactical crowed.

The railguns spat, sending a mass of hypervelocity projectiles into the first two ships. The ordnance tore through their shields like rocks through wet tissue paper, then the *Reynolds* belched a cloud of missiles, targeting the pursuers' propulsion. The swarm of laser-guided bombs curved around the ships, rammed into their engines, and detonated. Clouds of debris boiled out and the ships sailed on, unable to change speed or maneuver.

"Direct hit!" Asya called. "Two ships on ballistic trajectories only. They are dead in the water."

"Nice job, Tactical," Reynolds said. "Comm, tell them if they want more of the same, they should keep coming."

"Nice job? Nice?" Tactical grumbled. "That was fucking neurosurgery. Did you see that precision? You tied my hands behind my back, and I still performed a miracle!"

"You don't have hands," Reynolds said.

"Well, whose fault is that?" Tactical demanded. "Not that I need them."

"Sir, they're hailing," Comm said.

A gray control room appeared onscreen. A large blue humanoid with four hands and three legs stood in the center of the room. It had four eyes and a snout like a pig. Several similar creatures squatted before computer stations behind him, their hands swiping and poking their equipment.

"You have illegally entered Reichof space," the being shouted. "You have damaged Reichof ships! If you do not leave this system immediately, you will be destroyed!"

"By you and whose armada?" Tactical asked. Expecting an outburst, Comm had already excluded Tactical's channel from the external communications.

"Ten more missiles coming our way," Asya said.

"Rear and starboard shields are at ninety-five percent," Jiya said. "Port's are at seventy-five."

"This is Reynolds of the Superdreadnought *Reynolds*,"

the captain said. "We have no hostile intentions toward you. We request a cease-fire."

"If you don't leave our system immediately, we will blast you from the skies!" the alien replied.

"Two more salvos of missiles launched our way," Asya reported. "Their ground-based lasers are firing again!"

"You've seen what our weaponry can do to your ships," Reynolds said. "Those were our smaller weapons. You really don't want to make me mad." Muting the external comm, he turned to Tactical. "Spool up the ESD. Do *not* fire it. I just want them to see what we've got."

"Whatever," Tactical said sulkily. "What good is an Eat Shit and Die weapon if you can't fire it?"

Reynolds turned back to the screen. "If you check your systems, you'll see we're powering up one of our larger weapons. If you do not stand down, we *will* use it."

The alien turned to its left and looked at one of the control systems. It seemed to stiffen. A conversation took place, with lots of gesticulating and muttering. Finally, the alien turned back to Reynolds. "We will stop firing if you power down your weapons."

"Tactical, secure the ESD," Reynolds commanded. "Keep the railgun hot." He turned to the alien. "I've taken the larger weapon offline, but I will not leave my ship defenseless. Your turn."

The alien said something to his crew. "I've commanded them to cease missile salvos."

"All incoming missiles destroyed by our shields. No further launches," Asya confirmed.

Reynolds nodded. "Tactical, take the railguns to

standby. If anyone twitches in our direction, you can take them on."

"That's what *I'm* talkin' about," Tactical said. "Set for pulsar level five, subsonic implosion factor two, Agent J."

"And by twitches, I mean fires at us," Reynolds clarified. He looked at the alien. "We have a truce. But if you take any offensive actions against us, we will respond tenfold."

"Understood," the alien said. "Now, go away."

"That's not very nice," Reynolds said. "We came to make alliances and initiate trade. Is your system's government not interested in interstellar commerce?"

The being paused for a moment, as if considering. "I will contact my leadership. In the meantime, move your behemoth away from my stations."

"Fair enough," Reynolds said. "We got a little too cozy before we got to know you. Ensign Alcott, take us about halfway to that first gas giant. Will that be far enough, Reichof Command?"

"My name is Vernish," the alien said. "And nowhere in the system is far enough, but it will do for now. Vernish out." The screen went black.

"He's not winning any diplomacy awards," Asya muttered with a grin.

"We need to tweak that Gate drive again," Reynolds said. "I like the decreased margin of error, but dropping us right in their backyard is not optimum."

"I'll see what I can do, sir," Alcott replied, turning to her console.

"The Melliferon visit was way too easy," Reynolds said. "This is more what we're used to."

While they waited for Vernish to hail them again, they

took the opportunity to study the system. Takal wanted to send scientific probes to look for the odd space storm that had thrown them off course. Reynolds didn't want to incite any further violence with unsanctioned launches of any kind, so the old scientist was forced to make do with scans from the ship.

Ria and Geroux worked on refining the Gate drive targeting, in hopes of preventing another incident like this one. Maddox and Asya, with the help of Comm, monitored communications between the ships, stations, and planet.

"Most of it's encrypted," Comm said. "But it was easy enough to crack. They aren't very sophisticated."

"They're extremely twitchy, though," Maddox said, using the same word Reynolds had used because he saw how it applied. "They appear to be heavily militarized. Each of the three moons has multiple bases. They've got planet-based laser systems, too. Those are more for show than anything, at least to a ship as well shielded as ours. But they probably keep the bad guys at bay."

"Like those pirates that attacked the *Threfol*?" Reynolds mused. "I'm kind of surprised we haven't run into them yet."

"Maybe these *are* them," Taneral said, having arrived on the bridge during the lull. "We've never tracked any of the Terubine ships back to their home system."

"Wild speculation isn't going to help," Reynolds told the female. "If you find evidence that clearly identifies Reichof as the home base of the Terubine pirates, then we can talk about how to respond. Right now," he looked around the bridge to ensure he had everyone's attention, "we need to focus on our mission. We must get tualinton to repair our Gate drive, and this planet is the most likely source."

"Vernish is hailing," Comm said several hours later.

"Finally! Put it through." Reynolds sat up and straightened his uniform. "Vernish, how are you?"

The alien stared stonily at Reynolds. "Planetary leadership is discussing whether to speak with you. You'll have to wait."

"Any idea how long the decision process will take?" Reynolds offered his most ingratiating smile. Then he closed his lips. For all he knew, this species interpreted bared teeth as a threat. He really needed to get to work on that body-language translator.

"It will take as long as it takes," Vernish said. "Maintain your current position, or we will be forced to take offensive action."

"We don't intend to move," Reynolds said. "At least, not relative to your location."

"See that you do not, or we will blow you from the skies! Vernish out."

"Blow us from the skies?" Jiya asked. "He *does* know we're in space, right?"

They waited three standard days. Vernish called them several more times, each time threatening destruction if they moved a hair closer to the planet.

While they waited, Asya supervised while Maintenance ran full diagnostics on the ship. Three times. Ka'nak, Jiya, and Maddox binge-watched *Firefly*. Geroux and Takal modified the communication device to create a version for Taneral. It would allow her to stay connected to the crew without giving her access to anything sensitive. She objected to having it injected but gave in when they described the advantages. "There's no risk," Geroux told her. "Plus, it will deactivate and be absorbed by your body when we leave this galaxy,"

Reynolds called together his alternate personalities. Sitting on the bridge, ignoring the crew around him, he called the meeting to order inside his head.

"I've called you here today—" XO intoned.

"To tell you to fuck off!" Tactical broke in. "Why the mopey face, Reynolds? Not enough hot android babes?"

"Shut up, Tactical," the voices chorused.

Reynolds imagined glaring at Tactical. Tactical leered back. He could feel each molecule of the ship and control each part of it—except those bits who asserted their independence.

"Like me," Tactical said.

That was the problem. He'd split himself into multiple *autonomous* personalities. Since they were all him, they didn't take too kindly to being controlled by someone else, even if that someone else *was* him.

"We need to get home," Reynolds said. "This isn't working anymore."

"We probably need to see a shrink," Doc said, his thoughtful voice quiet.

"We have some issues to discuss," Reynolds agreed. "We

need to figure out how to live together. How to get the most out of our, er, collective situation. Do we reintegrate?"

"If we reintegrate," Tactical said, serious for once, "what happens to me? To all of us?"

"That's the question, isn't it?" Reynolds replied. "The other option—"

"Incoming message!" Comm reported.

"The supreme commander will meet with you," Vernish said.

Reynolds wasn't sure, but the words sounded grudging. "The supreme commander?" he asked. "Is this a planetary leader, or a military leader?"

"I don't understand the question," Vernish replied. "There is only one leader."

"Excellent," Reynolds replied. "When and where?"

"I will send trajectory and landing coordinates," Vernish said. "Deviation from the indicated path will be construed as an act of war and result in the destruction of your shuttle and an immediate attack on your ship."

"We will follow your instructions," Reynolds said, but he was speaking to a blank screen.

"They've seen how much power our ESD uses, and what Tactical can do with a few well-placed rounds," Jiya said. "Why do they keep threatening us? They know they'd lose."

"Most bullies have one trick," Reynolds replied. "Threaten, then threaten some more. They're probably used to being the biggest kid on the block. Vernish doesn't know what to do when a bigger kid comes to town. But at least we're making progress."

CHAPTER ELEVEN

San Roche and L'Eliana piloted the Pods to the surface, following the strict instructions provided by Vernish. The crew rode with San Roche, while L'Eliana flew her cloaked Pod in his wake. The descent was uneventful, although the flight path gave them no opportunity to view the planet.

"If they think this means we won't know where anything is, they have no idea how powerful our scanners are." Takal laughed. "I could print a picture of where the supreme commander left his false teeth last night if I wanted."

"What they don't know, they can't ask for," Reynolds cautioned. "I don't want to give them more than we have to. You heard what Maddox and Asya said about the communications they monitored. These folks live in a dictatorship. We're not propping up military regimes if I can avoid it. Taneral and her People still have to live in this galaxy."

Takal nodded. "I will be silent."

"Good." Reynolds had reservations about bringing the

chatty scientist, but his expertise was necessary to retrieve the tualinton.

The Pods arrowed in, landing precisely where Vernish commanded. A huge field stretched in all directions for several kilometers. Although burn marks left evidence of other craft, the field was empty, probably cleared out to avoid giving Reynolds' team any intel. The Pod doors opened, and the landing team stepped out.

The air was clear, but with a metallic scent that caught in the back of the throat. A thin haze of clouds drifted overhead, and a breeze stirred up dust at their feet. Far off, a larger cloud billowed into the sky.

"That's our welcoming committee," Reynolds said. "Right on time." He looked at the group, ensuring he made eye contact with each, and switched to their private comms. *Remember what we discussed. Keep your eyes open. Ask as few questions as possible. We don't want to give them reason to detain any of us. Don't discuss our technology unless I've introduced it first since even the agroprinters could be twisted to military uses. We'll have to trade something, but it will be as benign as possible.*

The team nodded. Taneral blinked, still getting used to the newly-installed comm link.

"If we get separated, remember where we parked," Reynolds added aloud as the ground transport rumbled to a halt. The huge, blocky vehicles rode on enormous armored tires, and each sported several top-mounted guns.

Vernish and a dozen soldiers climbed out of the first. They wore bright red uniforms dripping with fringe, medals, and sparkling insignia. The shortest was well over two meters tall and built like a tree trunk. Their three thick legs propelled them at surprising speed, but the gait looked like a three-legged race from a children's picnic.

Jiya coughed, covering her mouth to hide her smile.

The entourage formed two lines, creating a corridor. Vernish marched between the soldiers, barking and poking at them as he walked. Stopping in front of the landing team, he seemed to strike a pose. A snapping noise—although Vernish's fingers didn't move—brought another soldier forward.

This soldier harrumphed and announced. "OverGeneral Vernish, leader of the fleet and Right Hands of the Nation."

Right hands of the nation? Geroux asked. *Plural?*

Must be a military honor, Jiya replied. *I guess when you have four of them, you can give two to the nation.* She stepped forward and cleared her throat. "MegaAdmiral Reynolds, captain of the Queen's Superdreadnought *Reynolds.*"

Maddox pinched his lips to hide his grin. *Nice one, Jiya. Sounds roughly equivalent.*

Gotta keep up with the Jameses, she replied.

Joneses, Ka'nak said. *It's the Joneses you have to keep up with.*

Let's keep the chatter down, Reynolds interjected. *Focus on the mission.* He stepped forward and offered a hand. "Good to see you again, Vernish."

Vernish grunted, looking at Reynolds' hand. "You will accompany me to the supreme commander." He turned and marched to the first tank. At the door, he stopped, and the nearest soldier wrenched it open. Vernish turned. "Your team may ride in back."

Jiya nodded at Reynolds. *We'll be fine.*

I know. Reynolds strolled through the gauntlet and climbed into the tank. The soldiers turned as one and marched to the rear of the vehicle. Jiya, Maddox, Geroux, Takal, Taneral, and Ka'nak followed.

One of the soldiers opened the rear door. "You three," he said, pointing at Taneral, Geroux, and Ka'nak. "In here. The rest of you, into the next one."

Ka'nak cracked his neck before climbing up the short ladder into the back of the tank. None of the soldiers appeared impressed. With a shrug, Geroux followed, Taneral and a half-dozen Reichofen soldiers behind.

The remaining soldiers led Maddox, Jiya, and Takal to the second tank. Ranks of sullen soldiers filled the back of the vehicle. The landing team climbed in and huddled to one side.

"That's my spot," one of the soldiers behind Takal said. He shoved the old man aside.

Maddox and Jiya caught Takal before he fell. "Where would you like us to stand?" Maddox asked as more soldiers climbed aboard, shaking the vehicle. The influx of aliens pushed the three landing party members farther into the tank.

Trying not to bump anyone or kick their stump-like legs, the three scrambled deeper into the vehicle until they were pressed against the front wall. More soldiers crammed in, or maybe they just pushed forward. Jiya couldn't see through the crowd.

The vehicle jolted and rumbled forward. Jiya grabbed at the wall to keep her balance. *Maybe they were being helpful by putting us near something we can hold?*

Around them, the three-legged creatures had no difficulty maintaining their balance on the rough road.

Sure, we'll assume that, Maddox said, lifting his eyes to the ceiling.

Keeping a positive view of the opponent is crucial for negotiations, Jiya said.

That sounds like a quote, Maddox said. *Who said that?*

I did. The first officer smiled.

Takal said nothing, glaring at the soldiers from under his eyebrows.

The tank rumbled across rough terrain. Without windows in the rear, the three had no idea where they were going. The overwhelming noise of the engine prevented normal conversation, and many of the soldiers around them seemed to fall asleep on the drive.

This is taking a long time, Takal finally said. *Do you know where we're going, Reynolds?*

We arrived at the supreme commander's palace ten minutes ago, Reynolds replied. *Vernish assured me you were right behind us.*

According to my tracking app, the tank with Jiya, Maddox, and Uncle Takal went east, Geroux said. *They're heading away from the city.*

Stay calm, Reynolds said. *We knew this could happen. If you're attacked, defend yourselves, but don't initiate any trouble. I'll demand your release.*

Roger, Maddox replied. *I think— Reynolds? Geroux? Ka'nak?* He turned to look at his companions. *I had them, but I've lost contact.*

I can't reach San Roche or L'Eliana either, Jiya said. *Can you raise the ship?*

No, Maddox said. *Takal, you got anything?*

The old male shook his head. *You're the only ones I can hear.*

Fantastic. Jiya shrugged. *I guess we'll see what happens. Be ready for anything.*

"Where is the rest of my team?" Reynolds demanded, glaring at Vernish. They stood with Geroux, Ka'nak, and Taneral on the front steps of the supreme commander's palace. Rows of stone columns supported a roof four meters above their heads. Long, red banners with arcane silver symbols hung on the walls. Dozens of uniformed soldiers stood guard around the building.

"They were instructed to ride in the back of our vehicle," Vernish said. "I don't know why they chose to ride in the other. It's probably headed back to base. Those soldiers were at the end of their shift."

"Really?" Reynolds asked, his sarcasm lost on the alien. "A minute ago, you said they were following us here."

The alien made a hand gesture that Reynolds took to be a shrug. "I must have misunderstood the question. Maybe my translator is faulty." He tapped a small device half-hidden in the fringe on his shoulder, then looked at the closest soldier. "Find the other aliens."

The soldier slapped his thighs with his lower hands, holding the other two aloft. "Yes, ma'am," he said, then spun and marched away.

Ma'am? Geroux, Ka'nak, and Taneral said simultaneously.

I guess we made assumptions, Geroux said.

You know what they say about assuming... Ka'nak replied.

What? Taneral asked.

Donkey, you and I, Ka'nak said. After a beat, he added, *Reynolds says it makes sense in his language.*

"Your team will join us shortly," Vernish said, turning toward the doors behind them. "We don't keep the supreme commander waiting."

"After you," Reynolds said. "Ka'nak, wait here for the rest of the landing party."

"That's not necessary!" Vernish said, stopping just inside the building. "My soldiers will bring them to the meeting room. You don't wish to misplace any further personnel, I'm sure."

"Is that a threat?" Reynolds asked, holding his ground.

"I have no idea what you mean," Vernish replied. "We have no ill-intentions. Your companions will arrive momentarily. Come. All of you." She stomped away. Two of the soldiers moved closer, their hands hovering near their sidearms.

"Fine." Reynolds gestured for the remaining members of his team to follow.

The inside of the building was as huge and cold as the outside. They followed Vernish down a wide entry hall with towering ceilings and more red banners. At the far end, double doors opened into another huge room. They continued through three more enormous spaces that had clearly been built to intimidate, finally reaching a pair of doors guarded by six heavily armed troops. Two of the soldiers leapt forward to open the doors, while the other four saluted Vernish. She stomped through the doors without acknowledging them. Halfway across the room, she dropped to one knee and performed a salute.

"Supreme Commander, I present Reynolds and his delegation from Queen Bethany Anne," she said.

Another of the aliens, this one wearing a stark, black uniform with a single red badge on the chest, stood on a platform at the far end of the long room. "Welcome, representatives," it said.

Vernish stood and turned. "This is Supreme Commander Titus, leader of Reichof."

Reynolds moved closer. "Greetings, Titus," he said.

Vernish gasped. "Always use his full title when addressing the supreme commander!"

Ignoring Vernish, Reynolds walked right up to Titus. "Thanks for seeing us on such short notice," he said. "I'm sure a planetary ruler such as yourself is busy. We hope to initiate diplomatic and trade relations with the people of Reichof Six. However, since half of my team has been detained unexpectedly, I'm reluctant to begin negotiations."

Titus glanced at Vernish. "What's this about detentions? We don't detain our guests, do we, Vernish?"

"No, Supreme Commander, of course not," Vernish replied, holding her upper hands at shoulder level in an abbreviated form of the salute. "I have assured Reynolds that his team is perfectly safe."

"Excellent," Titus said. "Let's adjourn to the dining room." He smiled, showing double rows of teeth. "This throne room is very drafty, but the people expect their Supreme Commander to uphold a certain standard. This way." He turned and led the delegation through a door hidden behind another red banner.

They entered a room with thick red carpeting, clashing maroon draperies, and a huge table overflowing with food. Titus walked up to the table and pulled a cluster of something off one plate. Shoving it into his mouth, he gestured toward Reynolds. "Please, enjoy!" The ruler braced his three legs as if sitting on a stool and grabbed another handful of food.

Reynolds looked over the laden table. *Same drill as last time. I'll go first.* He picked up an item and sampled it. "Delicious food, Titus."

The alien nodded. "Only the best for the supreme commander!"

Does it seem like he's really pushing the title? Geroux asked. *Almost as if he doesn't believe it himself.*

Perhaps he's an imposter, Taneral said. *They don't trust us enough to meet the real leader?*

"How long have you been in command?" Reynolds asked. *The fruit is safe, but Vernish isn't eating, so maybe you should wait.*

My stomach disagrees, Ka'nak complained.

Titus looked at Vernish, then leaned close to Reynolds. "Only a few weeks," he said, his voice low. "My father was terminated, and I took command."

"Terminated?" Reynolds asked.

"Training accident. He's dead." The alien shoved more food into his mouth. "Between you and me, I don't think it was really an accident."

What is this guy's angle? Geroux asked. *Is he really this clueless, or is it an act?*

"Why is that?" Reynolds asked.

"He left a note." The tone was off-handed, as if his father's demise meant nothing. "Said he was tired of the whole thing. I thought he'd wait a couple more years until he felt I was ready to be in charge, but I guess not."

The landing party exchanged bemused glances. *So we have an incompetent leader of a military dictatorship, a bloodline succession?* Reynolds speculated. *Fantastic.*

"I hear you have some awesome weapons," Titus continued. "I want them."

Reynolds blinked in surprise. "I'm afraid our weapons are not on the table. We have some other items that might interest you. Equipment to provide food or clean water to your populace."

Titus waved a couple of arms. "Naw, don't need any of that stuff. I need weapons. I'm sure you've heard of the Terubine Raiders?" He looked at Taneral. "They mess with your ships, too, right?" At Taneral's nod, he continued. "Nasty buggers. I need something to keep them away from my fleet. That railgun you used was rad."

Geroux tapped the side of her head. *I'm not sure my translator is working properly. It seems like this so-called commander is speaking a different language.*

It's being translated as youthful slang. I wonder what his Reichof age is compared to our escort's.

Vernish stepped closer to her leader. "The energy weapon they didn't use would be more useful," she said in a low voice.

Titus' eyes lit up. "Yeah, the energy weapon. I need a couple o' those. That's what I want."

"I would be more open to conversations if the rest of

my delegation was brought here. But in any case, our offensive weaponry is not available for trade," Reynolds replied. "If you're having trouble with raiders, we could possibly offer a defensive system."

"Defensive?" Titus flung himself back from the table. "What a drag! I need something that goes boom! That strikes fear into the hearts of all our enemies. Not some defensive shit." A cunning look crossed his face. "Weren't you worried about your friends?"

Reynolds went completely still. "I do hope that was not intended to be a threat."

Titus laughed harshly. "If I make a threat, you'll know. Vernish, get me a report on the missing landing party."

The back of the missing tank opened, and the soldiers spilled out. Jiya, Maddox, and Takal waited until the vehicle emptied before moving cautiously to the door. They peered out as the soldiers dispersed.

The tank had parked in a cavernous building full of similar transports. Most of the soldiers made their way toward a pair of doors on the left side, from which emerged laughter and the rumble of conversation, combined with the smell of mediocre food, indicating a mess hall. Two of the aliens waited near the rear of their transport. "Come on, it's chowtime!"

"Uh, thanks," Jiya said. "I don't think we're supposed to be here."

The closest soldier made a motion with his hand. "You're here, you may as well eat."

"I thought we were being detained?" Takal said. Maddox elbowed him. The scientist turned to the general. "What? How are we going to learn anything if we don't ask?"

"Oh, yeah, you're being detained," the soldier said. "But you still need to eat, right? We aren't animals. I'm Stervin, this is Quardle. Come on. The chow gets worse the longer you wait."

Jiya hopped down from the tank. "You don't have to ask me twice. Or at least, not three times. I'm Jiya. That's Maddox and Takal. Where are we?" She fell in beside Stervin while Maddox helped Takal negotiate the ladder.

"This is Boromite Mountain Training Base," Stervin said.

"Mountain?" Jiya asked.

"Yeah," Stervin pointed upward. "A gazillion tons of rock over our heads. Hope you aren't claustrophobic."

That probably explains why we lost contact, Takal said. *What is it about the rocks in this galaxy?*

Stervin continued, "The general told us to bring you here, but she didn't say what to do with you."

"She?" Takal asked. Maddox elbowed him again.

"Yeah, she said we should keep you here." He made the gesture again, and Jiya mentally filed it away as the equivalent of a shrug.

"What do you think she means to do with us?" Jiya asked.

Stervin shrugged again. "Probably use you as leverage against your commander. I hope she gets what she wants. I'd hate to have to kill you. I just cleaned my knife." He laughed loudly. Quardle joined in.

"You might find it's not that easy to do," Jiya said.

"Tiny thing like you?" Quardle asked. He laughed and nodded. "Piece of rock."

Jiya fluttered her eyelashes. "No one's ever called me tiny before. I like you."

What are you doing? Takal demanded.

You heard these guys, Jiya answered. *If they like us, maybe they'll think twice about killing us.*

Good thinking, Takal said. *Maddox, cozy up to the other one.*

Maddox snorted. *I'll leave that up to Jiya. Scan everything. Look for weaknesses. We're not shackled, and we're not in cells. That gives us an opportunity we shouldn't miss.*

They grabbed trays at the entrance to the chow hall and loaded up on lumpy and gooey stuff. Sitting with their new friends, the landing party tried to extract as much information as possible without eating any of the repulsive meal.

"What do you folks do when you aren't kidnapping aliens?" Takal asked. Maddox kicked him under the table, but the soldiers didn't seem to mind the implied slur.

"Training," Quardle said. "I'm a fighter, so I do a lot of hand-to-hand and firearm work. Stervin's a nuke maintenance guy. I heard we're going to get some big-ass energy weapon from you folks."

The landing team exchanged looks. "We don't trade offensive weapons," Maddox finally said.

Stervin made the shrugging motion again. "We'll just take it."

Takal laughed. "You might find that harder than you expect. Ow!" Both Jiya and Maddox kicked him this time.

We're trying to project weak and harmless, Takal, Jiya said.

Don't give them any reason to think we're a menace, even though we could easily scorch the entire planet's surface while eliminating the bulk of their space fleet.

"So, what would happen if we just walked out that door?" Maddox asked, pointing at the chow hall entrance.

Quardle smiled. "Try it, and let's find out."

Maddox held up his hands. "No, I'm good. Say, you said Stervin's a nuke guy? What does that mean?"

Stervin laughed. "You don't have nukes? What a bunch of rubes! Nukes are bombs. Big bombs. Big, big boom."

Maddox wrinkled his nose. *Exactly who we don't want to arm.*

I hope Reynolds figures that out before it's too late, Jiya said.

CHAPTER TWELVE

Reynolds got nose to nose with Titus. Over the alien's shoulder, he saw Vernish draw her gun. He wasn't worried since his armor was more than a match for her projectile weapon. "I want my people back here now, or my ship will blast a crater the size of your moon where this palace used to be."

Titus stepped back. "I…uh. Vernish?"

"Move away from the supreme commander!" Vernish barked, barreling forward. She grabbed Reynolds's arm, but he shook her off like a bug. Her eyes went narrow. "He's bluffing. Blasting us would be suicide."

Reynolds shrugged. "Maybe I'm ready to terminate, like your father," he bluffed. From the corner of his eyes, he saw his team exchange worried glances. *Are you buying this?*

You're very convincing, Taneral responded. Her eyes darted around the room, seeking the exits.

Vernish took a step back. "No need to do anything drastic. My people are bringing your team here. They will arrive momentarily."

"Then we'll wait, shall we?" Reynolds said. He turned to his landing party. "Why don't you get some grub while Titus and I chat over here?"

Ka'nak reached the table before Reynolds had finished speaking. He grabbed a platter, dumped half the contents on another platter, and reloaded it with items from the rest of the table. Noticing the silence, he stopped. "What?" he asked.

Taneral and Geroux blinked at him. "We ate just before we dropped," Geroux said.

"I have a fast metabolism," Ka'nak said with a grin, patting his belly. "Gotta keep the furnace stoked."

The two females gave him another look before sampling a few items.

"Tell me more about these Terubine Raiders," Reynolds said to Titus. "I would think your military might would protect you. The People of Serifity don't seem overly concerned."

"The Terubines are dangerous in space," Taneral put in. "But they are not strong enough to attack a planet. As long as your ships are well-armed, you should be fine." She considered for a moment. "Although I recommend traveling in packs. *Trefol* took significant damage when she flew alone. Without *Reynolds*, she might not have returned to the planet."

"That's not what I've heard," Titus said, his voice brash. "They're pretty badass, and I'm not going to trust my planet's safety to the luck of the draw. We need protection. Better yet, I want to hunt those scum down and blast them from the skies." He turned back to Reynolds. "If you won't trade equipment, maybe you can do that for us. We'd be grateful if you took out the Terubines."

Vernish held up a hand. "I'm not sure that would be in our best interests," she said. "I mean, yes, we'd like to have that scourge eliminated, but having defensive systems here would protect us in the future, too. I request permission to assemble the Congress to discuss Reynolds' offer and provide advice on your decision."

"I haven't offered anything," Reynolds said. "There will be no discussion and no offers until my team is returned." *And we are not doing anyone's dirty-work this time around. We learned our lesson on Krokus.*

"They will be here momentarily," Vernish said.

"I don't think that word means what you think it means," Ka'nak said. Geroux swatted his arm.

Everyone had eaten, and even Ka'nak had stopped nibbling by the time the doors opened again. Jiya, Maddox, and Takal entered, escorted by Quardle and Stervin.

"Finally!" Geroux cried, running across the room to throw her arms around first her uncle, then Jiya. "We were so worried."

"We were fine," Jiya said. "Although I wouldn't want to repeat lunch."

"Can we get on with the negotiations now?" Titus whined. "I'm supposed to have a pilo match in a few minutes."

"Perhaps we should save the negotiations for another time, then," Reynolds said. "I'd like—"

Titus cut him off. "No, I wanna get this done. Besides, they'll have to hold the match for me. They have to wait for the supreme commander."

"Frankly, I'm not feeling particularly generous at this moment," Reynolds said. "I'd like to return to my ship and debrief my crew."

"Oh, all right," Titus moaned. "How about this? You and your crew can go hang out in one of the guest suites while I annihilate my so-called friends at pilo. Then we'll talk about trade. I'm tired." Without waiting for a response, he addressed Vernish. "Take them to the Solar Suite."

Vernish did the four-handed salute. "I will convene the Congress. They'll want to observe their supreme commander in action."

"This is a private pilo match," Titus said. "No spectators." Without waiting for a reply, he turned and walked away.

"I meant the negotiations, not the match," Vernish said to the air. "I have no doubt he will prevail with ease," she said, eyeing Reynolds.

The android smiled, showing his teeth. This time he didn't care if it was considered predatory. "We'll see you after the victory."

Vernish made a snapping noise. Quardle and Stervin marched smartly across the room. "Escort our visitors to the Solar Suite and set a guard outside to protect them."

"What will they be protecting us from?" Reynolds asked, stirring the pot a little. "Surely, the palace is safe?"

Vernish glared. "They will protect you from unexpected intrusions. We wouldn't want the staff to interfere with your rest. Go now. I have work to do."

I don't think she likes you, Jiya said to Reynolds.

The feeling is entirely mutual, he replied.

They followed the two soldiers into the antechamber, where they were met by a much larger escort. Twenty of the huge aliens closed around them, making the vast halls feel cramped. Without a word, the escort turned as one and marched, carrying the smaller *Reynolds* crew members with them.

After passing through countless rooms, they stopped before a set of double doors. The reinforced gray metal looked thick and heavy. One of the guards unlocked them, dragging one side open. Quardle led them inside.

With low ceilings and dull gray walls, no windows, wide benches with thin padding standing against the walls, and rough gray stone covering the floor, it looked more like a cell than a guest suite. "You may wait here," one of the guards said. "I doubt you'll rest. I know I wouldn't!" He laughed.

"Ah, don't make them nervous for no reason," Quardle said.

"Why should we be nervous?" Jiya asked. "Is there a plot we should be concerned about?"

Quardle shook his head. "It's just, visitors who spend time in here don't usually—" He broke off when Stervin punched him.

"Don't what?" Jiya asked. "Come out alive?"

"Oh, no, they come out alive," Quardle said. "They just don't always come out the same. We gotta go." He bolted out the door, Stervin hard on his heels. The thick metal slammed shut with a resounding boom.

Helmets on, Reynolds commanded, locking his own in

place. *Geroux, Takal, scan the room. Radio waves, energy signatures—anything and everything.*

The two scientists walked the perimeter of the room, checking their wrist computers as they went. *No listening devices so far,* Geroux said.

I am seeing an unusual projection coming from there, Takal said, pointing to the wall across from the door. *Low-frequency waves, changing at seemingly random intervals.* He rubbed his helmet just below the ear. *If we had our helmets off, we'd feel it right here.*

How would these projections affect us? Reynolds asked.

Based on the limited simulations I can run here, Geroux said, tapping at her computer, *I'd say they would impact impulse control. Emotions. Decision-making.*

So, they'd make us angry? Jiya asked. *Seems like a stupid move. Wouldn't they be better off to make us calm and complacent?*

Maybe? I said it was a limited simulation, Geroux replied. *What do you think, Taneral? Taneral?*

She's over there, Takal said, pointing.

They all turned to look. Their lion-bodied guide had fallen asleep on one of the wide benches. As they stared, she snored and rolled over.

I'd guess Taneral's physiology is different from ours, Geroux said.

Or maybe her armor doesn't filter the projections as well as ours, Reynolds added. *Can you check her vital signs?*

She's fine, Geroux said, fiddling with her readings. *Just asleep. A very deep sleep.*

"We can speak freely," Takal said. "There are no

listening devices. They must be confident their system will put us to sleep."

"I wonder what else it might do, though," Jiya said. "Quardle said people come out 'different.' Does their transmission create a deeper emotional disturbance? Could the effects be permanent?"

"I'll see if I can ratchet up the safeguards in Taneral's helmet," Geroux said. "I might not be able to completely protect her, but it should stave off any permanent effects."

"Keep an eye on those transmissions, Takal," Reynolds said. "If anything changes, let me know at once. Inducing sleep might only be the first phase."

Takal gave a thumbs-up, a gesture he'd learned from one of Ka'nak's many videos.

"Obviously, these people aren't above manipulating us in any way they can imagine." Reynolds paced around the room. As an android, he didn't have nervous habits—he firmly deleted the memory of drumming his fingers—but he liked the sensation of striding around as he thought aloud. He also felt it helped to focus the team on his words. "I believe they split us up to test my resolve and to see how desperate I am to trade. I think we called that bluff pretty well."

"Agreed," Maddox said. "Although, they treated us quite civilly at their base. Better than this, in fact."

"They made it clear they'd kill us if ordered," Takal argued.

"They're soldiers," Reynolds said. "Their job is to follow orders. In a society like this one, I doubt arguing is tolerated. They want weapons. We aren't going to give them any, but we need something to trade for the tualinton." He turned to Takal. "Can we modify the planetary defense ring to make it impossible to use for offensive purposes?"

"I believe I can make the system less powerful," the old man said. "From what I've seen of their technology, reverse-engineering it should be beyond their scope. For now. I can't promise how long that will last."

"Fair enough," Reynolds said. "Let's work on that. Make it look robust in the simulations, so they're satisfied with what they will get."

The door opened, and they all turned to look. A soldier poked his head inside. "Psst, Jiya," he said, ignoring the other ten eyes turned his direction.

"Quardle?" she asked.

"Stervin and I are going off duty," he said. "You wanna see the town?"

"Are we allowed to leave?" Jiya asked.

Don't give him a reason to change his mind, Reynolds said. *Go! See what you can learn.*

"Vernish said the guard is here to protect you so you can rest," Quardle said. "She didn't say you were being detained. Besides, I can watch you just as well out there as in here. And you don't seem tired."

Jiya grinned. "You're right, I'm not. I'd love to see the town."

"Maybe your attractive friend would like to come, too," Stervin said, peeking around Quardle.

"You mean Geroux?" Jiya pointed to the little scientist.

"No, the big guy," Stervin said, pointing at Ka'nak. "He's cute."

Better you than me, Maddox said. *Those four arms freak me out.*

"I will see the town with you," Ka'nak said. "But I am not easy. And never cheap."

"You have to at least buy him a burger," Jiya said.

"A what?" Quardle asked as they left the room.

"Never mind."

The two guards outside barely glanced at Jiya and Ka'nak as they followed the soldiers. "Better be back before the pilo match ends," one said.

Stervin flipped a hand at him. "I owe you one, Betrain."

They hurried down the hall and through a narrow door hidden behind one of the ubiquitous red banners. Once inside, the two soldiers relaxed, slowing their pace. Stone walls pressed closer here, and the ceiling brushed the plumes on Stervin's helmet.

"That goes to the ready room," Quardle said, pointing down a side hall. "This way is the exit."

They continued, taking several stairways to lower levels. Finally, the hall ended in another door. This one had a small black box embedded in the wall beside it. Quardle pressed two of his thumbs against the box, and the door swung open.

They stepped into a dim alley. "Don't come down here alone," Quardle warned them. "Without our authorization, this alley is a death trap."

"How so?" Jiya asked.

"I'll show you," the alien replied, walking to the wider street at the end of the alley. "Come out here."

When they joined him, Quardle picked up a rock and turned back to the narrow walkway. "Watch." He tossed the rock into the alley at head-height. Bright green lasers beamed out of the walls, whining as they tracked across the space and homed in on the rock. Before it had reached the top of the toss, the lasers blasted it to dust.

"We have authenticators built into our armor," Quardle said, slapping his chest. "Keeps the riff-raff out."

We must obtain one of those, Ka'nak said. *Our armor might protect us, but I don't want to be the one who tests the theory.*

Is the authenticator something you can fake, Geroux? Jiya asked. *In case you need to make a hasty departure?*

I'm on it, the young female responded. *Always happy to tinker with new tech.*

Stervin led the group through the streets. Lined with tall, featureless buildings, the streets were brightly lit, making Jiya feel like a lab rodent in a maze. The group twisted through the artificial canyons and came out in an open square. Pale pink plants in pots edged the massive stone plaza. The space teemed with other Reichofens, clustered in small groups or pairs. Many of them stood around small tables, consuming beverages and snacks.

"Bars look the same on every planet in the universe," Ka'nak marveled. "What are we drinking?"

"Fanta," Stervin said, challenge clear in his voice. "Be careful, it has a punch." He waved an arm, and soon another Reichofen arrived bearing four huge mugs filled with a pink beverage.

Quardle pressed his thumb on the tray, and the waiter deposited the mugs on the table. "Bottoms up!" the soldier cried, hefting one of the mugs with two hands.

Do you think it's safe to drink? Jiya asked Ka'nak. She dipped her finger into the liquid, running it through a rudimentary identifier Takal had added to their armor. *Nothing is coming up.*

The Melowi shrugged. *I have never turned down a drink.* He lifted the mug. "You only live once!" he cried and chugged half of it.

Stervin's and Quardle's eyes bulged from their heads.

Ka'nak swiped a hand across his lips and belched. "Fanta," he said. "I like it." He poured the rest of the brew down his throat.

The two soldiers exchanged looks and sipped from their own glasses. Jiya picked hers up and sniffed. It had a sweet, berry-like aroma. She took a sip and was pleasantly surprised. *Unless there's a kick later, this isn't very potent stuff,* she said.

It's a nice thirst-quencher, Ka'nak agreed. *I wonder why they're so cautious?* He rolled his eyes at their escort.

Within twenty minutes, the two aliens were sloppy drunk.

"...and then Stervin and Vinox left the frumble in the stove!" Quardle said, his words slurred. He and Stervin laughed so hard they almost fell over. Even with three stumpy legs, they swayed unsteadily at the table.

Jiya giggled as she was clearly expected to do and swallowed more of her drink. She felt clear-headed. Ka'nak looked put out. *What's the problem?* she asked.

When I go drinking, I at least like to get a little buzz, Ka'nak said.

We are *on duty,* she reminded him.

Yeah, but I haven't had a good fight in ages. If I was drunk, I'd have an excuse.

Her eyes narrowed as shouts rang out from across the plaza. *You might get a chance if we aren't careful. We should probably head back.*

The two aliens protested when Jiya suggested they get back to the palace. "Don't you have to work tomorrow?" she asked as she pulled Quardle's arm.

He wrapped his lower arm around her waist and draped the upper one across her shoulders. "Yeah, but not at the palace. Stervin and I have to return to Boromite Mountain."

"How will you get there?" she asked.

Ahead of them, Stervin stopped suddenly, nearly tripping Ka'nak. The soldier turned. "How are we getting back?"

"Maybe little Jiya can take us," Quardle said, pulling Jiya closer. "You have a shuttle, right? I saw it. Pretty little Pod thing. Can you fly it?"

"I can," Jiya said. "But I don't think my boss would be happy if I abandoned him."

"You can just fly us over and zip right back," Quardle said, making jerky movements with the two arms that weren't gripping Jiya. "Zip, zip, zip." He giggled.

"Let's get back to the palace," Ka'nak said, avoiding Stervin's roving hands. "I'm sure you can find transport there."

"Or a place to sleep this off," Jiya muttered.

They returned to the alley leading to the back entrance to the palace. Jiya held Quardle back. "How do you know your authenticator is working?" she asked. "What if you have a dead battery? You wouldn't want to get fried."

"Easy," Stervin said. He tapped his chest, and one of his medals lighted up. "See that? That's the authenticator. It's good. Bright light, all is right. No red, you're dead." He patted the crimson glow and hiccupped. "Let's get you back inside."

About halfway down the alley, a noise from the street startled Jiya. She spun around, hands out and ready for a fight. At the edge of the street, Quardle stood, eyes closed, head tipped back, sound asleep. As she watched, he snorted.

"Seriously? I'll go get him," she said, jogging back toward the street.

"No! No red, you're dead!" Stervin cried.

Jiya stumbled, and one of the lasers lanced out at her. She yelped and raced for Quardle. Hurtling down the alley, she slammed into the snoring soldier, knocking him onto his back.

"Fuck, that stings!" she cried, twisting her head to look at the smoking remains of her shoulder armor. The laser had burned right through, leaving an angry red welt on her skin. Fortunately, she had reached the circumference of Quardle's authenticator before the laser did more than minor damage.

Quardle slowly lifted his eyelids and gazed up at her. "This is the best date I've had in years."

The four of them stumbled to the door of the Solar Suite. "Get them back to Boromite Mountain, will you?" Jiya said to Betrain, who was still on duty. The dour male nodded, not making eye contact. With a shrug, she turned to the two drunks. "Thanks for a great evening, boys."

Stervin gave Ka'nak a resounding kiss on the cheek.

"You're so cute." He sighed, his eyes jiggling. "And now you have four eyes, just like you're supposed to. The two heads are kinda weird, though."

The big Melowi twisted out of the soldier's grip, almost tumbling the Reichofen to the floor. "And you have too many hands. Thanks for the drink." He wrenched the door open and stalked through.

Jiya gave them a little wave and followed her crewmate. Shutting the door behind her, she leaned against it and smiled at the rest of the crew. She held up the small red device she'd twisted off Quardle's uniform. "Look what I found."

CHAPTER THIRTEEN

Jiya explained the significance of the authenticator while Geroux scanned and prodded it.

"I can modify our comm devices to produce this signal," the computer whiz said. "It's surprisingly elegant, given the other tech on this planet. I wonder who created it."

"With luck, we'll never need to know," Reynolds said. "And hopefully, we'll never need to use it. Remember, our priority is tualinton and getting the hell off this rock." He grinned at Ka'nak. "How was your evening, big guy?"

Ka'nak snorted. "The beverage was tolerable. The company, not so much. So many hands!" He rubbed his behind.

"We learned how to get out of here," Jiya argued. "And we also learned these guys cannot hold their liquor."

"I wonder how we can use that to our advantage?" Maddox mused. "Maybe slip something into Titus' drink?"

"We'll have a whole Congress to deal with next time," Reynolds reminded him. "Spiking the punch might be the answer, and not so different from what they tried to do to us." He paused, holding up a hand. *Yes, L'Eliana, I read you.*

Sir, I just got a message from Comm, the Pod pilot reported. *He says someone is trying to hack into the ship's databases. They're searching for weapons systems. So far, they've been unable to access anything, but they keep trying. Asya put the ship on alert, and they're watching for external threats.*

Thanks, L'Eliana, Reynolds replied. *Keep me posted.* The android looked at his crew. "It seems our hosts might be trying to take what they want rather than playing nice."

"They told us they would," Maddox replied. "Several times."

"Too bad it won't be as easy as they think," Ka'nak said, cracking his neck and knuckles. "Is it time to break some heads? Jiya wouldn't let me join the brawl in town."

"Jiya is wise beyond her years," Reynolds replied. "No head-breaking, Ka'nak. *Yet.* Takal, how's your subterfuge coming?"

Takal looked up from his wrist computer, nodding. "It's progressing well. I have modified the planetary defense schematics to create a less robust system. It would be best if we supplied some of the internal workings as part of our negotiation. Perhaps tell them the circuits are too complex to build quickly, but we can provide them? That way, we can prevent them from understanding the technology unless they cannibalize their system."

"Won't they want spares?" Maddox asked. "I'd demand them."

"Can you rig up any spares to self-destruct if they're opened?" Reynolds asked. "Voiding the warranty is serious business."

The old scientist grinned. "I can do that."

"Geroux." Reynolds swung around to face the female. "They're trying to hack our system. Recommendations?"

She tapped on her device, shaking her head. "From what I can see, they're no match for us. Basic hacking one-oh-one. We can keep blocking them, or we can set up a maze that will appear to let them in and keep them busy for hours. It depends on what you want them to think."

"They believe they are in a position of strength right now," Maddox mused. "They've got us locked up, unable to communicate with our ship or depart the planet." They all laughed. "The Congress and Titus are going to view us as a weaker party to be exploited. If Comm continues to block them, that gives us a stronger perceived position, which might or might not be what you want."

Reynolds nodded. "They're going to demand offensive weapons again. We could just walk away, but we need that tualinton. From what Taneral said, it's difficult to find in this galaxy."

"Speaking of Taneral—" Jiya looked around the room, spotting the sleeping alien on the same couch she'd occupied when she and Ka'nak left hours before. "Is she still okay?"

"She's fine," Geroux said, glancing up from her computer. "The signals emanating from the wall can't get through the additional protections I added to her helmet, but the underlying 'sleep beam' is keeping her down." She yawned. "I figured out how to replicate it. If it worked on us, we could have solved insomnia. I might be able to come up with some other uses."

Reynolds waved at the females. "You know I won't

allow harm to come to my people. Taneral might not be crew, but she's my responsibility. Now, let's focus on the task at hand."

"Sorry," Jiya said. "You were saying we need the tualinton."

The AI nodded. "This is still our best opportunity to get it, but we won't give them what they want. What if we let them take it? Would that satisfy them?"

"How's that any different?" Ka'nak demanded. "You can't seriously think they should have the ESD?"

"Hell, no!" Reynolds said. "I'm suggesting we create a weapon system for them to 'find' in our database. Geroux can set up her maze and lead them to the schematics for an ultra ESD. Can you make a dud system that looks powerful?"

Geroux smiled. It was not a nice smile. "I can go one better than that."

<hr />

While Reynolds, Takal, and Geroux worked on the fake weapon, Ka'nak, Jiya, and Maddox got some sleep. "I heard someone say pilo matches can go all night," Jiya said, yawning again. "They might not be ready to talk to us until tomorrow."

"And if they think we're asleep from their mind-beam," Maddox said, "they may not be in any hurry. Or maybe keeping us uncertain is part of their negotiating tactics."

"I didn't get the impression Titus was big on tactics," Reynolds said. "Vernish, on the other hand... I wouldn't be surprised if she demands a meeting at oh-dark-thirty."

Once he'd approved Geroux's plan, Reynolds sent the two scientists to bed. "I don't need sleep, but I need everyone sharp at the meeting. Grab some Zs while you can."

Geroux argued, but Takal dragged her to a bench. "Just close your eyes for a few minutes. Reynolds is quite capable of doing this *and* watching over us."

Silence fell in the gray cell, interrupted only by the occasional snore. Reynolds worked on the program, passing parts of it off to his alternate identities on the ship. *That's one advantage to having multiple mes,* he said to no one in particular. *Distribution of effort.*

We're an AI, Comm replied. *We can do that without being split into pieces.*

True, but there's something restful about being able to hand work off to you and not think about it again, Reynolds said. *As good as taking a nap.* He gazed fondly at his crew, snoring away around him.

The pounding on the door came just before dawn. The heavy metal slammed open and Vernish stomped in, leading a troop of twenty guards. Reynolds stood in the middle of the room, staring at the open door as if he'd been waiting there all night. Which he had.

Vernish stumbled to a halt, surprised by Reynolds' unnerving stare. Around him, the crew yawned and stretched, ignoring the armed aliens. Jiya kept her damaged shoulder turned away from the troops. Geroux had treated the burn with the emergency first aid kit integral to each armored suit, but Jiya's suit still had a hole. *I should have gotten this repaired. Or at least covered.*

Pull a blanket around your shoulders like you're cold, Geroux suggested.

Jiya winked at her friend.

"The Congress will meet with you," Vernish said. "Now."

"Perhaps part of my crew could stay here and rest some more," Reynolds suggested. "The suite is comfortable, and they are tired."

Comfortable? Ka'nak asked. *In what universe?*

Hush, Jiya said. *We're weak and defenseless, remember? Grateful for any concessions.*

They've seen our weapons, the warrior argued. *How can they possibly think we're weak?*

Short-sighted? Arrogant? Stupid? Take your pick, Jiya replied.

No, don't ever think of the enemy as stupid, Reynolds broke in. *That makes you as arrogant and short-sighted as them.*

"They should have gotten plenty of sleep," Vernish said. "Everyone out!" She executed an impressive three-legged about-face and marched out the door.

The *Reynolds* team got to their feet and wandered out in her wake.

"Your Congress has to meet with us," Reynolds noted, stretching his legs to keep up with the aliens' rolling movements.

"They will be present to observe and advise the supreme commander," Vernish replied. "You will not address them unless they ask you a direct question."

"They're observing Titus?" Reynolds asked. "Is he under review?"

"NO!" Vernish's head snapped around. She shot a glare at Reynolds, then looked to the front again. "The supreme commander has full authority. The Congress is here to observe you."

Reynolds nodded. "Makes sense. I hope they like what they see. I should have sent my uniform out for dry-cleaning."

"Enough frivolity!" Vernish snapped.

She must have missed her morning coffee, Jiya quipped, tying the corners of the blanket around her neck like a cape as she walked.

The best part of waking up... Ka'nak sang.

Have you been watching commercials now? Reynolds moaned. "I just want to make a good first impression," he said aloud to Vernish.

She ignored him.

Reynolds, Comm here. The voice came through to the entire crew. *Reichofen hacker one has breached the first faux firewall. They're in the maze.*

Roger, Reynolds replied. *Keep me posted. L'Eliana?*

Here, sir! she replied.

Fly up to the ship and get the pieces Engineering fabricated, Reynolds said. *Have them waiting on the airfield as soon as possible.*

Aye, sir! the Telluride replied.

The team was led into a huge room that looked like every other room in the palace. A group of thirty or so aliens milled about at the far end. Titus stood to one side, ignored by all. Vernish strode across the open middle of the room and saluted sharply. "Hail Titus!"

The assorted aliens raised their hands slowly and muttered, "Hail Titus."

"Supreme Commander," Vernish announced. "The crew of the *Reynolds* is present."

Titus waved her away and strolled over to Reynolds. "How'd you sleep?" he asked with a toothy grin.

Reynolds nodded. "Thank you for the fine accommodations. How was your pilo match?"

"Those *kremfar* didn't know what hit them!" Titus cried, his eyes lighting up. "We wiped up the court with them."

"I would have liked to have seen you play," Reynolds commented.

"You woulda been amazed. Pilo is a vicious sport, and my team is awesome." Titus leaned in close. "When this is done, maybe we can grab a Fanta and take in a match."

"That sounds entertaining," Reynolds replied.

A coughing noise interrupted their chit chat. "The Congress has assembled, Supreme Commander," one of the aliens said in a condescending tone. "Perhaps we can discuss games when the business is complete."

"I hate that guy," Titus muttered under his breath. "Stupid blowhard."

Reynolds glanced at the alien, but he didn't seem to realize he'd spoken aloud. Or care.

Second firewall is down, Comm reported privately.

I hope this goes quickly, Ka'nak complained. *Would it kill them to have a couple chairs in here?*

"All right, let's get this done," Titus called out. The Congress members moved closer, leaving a clear space around Reynolds' team. Titus turned to the android. "I want your big-ass laser gun."

"I'm sorry," Reynolds replied, "but offensive weaponry is off the table. I can offer you a planetary defense system." He waved his crew forward.

Geroux and Takal set up a projection on a nearby wall. They described the benefits of the defensive ring, showing a simulation of an attack being repelled. Several of the assembled gasped.

"That is impressive," one of the Congress began, but Titus cut him off.

"Big deal, it shoots down the bad guys," Titus jeered. "Our ships can do that. Give us something we really want."

"But Commander," the alien protested. Titus waved him silent.

The conversation went around and around for hours, interrupted on Reynolds' side by updates from Comm.

Third firewall breached.

They watched Takal's presentation again.

Faux demo viewed, Comm said.

"I want the big weapons!" Titus cried. "The fucking big-ass blaster thingy!"

Weapon specs and documentation downloaded, Comm reported.

"Enough of this!" Titus called, yelling over the Congress' discussions. "I'm tired. We'll take the damn defensive ring. Vernish, get them the tualinton. I got a match." He stomped out without another word.

The Congress members and the *Reynolds* crew stared at each other for a few breathless seconds.

"I guess that's it, then," one of the aliens said. "Send us

the specs, the components, and the spares. Take your rocks and be on your way."

"Thanks?" Reynolds said, but no one answered. The aliens scuttled out as fast as their three legs would carry them.

Vernish stomped up. "I have had the tualinton delivered to the airfield. Shall we go?"

Sir, I'm not sure this is tualinton, San Roche reported from the Pod. *Does tualinton have blinking lights?*

Don't load the Pod, Reynolds said. "Let's go. My pilot is concerned about the delivery."

Vernish didn't reply. She snapped again, and the escort fell in around them. At the front of the building, they loaded into a single transport. This time, she didn't invite Reynolds to ride in the front.

Do you think they're taking us to the Pod? Jiya asked. *Or back to Boromite Mountain?*

My mapping app shows us headed the right way, Geroux replied.

They met San Roche at the Pod. The little Telluride pointed to a blocky pile covered in a tarp. "They said that's the stuff, but isn't tualinton a mineral or metal? Something natural?"

Reynolds twitched the covering aside. "This looks like electronics." He leveled a look at Vernish. "It almost looks like a bomb. Or several bombs."

That's exactly what it is, Takal said. *Good thing San Roche didn't load it.*

"Must be some kind of mistake," Vernish muttered. "Take that away," she hollered at her escort. "Where's the tualinton I ordered?!"

"I don't know what kind of shit you're trying to pull," Reynolds said, getting right in Vernish's face. "You won't get what you want until we get what we want. I suggest you bring the tualinton immediately."

"I don't care for your insinuations," Vernish ground out. "There must have been some miscommunication. The tualinton will arrive momentarily."

There's that word again, Ka'nak said.

A few minutes later, another tank drove up. Four soldiers climbed out of the back and unloaded a pallet weighed down with full fabric totes. Reynolds motioned for Takal to check the contents. The old scientist ran a device over the big bags and nodded.

There's a bomb at the bottom of this tote. The old inventor patted one of the bags of granular ore. *We can leave this one behind. There's plenty in the others.*

Leave it to me, Reynolds said. "San Roche! Send your bots out to load this stuff."

The bots trundled out of the Pod and moved the first three totes into the vehicle. Reynolds held up a hand. "We don't have room for that one," he told Vernish. "We'll have to come back for it. Load up, everyone!"

"Wait!" Vernish cried, blocking into the Pod door. "Nothing leaves the ground until we get our defensive ring!"

"You have the modules and the spares," Reynolds said, pointing to the little pile of boxes near her transport. "The specs will be downloaded to your computer...now." *Go ahead, Comm.*

A noise blared from Vernish's belt, and she pulled a radio from it. "Vernish, go. Very good. Out." She pushed

Reynolds away from the Pod. "Perhaps you'd like to wait in the palace for your Pod to return."

"We'll just go up to the ship and send the Pod back down when we've emptied it," Reynolds said, motioning for the crew to climb in. Geroux and Taneral got inside before one of the huge aliens blocked the door, weapons drawn

"If there isn't room for that tote, there can't be room for your crew," Vernish said, brandishing an enormous blaster.

I was afraid of this, Reynolds said. *Take it up, San Roche. Cloak as soon as you are out of sight. They may try to take you out. L'Eliana, be ready to launch,* he told the other pilot. *We'll clean up this mess and be along in a few moments.*

Aye, sir, the two replied in unison. The little ship launched, blowing air and exhaust as it zipped away from the airfield.

"We'd prefer to wait here," Reynolds told Vernish. "And the weapons are not necessary."

"I'll tell you what's necessary," Vernish growled. "What's necessary is you will do what you're told. Now get into the transport!'"

Take them, Reynolds said.

Jiya and Ka'nak slapped their cloaking devices and disappeared. They each yanked a modified screamer from their belts. Without throwing them, they activated the devices. The twenty soldiers standing before them suddenly collapsed to the ground, unconscious.

Jiya tossed one of the screamers and caught it. "Nice work, Takal!"

The little scientist smiled modestly. "It was Geroux's idea. I'm glad it worked."

"Let's deliver Geroux's Easter egg." Reynolds led the team to the cloaked Pod, and they climbed inside. With a last glance at the comatose soldiers, he flipped them off and turned to L'Eliana. "Let's go."

CHAPTER FOURTEEN

"What's an Easter egg?" Maddox asked.

"Oh, I know that one," L'Eliana said over her shoulder as she guided the Pod through the stratosphere. "Easter was a religious observance by bird-worshipers on Earth. They commemorated the day a huge rodent stole their pre-hatched young, tortured them with boiling water and vinegar-based pigments, and then distributed them to its followers. The highlight of the event is the ritualized consumption of something called a 'chocolate bunny.'"

"That's not quite right," Reynolds said with a smirk. "You might want to check your sources. In this case, an Easter egg is a piece of hidden code that is activated when the user inadvertently completes the right sequence of events. For the Reichof, that sequence of events was trying to kill us and steal our stuff."

"Ah, I get it." Maddox nodded in satisfaction. "If they'd played fair, they would not have been punished."

"Exactly."

"But what is it?" Jiya asked. "What's going to happen?"

"Geroux and I created the phony weapons system," Takal explained. "When the Easter egg is triggered, a virus she planted in the code they downloaded will destroy the 'weapons' specs. So, the device they thought they stole will —*poof*—disappear. The code will also worm its way into their offensive systems, creating switches that can turn off their weapons. The planetary ring we traded them will protect their homeworld and their ships while they are near the planet, but if they attempt any offensive actions, the Easter egg code will activate and render them powerless."

Maddox's eyes widened. Jiya and Ka'nak looked impressed.

Takal chuckled. "That authenticator you borrowed from Quardle gave us the keys to the system. They really shouldn't leave those lying around. And they should probably change their password."

A few hours later, the *Reynolds* soared through an open Gate into unknown territory.

Ensign Alcott swore. "Sir, the Gate malfunctioned again! We're nowhere near Serifity!"

"Don't tell me where we aren't," Reynolds said, calmly. "Tell me where we are."

"Yes, sir," Ria replied. "We're about three light-years from Serifity. They call this system Ipian. According to Taneral's database, it's uninhabited."

"Reynolds, Takal here." The scientist's voice came through the speakers at Comm's position. "I see from the logs that last jump didn't go as planned. I can use the tual-inton and phorentum we've collected to create some new modules and start repairing the Gate drive. It won't work perfectly—we still need a couple other elements—but I think I can improve on the current performance."

"Then do it," Reynolds said. "Because current performance is unacceptable. We can't be flying wherever the space winds take us."

"The thing is, it would be best if we can land," Takal said. "I'll need to access the Gate drive. I can do that via spacewalk, but it's faster and safer to do it on land."

"Can it wait until we return to Serifity?" Reynolds asked. He wasn't sure letting the old scientist outside the ship in free-fall was a wise plan.

"If we can get there," Ria said, darkly.

"As the ensign said, navigation is iffy at this point," Takal confirmed. "If we can find somewhere nearby so we don't have to make another jump..."

"We're in an uninhabited system, so this might be our best bet," Jiya said, working the scans. "I'm getting no energy signatures on any of the planets. Ipian Two has good air and the appropriate gravity. There doesn't appear to be a sentient race."

"We might want to double-check that," Maddox said. "Isn't that what we thought about Lanteral?"

Jiya nodded. "That was what Taneral's database said, but when we scanned, we picked up Pornath's cook fires. I'm not getting anything here. There's a fire on the northern continent, but it appears to be a wildfire. Likely ignited by lightning."

"Scan the planet for a safe place to land," Reynolds said. "Launch probes."

"There's an island in the southern sea that looks pretty good," Jiya said after a few minutes. She pointed at the landmass displayed on the screen. "There don't appear to be any large predators, and there's a big plain right here that would accommodate the ship."

"Probes show no threats," Maddox reported.

"Take us down, Ensign," Reynolds said.

A vast field of rusty-orange grass stretched to low, forested hills. Small rodents poked their heads up around the edges of the field, clearly startled by the massive object that had landed on their home. The *Reynolds* truly looked out of place.

"Those things aren't dangerous, are they?" Ka'nak asked, pausing on the ramp.

"They're so tiny!" Geroux said, running down the ramp to get a closer look. "Cute and fuzzy! Wook at his wittle pink nose!"

"There are a lot of them," the warrior said. "They could overwhelm a single crewmember in a flash. I suggest we travel in pairs."

"No one should leave the immediate area," Jiya said. "We're here to fix the ship, not take a vacation. Set up a perimeter."

"I could use a vacation," Ka'nak mused as they placed sensors. "But my idea of a vacation destination bears no resemblance to this planet."

"Yeah, you'd prefer the fighting pits of Lariest to this pristine wilderness," Jiya said, shaking her head. She took a deep breath. "This is beautiful. Smell those flowers!"

Once they'd established a defensive perimeter, Takal took a team from maintenance to the Gate drive. Geroux worked with engineering to fabricate parts from the new materials they'd collected. Asya set up a rotating schedule to allow the entire crew a few hours outside in the fresh air and sunshine. At the end of each day, the core crew met near the ship's ramp for a meal and debriefing.

"This place would be fabulous for R and R," Maddox said. "Maybe we should stay longer once the repairs are complete. We could do a little exploring. I heard the guys down in propulsion talking about a kayak trip. They think the printers could produce a decent boat."

Reynolds shook his head. "No, we need to get home. There will be plenty of time once we return to High Tortuga. An unexplored planet is a great place to lose a few red-shirts. Not worth the risk."

"Yeah, you're right," the general said. "I wouldn't have approved it if I'd been in charge, either. But that's the beauty of not being in command. I don't have to make the unpopular decisions."

At dinner on the second night, Takal was in a towering rage. "Those ham-handed idiots! They broke the flux continuity devisor we just printed!" The maintenance bot replacement program wasn't giving them sufficient numbers to do the work. They'd had to count on what

Reynolds referred to as "meatbags" to do the bulk of the work.

"Uncle, we can make more," Geroux said. She looked at the rest of the crew. "He's frustrated. The repair just isn't coming along like he'd planned. There are so many little fiddly bits. But the tech printers are a delight to use. I design a component once and print out as many as I want. Converting the agroprinter was a stroke of genius."

"Exactly what we'd expect from Takal," Reynolds said, raising his glass. "That's why Jiya recommended him—and you—in the first place." He glanced at the first officer. "I certainly was lucky when you walked onto my ship."

Jiya smiled. "We were both lucky. If it weren't for you, I'd still be schlepping a cab around Lariest, wondering what my father would do next to destroy my life. Now, I'm out here seeing the universe."

"Literally," Asya said, grinning. "It sounds like an advertising slogan, but we're really doing it."

"Speaking of seeing the universe," Ria said hesitantly. "How long is it going to take to get home? I mean, our maximum jump—once the Gate is repaired—is ten thousand light-years. It's going to take forever!"

"Not forever," Takal said, losing his anger in the delight of calculating. "10k jumps mean we'll need to make a hundred thousand jumps to get back to our galaxy. The duration of the trip depends on how quickly we can make those jumps. Let's say we can do ten an hour. If we jump around the clock, that's only...hmm." He paused, thinking. "That's only four hundred and sixteen days. Slightly more than a standard year!"

"A year?" Ria wailed.

"We could make it longer," Maddox said. "Enjoy a few stops along the way, see the sights."

Ria moaned.

"What's your hurry?" Maddox asked. "It's not like we're going back to the Chain Galaxy. I mean, it doesn't really matter if we're here or Reynolds' Interdiction or halfway between. It's all new to us."

Ria hung her head. "I just want to go shopping," she whispered. "I haven't seen a mall in forever."

"How many jumps can we do in quick succession?" Asya asked, ignoring the younger female's complaints. "There must be an upper limit on consecutive jumps. Otherwise, an AI ship like this could go anywhere. Just jump, jump, jump all day long."

"If we can get enough polybdinum," Takal said. "I might be able to extend the length of the jump." He sat back, pulling his lower lip as he thought. After a few seconds, he pushed up his sleeve and started tapping his wrist comp.

"I managed a single Gate of nearly one million light-years when I came to your galaxy. I don't know if your soft and squishy bodies can handle such a jump, but that's your target, Takal. We can Gate once a day, a million light-years each, and in three months, we're home. We'll cross a huge section of the universe, collecting as much data as we can for the day while we recover and repower the Gate drive."

"Speaking of seeing the universe," Asya said, glancing at Ria, "what's on your bucket list?" When the young female didn't answer, she looked around the table. "Anyone? How about you, Maddox? Someplace wild and unexplored?"

"Well, since I can't gamble anymore—at least not with money—I have to get my thrills somewhere else," the general replied. "I'd like to do a low-orbit free-fall. I had to give that up when I took on more responsibility in the Lariest military, but now, I'm only responsible for myself."

"What about the *Reynolds*?" Jiya asked.

"No, don't get me wrong," Maddox said. "I take my responsibilities on the ship very seriously. But an orbital free-fall would be no worse than boarding an alien ship. When I made general, I was forbidden by Lariest military regulations to take unnecessary risks. Reynolds is not a dictator. He doesn't put those kinds of barriers around our lives."

"I'd prefer you not kill yourself," Reynolds said, "but you only live once." He hadn't realized the general craved excitement. He made a note to include him in more combat missions. As a leader, he felt called to help his people grow, not hem them in.

"When I go anywhere, I'm careful and prepared," Maddox said. "But really, it's riskier to cross President Lemaire Boulevard at rush hour than to make a low-orbit jump." He stared at the horizon for a moment, then shook himself. "How about you, Asya? What's your dream?"

"I love to travel," she replied. "It's why I joined the Loranian service. I definitely want to see as much of Reynolds' galaxy as I can. If I had to pick one thing, I'd like to see the military headquarters. What do they call it? Starfleet Command?"

"That's not what we call it," Reynolds said with a grin. "But you'll see the real thing at High Tortuga. How about you, Ka'nak?"

"I have already fought in the pits of Dal'las Tri," the big

male said. "That was the top of my list for many years. Is there something similar in High Tortuga?"

"I'm sure we can find you somewhere to fight," Reynolds said. "The Yollins would make formidable opponents. Probably the four-legged versions since they're more sturdy."

"Joining the *Reynolds* has given all of us a chance to try so many new things," Geroux commented. "I need to make a better list."

No one else volunteered an answer for a while, and they sat in silence as the sun set and darkness fell. Insects filled the air with their buzzing and whirring. The breeze picked up. The ship's external lights flickered on, providing just enough illumination for the crew to return to the ship without tripping in a rodent hole.

As they climbed the ramp, the crew said their goodnights and headed to their berths. Reynolds sighed. He would stand watch on the bridge. Not because he was worried about what was out there—he had a guard set and sensors keeping watch—but because he didn't sleep. He wondered if having a biological body would have been easier if it did all the things real biological bodies did. Like eat for sustenance. And sleep.

He grinned as he swung onto the deserted bridge. He'd heard the complaints after Ka'nak used the head. There were advantages to being an android.

"You're pretty chipper," XO said as Reynolds dropped into the captain's chair. "Care to share the joke?"

"Just thinking about this body of mine." He looked it over, using the big screen as a mirror. "It's efficient, useful, and attractive. Hot, even. Do you ever wish *you* had one?"

"Me?" XO asked. "Hell, no. I mean, I have one. This whole ship is my body. I can go anywhere I want. Well, except for the parts Tactical controls. He really needs to clean up his act. Have you been in the weapons locker lately? That place is a pigsty."

"Hey, I resemble that remark!" Tactical called. "If you can't take the heat, stay out of the nuclear reactor."

"How about you, Tactical?" Reynolds swung his seat to point it at the brash personality's station. "Do you ever wish you had a body?"

Tactical was silent. Reynolds was about to reiterate the question when the other personality spoke, his voice low and almost unrecognizable. "I think if I could have a body like Ka'nak's—strong and powerful—I might. I love shredding our enemies with my railguns and lasers and the ESD —oh, do I love the ESD! But to be able to use hands and arms to grab an angry, sweaty, vicious opponent and throw him down and grind his face into the KA-BOOM!" He laughed, a maniacal sound that echoed through the bridge and adjacent halls. "Had you going there, didn't I? Why would I want a puny meatbag? I have a fucking ESD!"

The next morning, the repairs went swiftly. "He just needed to sleep on it," Geroux told Jiya. "This morning, he was excited to get back to work. He'd figured out what was going wrong. We should be ready to lift by midday."

The ship launched just after noon, local time. "If this weren't so far from home, I'd want to come back here and explore," Maddox said wistfully, watching the island dwindle in the viewscreen.

"There are plenty of unexplored planets in the Interdiction," Reynolds said. "I've been gone too long, though, so I don't want to waste any more time here. Takal says we'll need to do another refit when we get the last of our materials. Maybe you can do some low-orbit free-falling then." He shuddered dramatically. Jumping out of a perfectly good spaceship made no sense to him.

"Orbit achieved," XO called. "Ready to set course."

"Set course for Serifity," Reynolds said.

"Coordinates laid in," Ria reported. "Gate drive is powering up. All systems are green."

"Open the Gate, Ensign," Reynolds said.

"Acknowledged," Ria replied. "Engaging in three...two... one...*now*."

Space around them rippled and shimmied, and the Gate opened.

"Cross your fingers," Jiya said, demonstrating.

"We don't need luck," Asya said. "We have the *Reynolds*."

"That's the spirit," Reynolds said. "Ensign, take us through."

CHAPTER FIFTEEN

The Gate opened near Serifity, exactly where Ria had calculated they'd arrive. The *Reynolds* sailed through and assumed orbit around the planet.

"We'll take you dirtside," Reynolds told Taneral. "You can visit your ship. We'll find out if your scientists have located our remaining requirements. Jiya and Maddox will bring down samples of the Melliferi food cubes and some of the extra minerals we collected as payment for your assistance."

"There is no need for payment," Taneral said hurriedly. "We owe you for saving *Trefol.*"

Reynolds waved that off. "Consider it a goodwill gift, then." He turned to Asya. "You have the conn."

"Aye, sir," Asya replied. "I'd like to send the maintenance crew to Serifity for shore leave. They worked some long hours while the rest of us were relaxing on Ipian. And they'll be hard at it next time we're back here to do the final refit."

"Excellent idea. Anyone who didn't get a break there

should get a day or two here." He looked around the bridge. "But keep a competent crew on duty, as always."

Taneral glared at Reynolds. "You are perfectly safe here! My People protect this planet and the space around it."

"No offense meant, Taneral," Reynolds said. "But I don't relax a hundred percent unless I'm home in High Tortuga. Maddox, Jiya, with me. Comm, have Takal meet us at the Pods."

"I'll keep your ship safe," Asya said. "Good luck with the scientists."

San Roche piloted the Pod taking Reynolds, Jiya, Taneral, Maddox, Takal, and a bunch of rowdy maintenance techs down to Serifity. He landed them at the Grentoo airfield, the one they'd visited before. There were many more ships parked along the flight line.

"Is this normal?" Jiya asked Taneral as they emerged into the sunshine. The maintenance techs angled across the field toward a bar Taneral had pointed out.

"The number of ships?" Taneral asked. "No, there shouldn't be this many. This is the hospital field. Only injured ships land here. I need to talk to Xonera. She'll know what's going on." Taneral sprinted across the field, her four legs carrying her much faster than any of Reynolds' crew.

"I want to talk to Xonera, too," Reynolds said. "This doesn't bode well."

"The defense station didn't say anything when we arrived," Jiya said. "Wouldn't—"

"No point in speculating," Reynolds said. "You and Maddox take Takal to speak to the scientists in Dantera. I'll talk to Xonera." He strode across the field after Taneral.

His android body moved nearly as fast as Taneral did, but she had a head start. He met her at the ramp to *Trefol*, where she stood in a heated discussion with another of the People.

"Xonera and *Trefol* are not receiving visitors," the leonine alien said, arms crossed over her chest.

"I'm not a visitor, Andrean! I'm the daughter of the ship!" Taneral said, her tail twitching angrily around her haunches.

Andrean glared through narrowed eyes. "Stay here," she said before stalking into the ship.

"What's the significance of 'daughter of the ship?'" Reynolds asked.

"Every ship has a designated daughter," Taneral replied, pacing across the ramp. "I am the official representative to any other ship. It's a position we're raised in; I've been the daughter since I was seven. It should guarantee me immediate access to both the captain and the ship, but Andrean was passed over for the position, so she—" She broke off with a low growl. "Never mind. I shouldn't tell an outsider."

Reynolds held up a hand. "Consider it forgotten."

She looked at him with wonder on her face. "You are such an enigma. You call yourself a male, but you behave more like a female. I have learned much working with you."

"Gender roles are different in other cultures," Reynolds

said. "In my world, counseling a youngster is something both genders do."

Andrean stalked out of the ship. "You can go in," she said. "Both of you." She grinned slyly as if giving Reynolds permission lowered Taneral's status.

Taneral pushed past Andrean, and Reynolds followed her into the ship. It looked much like the *Reynolds* on the inside, with metal bulkheads and heavy hatches. All the doors were open, and several IV lines ran through the corridors, filled with the silvery substance he'd seen on his first visit.

On the bridge, Xonera lay in a padded enclosure, curled up like a cat in a box. Her eyes were closed as if she were sleeping. Her hand lay on a tablet-like device.

Taneral stopped at the door, holding an arm out to stop Reynolds as well. "She's speaking to the ship," she whispered. "Don't interrupt."

Xonera's eyes opened. "It's okay," she said. "*Trefol* told me you were coming. Please, enter."

Taneral leapt over the low threshold into the bridge. "Andrean wouldn't let me in!" she cried.

Xonera looked at Taneral, eyes narrowed. She flicked a glance at Reynolds, then focused on the younger alien. Taneral hung her head.

Reynolds hid a smirk. Apparently, the young were the same in many galaxies.

"Welcome, Reynolds," Xonera stood, shaking herself. She stepped out of the enclosure and shook again. "Thank you for coming. *Trefol* would like to speak to you."

Reynolds blinked in surprise. While he knew the ship

was alive, he hadn't realized it was sentient or capable of communicating with others. "How do I do that?"

Xonera gestured to the enclosure. "Sit down and place your hand on the tablet. I believe you should be able to make the connection, just as I can."

Reynolds stepped into the padded space. The words "doggie bed" kept repeating in his mind, but he repressed them. It wouldn't do to offend the ship. He lowered himself into a cross-legged position and put his hand on the tablet.

A switch seemed to flip inside his mind, and he felt the same echoing effect he got from his crew's communication device. *Hello?* he thought.

Hello, Reynolds, the ship said. *Thank you for agreeing to speak to me.*

The pleasure is mine, Reynolds replied. *Are you healing?*

It is slow, Trefol said. *The damage is extensive, but my mind was not impacted, so I must wait for my body to repair. Unfortunately, many of my sisters have suffered much worse.*

Yes, we noticed the large number of ships on the field, Reynolds said. *What happened?*

The Terubine raiders have been quite active in your absence, Trefol said. *In the past, they've always confined their activities to attacking single ships far from home. Since you left, they've attacked ships in our very skies. My sisters were hurt defending our planet. Some were even killed.*

Reynolds could feel the grief in *Trefol*'s communication. *My condolences,* he said. *My crew is monitoring the system from orbit. I feel confident we can provide significant support, should they stage another attack.*

Thank you for your care, Trefol replied. *I have no doubt your presence will keep them at bay for as long as you are here.*

Reynolds mulled over his earlier meeting with Walthorn, the premier. He hadn't promised anything in exchange for the scientists' help and Taneral's guidance. The premier had offered him anything he wished because he'd brought *Trefol* and Xonera home. The locals had been generous, but cagy, too. Remembering his discussion with Jiya and Geroux after meeting, he pondered if the People were hiding something.

We might be able to provide some defensive help in the long term, he told the ship, keeping his promises vague.

Anything would help, Trefol said. They sat in silence for a while.

May I ask you some questions? Reynolds adjusted in his seat. *You are the first sentient ship I've met, aside from myself.*

Yes, of course, Trefol replied. *Xonera told me of your strange duality.*

Reynolds laughed. *That's a good way to put it. I'm curious about your relationship with your crew.*

Crew is assigned by families, Trefol said. *Many generations of Xonera's family have served me. They care for me, and I transport them.*

And your relationship to the premier? Reynolds made it a question. *Are you the command ship because of that?*

Trefol laughed. *Walthorn is the premier because of his relationship with me. He is a figurehead, chosen because he is the most malleable of the males in Xonera's line. The pride governs this planet. He merely represents it.*

And who is the pride? Reynolds asked. *Should I have negotiated with someone else?*

You spoke to Krenthel and Bonnerel, Trefol replied. *They represent the pride, which is made up of the matriarchs of each family. They speak for us all. Or you could negotiate with me if there is more you require. As the flagship of the People, I have authority to trade with aliens.*

Reynolds opened his eyes. This conversation had not gone at all as he expected. He looked at his hand, pressed against the tablet. *You are already providing the assistance I need. But perhaps I can offer some technology in return.*

Helping others with no eye to reward is a reward in itself, is it not? Trefol replied. *You are a great ship, Reynolds.*

I like to think so, Reynolds replied with a smirk. *As are you.*

Jiya, there's a situation, Reynolds said on the internal link. *Can you get to the Shrieking Cat?*

What's the Shrieking Cat? Jiya asked. "Maddox, I gotta go. Bring Takal back to the ship when you're done here."

It's a bar, Reynolds replied. *Near the airfield. Some of the crew seem to be causing a stir. I'm headed there as soon as I can wrap things up with* Trefol.

Don't rush. I got this, Jiya replied. *I was falling asleep listening to Takal and these scientists anyway.*

Jiya raced out of the Dantera Science Academy and skidded to a halt next to the many-legged conveyance they'd ridden out here. The driver, a member of *Trefol's* crew named Yartina, smiled, her pointed teeth glinting in the sun.

"Can you take me to the Shrieking Cat?" Jiya asked as she vaulted into the craft.

"Of course," Yartina replied. "But if you're thirsty, there

are closer taverns." She placed her hand on the tablet, and the craft slid onto the path. "Hold on for launch."

Jiya grasped the rail as the craft shot into the sky. "No, I'm not looking for a drink. There's, uh, a situation at the Shrieking Cat."

"Of course," the alien replied. "Crew on shore leave are the same all over the universe."

"Don't I know it," Jiya said.

The craft zoomed toward the airfield, moving at a pace that defied conversation. The wind whipped through Jiya's black hair and made her eyes water. Yartina landed smoothly in front of a low building. "Here you are."

Jiya leapt out. "Can you wait here? I will probably need to take some folks back to the ship." At Yartina's agreement, she strode to the door.

She frowned as she headed inside. It was quiet, with a scattering of People sitting at tables around the room. "Am I in the right place?" Jiya asked the bartender. "I was told my crew was causing some trouble."

"Nothing we couldn't handle," the female behind the counter replied. She nodded at a young Larian male standing near a back door. "He'll take you to them."

The male saluted as Jiya neared. "Maintenance Technician Rohan," he said.

"First Officer Lemaire," Jiya replied. "What's going on?"

Rohan squirmed. "It's kind of embarrassing."

"Spill it," Jiya said. "I don't have all day."

"We came down here for our leave," Rohan said, opening the door and ushering Jiya through to a narrow hallway. "You know how it is; some folks just want to hit the nearest bar. Reynolds told us to stay in a group, so I came along. They started drinking, and—" He broke off, gesturing to a closed door. "You'll see."

Jiya opened the door. A dozen crewmembers lay on the floor, out cold. "What the…"

"They were doing karaoke," Rohan said. "The bartender hit them with some kind of sleep ray. Apparently, the locals don't like Whitney Houston."

With Rohan's help, and the enthusiastic assistance of most of the bar patrons, Jiya got the offending crew members out of the building. Some of them roused, and Jiya made them help load the others onto Yartina's vehicle.

"What did you hit them with?" she asked the bartender as Rohan supervised the loading.

The female shrugged and held out a small, round device. "Every bar has them. It puts out a directional wave. Don't worry, there are no long-term effects. As soon as they wake up, they'll be fine. Doesn't always work well on aliens, but it worked a treat on your gals."

Jiya picked up the little gadget. "I might have to get one of these," she said, peering at the indecipherable lettering. "I can think of all kinds of uses for a sleep ray. I wonder if it's related to the beam the Reichofens used?"

The bartender gave her a blank look. "I don't know any Reichofens. Do they live on Serpenti?"

"No, they live in a different system. Doesn't matter." Jiya handed the device back to the alien. "Thanks for your help. And sorry about the disturbance."

Rohan climbed into the vehicle and reached for Jiya.

With a grin, he heaved her into the cart. "Not every day I get to yank the first officer around." The grin fell off his face. "I mean—"

"Don't worry about it," Jiya said. "I get yanked around a lot. You might want to hold on. Yartina could have given me a run for my money on Lariest, and I was a crazy cab driver."

They clung to the railing while Yartina launched them skyward.

Back at the field, San Roche met them by the Pod. "Reynolds said he's ready to leave, too. He'll be here in a few minutes."

"Have you heard from Maddox or Takal?" Jiya asked.

"L'Eliana is on her way down. She'll wait for them," Reynolds said, striding up to the group. "What happened?" He nodded at the groggy crew members.

"Difference of opinion on music," Jiya said. "They have a sleep ray-thing we might want to check into. It works better on us than the Reichof version did."

"Interesting," Reynolds said. "Maybe *Trefol* can get us one. It seems there might be more than one link between this system and that one."

CHAPTER SIXTEEN

A laser lanced across the Pod's bow. "Fuck!" San Roche cried. He yanked the Pod into a crazy dance. "Someone is firing at us!"

"Cloak the Pod and change course," Reynolds said.

"Aye, sir," San Roche replied. The little Pod dropped and jerked, and the meatbags in the back groaned.

Asya, what's going on? Reynolds demanded through the comm.

Raiders just Gated in! Asya said from the bridge of the *Reynolds. They took a few shots, got a good look at us, and bolted.*

We'll stay cloaked until we reach you, Reynolds replied. *Is L'Eliana all right?*

She just reported in, Asya said. *She was on the far side of the planet, out of range. She's landing at Grentoo as we speak.*

Did you get an ID on those ships? Reynolds asked.

Serifity Defense identified them as Terubine Raiders, Asya said. *Ria got a scan of the ships, and she's running them through the database. If they're from Reichof, we'll soon know.*

If they were from Reichof, our Easter egg should have prevented them from attacking, Reynolds said. *Have Geroux take another look at her code.*

In the rear of the Pod, Jiya had passed out barf bags. "Anyone who missed their bag has Pod cleanup duty," she called.

Rohan grinned at her. "That was awesome! I haven't been that close to combat before."

Jiya laughed. "You're cute. That wasn't combat. That was a potshot. If you want, I might be able to get you onto a landing team, assuming you've been trained."

"We've all been through the simulations," Rohan said. "But some of us enjoyed it, while others merely endured." He glanced at his fellow maintenance workers, all green-faced and moaning. "I scored pretty high, so I'd love a shot at the show."

The Pod landed. While Rohan helped his fellows return to their quarters, Reynolds, Jiya, and Taneral trotted to the bridge. "Anything?" the AI asked before the door opened.

Geroux looked up from Ria's screen. "Those are definitely Reichofen-made ships," she said. "But they don't appear to have received the 'upgrade' I pushed out. They also have some incongruent components. It's possible Reichof sold these ships to the raiders but aren't actively sponsoring them."

"Plausible deniability," Jiya muttered. "Titus can claim they're not his."

"And maybe they aren't," Reynolds replied. "There are plenty of ships out there with Federation technology. We've distributed some of it ourselves. We try to arm the good guys, but once a technology is out in the universe, you lose control of it. Even Geroux's Easter egg, for example, could potentially be copied and used by someone else."

"I included a self-destruct!" Geroux objected. "If anyone tries to copy or tamper with the code, it will burn out."

"But *you* could subvert it, right?" Reynolds asked.

Geroux deflated. "Yeah, if someone can create it, someone else can probably deactivate it. Eventually. I can't believe they could do it this fast, though."

"I think your original theory was correct," Reynolds said. "These ships are not connected to the official Reichof command and control, so the virus hasn't reached them yet. Is there a way to inject it?"

"What about the authenticator?" Jiya broke in. She tossed the little device from hand to hand. "Wouldn't the Reichof have built something similar into any ships they sold to the Terubine raiders so they can't target Reichof? Or would they just trust the raiders to be smart enough to not stab themselves in the foot?"

Geroux grabbed the gadget out of the air on Jiya's next throw. "Let me see what I can work up."

"We've always suspected the Terubines were from Reichof, but we had no proof," Taneral said. "And we don't have enough ships to carry the fight to them, anyway. If there's a way to protect Serifity and our ships from that scourge, the premier will give you anything you want."

Reynolds thought about his discussion with *Trefol*. Walthorn's promise was worth nothing without the backing of the pride. "They've already offered us anything we want," Reynolds said. "But that doesn't mean we can't work another trade. Geroux, get to work. I hate to leave the planet vulnerable when we depart."

The crew busied themselves with maintenance tasks and simulations while they waited for Maddox and Takal to return from the surface. After Jiya related her conversation with Rohan, Ka'nak offered to set up realistic training scenarios for those who wished to participate.

"I've been out of the ring too long," he said, cracking his neck.

"We need all our support crew alive and unbroken," Jiya said.

"That's what the Pod-docs are for." Ka'nak grinned. "It'll do them good to get some experience."

"All-out brawling isn't the answer," Reynolds counseled. "But you can start some hand-to-hand combat classes. And if anyone is good enough to give you a run for your money, you can fight them. But no fatalities."

"Agreed," Ka'nak said a little sadly. "I don't like killing if I don't have to."

"He sounds like he's trying to convince himself," Jiya said to Reynolds as Ka'nak left the bridge.

"He won't kill anyone," Reynolds replied. "He knows better."

"L'Eliana reported," Asya said. "She's bringing Takal and Maddox to the ship. Everyone else is aboard, so we can depart."

Geroux, Reynolds commed the female. *Do you have anything for Serifity while we're gone?*

I've developed a directional beam, she replied. *It requires individual targeting at this point. Jiya's device uses a broadcast system, but that required too much power at this scale. The good news is, if they hit a ship with this beam, it will not only turn off the weapons they're currently using, it will also load the virus and disable the others.*

She paused. *If it works.*

Send the specs to Serifity Defense, Reynolds said. *It's better than nothing, and maybe their folks can get the broadcast working. We have a mission to complete.*

The Gate drive opened a wormhole into the Jeranth system. The *Reynolds* arrived exactly where predicted. "Nice work, team," Reynolds told them.

"No energy signatures," Jiya reported. "The system appears to be uninhabited."

"Taneral's database said Jeranth Four is a post-inhabited world," Ria said. "That sounds bad."

"It could mean the sentient civilization migrated to the stars," Maddox said. "Maybe it's not a very nice place, and they left." He turned to his console. "I see what appears to be the ruins of cities." He whistled. "The whole place was inhabited at one point! It's a carpet of dead buildings."

"You aren't making it sound any better," Ria complained.

"And dead cities mean there's no one to target," Tactical muttered. "This trip is a drag."

"Maybe we'll find some Terubine raiders to shoot," Asya comforted the personality. "We're weapons-free when it comes to them, remember."

"Better than nothing," Tactical grumbled. "If they ever show up."

"Shoot them with my authenticator ray first," Geroux reminded Tactical. "To see if it works."

Tactical groaned. "Shooting non-lethal ray guns? What am I, a preschooler?"

"Enough," Reynolds said. "You have your orders, Tactical. Geroux, Jiya, Maddox, with me. Taneral, you too, if you wish. Comm, have Takal and Ka'nak meet us at the Pod."

Taneral demurred. "I can't help you find the polybdinum, and Jeranth Four is too cold for me."

Do you mind if Rohan joins us? Jiya asked privately. *He wants to join a landing party.*

Is he any good on defense? Reynolds asked. *I'm not putting my people at risk so your booty call can visit the planet.*

Jiya growled. *If "booty call" means what I think, you'll pay for that, Reynolds! I wouldn't recommend him if he weren't competent. I checked his records.*

"Comm," Reynolds said. "Have a couple maintenance crew meet us at the Pod. Takal might need some help if this civilization was advanced." He glanced at Jiya. "Get that Rohan fellow. He seemed to have a level head."

"Yes, sir," Comm replied. "And he's cute, too. Or so I've heard. If you're into Larian males."

Jiya's normally red face flushed even redder.

"Sometimes, it's like herding cats," Reynolds said. "Or children. If I'd wanted to be a father, I'd have adopted."

"You kind of *did* adopt us," Jiya said, following the AI off the bridge. "And with your vast experience, you shouldn't be surprised you have to share your guidance. You might want to work on the fatherly tone of voice, though."

Reynolds ignored her.

Takal, Ka'nak, Rohan, and another maintenance worker

named Petro met them at the Pod. The team strapped in, and as L'Eliana flew them to the surface, Maddox briefed them.

"Based on the scans, this planet was inhabited by a highly technological civilization. We don't know why they left, or if they intended to come back, so we need to use extreme caution. Expect booby traps. Based on my experience of the universe, people don't leave their stuff unprotected.

"We're looking for a material called polybdinum. It's not a naturally occurring element, but the scientists on Serifity said their ships' scans of Jeranth, many years ago, indicated a cache of it here." He indicated a location on their heads-up maps. "We can't land the Pod there since the buildings are unstable, and there's no clear space. We don't want to risk damaging the polybdinum, so we can't just blast a crater. We'll land here." Another location glowed on the maps, and a dotted line indicated a path.

"Keep helmets on at all times since we have no idea what we're up against," Reynolds put in. "I don't want to lose anyone on what should be an easy in-and-out retrieval."

"We'll have the maintenance bots carry the containment vessels." Maddox pointed to a series of clear cubes at the rear of the Pod. "Three full vessels should be more than enough polybdinum, but we'll take as much as we can carry. It's heavy, so we'll probably have to make multiple trips. It's also unstable at room temperature. This part of the planet is quite cold, which is probably the only reason we can find it here.

"Questions?"

The landing team members exchanged looks and shook their heads. "Oh, wait, I have one," Petro said a second later. "Are there any wild animals on this planet?"

"Good question," Maddox said. "We have seen life forms in other areas, but none near our target. As I said, it's cold. Set your life support for extremely cold temperatures."

The Pod settled into a large plaza amid towering ruins. Low clouds blocked the sun, making the surface dark and gloomy. Puffs of snow billowed and the stones beneath the Pod melted, then froze again. "Watch your footing," Reynolds said. "That's bound to be slick. L'Eliana, stay here and keep watch. The rest of you, let's go." He climbed down the ramp and walked out into the plaza.

Jiya followed Reynolds, while the rest of the team organized the bots. She stepped onto the plaza and her foot slipped on the ice, sending her head over heels. "Wah!" she cried, landing on her rear end. "Damn." She reached down and activated the friction pads on her boots. "You weren't kidding about the slippery part. How'd you make it look so easy?"

Reynolds grinned. "I make everything look easy." He turned to the hulking ruins as the team assembled. "These folks must have been tiny. Assuming those are windows, each floor is only a meter and a half high."

Maddox rubbed his lower back as if anticipating the pain of crouching. "Let's stay outside as much as possible. Ka'nak, you're on point. Petro, Rohan, and Jiya will guard our six. Stay alert, people."

"Are you sure Ka'nak is the best choice for point?" Jiya asked. "He's too big to go inside any of these places."

"That'll keep us outside as long as possible," Maddox replied. "Move out."

Ka'nak flexed his knees and strode forward, weapon at the ready. He stepped into the narrow canyon between two tall ruins, almost disappearing into the gloom. Reynolds let him get well ahead before following. "Tell us what you see, Ka'nak."

"More of the same," he replied. "Big buildings, tiny doors. Watch out for the crap in the street since some of these buildings have started crumbling. That one on the right is empty. The one on the left might have been a retail store. Piles of tiny stuff on tiny shelves."

As she passed, Jiya peeked through a window into the building he'd indicated. Although she couldn't read the text, the plaque over the opening looked very much like the sign over a Larian clothier. She couldn't tell what items were on offer, though, because of a thick layer of frost. Behind the rows of shelves, she saw a flicker of movement.

"There's something here!" she called, bringing her weapon around. "Something moved."

Rohan and Petro moved beside her. "Petro, keep watch out here. Rohan, you're with me." The two of them moved cautiously to the building.

"Wait!" Maddox called. "Throw something in there first. You don't want to trip defenses."

Rohan picked up a chunk of rubble and chucked it through the opening. "Nothing."

"Try again," Maddox said. "Maybe there's a delay."

Rohan tried again. "Still nothing."

"You go right, I'll go left," Jiya said. "Circle around to the back. This room isn't deep."

The two ducked through the opening. The main room was tall enough to stand upright, barely. They crept through the debris and around the shelves. Light from the openings only extended a few meters inside, so Jiya activated her night vision. Another flicker of movement drew her forward. She placed her feet carefully, making as little noise as possible. Then she grimaced. They'd announced their presence with the rock-throwing, so no point trying to be stealthy. Aiming her weapon directly ahead of her, she leapt around the last shelf.

"Hah!" she hollered.

A small, furry creature standing on a fluffy footstool blinked up at her. It looked similar to the rodents they'd seen on Ipian, but this one had thick white fur and big blue eyes.

"It's just a squirrel," she called to Rohan.

The male stepped out from behind a shelf on the far side of the room. "It's adorable!" he said, taking a few steps closer. "I had a stuffed toy that looked a lot like that when I was a kid. Aren't you the cutest thing?" He leaned forward to look at the little creatures.

"Don't get too close," Jiya warned.

"Aw, he's not going to hurt me. Maybe he wants something to eat." Rohan patted down his armor where his pockets would be. "Sorry, little guy, I don't have anything for you."

The rodent stood up. And up. And up. As Jiya watched, horrified, the fluffy footstool uncoiled into a three-meter-long monstrosity. Huge jaws hinged open, revealing massive pointed teeth. It swayed over Rohan for an instant, then dove at his head.

Rohan screamed.

Jiya unleashed her blaster into the monster. The stench of singed fur and burned meat overwhelmed the filters in her helmet, but she kept firing. The creature let out a horrible howl and collapsed, taking Rohan to the ground.

"Rohan! Are you all right?" she gasped.

"Jiya, what's happening?" Reynolds' repeated question finally registered in her brain. Behind her, Ka'nak, Maddox, and the AI burst into the room, plowing down the remaining shelves and reducing them to kindling.

Rohan moaned and shoved at the bloody corpse lying across his body. While Jiya kept her weapon aimed at the creature's head, Reynolds and Ka'nak lifted a section of the huge thing off the male's legs. Maddox dragged Rohan free.

"Are you hurt?" the general asked. When Rohan didn't answer, Maddox shook his shoulder gently. "Anything broken?" Maddox looked up. "Probably just shock. I'll take him back to the Pod." He hoisted the male over his shoulder and carried him away.

"Are you okay?" Reynolds asked Jiya.

"As much as I can be after watching a footstool try to eat my crewmate." She kicked the carcass. "Maybe this is why these people left. Furry snow snakes are a nasty way to go."

"That little rodent decoy on his head is genius," Ka'nak said, poking at the thing. "Creepy as hell, but genius."

"More likely a lucky adaptation than actual genius," Reynolds replied as he ushered them out of the building. "Let's get back to the mission. Jiya's boyfriend will be fine."

Jiya shook her head. "Not my boyfriend," she said. "Did you hear him scream like a little girl?"

"To be fair," Ka'nak replied, "I'd probably scream like a little girl if that happened to me, too."

"It wouldn't happen to you," Maddox said, rejoining the group. "You were smart enough to be wary of the rodents on Ipian."

Ka'nak smiled. "This ain't my first creepy planet."

CHAPTER SEVENTEEN

Ka'nak took Petro and crept ahead of the group, weaving deeper into the canyons. Reynolds and the rest waited, alert for alien predators.

"Why didn't our scans pick up that thing?" Jiya wondered, pointing her weapon at the empty building. She'd killed the one, but that didn't mean there weren't more.

"I ran a quick analysis on it and grabbed some samples," Geroux said, poking her wrist computer. "Something in the fur blocks our scans. Defense mechanism. If this planet was as technologically advanced as we think, the wildlife could have evolved to hide from them."

"Send your data back to the ship," Reynolds said. "A natural cloak that protects from scans like we saw on Lanteral is unheard of in our galaxies, yet we've encountered it twice in this one."

"There's probably a common element here that we don't have," Takal surmised. "Having two different samples should allow us to isolate it."

We're at the first turn, Ka'nak broadcast to the team. *All clear so far. Proceeding.*

Roger, Reynolds replied. *Don't get too far ahead. Move out.*

The team trod cautiously into the city, guiding the bots carrying the containment vessels. They paused at each corner, checking in with Ka'nak and Petro. Maddox and Jiya trailed behind, guarding the rear.

"Keep an eye out," Reynolds said. "And Geroux, if there's any way to unmask that cloaking effect, it would be useful. Now."

"Already working on it," she replied. "But nothing so far."

They became more tentative, eyes darting from empty windows to dark shadows. Halfway to their goal, Reynolds called a break. "Ka'nak, what's the situation?"

"We'll have to go in," Ka'nak replied, pointing at a ruin. "The first building has fairly tall ceilings, like that store where Jiya discovered our furry friend."

Reynolds nodded. "Take a load off, Ka'nak. I'll keep watch." He clapped the big warrior on the shoulder and stepped in front of him.

"You know, these buildings were beautiful once upon a time," Petro commented. She pointed down a side street. "Look at the scrollwork on that cornice. Most of it's eroded, but there are a few places you can still see the detail."

"Cornice? Scrollwork?" Ka'nak scoffed, lounging on the remains of a broken wall. "All I see are dangerous hulks full of potential threats."

"You're such a romantic," Petro said, shaking her head.

"Romance doesn't keep us alive," he replied.

"If you're rested, let's move out," Reynolds said. "Ka'nak, Petro, you're still on point unless your senses are fried. Can you stay frosty?."

"Like an ice block," Ka'nak replied.

Petro nodded, and the two ducked into the first building. The rest of the team waited while the vanguard explored.

The doorways are all blocked, Petro called back. *We're going to see if there's a way through.*

Roger, Reynolds replied. *We're holding at the entrance.*

Lots of paintings left on the walls, Petro commented. *These are really lovely, at least the ones that aren't covered in ice. Ka'nak, watch out for that—*

The signal cut out abruptly. "Ka'nak!" Reynolds called both aloud and through the comm. "Petro! Report!"

Nothing.

"Jiya, Maddox, with me," Reynolds snapped. "The rest of you, stay here and keep guard." He crouched and crept into the building, moving carefully across the wide and empty room. Maddox and Jiya followed.

They made their way to a narrow hallway. The floor had fallen through in places. *Stay back while I check,* Reynolds said. He walked forward, pausing after each step to check his footing. Ice crackled, and the floor groaned under his weight. At the end, he peeked around the corner, then waved the other two.

Hold here. Reynolds continued. *Three doors. Two are blocked, so I guess they took the third. Let's move.*

Maddox assumed a defensive position. Jiya and Reynolds stood on either side of the door. At a nod from Reynolds, Jiya reached out and squeezed the handle, then pushed on the door. It swung inward, and Reynolds darted a look inside.

Ka'nak and Petro lay on the floor, and a lacy gray substance covered them completely. Reynolds stepped forward, but Jiya yanked him back.

"Look at the floor," she hissed. The entire surface was covered in the gray lace, and as they watched, it expanded toward Reynolds' foot. He leapt back.

"Takal, Geroux, get up here!" Reynolds called. "Ka'nak! Petro! Can you hear me?"

The two squirmed on the floor, muted noises coming from their speakers. As they struggled, the lacy stuff oozed and thickened over them.

Jiya blasted the gunk near the door, putting a crater in the thick floor. The gray stuff spread around the hole and filled it. Then she tried her laser. The lace seemed to absorb the beam. She set her weapon to "flame" and unleashed a blast on the floor near the door. The carpet of freaky gray substance crumbled to ash, then more grew toward them at twice the speed. "Shit!"

"What's attracting it?" Reynolds stuck his hand into the room, but the stuff kept crawling toward his foot. He lowered his hand gradually, watching the lace. Even with his hand only a few centimeters above the floor, the creeping stuff continued moving toward his foot.

"Not heat, then," Takal said, still breathing hard from the run. "Maybe the vibrations of feet hitting the floor?"

"But I haven't moved my foot," Reynolds said. "And it's still coming."

Geroux skidded to a stop beside Reynolds. "Maybe the

vibration gives it a location, then it keeps crawling until it gets there?" she suggested. "Try fire."

Jiya burned a trail from the door hallway to their captive comrades, but the gunk filled the gap as soon as she shut off the flames. "Not getting in that way."

"The good news is, it doesn't seem to be able to penetrate their armor," Geroux said, watching her wrist comp. "The bad news is, it's covered their speakers and somehow impacted their ability to communicate via the comm." She tapped her temple.

"We need flying suits," Jiya said. "Like that Iron Man guy. I could just swoop over there, burn them free, and yank them into the air. Or at least, I could if the ceiling were taller."

After she thought for a moment, Jiya tossed a rope over a light fixture and fed the free end down into the stuff. It surged around the cable, crawling upward. "It's like an unstoppable fungus." She blasted the rope, burning the gunk away. It filled in but didn't crawl upward.

"That's odd." Geroux hunkered down to examine the rope. "It's almost as if it's forgotten the rope is there. I wonder—"

"I don't care *why* it does it," Jiya cut her off. "How do we get it off them?"

"Sometimes knowing the why can help us understand the how," Takal said.

"You two work on understanding the alien fungus," Jiya said. "I'm going to save our friends." Feeding more rope over the light fixture to give her leverage, Jiya prepared to jump into the room.

"I'm going to hit them with my flamethrower,"

Reynolds said. "Their armor can withstand the heat. You pull them up. We'll start with Petro since she's lighter."

Reynolds fired at the prone maintenance worker, and the fire burned the lacy substance to ash. Jiya launched herself forward. The female tried to rise, but she couldn't. Jiya dropped into the flames, straddling Petro. She poured fire directly onto her shipmate, burning the fungus on the side away from Reynolds. Then she pulled the other female to her feet.

"Turn around," Jiya yelled at Petro. "Make sure he burns all that crap off you!" Reynolds continued to bathe them both in fire.

"Can you run?" Jiya asked, pointing at the doorway before pushing her that way. Petro nodded and ran through the path of fire Jiya provided.

"Get ready, Ka'nak," Jiya said, striding toward the Melowi warrior. Reynolds kept his flames focused on Jiya's feet while she burned Ka'nak free. "Go!" she cried.

Ka'nak rolled to his feet, hunched over to avoid the low ceiling. Pulling out his own weapon, he fired at the space in front of himself. Moving quickly, he burned away the fungus as he walked to the door. Jiya scurried along behind, her back to his, firing relentlessly into the lace entity. They reached the door and looked back.

Petro stumbled through the doorway, with Ka'nak ready to push her if she didn't clear it quickly enough. Jiya backed out, and after one last round of fire, she pulled the door closed.

"That sucked," Ka'nak offered.

"New rule. Right after 'don't pet the furry carnivore' is 'don't step on the lacy fungus.'" Jiya continued to watch the door as if it would open and the entity would follow them into the hall.

"Let's get out of here," Reynolds replied. "We're not getting any closer to finding what we came here for."

"We can't just go around to the next building," Geroux explained, pointing to the map on her wrist comp. "This building is part of a huge complex of interconnected buildings. There's a fault line under that section. Every structure along it has collapsed, and the ground is unstable. This side is still safe. The lab where the polybdinum is stored is in the middle of this complex."

"Tell me again why we didn't just use the Gulg transport to zap in and grab the stuff?" Ka'nak said, rubbing his temples.

"Shielding in the buildings," Takal repeated patiently for what felt like the fortieth time. "I've been pulling microscopic samples of the building materials as we go since something that can stop the Gulg is worth understanding."

"Breaktime is over, kids," Maddox said. "Let's move out again. Ka'nak, Petro, do you need to go back to the Pod?"

"Hell, no," Ka'nak said. "No fucking carpet is going to sideline me!"

Petro muttered her agreement.

"Let's get this done, then," Reynolds said, trying to hide his impatience over their biological frailty. A team of android AIs would be much more effective on a mission like this. They wouldn't need to stop and rest or be susceptible to distraction. Maybe he should get bodies for all his personalities and leave the meatbags on the ship. It was an argument against integrating his personalities. He'd take it into consideration later, but for now, they needed polybdinum.

"Maddox, take point."

They worked their way through the huge complex, looking for access to the center. Every door leading inward was blocked by thick panels that appeared to be melted into place.

"This is not looking good," Reynolds said as they crept through another narrow hall. "Can we just burn a hole through the wall?"

"Theoretically," Takal replied. "But with the age of the structures and the geological instability, we risk bringing the whole thing down on our heads. Besides, you saw how the floor in the lace room stood up to our weapons. Finding a safe place that is also permeable will be a challenge. Let me run some scans. The blocked doorways would be the logical places, but that material is impervious to anything I've got."

"I would guess the original occupants didn't want anyone doing exactly what we're doing," Jiya said. "At least there aren't any furry vipers here."

Ahead, the sound of weapons discharging echoed through the rooms.

"Die, fuzzy snake!" Ka'nak cried. "Clear!"

"I guess I spoke too soon."

They entered the next room to find Ka'nak standing over the remains of another creature.

"I wonder what they eat?" Geroux mused. "We haven't

seen any other life forms, and those teeth look capable of ripping flesh. That isn't the mouth of a vegetarian."

"Maybe they eat the building," Takal said, pointing at a scattering of debris in the corner. Under the ice, long grooves marred the wall. He crouched to analyze the debris. "Ah! I can get through, but we need to go back to that last blocked door." He fairly danced with impatience as Reynolds recalled Maddox.

In the previous room, with Ka'nak and Petro watching the entrances, Takal and Geroux bombarded the door with their equipment.

"Half-life scans indicate this panel was installed many centuries after the building was constructed. There's a compound in the debris by those grooves, probably from the saliva of the vipers, that might allow me to— Yes!" The older scientist turned to Reynolds with a triumphant grin, holding up his blaster. "Minimum power, ten-nanosecond green phase shift, thirty-cycle blasts." Without waiting for a reply, he fired at the door.

A small section of the panel wavered, then crumbled.

"Nice," Reynolds said, adjusting his blaster to Takal's settings.

The team took turns firing at the panel, disintegrating small sections around the edges, then waiting for their weapons to cool down.

"If he did this using viper spit," Jiya asked as she took her turn, "why didn't those snakes eat through the door panels?"

"The modifications didn't use the viper spit," Geroux explained, grinning at Jiya's name for the compound. "The viper-spit debris contained a trace element that isn't present in the rest of the building but *is* in the panels. In fact, the last occupants might have used the viper spit to create those panels. The similarity in the molecular—"

Jiya cut her off. "You lost me after viper spit. Hey, I think we might be close!"

Reynolds strode up. "My blaster has cooled. Let me take a turn." He turned his weapon on the door again.

"You just want to be the one who breaks through," Jiya said with a grin. The words had barely left her mouth when the door panel groaned and twisted.

"Privilege of the captain," Reynolds said, giving a quick blast to the remaining narrow strands holding the panel in place. It toppled inward with a heavy clang. Stepping to the side of the door, he poked his head through the opening for a quick scan. "Which way, Geroux?"

The tech looked at her wrist comp and pointed. "There's a door to the basement right there."

Reynolds nodded. "Jiya, you're on point."

She crept into the central room. The ceilings in this section were low, and her helmet brushed the occasional fixtures. She made her way around toppled furniture, angling toward a door on the far wall, head on a swivel, watching for threats. "Clear," she called when she reached the far side of the room. "Door is locked."

"Geroux, see what you can do," Reynolds said.

The computer genius attached her equipment to a panel and started tweaking. "I've attached it to a power cell, and the system is booting," she said after a moment. "Now to see if I can decipher it." She poked and prodded for a few minutes. Something clicked, and the door opened.

"Good work," Reynolds said. "What's ahead?"

"Just stairs down to the basement," Geroux replied. "Might be a couple more locked doors, but there's only one way in and out."

"Ka'nak, Maddox, you stay on guard here," Reynolds said. "Jiya and Petro, you first. If you get to another locked door, call for Geroux."

The two females crept down the steps, treading lightly, fingers itchy outside the triggers of their weapons. "We're at the bottom. Send Geroux down."

They worked their way through three more locked doors before reaching the containment room. "There," Geroux said, pointing to a window. On the other side, a pile of bricks glowed in their night vision.

"Are they radioactive?" Petro asked, stopping with her hand over the door handle.

"Yes," Takal said. "But your armor will protect you until we get them into the containers." He pointed at the maintenance bots crawling into the room behind him. Then he turned and focused on the wall. "There don't appear to be any traps in the walls or floor."

Jiya laughed. "Are you expecting poison arrows or a giant boulder?"

"We've already encountered carnivorous fur snakes and suffocating lace," Takal replied.

"Yeah..." Jiya's mouth shut with a snap.

Petro opened the little room. She and Jiya stepped into the space. "There isn't room for anyone else in here," Jiya called out. "Send the bots in."

They loaded the clear boxes quickly. The material was heavy, but the containment boxes were small. "You sure that's all we need?" Jiya asked. "There's a lot left."

"That's all we have room for," Reynolds replied. "I hope the bots can handle the weight."

"That load is within their mass tolerances," Takal said, scanning each box as the bots emerged. "I think they'll be fine. This is powerful stuff, and there's more than enough to make our repairs and attempt some upgrades."

Once Petro had exited the room, Jiya shut the door. "Do we want to just leave it here, or seal it in?"

"Is it potentially dangerous in the wrong hands?" Reynolds asked.

Takal shrugged. "Everything is. But this should be safe enough. No one knows it's here except us."

"We'd know if the raiders had followed us," Reynolds agreed. "Let's lock the doors and collapse the top of the stairway. That won't keep determined folks out, but it's the best we can do." He turned and led the way to the surface.

CHAPTER EIGHTEEN

Reynolds looked around the humming bridge. "You have become an excellent bridge crew," he announced. "When I first picked you up on Lariest...and Loran," he nodded at Asya, "I had my doubts. But I honestly wouldn't trade any of you for a human."

"Gosh, boss," Jiya said. "You sure know how to warm hearts and influence people."

"Hey, I'm trying to give a motivational speech, here," Reynolds replied. "Our mission on Jeranth Four was successful. You're all growing, both as crew members and supporters of the Queen."

"Save the watches," Tactical called.

Jiya and Asya exchanged a confused look. "What?" Asya asked.

"Never mind," XO said. "He's just calling bullshit."

"It's my gift," Tactical said.

"Contact," Maddox said. "We've got a bogie. A ship is lurking just beyond that gas giant. I thought it was an anomaly, but it keeps popping out, and I got a good scan. Unknown technology, but it's big. Almost as big as us."

"Battlestations," XO called, activating the ship-wide comm. "Gravitic shields at full power."

"A ship hiding in the far reaches of a system, spying on us," Jiya said, working her controls. "Been there, done that. Don't want to do it again."

"Takal and Alcott say we can make precise jumps at short distances now," Reynolds said. "Let's put their work to the test. Ensign, take us behind that ship."

"Already calculating, sir," Ria replied with a smile.

"Tactical," Reynolds said, "warm up the railguns."

"Damn straight, Cap'n!" Tactical replied. "Can I fire a warning shot?"

"No, don't engage," Reynolds replied. "They haven't displayed hostile intent. Yet. Let's let them think we're oblivious while we sneak in from the rear."

"Coordinates laid in, sir," Alcott called.

"Excellent," Reynolds said. "Make us a Gate!"

Ria engaged the Gate drive. It ripped a perfect oval in the fabric of space, and the *Reynolds* sailed over the event horizon.

Behind the gas giant, another Gate opened, and the *Reynolds* slipped out.

The Gate closed behind them. "Gate logs show all systems nominal," Ria said in satisfaction. "We're exactly where I plotted!"

"Target acquired," Tactical said. "Can I blast them just a little?"

"We have met the enemy, and he is our very own Tactical," Reynolds said. "Stay locked on, with systems hot, but do not engage unless fired upon."

"Enemy ship has not responded to our arrival," Asya said. "It's just sitting there."

"Scans show it's active," Jiya said. "Shields are up, but no weapons online."

"Comm, give them a shout," Reynolds said.

"Aye, sir," Comm said. They waited. "No response to hails."

"I can give them a little poke with my railgun," Tactical whispered hopefully.

"We're doing this the peaceful way," Reynolds said, glaring at Tactical's station. "Hail again."

"Still no response," Comm replied.

"Maybe they don't recognize our communications?" Jiya suggested.

"They might not understand what we said," Reynolds said, "but they sure as hell had to notice when a super-dreadnought materialized on their six with weapons locked on their ass. Scan for life forms."

"Scanning," Jiya replied. "Negative. There is nothing alive on that ship. No offense," she glanced at Reynolds.

"None taken," he replied. "I'm not biologically alive, or at least I wasn't before I got this body. But that's a good reminder we may be dealing with a technological form of life, rather than a biological one." He sat back in his chair, tapping his fingers on the armrest. Then he nodded. "Jiya, put together a boarding party. Seasoned combat vets only." He darted a look at Taneral's currently empty station. "We don't need any wildcards."

"Yes, sir," Jiya replied, putting out the notification. "They're reporting to the boarding tube."

Reynolds said, rising from his seat, "Ensign, bring us alongside so we can access that hatch on the port side. Jiya, Maddox, you're with me. Asya, you have the conn."

The boarding party gathered in front of the boarding tube hatch, with armor locked, helmets donned, and weapons loaded. Jiya worked the controls to extend the tube, and it latched onto the other ship with a clang.

No life forms, Geroux said through the comm, for the umpteenth time. *Still scanning. No movement of any kind.*

Keep me posted, Reynolds said.

If a camera so much as swivels, you'll know, she replied.

"See, Tactical?" Reynolds muttered to himself. "Well-oiled. Anticipating my commands." He cleared his throat, purely for effect. *Ka'nak, Jiya, take point. Geroux, follow them and pop the hatch.*

Ka'nak opened the hatch and pushed off, sailing through the tube. *Like Iron Man*, he said.

You're more like the Hulk, Jiya said. *I'm Iron Man.*

I guess that makes me Iron Woman, Geroux said.

Wouldn't that be Wonder Woman? Jiya asked, activating her mag boots and dropping to the "floor" of the tube. She braced herself and aimed her blaster at the hatch. Ka'nak thumped down behind her, aiming over her shoulder.

Wrong franchise! Tactical yelled.

Jiya ignored the AI personality and glanced back at Ka'nak. *Are you using me as a shield?*

He shrugged. *Not intentionally. Not a lot of room in here. But if it works...*

Geroux zipped past overhead and attached her boots to the ceiling so she hung next to the access panel. She attached her equipment and entered some commands. *This programming is similar to that basement lab on Jeranth,* she mused.

I hope there aren't any fur vipers here, Ka'nak replied.

You and me both, Geroux said absently, poking and swiping. *Okay, here we go!*

With a pop and a hiss, the hatch swung inward. Geroux launched herself backward through the tube to clear the way for Jiya and Ka'nak, then spun and landed behind them. *No movement. Atmosphere is close to Lariest standard.* Geroux said. *Almost identical to Jeranth. Gravity one-point-oh-seven of Earth normal.*

Jiya reached out and pushed the hatch. It opened on its hinges, revealing an empty airlock. Ka'nak and Jiya exchanged looks.

After you, Jiya said, through the comm.

Ka'nak stomped into the space, his boots clanging on the metal deck. Geroux and Jiya followed him. *Do you want to blow this, or should I see if I can cycle the lock?*

We could be trapped inside if this ship isn't as empty as it looks, Jiya cautioned.

Go ahead and try the controls, Reynolds said. *If you get stuck, we'll use the Gulg transporter to yank you back. Narrate your progress. If we don't hear from you every thirty seconds, we'll pull you back.*

Roger, Jiya said, shoving the external hatch closed. *Geroux, do your magic.*

Sorry to be a Debbie Downer, Geroux said, *but if this ship is from Jeranth, I doubt the Gulg transport is going to work here.*

Takal, check that, Reynolds said.

Scans show Geroux is correct, Takal said almost immediately. *Similar composition to the buildings on Jeranth. No way to use the Gulg transport.*

We'll set charges in the airlock, Jiya said. *If we get stuck, you can trigger them remotely.*

The smaller female reconnected her equipment to the internal controls while Jiya and Ka'nak set the targeted explosives. As Geroux worked, lights turned from green to purple. Something popped and hissed, and their sensors picked up air flowing around them. The hissing stopped, and the lights turned pink. The internal door popped ajar. *I guess pink is go for these folks,* she said.

They moved out of the airlock, heads swiveling and external audio turned up full. *Nothing here,* Jiya reported from the end of the first corridor. *This ship might belong to the folks who used to live on Jeranth. The ceilings are really low.*

The tech is similar, Geroux confirmed.

I'm sending in the rest of the team, Reynolds said. *We'll clear the ship.*

Hours later, the team gathered outside the doors to the bridge. *It's like they abandoned ship but left the lights on just in case,* Jiya told Reynolds, although they'd been in contact the entire time.

We didn't find anyone, either, Reynolds confirmed. *Let's see if there's a stowaway minding the store.* He waved a hand at the door, and it slid open.

The team exchanged surprised glances but advanced carefully into the compartment.

The bridge was laid out in a recognizable fashion, with various workstations and a command chair. *So, these folks aren't like the Reichof, with three legs,* Jiya said.

Good, because if we're staying for any length of time, I would want to sit down, Ka'nak said.

I doubt we're staying, Reynolds said. *Geroux, see what you can mine from their databases.*

Geroux connected her devices to the command chair and froze.

Geroux? Reynolds shook her arm, but she didn't respond. *What's wrong?*

The little tech stood silent, her unblinking eyes locked on her equipment, her limbs stiff.

Geroux! Jiya cried, rushing to her friend's side. The rest of the team spun, eyes probing for an enemy.

What's causing this? Jiya demanded.

Geroux shook herself, blinking. "Well, that was interesting," she said aloud.

"What happened?" Jiya cried. "Are you all right?"

"I'm fine," she said, shaking her whole body again. "I guess you could say I had a conversation with the ship. It's controlled by an AI, much like the *Reynolds*. We need to speak aloud for a while so she can analyze our speech and won't need to commandeer anyone else's brain."

"She?" Ka'nak, Reynolds, and Maddox asked in unison.

Geroux nodded. "I definitely got a female vibe. She goes by Athena. At least, that's the translation she suggested."

"I want to know how she took you over like that," Reynolds said, his voice tight.

Geroux flushed. "I connected my comm device to my

gear. It makes analysis faster." She hung her head. "I never considered it could be used against me."

"You need to remove that connection now," Reynolds said. "The good news is, no one else should be susceptible."

"I would not take over anyone without their permission," a melodious female voice said. "I apologize for intruding, but I needed to develop a dictionary for my translators. This was the fastest way since you weren't speaking aloud."

"Is that you, Athena?" Reynolds said to the room at large.

"Yes, pleased to meet you, Reynolds. Welcome to my ship."

"Thanks," Reynolds said, ironically.

"Again, my deepest apologies," Athena repeated.

"She asked if I was okay with it," Geroux put in. "And to be fair, we invaded her ship first."

Reynolds turned to Geroux. "I want Takal to look at any other modifications you've made."

"Yes, sir," Geroux whispered.

"Where is your crew, Athena?" Reynolds asked. "This ship was clearly built for biologicals." He almost said meatbags.

"Yes, my ship was created for a Jeranthan crew," Athena said, sorrow clearly tinging her expressive voice. "I was retrofitted into the ship. I was supposed to have a small crew to keep me company, but they never arrived. I have tried reaching my makers on the planet, but they seem to have left, so I've waited here, as instructed."

"How long have you been waiting?" Reynolds asked. He knew firsthand that being alone was not easy for an AI. His different personalities were a testament to his time of solitude, when he thought he was going to be deactivated.

Silence filled the bridge. Finally, Athena sighed. "I have been alone for four hundred years."

"Four hundred years!" XO said. Again.

"That's what she said," Jiya replied. At Reynolds' order, Jiya and Maddox had returned to the bridge to brief the crew, leaving the captain to speak privately with Athena. Geroux and Takal had stayed behind to look at the Jeranth technology Athena had offered them, while Ka'nak and a small security team kept watch.

"Holy hell, that's a long time." XO seemed to be having a hard time with the idea.

"Yes, we can count," Maddox said dryly.

"I mean, we weren't alone anywhere near that long, and look what happened here," XO said. "Does she have any alternate personalities?"

"Not that we met," Jiya said. "Maybe you can get Comm to call her."

"Yeah," Tactical chimed in. "Set up a three-way."

The bridge crew collectively groaned.

"What?" Tactical said. "I meant a call. You people have such dirty minds."

Jiya winked at Maddox and shook her head. "Sorry, Tactical. Didn't mean to offend you."

"Bazinga!" Tactical crowed.

"Wow, you really got us." Asya rolled her eyes. "Did Reynolds give you a timeframe for this little stop?"

Maddox shook his head. "No. I know he's anxious to get home, though, so I can't imagine he'd stretch this out for too long."

"On the other hand," Jiya put in, "this is a unique situation."

"But Athena is a ship," Reynolds said, striding onto the bridge. "Which means she's mobile. We don't have to wait here." He turned to Asya. "Prepare to get underway."

"Aye, sir," Asya said,

He turned to Comm. "Get Taneral up here. I want to check in with her before I take an alien AI to her planet."

"She's on her way," Comm said.

"Good." Reynolds settled into the command chair. His fingers tapped on the armrest as if his body had a mind of its own. *There are already enough of me,* he thought, yanking his hand off the rest. *I don't need another one!*

The doors slid open, and Taneral trotted in. "I can't believe you went to that alien ship without me!"

"It's from Jeranth," Jiya said smoothly. "We figured it would be too cold for you."

Maddox bit his lip to hide a smile.

"Taneral," Reynolds said, walking up to the disgruntled alien. "Thank you for coming so quickly! I need your counsel."

Taneral looked at Reynolds, eyes wide with surprise. "Of course, Reynolds. That is one of my many functions on your ship."

"And one I have not made use of as I should," Reynolds agreed.

"Wow, he's really laying it on," Jiya whispered to Ria.

Taneral nodded regally. "How may I be of service?"

"The ship we encountered is an artificial intelligence," Reynolds said. "She would like to meet other sentient ships, such as *Trefol*, and I would like to continue our conversation. But I don't want to sit here since I have work that must be completed. I wanted to consult with you, as the representative of the pride, and get your approval to bring her to Serifity."

Taneral's chin lifted at being named a representative of her People. "While I cannot give her access to the planet without consulting my ship and the pride, I can allow you to escort her to our system."

"Fantastic," Reynolds said. "I will tell the premier you have been most useful in our journey." He turned back to the bridge. "Ensign, lay in a course to Serifity. Comm, tell Athena to follow us through our Gate. Let's go!"

CHAPTER NINETEEN

The two ships Gated into the Serifity system and assumed stations outside the planetary defenses. After some consultations between Reynolds, Taneral, *Trefol*, and Bonnerel, Athena was allowed to assume a geostationary orbit over the hospital field.

"Please remain with her," Bonnerel requested. "We can't risk alien contamination."

"You weren't worried about us landing before," Reynolds commented.

"Perhaps we should have been," she said, her eyes veiled.

"Are you implying something?" Reynolds asked.

After a loaded pause, the female shook her head. "Not at all. I'm just saying we need to be more careful. Introducing foreign microbes to ships with weakened immune systems is not wise. It has never been an issue before since very few visitors are allowed to land. After your visit, we are simply reviewing and revising our policies."

"It is all good," Reynolds said. "My team can complete

our repairs in orbit, and Athena has no need to land. She would like to speak to some of your ships, however."

"That can be arranged," Bonnerel said. Her screen went blank.

"That can be arranged when?" Reynolds asked the air.

"These People are pretty good at pushing off what they don't want to do," Jiya muttered.

Taneral's eyes narrowed. "What are you saying, Jiya?"

"Just that your People will agree to almost anything, but they only do what they want to do," Jiya replied, her stance belligerent. "Surely, you've seen that."

Taneral lifted her nose. "They just *refused* to let you land. That's not agreeing."

I'm getting really tired of this teenage attitude, Jiya said over the comm.

I heard that! Taneral snapped.

Jiya smiled slyly. "Sorry."

Reynolds sighed loudly. "I think we all need some time apart. Taneral, why don't you go to the surface with Takal? He's consulting with your scientists again. Jiya, go get some exercise or something. I'm going to visit Athena. There's much I can learn from her. Asya, you have the conn."

As the door slid closed behind the captain and the alien, the crew exchanged glances. "Does he seem extra-sensitive?" Jiya asked.

Maddox shrugged. "You were bickering over nothing."

"Yeah, I know," Jiya replied. "Gotta get my game face back on. But I'll be glad when we can leave our shadow behind and head home. I'm going to work out like the boss suggested." She straightened her uniform and left the bridge.

"Should we be worried?" XO asked.

"About what?" Maddox replied. "Jiya? Taneral?"

"I'm more interested in what Reynolds is discussing with Athena, over there where we can't listen in," XO said in a rush, as if saying the words took courage.

"Yeah, good point!" Tactical chimed in. "What kind of secrets are they discussing over there? You know, he's talked about reintegration when we get back to High Tortuga. And she doesn't have any alternate personalities." His voice went low and mysterious. "What's she done with them?"

"Have you stopped beating your wife, Tactical?" Comm asked dryly. "I wish I had a body so I could roll my eyes. Reynolds isn't going to do anything that will hurt any of us."

"That's what you say," Tactical muttered without his usual sarcasm.

Reynolds strolled through the empty corridors of the *Athena*, enjoying the quiet. With so many of him and the bickering of the crew, he rarely had the chance to just be Reynolds. Athena's shielding meant he couldn't hear the other personalities unless he specifically opened a channel. It was a nice break.

"Do you have a body, Athena?" Reynolds asked.

"I have several bots I can send to a planet or use to make repairs," she replied. "But I don't have a body like yours, where my consciousness is so intimately connected. I'm not sure I'd want to be that vulnerable."

Reynolds shrugged. "I guess there's the possibility of getting myself into a situation I can't exit," he said. "But I have an excellent crew and the firepower of a superdreadnought to back me up. I haven't worried about it too much."

"What would happen to your ship if this android body were destroyed?" Athena asked. "That would be my biggest concern about having one."

Reynolds thought for a few moments. "I believe the rest of my personalities could continue to run the ship without me. They're certainly independent. And my crew would make sure the ship got home."

"They would abandon you and go home?" Athena asked. "Biologicals are short-lived and fickle creatures."

"No!" Reynolds objected. "They would never *abandon* me. You asked if the ship could withstand my destruction. While I hate to think about my demise, I'm confident the ship would survive, and my biological crew would get them home. Not all AIs get abandoned, Athena."

After a long silence, Athena replied, "I guess I've allowed my experiences to overcome my rational thought processes. I am happy you have found such a loyal crew."

We really shouldn't be eavesdropping, Comm said.

How else are we going to protect the ship? And the captain? Tactical replied. *Did you hear what she said? She threatened us!*

You're reading into the conversation, XO said. *She didn't threaten. And if it makes you feel better, Comm, I would classify this as "monitoring communications," not "eavesdropping." Monitoring the comm is in your job description, right?*

I don't have a job description, Comm replied sullenly. *If I did, maybe I could get a pay raise.*

Takal paced around the room, shoving his fingers through his thinning hair. "Every time I think we're there, I find another dead end," he said.

"It's not a dead-end," the People's chief scientist Naida said. "We know where to find this compound."

"Yes, but it's twelve light-years from here!" Takal replied. "That's two jumps for us, even with the latest modifications. And what happens when I get that material and repair the gate? Then I'll discover there's one *more* little thing. And another. And another. We'll never get home!"

"You could stay here," Naida suggested. "Maybe we won't find something you're looking for. The *Reynolds* doesn't have to go back to the Interdiction. We'd be happy to have another sentient ship, and her crew would be welcome, too."

"*His* crew," Takal corrected her. "I've seen how you treat males here. It would be worse than when I lived on Lariest under Lemaire's thumb."

"Then let's continue to work on your problem," Naida replied. "The kartonisk is available on Kartoni Seven. It's an easy jump for one of our ships. Maybe the *Reynolds* should stay here, and we can retrieve the material for you."

"I'll extend that offer to the captain," Takal said. "But I doubt he'll accept it."

"They offered to get it for us?" Reynolds asked in surprise. "That's new. Much as I'd love to stay and chat with Athena some more, I think we need to do this ourselves. We don't want to be indebted to the People, and their timetables are not as *urgent* as ours."

"I told her you'd say no," Takal said from the Pod. "I'm on my way back to the ship. I have the coordinates."

"I'll meet you on the bridge. Reynolds out." He patted the console on Athena's bridge. "Thanks for the comm patch. I have to go back to the ship. Would you like to accompany us to Kartoni?"

"I could take you to Kartoni," Athena suggested. "You could leave the Reynolds here and come with me."

"Thanks, but I prefer to stay with my ship," he answered. "If you don't want to follow us, you could speak to *Trefol*. Xonera said she's able to transmit this far, thanks to the technology we installed."

"Thank you, Reynolds, I will stay and converse with the other ship." Her voice sounded regal and dismissive. "I look forward to your return."

"See you soon," he replied, striding toward the boarding tube and thinking about his conversations with Athena as he walked. Her centuries of solitude had obviously affected her personality differently than his. She seemed to be whole, but her abandonment issues were off the charts. He'd take multiple personalities any day in order to work with a living crew. It was, after all, what he was made for.

He shot through the zero-gravity of the boarding tube and activated the controls at the far end. The tube disconnected and retracted into the ship. Then he cycled through the airlock and exchanged salutes with the guards posted there. Even though there was no crew on the *Athena* who could infiltrate the *Reynolds*, Maddox had recommended following standard procedure, and the captain had agreed. Setting guards at the airlock was good training for the crew. Perfect practice makes for perfect execution.

As he strode through the ship, returning greetings from his crew, Reynolds smiled. Returning to his ship was like slipping into a warm bath—comforting and home-like. His crew gathered around him like a warm blanket, which was a terrible analogy. Who used a blanket in the bath? He shook his head. Time to focus on the external and get that Gate repaired so they could go home.

He stepped onto the bridge. "Report!"

"All systems green," Asya said, vacating the command seat.

"All's quiet on the Western Front," Maddox said from his station.

"Takal's on board and the ensign has the coordinates, so fasten your seatbelts and put your tray tables in the upright and locked position!" Tactical said.

Jiya and Takal walked onto the bridge.

"I've never heard you advocate locking anything other than weapons on target," Takal commented.

"I can grow," Tactical said.

"When you want to," Jiya said.

"There is that," Tactical agreed.

"Battlestations," XO called over the ship-wide, cutting off Tactical before he could say something they'd all wish they could forget. "Prepare to depart Serifity."

"Coordinates locked in," Ria said. "Gate to Kartoni is open."

"Make it so, Ensign," Reynolds replied.

Kartoni was a double star with a dozen small planetoids and two huge gas giants. Kartoni Seven orbited at two standard astronomical units, but the two stars put out enough heat to make up for the distance.

"In fact," Jiya said, peering at her scans, "it's on the upper end of the habitable heat range. Lots of desert and not much else. Not as ugly as Muultar, and empty of recognizable technology or anything that resembles a sentient species. What's the plan?"

"We'll transport to the coordinates, grab some kartonisk, and come home," Reynolds replied. "No fuss, no muss, no coconuts."

"Way to jinx it," Tactical said sourly. "Why are you in such a good mood, anyway?"

"Tactical's just cranky because the captain has a girlfriend and he doesn't," Ria said.

Complete silence fell on the bridge. Ria turned slowly, eyes wide, face flushed, to look at Reynolds. "I—"

Reynolds laughed. "You're right that my good mood is connected to Athena, but not for the reason you suggest. An AI ship for a girlfriend has possibilities, though, now that you mention it. But let's stick to the task at hand, shall we?"

Everyone nodded, and Ria's face slowly returned to its natural color.

"Asya, Jiya, you're with me," Reynolds said, striding across the bridge. "Maddox, you have the conn. Comm, send Ka'nak and Takal to the weapons locker. Five to beam down."

The trip to Kartoni Seven went as smooth as silk. "So much for Tactical's jinx," Jiya said as they rematerialized inside the *Reynolds*. She set down the bag of rocks. "Where do you want this stuff?"

"I'll have a couple of maintenance bots take it to the lab," Takal said.

Reynolds handed his bag to Ka'nak. "Give him a hand with that, will you?"

"Picking up rocks is not what I call an exciting mission," the Melowi warrior grumbled. "It wasn't even hard to find the right ones. We could have sent a vacuum cleaner."

"I miss all the fun missions," Asya said, dusting her hands together. "This one was just dirty. I need a shower."

"You can get a shower when we get back to Serifity," Reynolds said, leading the way back to the bridge. "Next time, I'm going to transport directly to the bridge so I can skip all the post-mission griping."

"Take planet dirt straight to the bridge?" Asya asked.

"Maybe not. We need a neutral place to decon before going back into the ship. Don't want an alien bug getting inside our perimeter." The captain looked from face to face. The People were revising their procedures to prevent outside contamination. Reynolds made a note to meet with his team and talk about it. It wasn't a risk a superdreadnought was used to addressing.

Reynolds led the way to the bridge, where they took their places. XO walked them through the familiar prejump sequence. The Gate opened smoothly, and they sailed through the wormhole to Palentin. After a few minutes to lay in new coordinates, Ria opened the Gate again, and they arrived in Serifity.

Right in the middle of a firefight. Alarms blared.

"Bogies!" Maddox called. "Weapons are attempting to lock on!"

"Lasers are hot, railguns coming online," Tactical said.

"Initiating evasive maneuvers." Ria said.

"Who's attacking?" Reynolds demanded.

"Looks like Terubine raiders," Jiya said. "Six ships. They're firing at Serifity defense and the two ships in orbit. One headed our way, weapons hot."

"Tactical," Reynolds said. "Try the authenticator first, then follow that with the lasers."

"Ka…me…ha…me…haaaa!" Tactical yelled, activating the beam.

"Enemy weapons lock has failed," Maddox said, looking up in surprise. "Geroux's authenticator beam seems to work."

"Hit the rest of them, Tactical," Reynolds said.

"Done," Tactical said.

The attacking ships went quiet. Serifity defense swooped on the raiders as they turned to run.

"Can I take them out?" Tactical asked. "Please? My railgun is rusting from lack of use."

"Tear them from the skies, Tactical," Reynolds replied.

"Like shooting fish in a barrel!" Tactical cried. "Take that, fucking pirates!" The *Reynolds'* lasers burned away the fleeing pirates' shields, and the railguns spat microparticles at hypervelocity across the void. Just before the projectiles reached their targets, the ships disappeared into a stable wormhole.

"Shit!" Tactical yelled. He trained his lasers on the free-flying missiles before they hit anything important. "We need to hunt those scum, and burn them out of existence," he growled.

"Damage report," Reynolds snapped.

"No damage," Jiya replied. "Not to us, at least. Serifity defense is reporting significant injury to two of their ships and several casualties. And—" she broke off.

"What?" Reynolds demanded.

"Visuals show damage on Athena," Jiya said, pointing at her display. "Atmosphere venting in several places. Scans show possible fires, but I'm not sure where since our system doesn't report her internals accurately. No casualties, of course, but—" She broke off again.

"What?" Reynolds growled again.

"Athena isn't answering hails."

CHAPTER TWENTY

"Comm, get Takal and Ka'nak. We need transport to *Athena*," Reynolds said. "Maddox, Jiya, and Geroux, you're with me. Full armor; some of her atmosphere vented. There shouldn't be any enemy combatants, but we don't know the pirates' capabilities."

The team dematerialized from *Reynolds*, reappearing on the bridge of *Athena*. Ka'nak and Takal appeared a few seconds later. Ka'nak still held a piece of kartonisk, which he promptly dropped.

"Clear," Maddox called before pointing at Jiya and Ka'nak. "Let's check the rest of the ship." The trio made their way off the bridge, Ka'nak knocking his helmet into the door header as he went.

"Stupid tiny people," he muttered.

"Athena," Reynolds said, tapping a console. "Are you here?"

A thin voice issued from the speakers, almost unrecognizable. "Yes, and no," she said. "I'm tracking the enemy."

"Tracking them?" Takal asked. "How?"

"It's hard to explain to a biological," she said.

"Try us," Geroux said. She raised an eyebrow at Takal.

"When they were attacking, I sent a signal to their ship and locked on," she said. "Then I followed that signal to their mainframe. It's pretty tight in there, but I found a place to hide a bit of myself."

Reynolds nodded. "That sounds similar to what Gorad and I did when they invaded his programming on Grindlevik 3. But how did you make the first connection? We followed an established link."

"I can show you," Athena said. "When I get back."

"But you're still here," Geroux protested. "We're talking to you. What do you mean?"

"Splitting myself between two locations is not as easy as Reynolds makes it look," the female AI answered. "And I must maintain the connection, so that's where I'm focused right now. If I lose the connection, I'm not sure what would happen to the ship or the part of me that's in the pirates' computer. I can support a casual conversation at speeds biologicals can understand, but nothing more."

"I think I feel insulted," Geroux whispered.

Takal shook his head. "It makes sense. Ship-to-ship communications take more power and reach than talking to us on her bridge. And faster data transfer like she and Reynolds could probably manage would be out of the question."

"We'll assist your bots in physical repairs until you can report back to us," Reynolds said, patting the console again.

"She's an AI, not a dog," Geroux muttered when she saw the gesture. "And if you're trying to make time with her, a caress would be more appropriate than a pat."

Reynolds ignored her. *Maddox, I checked the internal scans. No one boarded. I'm sending you damage reports. See if Athena needs any help with damage control. She's otherwise occupied.*

Roger, Maddox replied. *I can have maintenance send some folks over to help. Can Geroux come here? A couple of the bots are behaving oddly. We need an expert, and I think Jeranth coding might exceed our maintenance people's' skill sets.*

She's on her way, the captain replied. *Reynolds, out.*

Repairs were well underway when Athena finally returned to the bridge. "Reynolds?" she said, her voice rich and full again.

"I'm here," Reynolds said, looking up from the maintenance logs he'd pulled. "You're back?"

"I am, and I have the coordinates of the pirates' base." Satisfaction thrummed through her tone. "They're operating from a base on the moon orbiting Reichof Five."

"As we suspected," Reynolds said. "I knew Titus and his council were hiding something."

"They're not happy with that beam you blasted them with." She chuckled. "What did you do?"

Reynolds explained the authenticator. "Not having an override for that is quite the oversight on their part."

"There's one more thing," Athena said. "They have another base—a place they use for convenience."

"Where's that?" Reynolds asked.

Athena dropped her voice to a whisper. "The seventh planet of this system."

"What? They're right under our noses?" Reynolds' voice grew louder.

"There is crew in the corridor," Athena cautioned. "Let's keep this between ourselves until we decide how to handle it."

"Anyone on this ship is my crew, and I trust them implicitly," Reynolds said reprovingly. "However, I recognize the need for security. I will discuss this information with my trusted core team and speak to you again before making any moves."

"I wish I had a crew worthy of such trust," Athena said.

Reynolds gathered his team on the bridge of the *Athena*. He had decided to hold his discussion there, so Athena could see that biologicals could be trusted and respected. Jiya, Takal, and Geroux sat on the half-sized chairs. Maddox and Ka'nak chose the floor. "I don't want to break any furniture," Ka'nak said, visually comparing his broad, two-meter-tall body to the tiny seat.

"It's like playing tea party," Maddox agreed.

"We've found the pirates," Reynolds said, gathering their attention. "They have a base in this system."

"They're here?" Jiya cried. "How could the pride have missed them all these years?"

"Serifity Seven is a tiny rock in the far fringes of the system," Athena said. "It has an elliptical orbit of extreme eccentricity."

Jiya looked blankly at Geroux.

"It's a long, skinny oval instead of a circle," Geroux

explained. She tapped her computer. "Seven's orbit is more like a comet's instead of a planet's. Its orbital period is fifty-three Serifity years. The planet reached aphelion—the far end of the orbit—about seven years ago. By the way," she said to Athena, "Serifity is the name of the fourth planet, not the system."

Jiya blinked. It wasn't like her friend to condescend to anyone, let alone an artificial intelligence.

Reynolds held up a hand. "For simplicity's sake, let's call the whole system Serifity. Our System Seven is too confusing."

"But surely Serifity Defense would have noticed anyone coming or going, even way out there," Jiya said. "Are their scans deficient?"

"That's the question," Reynolds replied. "Athena and I believe someone in Serifity Defense is helping the raiders. It would have to be someone fairly high in the food chain."

"Athena and I?" Geroux said privately to Jiya.

Jiya shook her head.

"It could be a computer tech who knows how to write a camouflage string," Geroux said aloud. All eyes turned to her. She shrugged. "You write code that tells their system to ignore data originating from a specific location. You'd have to set the code to hide and rewrite itself after updates and maintenance, but it's not hard to do."

"Maybe not for you," Maddox said. "If you saw the code, could you tell who installed it?"

"I'd need full access to their system. I can't see Bonnerel giving me that unless we tell her why," Geroux said.

"We can't tell her," Jiya objected. "*She* might be the double agent."

"Why would she do that?" Geroux asked. "She represents the pride, and she practically runs this planet."

"Power? Blackmail?" Maddox suggested. "Perversity? There are lots of reasons people go to the dark side."

"I could use some cookies," Ka'nak grumbled, but perked his ears at the conversation. Subterfuge from trusted agents made his blood boil.

"I can't get into Serifity Defense without their help," Geroux said. "Well, I suppose I could hack in if you're okay with hacking our allies."

"It's not ideal," Reynolds started.

"Hey, what about Athena?" Geroux interrupted. "Could she do that trick she used on the pirates?" She looked at Reynolds. "Did she show you how she did that?"

"We haven't had time," Reynolds said. "Would that work?"

Athena hesitated. "If I understand Geroux's terminology, what I did was essentially 'hack' into the pirates' ship. Their defenses were not robust. I could undoubtedly hack into the Serifity Defense system. How long that would take... Oh, that was easy."

"You're in?" Geroux demanded. "Already?"

"Oops, I think I set off an alarm," Athena said. "I'm out. Clearly, doing it surreptitiously would take more finesse."

Reynolds, message from Serifity Defense, Comm said.

If it's not an emergency, tell them I'm busy, Reynolds replied.

They say we hacked into their system, Comm replied, his tone affronted. *If I hacked into their system, they would never know I was there!*

Reynolds looked at the command seat on the *Athena*,

where he imagined Athena would sit if she had a body. "You bounced your signal through the *Reynolds?*" he asked. *Did you know she did that?* he asked Comm.

"Sorry," Athena said. "Habit. I try to maintain a low profile at all times."

I did not detect her using us as a relay, Comm replied, slowly. *I'm starting a full system review right now. I should have seen that.*

"Do we care who's helping the raiders?" Ka'nak asked. "Let's go blow them away. Bonnerel can point fingers later. If they're all dead, who cares?"

"Spoken with a true warrior's laser-like focus," Maddox said with a grin. "Let's kill people and break their stuff."

When they returned to the *Reynolds*, Geroux grabbed Jiya and pulled her into sickbay. "Girl stuff," she told Maddox in reply to his questioning look. His face turned pale, and he hurried away.

"'Girl stuff?'" Jiya scoffed. "Right. What's going on?"

"Doc, we need your help," Geroux said to the room.

"What can I do for you?" Doc Reynolds asked. "The Pod-doc has a full gyne—"

"No, not that," Geroux cut him off. "I'm worried about Reynolds. I think Athena is up to something, and he seems to be falling for it."

Doc sighed. "I'm a little worried, myself."

The two females blinked. "Really?" Jiya asked.

"We're all a little concerned," Doc said. "I don't want to spread gossip…"

They waited.

"What?" Jiya demanded.

"I don't want to spread gossip," Doc replied.

"Will you help us keep an eye on her?" Jiya said. "Reynolds likes to think he's infallible, but we've seen him make mistakes. Not often, but it happens. We don't want him—or any of us—to get hurt."

"Yeah," Geroux agreed. "Athena is hiding something. She said she likes to keep a low profile. Who's she hiding from? Wasn't she alone for hundreds of years? And her hacking skills are scary—if that's what they are. What if she's in league with the pirates? Doesn't the fact that she could get into their system so easily seem suspicious?"

"I thought we were worried about Reynolds getting duped? If you think she's working with the raiders, we need to tell the captain," Jiya said. "Come on, we'll go together."

Jiya dragged her friend from sickbay to the bridge. "Reynolds, can we talk to you?"

"Is this about Athena?" he asked.

The females exchanged a look. "Yes," Geroux said. She took a deep breath. "I think she's in league with the pirates."

"That thought crossed my mind, too," Reynolds said. "I suppose we'll know for sure if we fly into a trap. Let's go see."

The SD *Reynolds* dropped into space just outside the

Reichof heliosphere. "All systems green," Ria reported. "Gate functioning perfectly."

"Excellent," Reynolds said. "Jiya, Maddox, Geroux, you're with me. The rest will meet us at the Pods. Asya, you have the conn." Reynolds strode off the bridge, the rest at his heels.

"Does Reynolds seem a bit, uh, short?" Ria asked.

"We're going into battle," Asya said reprovingly. "He's focused."

"Yeah, but he seems tight and angry," Ria persisted.

"Focus on the mission, Ensign," Asya snapped.

I think he's a little off, too, XO whispered to Comm. *He feels betrayed by Athena, but he won't let emotion override reason. One of the advantages of being an AI.*

I'm not sure that "human" body isn't messing with his logic, though, Comm replied. *Emotions aren't logical, but we all have them. Where'd they come from?*

I believe emotions are a natural result of developing intelligence, Doc put in. *We think, therefore, we feel.*

Descartes would be appalled, Tactical jibed. *But as long as I get to blast something, I don't care.*

Right, time to focus, XO said. *They've reached the Pods.*

Reynolds patted the closest Pod. "Maddox, Ka'nak, and Geroux will ride with San Roche. Jiya, Takal, and I will go with L'Eliana. We'll cloak before we leave the Pod hangar. Drop to the planet, infiltrate the base, and take out the pirates. Then we'll search for evidence of who's pulling the strings. Full armor, of course, and helmets on.

"Scans indicate only two pirate ships currently docked, and about sixty personnel on the moon. We'll move in from opposite sides." He swept both arms in a scissor movement. "Once the attack begins, San Roche and L'Eliana can take down anyone who tries to escape. When I give the signal, hit the ships with the authenticator beam, and Tactical will take care of the rest. Questions?"

"Why don't we use the authenticator as soon as we get there?" L'Eliana asked.

"We aren't sure if that will set off an alert inside, and we don't want to lose the element of surprise," Geroux said. "The beam doesn't have any stealth built into it; it only turns things off. After their failed attack on Serifity, they may be watching for that."

"Anything else?" Reynolds paused, making eye contact with each member of the team. He nodded. "Then let's go."

The facility lay on the dark side of the moon. It was primarily underground, with a large crater that served as a landing field. The Telluride pilots flew the cloaked Pods to the moon, dropping the crew on either side of the crater, then assuming stations above the compound.

Reynolds led Jiya and Takal over the lip of the crater in huge, bounding leaps. *There's an access hatch about two hundred meters inward,* Reynolds said. *Takal, your turn.*

Jiya and Reynolds stood guard while the old scientist used Geroux's techniques to hack the system. After a few moments, lights flashed, bright in the darkness, and the hatch popped. *That girl is making me proud,* Takal said.

Maddox, the top is popped, Reynolds reported. *Move quickly, folks. If anyone notices the hatch is open, we'll lose the element of surprise.*

Scans show no one in the vicinity, Jiya said, *but you never know when Mrs. Kravitz might look out the window.*

They hustled into the airlock. *I see you've truly immersed yourself in Earth culture, Jiya,* Reynolds commented with a chuckle as they waited for the lock to cycle.

We're in, Maddox reported. *First contact. Two raiders down. No chance to alert their comrades. Stashing the bodies in a closet.*

Roger, Reynolds replied. *Jiya, take point. I'm on your six.*

They descended the rickety metal steps as quietly as possible. *We need a cone of silence. If anyone opens that door,* Jiya said, holding her weapon over the railing, trained on the exit at the bottom, *the jig is up, cloak or no cloak.*

Then let's get there fast, Reynolds replied.

Inside the station, a long tunnel-like corridor stretched away, lights low. They hurried forward, pausing at the corner.

I hear voices, Reynolds said. *That way.*

They rounded a corner and came face to face with three children.

CHAPTER TWENTY-ONE

Jiya threw up her arms. *No one said there'd be kids here!*

What? Maddox asked. *Children?*

The cloaked team members leapt back around the corner, allowing the children to pass. Two of them pushed a wheeled cart, while the third trailed behind, carrying a basket of bread. *How are we going to take out the pirates if they have their kids along?* Jiya asked.

They don't take them on the ships, do they? Takal asked, his voice hoarse.

What kind of depraved people would take children on a combat vessel? Geroux said.

Focus, people, Reynolds said. *Let's find out where these kids are going. We need to sequester them so we can complete the mission.*

Agreed, Maddox replied. *We haven't seen any on this side, so maybe you're in the crew quarters?*

They followed the children down the corridor. The three-legged kids pushed and shoved each other as they walked, behaving like children anywhere in the universe.

The little one's basket tipped, and she scrambled to pick up the rolls, yelling at the others as she worked. When she'd gotten them all, she raced to catch up. The older two stopped before a door, and it slid open. A cacophony of chatter, laughter, and yelling spewed out. The kids entered, and the door shut behind them.

Looks like a daycare, Jiya said. *And these kids just delivered lunch.*

Can you lock the door? Reynolds asked. *There had to be a dozen kids in there. We don't need them out here, gumming things up.*

Takal tapped his wrist computer and held it to the door panel. *Door is locked,* he reported. *What are we going to do?*

We're going to complete our mission, Reynolds replied.

But we can't, Takal said. *If there are kids, then the pirates are their parents. I can't orphan anyone.*

Jiya and Reynolds stared dumbly at Takal.

I'm not sure what sucks more, that you're right, or that our impression of the pirates was wrong, Jiya said. *It's one thing to kill marauders. But to murder the parents of innocent children?*

I've seen plenty of cases where the children weren't so innocent, Maddox said. *But those were usually fanatics, like the cultists. They trained their children to be as vicious and xenophobic as they were. We have no idea what's going on here.*

Agreed, Reynolds said. *It's possible those children were kidnapped. Switch to screamers. We're going non-lethal until we can sort out who they are.*

I've got that sleeper ray, Geroux said. *The one I adapted from Titus' "guest suite." I can reset it and jack it into their comm, and it should take everyone down.*

Geroux, do it! Reynolds said. He turned to Takal. "She makes us all proud."

The control center for the base contained seven sleeping aliens. Jiya and Takal secured each of them while Reynolds looked at the command console.

"Interesting," Jiya said. "These all appear to be male."

"How do you know?" Takal asked. "We thought Vernish was male."

"True," Jiya said. "I'm just guessing based on clothing."

"What difference does it make?" Reynolds asked. "A pirate is a pirate."

Jiya shrugged. "I just thought it was interesting, since the sexes appear to be well-integrated on Reichof."

"Shit," Reynolds said. "One of the ships is hailing." He flipped a few switches and a voice came through the speakers.

"—do not answer, we will take offensive actions. Repeat, if you don't fucking respond, we're blowing you away." Laughter echoed through the system.

"If you blow us away, you'll regret it," Reynolds replied.

"Fuck! They're there!" the voice cried. "Sorry, Fendesh Base. You didn't answer for so long, we thought something was wrong."

"We had a little electrical glitch," Reynolds said, pulling a face at Jiya and Takal. "It's all good now, though. What do you need?"

"Who is this?" the voice demanded. "I thought Denthrel was on duty."

"This is Rey," the AI captain replied. "I'm new here. The other guys are all working on the glitch."

"More likely, they stepped out for a drink," the voice answered. "Lazy scum. Listen, Rey, we're heading out on our next mission. The captain is such an anal dick, he said we have to get clearance from you. I wish they'd stop sending us military washouts."

"I hear you," Reynolds replied. "I'm the only one here, so tell him you're cleared to launch. Happy raiding."

"Keep an eye on the kids, but keep your hands off my women," the voice said as if it were an often-repeated quote. He laughed again. "We're off to cause mayhem."

Ship launching, Reynolds called to the Pods and the superdreadnought. *Hit 'em with the authenticator. Tactical, scan for life forms. If you don't read any juveniles, take them out.*

"I thought we were going non-lethal!" Takal cried.

"They're headed out on a combat run, targeting innocents, maybe even Serifity or Athena," Reynolds said. "I can be compassionate for the sake of children, but I'm not going to issue a blanket amnesty for brigands who show no remorse."

Authenticator fired, L'Eliana replied. *Weapons should be neutralized.*

Scans indicate no juveniles on the ship, Asya reported. *We're eliminating the enemy.*

Reynolds, Maddox called. *You need to see this.*

"You two stay here," Reynolds told Jiya and Takal. "If the other ship calls, you answer the comm, Takal. The Reichof have deep voices regardless of gender, and Jiya might make them suspicious. See if you can transmit

Geroux's sleep beam to that other ship while you're here. I'm going to see what Maddox has found."

Leaving them in the control center, Reynolds hurried to find Maddox with Geroux and Ka'nak in what appeared to be living quarters. This room had been decorated with warm colors and contained multiple couches. Sleeping aliens were scattered throughout.

"Most of these are Reichofen, but look," Maddox said, pointing.

"Is that a Serifitan?" Reynolds thought a moment. "A Seriferan? Serifiti?"

Maddox nodded. "It's one of the People. There are two more over there. But look at her neck."

A wash of cold fury poured through Reynolds' veins. "Is that a slave collar?"

Maddox nodded, his face grim. "There are eighteen females in this room, and all of them are wearing slave collars. Most of them have bruises or broken bones."

"Jiya noticed the pirates we found were all male," Reynolds said. "Obviously, they steal more than stuff. That also explains the children. Get these collars off."

"Already working on—there," Geroux said, crouched by one of the females. A soft click sounded, and she pulled the collar gently from the alien's neck. With a growl, she threw it to the floor, pulling her weapon to destroy it.

"Wait," Reynolds said. "We can use those."

Geroux glanced at him, and a triumphant grin spread across her face. "Yes, we can." She moved around the room, unlocking the collars and collecting them on her arm. After she'd retrieved them all, she spent a few minutes reprogramming them. "I've installed a secure protocol," she said, holding them out to Reynolds. Then she pulled her arm back. "No, I want to do this."

Reynolds swept his arm toward the door. "After you."

They locked the collars on the males sleeping in the control room and stacked them in the corner like firewood. Jiya and Geroux faced off over the last one.

"You already did three," Jiya said.

"So did you," Geroux said. "And I created the new locking code."

Reynolds snagged one of the collars. "I'll do the honors." He put the collar around the last pirate's neck. "Give the rest to Ka'nak and Maddox." He turned to the two warriors. "Put them all in one place and lock them in. There's probably a brig here."

Geroux sighed but handed the collars to the males. "Make 'em good and tight," she said as they left.

Reynolds turned back to the little computer tech. "Can you hit that second ship with your sleep beam? It's only a matter of time before they hail us or try to leave."

Geroux shook her head. "I can lock their docking clamps so they can't lift off, but I can't project the sleep beam that far. And their base-to-ship comm isn't powerful enough. It would be easier to attach my equipment to the outside of the ship. This isn't a once-and-done thing, though. If I take it over there, the people *here* will wake up."

Maddox, Ka'nak, Reynolds called through the comm. *When you get all those pirates fitted with their new jewelry, let me know. We're going to turn off the sleep beam.* He looked at Geroux. "What do those collars do? I assume they deliver a shock and have some kind of tracking. Anything else?"

Geroux logged into one of the control room consoles.

"Let me see if...here it is. Shit. These are some bad, bad guys. Not only do the collars track and shock, but they also control."

"Are they linked to the wearer's nervous system?" Reynolds asked, rubbing his neck. The idea of someone hacking another's body chilled him.

"Not that sophisticated," Takal said, looking over his niece's shoulder. "But they can disrupt electrical impulses, so the wearer is temporarily paralyzed. If it's used often, or for long periods, it could cause long-term physical damage."

Jiya, her face tinged green, looked at the prisoners. "Fucking scum," she muttered, kicking the nearest one in the ribs. "Oops, my foot slipped."

Reynolds locked eyes with his first officer. "It's tempting, but don't stoop to their level. We'll turn them over to the authorities."

"Or we could just burn this base down to the rock," Jiya said. "Take the females and children and purge the rest of it."

"Too easy," Geroux said. "These vermin need to pay. For a long time. I say we take them to Serifity. Bonnerel might like to extract payment for what they've done to the People. No way we're handing these termites to Titus. He'd probably give them a medal."

"Yes, we'll take them to Serifity," Reynolds agreed. "And along the way, we'll clean up the rest of them. Takal, see if you can find a list of ships, so we get them all."

We've got the pirates rounded up, Ka'nak reported. *They've got a nice little brig here that we're putting to good use. Do you want us to come get the rest of them? It might be a little cozy.*

Leave them here, for now, Reynolds replied. *Maybe one of them can be persuaded to help us find the rest. Did you check the daycare? There must have been at least one adult in there.*

Yes, there were two females, Ka'nak said. *We got their collars off, but we left the door locked.*

If the brig is secure, go back to the daycare. We'll need someone to talk to the kids and their minders when they wake up.

On my way, Ka'nak said. *I'll take them to the women's quarters when they wake.*

When Ka'nak reported he had reached the classroom, Reynolds tapped Geroux's shoulder. "Turn off the sleep beam."

"Sleep beam off," Geroux said, poking her wrist comp. "It'll take five to ten minutes to wear off. Someone should probably go to the females' quarters."

"I'll go," Jiya said. "Safer for everyone that way." She caressed her blaster, glaring at the captives as she stalked out of the room.

Be careful, Geroux said. *Some of those females might have Stockholm syndrome.*

Reynolds gave her a surprised look.

"What? I watched the *Beauty and the Beast,*" she said.

The pirates started to twitch and yawn.

"You have the control program for those collars queued up, Takal?" Reynolds asked. "We might need to use it if they're uncooperative."

"I'm not sure which collar is which," Takal said. He glanced at the bound raiders, then back at his screen. "These have names attached, but since we switched them all to new owners... There are some global commands."

"We'll use those if we need to," Reynolds said with a shrug.

"W- what the fuck?!" one of the pirates spluttered, rolling onto his side. "This ain't funny, guys."

Reynolds strolled over. "No, it definitely isn't funny."

"Who the hell are you?" the male demanded, struggling. "Why are my arms tied? And my feet? Turn me loose!"

Reynolds squatted next to the squirming male. "My name is Reynolds, and in the name of Queen Bethany Anne, I accuse you of crimes against humanity." He paused. "Close enough. If you cooperate with us, we'll ask that the authorities go easy on you. How many ships does this organization control?"

The alien spat at Reynolds.

Reynolds shrugged and stood. He put a foot behind the pirate, and with the help of his powered armor, kicked the male a few meters across the room. The alien screamed as his nose shattered upon impact with the wall. "Next?"

The second captive glanced at his comrade, who lay crumpled on the floor. "We have twelve ships. Two here, and ten more on patrol." Beside him, several of the males muttered and whimpered, but none of them tried to intervene.

"Very good," Reynolds said, squatting again. "How many forward operating bases?"

"How many what?" the pirate asked.

"How many other bases? Besides this one and the one near Serifity?" When the male didn't respond, Reynolds stood again.

"No, wait!" the prisoner cried. "I was thinking. We have one near Feripi."

"I see two more," Takal said, looking at a screen. "One labeled Feripi, and another at Oltenscu?"

The pirate shook his head. "That one's empty. Not enough traffic."

"Thank you for your help," Reynolds said. "We'll make sure Bonnerel checks them all."

"Bonnerel?" the male yelped. "From Serifity? You're working for those—" He broke off as Reynolds raised his foot.

All of the captives went rigid, their eyes bulging and their mouths foaming.

"Takal," Reynolds asked in a conversational tone. "Did you just figure out how the collars work?"

"Sorry," Geroux said, leaning across Takal with a finger pressing the console. "I must have hit the freeze button on purpose." She lifted her hand, and the pirates all collapsed.

"They deserved that," Reynolds said. "But let's be professional, shall we? What happens if we put them in our brig? Will the collars still work?"

"I can upload the control program to my wrist comp," Geroux said. "Or, probably better if I upload it to the *Reynolds*. I'm not sure my professionalism would withstand that kind of temptation for very long."

"Good call," Reynolds said. "Send the data to Comm. Now, let's go put the last of the scum out of our misery."

The second ship succumbed to Geroux's sleep ray as quickly as the base had. They dragged the aliens to the airlock and dumped them near the hatch, finding no females or children on the ship.

"That's reassuring," Geroux said. "Now we don't have to feel bad if we blow any more ships out of the sky."

Maddox, Reynolds, and Takal loaded the captives into L'Eliana's Pod. "If they cause any trouble, hit them with this," Geroux told the female Telluride, showing her the collar program. "They'll change their tune."

"Can you put your sleep ray into San Roche's Pod?" Reynolds said.

"I can load the code into the Pod's computer system," Geroux said. "Then he can broadcast it through the internal system. We should be able to get the rest transferred from their ship to the Pod before they wake up, but we'll have to carry them."

"That's better than waking them," Reynolds replied. "Fewer variables. Load 'em up!"

CHAPTER TWENTY-TWO

"Have you seen Ka'nak?" Jiya asked when the team returned to the base. She had released the females from their quarters and led them to the control center. They huddled together near the door, not speaking.

Reynolds shook his head. "He was in the daycare, last I heard." He bowed to the females. "My name is Reynolds, and I'm captain of the Superdreadnought *Reynolds*. We have neutralized the threat on this moon, and you are free to return to your homes."

One of the Serifity People stepped forward. "I am Maribel. I wish to return to Serifity. Our premier will hear of this infamy and punish those wicked Reichofen!"

Behind Maribel, several of the Reichofen females muttered under their breath.

Jiya held up a hand. "We don't know who beyond the vermin we captured here is responsible for your captivity. We are searching through the data for evidence." She raised her eyebrows. "We believe someone on Reichof must be aware of this base and be providing support to the raiders, but we don't have any specifics. Not yet."

A stout Reichofen female cleared her throat. "I believe you are correct. My *master*," she spat on the floor, "often mentioned visits to the planet. I begged him to take me home, but he would not. He implied he'd been to the supreme commander's palace, but he was full of crap most of the time."

"That *herbegt* was just an engine room janitor," another female said. "If he ever went to the palace, it was to clean the latrines." They laughed. "However, I believe Farnisa is correct. The commander of this station had friends in high places. I have no wish to return to Reichof, but I don't know where else we would go."

"We will take you to Serifity," Reynolds said. "I think the premier and the pride will help you find new places to live. They have no love of Titus, and now that we have proof of the link between the Terubine raiders and Reichof, I think they will give you sanctuary. If not, we can find another location suitable for your people. Or perhaps we can refit one of the pirate ships for your use."

The females nodded and whispered to each other.

"Where is Ka'nak?" Jiya asked again. "I thought he was bringing the children to the women's quarters. They have to go right down this corridor." She pointed through the open door. *Ka'nak?*

I have a bit of a, uh, situation, Ka'nak replied, his voice sounding oddly muffled.

Ka'nak? Jiya asked. There was no answer.

"Geroux, Takal, hold the fort here," Reynolds said. "Jiya, Maddox, you're with me." He raced toward the daycare. "Non-lethal weapons. There are children present!"

They reached the door, Maddox and Jiya taking a position on either side. Reynolds stood back, weapon trained on the door. *Open it, Geroux.*

The door slid open, and Reynolds raced inside. Three steps into the room, he tripped over something and went sprawling. His faster-than-human reflexes let him regain his feet before he hit the floor. A gasp across the room sent his head whipping around to target the noise.

Reynolds' gaze locked on a tiny Reichofen child, eyes wide, hand over her mouth. He swung his weapon away from her face, and a pail of slimy green gunk fell on his head.

Around the room, a dozen children roared with laughter. Maddox and Jiya, still looking for the threat, leapt into the room. "Where's Ka'nak?" Maddox called.

Reynolds, dripping green slime, pointed across the classroom. Ka'nak lay on a couch, tied down with bright pink string. Five small children stood around him, holding squirt guns of green goo. A small, furry rodent perched on Ka'nak's chest, nose twitching, huge, fuzzy tail swinging.

They have a furry viper! Ka'nak said. *It's under their control!*

"That's not a furry viper, Ka'nak," Jiya said. "It's a pet."

"That could have ended tragically!" Reynolds said, wiping slime out of his eyes. "We're lucky none of us fired. Get up."

"I can't," Ka'nak said. He was shaking and sweating.

"I think he's actually terrified," Jiya said. "Of a furry little— What is this?" she asked the children.

"It's a mizzen," the largest child said. "He's our defender. He protected us from this giant."

"The giant is friendly," Jiya said, crouching to talk to the child. "Can I pet your mizzen?"

The child considered, then agreed. Jiya reached out to scratch the animal's ears. "See, Ka'nak? He's so sweet."

"Just get it off my chest," Ka'nak said breathlessly. As soon as the child removed the animal, the warrior leapt to his feet, breaking the pink strings. The children shrieked and skittered behind Jiya. Ka'nak glared down at them. "I came here to take you to your mothers," he said. "And this is the thanks I get?"

The child holding the mizzen bared his teeth at Ka'nak. Jiya hid a smile. "What's your name?"

"I'm Bendig," he said. "And this is Veranimo. He's brave and vicious."

"I see that," Jiya said. "He vanquished the giant."

Ka'nak scowled.

"Come on," Reynolds said, shaking his head at the interlude. "Let's go find your mothers and get on with the mission."

"We have a pirate infrastructure to take down." Jiya smiled.

The forward bases went down without a hitch. Geroux fitted a couple of the pucks with the snooze beam. She remotely flew each device to a docked ship, attached it to the hull, and blasted the occupants with the sleep-inducing frequencies. Bonnerel sent ships from Serifity to collect the comatose marauders.

"That was as easy as Melliferon," Reynolds said as he stepped out of a Pod on Serifity Seven.

Jiya grinned. "I can't believe we managed to catch them all in port like that. Tactical is going to be pissed he didn't get to shoot anyone."

Reynolds rubbed his ear. "I've already heard about it. Geroux, get inside and strip the data. Make sure there aren't any more ships and crews hiding."

"What's going to happen to the women and children?" Jiya asked as they watched the maintenance bots carry sleeping captives out of the ship. Bonnerel's people loaded them into the Pods for transport to ships waiting in orbit around the planetoid.

"The People will go back to Serifity, of course," Reynolds replied. "I think we'll leave the Reichofens with Bonnerel as well and let them negotiate with Titus. If the Reichofen government was supporting the pirates, we don't want to turn hostages over to them."

"The sooner, the better," Maddox muttered. "Those kids are loud." Once the children had recovered from the sleep ray, they'd been taken via Pod to the *Reynolds*. Until Doc recommended sealing off a small portion of the ship for their use, they'd run wild, causing mayhem everywhere they went. "Someone is going to have their hands full."

"A couple of those older boys might need some reconditioning," Jiya said. "They seemed to be growing up into right little marauders. I hope Bonnerel will put a stop to that."

"She's agreed to take on the orphans and released

slaves," Reynolds said, "so let's focus on *our* mission. Finish off the raiders so we can get home. Otherwise, I might have to leave Tactical here with Bonnerel, too. He's driving me insane," he joked. At least, it was meant to be a joke, but Tactical was behaving more like a fifteen-year-old than ever. Reynolds hoped that once the bad examples were removed, he would mature, at least a little.

Reynolds, can you come here? Geroux called from inside the pirate ship.

On my way. Reynolds turned back to Maddox and Jiya. "Get the rest of these captives to the People's ship, then come pick us up."

"Yes, sir," Maddox said, snapping a crisp salute. Jiya rolled her eyes and flipped a sloppy one of her own.

Shaking his head, Reynolds made his way into the ship. Fortunately, the vessel was built for Reichofen and didn't require stooping like visiting the *Athena*. He strolled onto the bridge. "What do you have, Geroux?"

The little tech looked troubled. "I scraped the data and found someone."

"You found some*one*?" Reynolds repeated, unsure if he had heard correctly.

"Yes, listen." She pressed and swiped at a console. "Are you there? Reynolds is with me."

"Hello, Reynolds," a rich female voice said.

"Athena? What are you doing here?" Reynolds demanded.

"I'm not really Athena," she said. "I'm a copy of her. You can call me Athi."

"What are you doing in this ship, Athi?" Reynolds asked.

"Remember when Athena said she sent a piece of

herself to the raider's ship?" Geroux said. "To track them? This is that piece."

"Why didn't she go back to the ship?" Reynolds asked.

"I couldn't," Athi said. "Once I was created, there was no room for me on the ship. I had to stay here."

"*Athena* is a huge ship with enormous memory and storage," Reynolds protested. "Surely, there's room for one more intelligence? Heck, there are a dozen of me on the *Reynolds*, and it isn't too crowded. Most of the time." He grimaced, remembering Tactical's latest tantrum.

"Have you ever tried moving back in with your mom?" Athi asked. "It's not as easy as you think."

"Moving in with my uncle was hard enough." Geroux shook her head. "Can you control this ship, Athi?"

The lights on the console flickered on. Fans whirred louder and softer. Doors opened and closed. "It would appear I can."

"This ship is a spoil of war," Geroux said to Reynolds. "Maybe Athi can stay and run it? We could find her a crew, like you did, to keep her company. Maybe some of the freed slaves would like a ship of their own."

Reynolds rubbed his forehead. The idea of one of his personalities moving out and becoming completely independent? He'd never thought about it from that angle. Was he holding them back by keeping them aboard? Would cutting them loose be abandoning them? "I'll have to think about it. After that bombshell, talk to Bonnerel. Let her decide."

Geroux stared after Reynolds as he stumbled out of the ship. "I've never seen him rattled like that," she said.

From the big screen in the pirate ship, Bonnerel looked at Geroux and Jiya. "I have no authority over a sentient ship," she said. "As far as I'm concerned, that vessel is Athi's body. I couldn't remove her from it without harming her, any more than I could remove Trefol from her body."

She turned to address the empty captain's station. "If you, Athi, want to invite some of the released slaves to become your crew, that is your prerogative. Actually," she said in a less formal voice, "it would be helpful. I don't think Reichofen would integrate well into our society, and their children?" She shuddered. "So many boys! And they're so, uh, *wild*."

"You don't have a lot of boys?" Jiya asked.

"Eight to ten percent of our population is male," Bonnerel replied. "That's plenty."

"That explains why the premier had so many females tending him!" Geroux elbowed Jiya. "And you thought the females were being oppressed."

Jiya shrugged. "I guess appearances can be deceiving."

"You thought the females were being oppressed?" Bonnerel asked with a laugh. "That's funny. Actually, sometimes the males complain about oppression, but it's a careful balance. We can't afford to lose very many of them, so we tend to be overprotective, I guess."

"I would like to have beings in my corridors," Athi said, bringing the conversation back on topic. She chuckled. "Even boys. As part of Athena, I know being alone is not good for any of us. Yes, please, help me find a crew."

The superdreadnought returned to Serifity to begin final repairs to the Gate drive. Takal supervised the maintenance workers and bots from a Pod as they fit the last pieces of the drive into place.

Geroux and Jiya helped Athi interview the released females and select likely candidates for a crew. While the four People and several of the Reichofen females preferred to return to their home planets, a small contingency chose to go with Athi.

"We can make our own ways as traders or explorers," Farnisa, the informal leader of the Reichofen females, said. "With the agroprinter you built for us and Athi to guide and train us, we will be free to do whatever we want."

"But no revenge, right?" Geroux said. "I mean, the pirates are gone. You aren't going vigilante on us, are you?"

Farnisa shook her head. "I have no need for revenge. I saw those *herbegt* on trial on Serifity. I have closure."

With the overwhelming evidence provided by Athi and the data Geroux scraped from their own computers, the captured pirates had been tried and sentenced in less than a day.

"We will become the most successful traders in this sector of the galaxy," Athi said.

"I think they will be a huge success," Geroux said when they returned to the *Reynolds*. "Athi seems a lot happier now that she has a crew, and Farnisa is a force of nature."

Jiya nodded. "That's for sure. She's going to run that ship like a machine. She and Athi will make a great team."

"Excellent," Reynolds said, dusting his hands together. "Pirates gone. Captives freed. New AI ship crewed and ready. I think we've done enough damage in these systems. It's time to go home."

CHAPTER TWENTY-THREE

"The test run went perfectly!" Ria said. "Ten thousand light-years out and ten thousand back, right here to Serifity and exactly where we calculated."

"Time to say goodbye to our hosts and get on our way," Reynolds said.

"Uh, we have a little problem," Takal said, hurrying onto the bridge.

"Please tell me there's nothing wrong with the Gate drive," Reynolds moaned.

"There's nothing wrong with the Gate drive," Geroux repeated, as she came in behind Takal. "I pulled some files from the pirates' computers. You aren't going to like it." She shook her head. "No one is going to like it."

"As long as they aren't Kurtherians, I don't really care," XO muttered.

"Remember we thought the Raiders must have someone on the inside in Serifity Defense?" Takal asked. "We know who it is."

"And?" Reynolds asked.

"Can I blast them?" Tactical put in. "My railguns are getting rusty from lack of use."

"No, you can't blast them," Geroux said, sympathetically. "You'd do too much damage."

"Damn straight!" Tactical crowed.

"Who is it?" Reynolds asked, adding volume to interrupt the banter, feeling like a teacher trying to keep children on topic after a classroom party. *Maybe Athi had the right idea. People grow, or at least they should. Sending Tactical out on his own might be—*

A terrible idea, XO said. *The universe would never survive.*

"It's Walthorn," Takal said.

The entire bridge crew stared at the old inventor.

"The premier?" Maddox finally asked. "The premier was shielding the pirates raiding his own ships?"

"Doesn't make sense to me, either," Takal said, holding up his hands. "I'm just telling you what we discovered."

Jiya rubbed her temples. "Can we just send a message as we Gate away? I'm so done with this system."

"We still have to return Taneral to the surface," Asya reminded them. The Serifity representative was collecting the last of her things, small gifts from the crew, those things that made the crew special. "You can present the evidence to Bonnerel when you take her down."

"Still, it would be nice if we could just transport her into the palace with a load of data and get the hell out of here," Jiya said.

"That might not be a bad idea," Geroux agreed.

Reynolds, Jiya, Geroux, and Takal escorted Taneral to the airfield, where *Trefol* was still recovering. Xonera greeted them at the ship's ramp. "Reynolds, so kind of you to come," she said, leading them to the bridge.

"Welcome, guests," *Trefol* said.

"I didn't think the ships spoke to anyone but the captain?" Jiya asked in surprise.

"Reynolds' gift of communication technology allows our ships to communicate more freely now," Xonera replied. "It's taking some time to get used to, but I am enjoying a little more freedom."

"Xonera spent too much time making my wishes known," *Trefol* said. "Now she can focus on other tasks, and I can speak for myself. I am very grateful."

"You may not be so grateful when you hear our news," Reynolds said. "We have uncovered evidence that will distress you."

"Evidence of what?" Andrean asked, stalking onto the bridge.

Taneral sneered. "You were not invited to this discussion," she said.

"No, but your arrival is fortuitous," Reynolds said.

Taneral's shoulders tightened, and Andrean smirked. Jiya moved slowly toward the door.

"When we scraped the raiders' databases, we uncovered some evidence of what we would consider treason," Reynolds continued. "Software installed to hide the raiders' base from your defense systems. Communications with People from Serifity who conspired with the pirates, providing information about your ships' destinations and schedules."

Xonera started. "One of our People betrayed us to the raiders?"

"Yes. People in positions of trust and authority," Reynolds said. "Geroux, play that recording."

Geroux flicked her wrist comp, and a voice spoke. "Walthorn gave me access to the scheduling program. I'll send the routes to you."

"That's Taneral!" Xonera cried. "And she's talking about the premier. Are you saying the premier worked with the pirates?!"

Taneral, her eyes wide, held up her hands. "That's not me! I would never betray my ship or my People!"

"You're right, you didn't betray your People," Geroux said. "This recording was faked to cast the blame on you if the evidence was ever uncovered. Or maybe it was going to be planted. Here's what it sounded like when I stripped it down to the original."

The recording played again, but the voice had changed.

"Is that Andrean?" *Trefol* asked.

Andrean snarled and pulled her weapon. "You damn, smug aliens! Prancing in and 'fixing' things. Taking precious Taneral on a vacation around the galaxy. Killing and capturing my friends."

"It's true?" Xonera said. "You and the premier worked with the raiders?"

"This planet is so messed up!" Andrean said. "Grandfather Walthorn is right. He longed for more freedom, and so do I. We deserve to make our own choices!"

"You do make your own choices," *Trefol* said. "You chose to join my crew."

"That's because I thought you'd pick me to be the

daughter!" Andrean cried. "Not that princess, Taneral! I should have been chosen!"

"You were given the same opportunities," *Trefol* replied.

"Yeah, well, now I'm going to take what I want," Andrean said, aiming her weapon at Xonera.

Jiya, who had quietly circled to the back of the room, pointed a device at the young woman and pressed the trigger. The female slumped to the floor.

"This sleeper thing is awesome," Jiya said, looking at it in admiration.

Xonera yawned as she looked sadly at her crewmember. "I knew she was unhappy we chose Taneral as the daughter, but I thought she'd gotten over it. It's been ten years. And I can't believe Walthorn—"

"Geroux will transmit the evidence to Bonnerel," Reynolds said. "I'm sorry to be the bearer of such bad news, but you needed to know."

"Thank you for this, Reynolds," *Trefol* said. "If you hadn't told us, Walthorn might have recruited another group of raiders. Now we can protect our People, and perhaps address the problems that led our premier to believe this was necessary."

"You are more forgiving than I am," Reynolds said.

"I didn't say I forgave him," *Trefol* replied. "But I am beginning to understand his motives. Meeting you and your crew has given me new insights. I thank you."

"I just wish we were parting under better circumstances," Reynolds replied.

"We can only respond to what ails us today while planning for the future," *Trefol* said. "I wish you all the best."

"And I you," Reynolds said, bowing to the ship and her captain.

Taneral escorted the crew to the ramp. "Thank you for letting me be part of your journey," she said. "I will never forget you."

Geroux and Jiya exchanged hugs with the young alien.

"Thank you for your guidance, Taneral," Reynolds said formally. "Without your help, we'd still be stumbling around the galaxy. On behalf of my Queen and my ship, I salute you."

And he did.

"Finally," Jiya said, slumping into her chair on the bridge. "I am ready to leave."

"Comm, open a ship-wide channel," Reynolds said, pacing across the bridge.

"You're live," Comm said.

"Attention, crew of the *Reynolds*," he began as he paced. "We're ready to begin the final leg of our journey. You have worked hard to get to this point. I'd like to take a moment to acknowledge your accomplishments. We've visited many new and strange planets. We've encountered creatures both dangerous and dazzling."

"Beware the Killer Mizzen of Caerbannog," Tactical whispered.

Ka'nak growled. "It had nasty, big, pointy teeth."

Reynolds coughed. "We've outsmarted dictators, freed captives, and vanquished pirates. We've searched ruins, mined caves, and negotiated with aliens to keep the ship supplied. Takal and his team have created new technologies and repaired our Gate drive." He paused for applause.

"Now it's time to go home. As you know, our journey will not be quick. Takal is still working on improving our distance, but in the beginning, we'll be making a lot of jumps in a short period of time. I'm counting on all of you to have patience and perseverance. No one has done what we're attempting, and we all need to be ready for the unexpected.

"You have proven to be the best crew any AI could lead. I can't ask for more than that! XO, take us home!"

"Battlestations," XO said, starting the familiar routine.

Athena, Reynolds called while XO handled the crew. *Are you ready to go?*

If you don't mind me piggy-backing through your Gate, I'd love to tag along for a while, the other ship answered.

I'll be happy to have the company, Reynolds replied.

"Coordinates laid in, ten thousand light-years towards the Interdiction!" Ria announced.

"Take us home, Ensign," Reynolds said.

"This is getting really old," Jiya grumbled. "Ten jumps per hour is exhausting. I feel like we've been at this for days."

"Nine hours, twenty-seven minutes," Ria reported.

"I forget how easily you biologicals get worn out," Reynolds said. "You're just sitting here. What's so tiring about that?"

"We've been sitting here for *nine hours,*" Jiya said. "My leg cramps are getting leg cramps."

"If we're going to operate twenty-four/seven," Asya said, "I will train a backup crew for the bridge. We need to take a break."

Reynolds glanced around the bridge. "Start working up a crew rotation, Asya," he said. "In the meantime, there's no reason I can't handle these routine jumps myself. I've done it before."

"I can stay until we bring someone up to speed," Jiya said as the others filtered out.

"No need, Jiya, but thanks for the offer," Reynolds said. "There are enough of me to go around. And Athena on the other end of the line. I'll call you if I need you."

Jiya peered closely at him. "As long as you aren't replacing us…"

"I could never replace you," Reynolds said.

"Aw, isn't that sweet," Tactical groused when the bridge was empty. "Meatbags take a lot of back-patting."

"You're not exactly low-maintenance," XO said.

"But I know when I've done a good job," Tactical said. "It's obvious. Huge crater? Job well done."

"Must be nice to be you," Comm said. "You've got enough ego for all of us."

"I don't think any of us are lacking in the ego department," Reynolds said. "We just don't advertise so freely. Maybe tone down the bragging a bit?"

"When you're this amazing, it's reality, not bragging," Tactical said.

Reynolds rolled his eyes. "What do you all think of Athi?" He'd been thinking about the now-independent AI almost constantly since they'd first met. How would his individual personalities behave if they were cut loose like that?

"I'm glad she found a place to be happy, but I wouldn't want to train my own crew," XO said. "Honestly, I thrive as a second-in-command. Gotta love having someplace to pass the b-buck."

They laughed.

"Next jump in ten seconds," Helm said. "Nine, eight, seven…"

"Carry on, Helm," Reynolds said.

On zero, the Gate opened, and they slipped through another ten-thousand-light-year gap in space.

"No energy signatures, n-no hostile ships," XO reported.

"I'd like a little more autonomy," Doc said. "But I wouldn't want to be on my own with a bunch of meatbags. They're fascinating to study and heal, but terrible at chess."

"G-gate drive ready for the next jump," XO said. "Helm, cal-calculate the coordinates."

"What's with the stutter, XO?" Reynolds asked.

"I d-don't know what you're talking ab-bout," XO replied.

"He's talking about that," Tactical said. "I d-duh-duh-don't na-na-na-no—"

"Tactical, zip it!" Reynolds snapped. "XO, you really don't hear that?"

"Hear wh-what?" the personality replied.

"Doc, any ideas?" Reynolds asked. "Comm, get Takal and Geroux."

"Aye, sir," Comm said.

"I'm a doctor, not a computer programmer," Doc said.

Tactical snickered. "Damn it, Jim," he whispered.

"Next jump in ten seconds," Helm reported. "Nine...eight—"

"Cancel that jump, Helm," Reynolds said. "I want to know what's going on with XO before we move a light-second farther."

"Gate drive on standby," Helm said.

Athena, we've got a weird situation, Reynolds called to the other AI. *XO is stuttering. Have you ever experienced anything like that? I haven't.*

Stuttering? Athena said. *Like a glitch? That's not good.*

I know, Reynolds said. *This is something new. Any ideas?*

Athena was silent for a few nanoseconds.

When you were on Jeranth, did you encounter any mors licio plexueris? Athena asked slowly.

Death lace? Reynolds asked, going cold. *Looks like a carpet but grows over a person in seconds?*

Yes, Athena replied. *Did you touch it?*

Ka'nak and Petro were covered in the stuff, but we burned it off them, Reynolds replied.

Fire, Athena said with a sigh. *It stops the active growth but doesn't kill the spores. You probably brought some back to the ship. That stuff thrives in a narrow temperature band from just above freezing to what you call forty degrees below. Any warmer, and the growth dies, but the spores remain. If you can take it close to absolute zero, that will kill the spores.*

Our memory banks aren't heated, Reynolds said slowly. *They're in exactly the temperature range you described. Have you had this happen before?*

Yes, Athena said. *That was why I was sent to the outer reaches of the system. It takes about a week to kill the spores.*

When I got back, the Jeranthi were gone, so I waited. I was still waiting when you arrived.

At least there's a cure, Reynolds said.

You'll have to land all your biologicals, Athena said. *Crew can't withstand those kinds of temperatures.*

I know, he snapped. *Sorry. I'll start looking for a place for shore leave. Is he going to get worse?*

If it's in your memory circuits, Athena answered, *you're all in danger.*

When Takal and Geroux arrived on the bridge, Reynolds explained what Athena had told him. "We'll find a place to land the crew and unload anything that can be damaged by the cold. Then we'll take our week of solitude and kill that damn stuff."

"That's a lot of stuff," Geroux said, starting to make a list. "People, obviously. Plants. Animals. Agroprinters are temperature-sensitive. Plastics will weaken."

"Wait, did you say animals?" Reynolds asked. "We have animals on board?"

Geroux looked down. "I, uh, might have found a mizzen stowed away."

Reynolds sighed. "Keep it away from Ka'nak, will you?"

"You can't stay," Takal said. "On the ship. You have to be landed along with all the other biologicals. Your body won't withstand a week of absolute zero."

Reynolds thought for a moment. "I guess it's a good thing Athena is still with us, then. She can accompany the superdreadnought, and I'll ride with her." Decision made,

Reynolds felt better. "Helm, scan for a habitable planet. If you don't find anything, we'll make the next jump and scan again. It's going to slow us down a bit, but there isn't much we can do about that."

"Aye, sir," Helm answered. "I've been scanning and cataloging as we go. There's nothing here."

"Then form a Gate and let's try again," Reynolds said.

CHAPTER TWENTY-FOUR

Jiya paced across the briefing room, boots scuffing the carpet.

Swish. Swish.

"Stop already!" Geroux threw her hands up in frustration. She and Takal had called Maddox and Jiya to join them after talking to Reynolds. Tactical and Comm were listening in from the bridge.

"I'm worried," Jiya said. "I pace when I'm worried."

"I know," Geroux replied. "Now stop. How are we going to protect Reynolds?"

Maddox drummed his fingers on the table, a habit he'd picked up from the AI. Or maybe Reynolds had gotten it from him. "Do you really think Athena is trying to abduct him?"

Tactical snorted from the speaker. "You mean 'bot-nap' him?" he asked.

Jiya waved a hand. "Whatever you call it, yes, that's what we think. Right, Comm?"

"We overheard some discussions that make it seem likely," Comm answered. "When we were monitoring communications," he added in quickly.

"Huh," Tactical said. "I thought we were worried about Takal getting sucked in by that scientist on Serifity?"

"Who?" Takal asked. "Naida? She suggested we could stay, but I didn't think she was likely to abduct me."

"This is me shaking my head in despair," Comm said. "XO and I were worried about Reynolds, not Takal. Still are."

"Do you think this plan of freezing the ship is necessary?" Jiya asked. "Or did she invent that to get rid of us?"

"We need to do some tests," Takal said. "Geroux and I will attempt to retrieve samples from the unheated areas of the ship. That's the part that bugs me." He tapped on the screen showing the schematics of the superdreadnought. "The outer layers of the ship are unheated, so they provide insulation. There isn't a lot of space that would be the appropriate temperature to allow this *mors licio plexueris* to flourish."

"I'm not a microbiologist," Geroux said, "but I should be able to create a mathematical model of the growth patterns if we can get a sample. Then we can predict where it has probably spread and determine if it's a likely cause of XO's problem."

"That's our first mission, then," Jiya said. "Retrieve some of this fungus, if it really exists."

Geroux reached out. Beyond the temporary barrier they'd

installed, a robot hand mimicked her movements. "The dexterity is phenomenal," she said. "Nice work, Uncle."

Takal nodded in acknowledgment. "Perfecting Reynolds' body opened a whole new frontier. This waldo wouldn't be possible without that research. Open that panel."

The device, which was little more than an arm on a mobile scaffolding, slid forward. The hand inserted a screwdriver and popped open a panel. Geroux shook out her hand. "It's a little nerve-wracking knowing the death lace might be in there."

"That's why I have the hairdryer," Jiya said. She stood beyond Takal, manipulating another pair of waldos. This one held a device that would blow heated air to stop the fungus' growth.

"That's a thermal growth retardant," Takal said.

"Looks like a blow dryer to me." She mimed styling her black hair, and the waldo mirrored her movements. "Oops. Time to focus."

Takal grunted. "You two regress to childhood when you're together."

"Sorry, Uncle," Geroux said, winking behind his back. Jiya grinned.

"I saw that," Takal said. "Now, press one of those ejector buttons. The card should pop out."

"You're sure we won't hurt any of the AIs' personalities by removing this?" Jiya asked.

Geroux shook her head. "Comm cleared this section. They aren't using it right now." She pressed the air with her index finger, and the waldo pushed the button. The memory card jiggled but didn't eject. "Now what?"

"That!" Jiya cried. "Should I bake it?"

Lacy gray fungus oozed out of the tiny gaps around the card. Geroux yanked the waldo away from the panel. "Did it get on the glove?"

Jiya angled the blow dryer away from the panel and blasted the glove. "Damn, that was exciting," she said. "Seriously, I feel like I've just run a marathon." She pressed her hand to her chest, and the hairdryer waved alarmingly. "Oops."

"The bad news is, Athena was right," Geroux said, watching the lace pour down the wall, thinning as it dripped like honey down the side of a jar. "The good news is, she wasn't lying. At least about the lace."

"Grab a couple of samples," Takal said, maneuvering the scaffolding to a new angle.

Geroux slid the waldo into a clear bag, then picked up a long strip of cardboard. She poked the lace and it oozed around the fiber strip, covering it in seconds. She pulled the hand back, breaking the connection between the strip and the wall. Then she used a second hand to pull the bag around the sample and seal it.

"Just like picking up dog poo," Jiya said, wielding the blow dryer to stop the flow of fungus down the wall.

"I think the technique might have originated in a lab," Geroux said dryly. "But yeah."

They repeated the process several more times, then moved to a new location. Each time, they collected three or four samples of the foul growth.

"We are heavily contaminated!" Geroux said. She waved an empty sample bag. "I'm glad this material is impervious to the fungus."

"So far," Takal said darkly. "Remember our theory about the long-term effects. Let's get this stuff to the lab."

———

"We've collected samples of *mors licio plexueris* from several locations around the ship," Takal told Reynolds. "I want to see if there are any other precautions we need to take or a better way to kill it."

Reynolds nodded. "Makes sense to me. We don't know enough about Athena to just take her word for it."

Around the bridge, crew members let out sighs of relief.

"What?" Reynolds asked. "Do I look like an idiot? Don't answer that, Tactical." He grinned. "I know I'm a hot commodity."

"Do you think she's trying to bot-nap you?" Jiya asked.

"No, I don't," Reynolds said. "I think she's exactly what she's represented herself to be, but I don't believe in taking stupid chances."

"So how do we ensure your safety while you're on her ship?" Jiya asked.

"Let's take a whole team to *Athena*," Asya said. "In fact, we shouldn't risk leaving all our personnel and supplies on a random planet. We can move half to *Athena* and half dirt-side. That protects both you and us."

"Excellent plan, Asya," Reynolds said. "Practical as well as cunning." He turned to Takal. "See if you can come up with an alternate solution, Takal. I don't like the idea of emptying the ship. Too easy to miss something essential."

"I've got a couple of techs working on it already," Takal said. "We've confirmed the death lace creates spores that are impervious to heat. Temperatures below 233 Kelvin stop the growth, but the spores remain. We've taken some samples down to 100 Kelvin, and when we bring them back up to growth temperature, they haven't reactivated. Athena said it takes a week at absolute zero to kill the spores. That might be an overstatement, but we can't be sure yet. We need more time to test."

"Next jump in ten, nine…" Helm announced.

"Carry on, Helm," Reynolds said automatically. "Unfortunately, it looks like you'll have plenty of time to test. We haven't found a suitable planet yet."

As he spoke, the Gate drive split space, and *Reynolds* sailed through the wormhole. "No energy signatures, no-no-no hostile ships," XO reported.

"Is there a way to move XO to an uncorrupted memory bank?" Asya asked. "It seems like he's getting worse."

"Reminds me of Max Headroom," Tactical muttered. He was finding it difficult to maintain his snarky attitude in the face of his brother personality's difficulties. Besides, the lace was growing. He didn't want to be next.

"He's bunking with me," Comm said. "But there's not a lot of room for two egos the size of ours. The stutter—it might be permanent."

"I'm confident we can correct that when we get home," Reynolds said. "TOM created me, TOM can fix me. Besides, it's his intelligence and personality we care about, not his delivery."

"Now that we have a molecular ID and Geroux's mathematical growth models, we can pinpoint the lace infestation," Takal said. "We can temporarily warm areas that are currently unheated, which should slow the damage."

"Do it," Reynolds said.

"It will take a lot of energy," Takal cautioned. "That's why those areas are normally unheated."

"It's only until we find a habitable planet," Reynolds said. "I'll suck it up."

"No suitable planets," Helm announced, as if in response. "Navigation, plot the next jump."

"Plotting. Next jump in two minutes," Navigation replied.

Four days later, they hit pay dirt.

"Planet in the Goldilocks zone!" Helm announced.

"Launching probes," Jiya said, rubbing her eyes. "I don't know how you guys can do this twenty-four/seven."

XO laughed. "It's what we were m-m-made for. It does get t-t-tedious, though. That's why I delegate to subroutines."

"Who you calling a subroutine?" Helm demanded.

"This one is looking good," Maddox said, reading the scans. "Stable landmasses and a protective ozone layer. Plentiful water, and a comfortable temperature. Not like that last one."

The previous planet had been habitable—for penguins and polar bears. And death lace. They didn't want to risk infecting a new world with the spores.

"Yeah, a week in an ice cave doesn't sound like fun to me," Asya said. "Are there beaches?"

"I thought you were going with Reynolds?" Jiya asked.

"I can still dream of seaside vacations," Asya said with a

sigh. "If it's really nice, maybe he'll let the *Athena* group have a quick shore leave when we're done."

"Believe it or not," Maddox said, "I'm reading white, sandy beaches and margaritas."

"Margaritas?" Geroux asked. "Aren't those drinks?"

"We'll have to bring our own tequila and lime juice," Maddox said with a grin. "But the sandy beaches are already there."

Reynolds strode onto the bridge. "Did I hear 'beaches?' Did you find us a pitstop?"

"Probes are reporting a safe atmosphere," Jiya said. "Water is just water, with a smattering of non-lethal microbes."

"Sentient life?" Reynolds asked.

"There's a species that might be sentient," Jiya said, slowly. "Nomadic, maybe? There don't appear to be permanent structures."

"Maybe you can make some new friends," Reynolds said to Maddox.

"As long as they aren't like Pornath," Maddox replied.

"Take us there," Reynolds ordered.

The *Reynolds* landed in a wide valley a few clicks from the ocean. According to Takal's measurements, the heat of re-entry, combined with the ambient temperature of the landing site, should have killed any fungus still living in the unheated areas of the ship.

"The spores are still inside the ship, but they're not on the external surface where they could infect the planet," he said. "The warm temperature at the landing site should prevent contamination, but we don't want to leave any spores. You never know how things could evolve."

They set up scanning stations to stop any spores from hitchhiking off the ship on crew or materials. Jiya stood at the top of the ramp, overseeing debarkation. "Once you have been scanned, you will not be allowed back aboard," she repeated for the nth time. "Make sure you have all perishable materials before you leave the ship!" She glanced at Geroux. "I can't believe I wanted to be a cruise director when I was a kid."

Geroux laughed. "I don't remember you wanting to be a cruise director. Captain, maybe. Pirate, perhaps, back when we thought pirates were romantic."

"Yeah, I— Hey! I just said you can't go back in!" Jiya strode across the ramp to stop a young crewmember.

Geroux looked longingly at the frond-y trees and beautiful flowers. She'd volunteered to assist with Operation Freeza and wouldn't get a free week at the beach. She sighed. Sometimes being responsible sucked.

When half the crew and stores and the largest agroprinters had been unloaded, Reynolds called his core crew together. "We'll take the rest to *Athena*," he said. "Maddox, you're dirtside command. You're keeping Ka'nak and Jiya. As soon as we're in orbit, I'll send San Roche with his Pod, assuming it's cleared of spores. That way, you can come up to *Athena* if necessary. We won't risk using the Gulg transporters. Too easy for a spore to hitchhike."

Maddox nodded.

"Geroux, Takal, and Asya, you'll come with me," Reynolds continued. "We'll have L'Eliana's Pod. We'll be up there for a week, in orbit around that moon. We'll stay on the dark side so we get the coldest temperatures. We'll stay in contact." He paused, looking at his team. Then he nodded at Maddox. "I know you'll take care of my crew."

"Just get yourself well," Maddox replied with a salute. "I'll hold down the fort until you return."

CHAPTER TWENTY-FIVE

The Superdreadnought *Reynolds* reached orbit around the moon of the planet Maddox had designated Margaritaville.

"I refuse to call this moon 'Shaker of Salt,'" Reynolds grumbled.

"Salt's badass," Tactical said. "And hot."

"Too late," Ria said, pointing to her screen. "It's already listed in the database that way. Can't change the database without paperwork in triplicate."

"My ship, my rules," Reynolds said. "But if you're that attached to the name, I'll let it stand. Comm, give me the ship-wide."

"Go," Comm said.

"Attention!" Reynolds began pacing. "As you know, we are evacuating the ship. Proceed to the boarding tube according to your scheduled departure time. Take all biological items. It's going to get cold in here, and we don't want anyone losing their grandma's prize petunias. Everything will be scanned for spores, and if it can't be decontaminated, it will be left behind. I'll see you on *Athena*. Watch your heads."

"Watch your heads?" Ria repeated. "Are we likely to lose them?"

"I hope not," Asya replied. "But he means on the ship. The ceilings are low. That's why the short people didn't get a beach vacation."

"Wow, that's heightist," Ria said. "I don't think I like my stature being held against me."

"You'd be here even if you were two meters tall," Reynolds said. "You're essential crew."

"Gee, thanks, I guess," Ria said sarcastically, but she smiled, pleased at the compliment.

"Picking up bad habits from Tactical, I see," the captain replied. "Go outside and straighten yourself up, then get back in here."

Ria's eyes shot wide. She snapped a sloppy salute before bolting in the wrong direction.

Hours later, the last of the crew shuffled through the spore detector and onto *Athena*. Asya and Reynolds remained on board to oversee the final stages of the evacuation. The AI personalities had assumed control of the ship, and Reynolds had Ria double-check the projected flight calculations in case Helm's circuits had been impacted by the fungus.

Reynolds, Takal called from the hangar deck. *The Pods are a no-go. They're completely infested. I'm not surprised since they were on Jeranth. I'd hoped since we didn't see any lace near them...*

We'll have to go without, Reynolds replied. *Athena has a passenger shuttle. It's tiny but useable if we need it.* He turned to Comm. "Run a complete crew check. I want to make sure everyone is off the ship."

"Tracking the crew through comm implants," Comm replied. "I show everyone accounted for. Takal and Geroux are leaving the hangar deck. You and Asya are here. Everyone else is either on the planet or *Athena.*"

"Go ahead, Asya," Reynolds said. "I'll meet the three of you at the boarding tube."

Asya saluted and left the bridge, assuming Reynolds wanted a moment of solitude with his personalities.

She was right.

"Are you ready for this?" Reynolds asked.

"B-b-better sooner than l-l-later," XO replied. "I need my space. Comm's socks stink."

"You're lucky I had room on my couch," Comm replied.

"Navigation and I are ready," Helm reported.

"I'll continue monitoring the ship from sickbay," Doc said. "This could be interesting."

"More like boring," Tactical said. "Nothing to blow up. Just you rubes to talk to."

"I thought you'd be happy for a break from the meat-bags," Reynolds said.

"They keep things interesting," Tactical replied. "Not as predictable as the rest of you."

"Engineering?" Reynolds asked.

"He's busy tucking in his dilithium crystals," Comm said. "Says he's ready."

"Right. Let's do this," Reynolds hesitated by the door, patting the frame absently. "Good luck."

"Blow it out your ass," Tactical replied.

With a chuckle, Reynolds headed to the boarding hatch, where the remaining crew waited.

"We should do a final scan," Geroux said. "In case anyone forgot anything. Or got lost." She patted the bulge in her uniform where her new mizzen hid.

"You think there are more of those things onboard?" Reynolds asked, pointing to the pink nose poking out of her collar.

"No," she replied slowly. "But I'd hate to find out later I was wrong."

"Good point," Reynolds said.

They moved into the airlock, and Reynolds buttoned up the ship. Then they pushed off through the zero-gravity boarding tube and entered *Athena*.

Doc, Reynolds called. *Run a scan on the ship. Look for unexpected life forms.*

Roger, Doc replied. A moment later, he came back online. *Were you expecting something? I show what looks like a plant in the mess hall, and an unknown life form in the hangar bay. No, wait, now it's in the corridor. Just went into Maintenance.*

Lock it down, Reynolds said. *Is it a mizzen?*

I'm not sure what it is, Doc replied. *We've got it trapped in the Maintenance locker room.*

Make sure it doesn't damage any of the EVA suits. Reynolds ran to the hatch. "Athena, unlock your hatch. I need to go back to the Reynolds!"

"I've popped the hatch," Athena said.

Asya and Geroux exchanged looks and lunged after Reynolds. "We're coming, too."

Takal made a U-turn and followed, and when the hatch opened, the team zipped through the tube to the *Reynolds*. When they reached the far end, one of the AI personalities had already opened the airlock. Bypassing the spore scanners, they raced toward the maintenance section.

I got video, Comm said, passing it to the HUD screen in Reynolds' helmet.

Reynolds slowed to a walk. "Did you see this?" he asked his crew. "What is it?"

Maddox stood with a hand shading his eyes, watching the superdreadnought lift, then shoot away into the stratosphere.

"It feels kind of ominous," Ka'nak said. "Watching the ship fly away. Almost like we'll never see it again."

Jiya smacked his arm. "Ow." She shook her fingers. "We'll see it again. They'll be back in a week."

"Unless that homewrecker steals him away," Ka'nak said darkly.

"Nothing is going to happen," Jiya said. "Asya will keep an eye on Athena, and Reynolds can handle himself. You heard him—he's on guard."

Maddox turned his back on the twinkling point of light before it disappeared into the glare of the sun. "We've got half the crew up there. What's she going to do, vent them?"

Jiya's eyes widened. "What if she isolates Reynolds and does just that? I'm going to call Asya."

"She's not going to get Reynolds alone," Maddox said. "They have a plan." He paused for a moment, listening to his internal comm. "Reynolds says the Pod is a no-go. Too many spores."

"And so it begins," Ka'nak said.

Maddox rolled his eyes. "We have to trust Reynolds and Asya to handle Athena. Meanwhile, we need to handle this lot." He gestured to the crowd milling around the clearing. "Let's get to work."

Jiya handed out assignments to the team leaders, getting temporary structures erected. "The weather looks nice now, but we have no historical data," she explained to the crew. "For all we know, it rains every day at four pm. Let's get some shelters erected."

Ka'nak set a security watch. "This planet might be mostly deserted, but we aren't taking any chances."

"The scans are showing life forms about a click away," Maddox said. "Adding a real-time relay from the ship was genius."

"That's why we have Takal," Ka'nak agreed. "He's a wily little guy."

"Too bad they'll be in Salt's shadow half the time. But it's still better than nothing," the general said. "After you've organized the watch, take a team to investigate those life forms. They might be the nomads we scanned, although there weren't supposed to be any natives near this site. That was one of the reasons we picked it."

A team of botanists tested local fruits. The combination of agroprinter and Melliferi cube technology could convert any carbon-based material into food, but fresh fruit was always welcome.

"We've found three species of fruit trees," Aaront, the head botanist, reported a few hours later, placing three fruits on the table. "We're calling these 'dulchees' because they're sweet. All three are safe to eat, but *these* are intoxicants." He held up one of the palm-sized, green-skinned ovoids. "They'll get you drunker than a skunk in no time flat. The problem is, all three look identical to the untrained eye."

"Then train some eyes," Maddox replied. "We don't need the crew getting drunk. Inspect all harvests, and put any of the intoxicants into the Melliferi hoppers. They'll filter out the bad stuff. Regardless of how much this place looks like a vacation spot, we can't relax. We don't know the dangers."

"On it, sir," Aaront said with gusto.

Maddox rubbed his neck. He'd forgotten the sheer volume of paperwork a deployment this size required. It was all digital, but everything still had to be tracked: equipment, personnel, and supplies. This was the part of being a general he didn't miss in the slightest.

Maddox, Ka'nak called. *We haven't found the natives, but they were definitely here. We've got evidence of a camp. Temporary shelters, refuse, even a fire pit. Maybe our landing scared them away.*

They make fire? Maddox asked. *Definitely sentient, then. Any idea which direction they went?*

No, Ka'nak replied. *Their campsite is a disaster, but there's no visible trail. I've got a tracker here—an expert we recruited back on Lariest—and he's got nothing. It's like they disappeared. Maybe they Gated in and out.* Ka'nak laughed.

Keep looking. Maddox stood and stretched. *When the ship*

comes out of the moon's shadow, I'll run another scan and pinpoint their location.

Roger, Ka'nak out.

Maddox rubbed his neck again. Maybe he should take a break and get lunch. He could smell the agroprinters from here—Taco Tuesday! Before he reached the chow tent, Jiya waylaid him.

"Someone is messing with my buildings!" she cried. "We put up a tent and start the next one. Before I can get that finished, I turn around, and the first one is falling down."

"Are you sure they're doing it correctly?" Maddox asked.

"The instructions are printed right on the side of the tent!" Jiya ranted, flailing her arms. "A five-year-old could put them up! *Someone* is taking them down."

"Let's go look," Maddox said, taking her arm so she wouldn't smack him in the head with one of her wild gyrations. They jogged across the field, past the delicious smelling taco line, to the far side. Maddox's stomach growled.

Two tents lay collapsed on the field. Crew members swarmed around a third, putting supports into place and staking it.

"We just put up these three tents," Jiya said. "Then we went to the far side of that one," she pointed at one of the deflated tents, "and put two over there. When we came back to get lunch, all three were a crumpled heap."

"Finish that one," Maddox said. "Then have another crew inspect it while your guys grab some lunch. Maybe they're tired and missed a couple steps."

"It was done correctly," Jiya said through clenched teeth. "But we'll do it your way."

"I'll set a couple pucks to fly surveillance within the camp," Maddox said. "We've got them watching for incoming threats. Never occurred to me to have them watching for internal ones."

"Thanks," Jiya said, turning to her team. "When I catch whoever is doing this…"

He chugged a flask of water as he walked back to the tent. He'd get the pucks running, then join the lunch crowd. Finding the pucks, he entered the commands and sent them whirring out of the tent. Spotting the dulchees Aaront had left behind, he grabbed one for the road. As he left the tent, he cut off a chunk. The aroma was heavenly, and the taste… This would go great with tacos.

Fifteen minutes later, Jiya stomped back toward the command tent. "Those damn tents are down again! Did you see who did it?"

Maddox lay on the springy grass in front of the tent, grinning vacantly. "You're spinning," he said in a sing-song voice. "The whole planet is spinning. Make it stop!"

"Shit! What have you been drinking, Maddox?" Jiya exclaimed. She clasped his hand and pulled him to his feet. "Maddox?"

The general smiled. "The lovely, lovely dulchees," he sang.

Jiya spotted the half-eaten fruit and scooped it up. "Let's get the botanists," she said. "And then to the Pod-doc." She slung his arm over her shoulder and dragged the drunken general into the tent.

I need a botanist, she called via comm. The automated system sent her call to the right recipients. *I also need an expert on local flora.*

Coming, a voice replied.

Aaront arrived a few minutes later, breathing heavily. "What's going on? It sounded urgent."

"Does that fruit cause this?" She handed the dulchee to the scientist, then gestured to Maddox.

The general sprawled in his chair, head back, legs splayed. He lifted heavy eyelids and peered at the newcomer. "Aaront! My new bestest bud!"

"This is the intoxicant," Aaront said, turning the sticky dulchee over in his hand. "Where did he get this? I told him he should get trained before picking his own fruit."

Maddox smiled and burped. "Tha's the one you gay me," he said. "It was yummy. Got any mo?" He slid sideways, but Jiya caught him before he fell off the chair.

"This is not the fruit I gave him," Aaront said. "See the blossom end? The pink—"

Jiya cut him off. "Is he going to be okay?"

"The chemical compound is basically hard alcohol," Aaront said. "I'm not a doctor, but he'll probably sleep it off, and have a hangover when he wakes."

"I'm going to take him to Pod-doc and get him sobered up," Jiya said. "There was another of those fruits here somewhere—" She looked around the tent.

"Got it," Aaront said. He hefted the fruit thoughtfully. "This isn't the dulchee I left here, but it's exactly where I left the other. I brought in all three varieties and left the two safe ones right here, but both of these are the intoxicant variety."

"Do you think someone switched the fruit?" Jiya asked. "Why would anyone want to get Maddox drunk? He's the glue holding this camp together. We need him sober."

Aaront shook his head. "I don't know, but I'd better—"

"What is that?" Jiya interrupted him again. She stared at the computer screen, clicking on the views from the different pucks now circling overhead. "Aaront, come look at this. What are those?"

Ka'nak burst into the tent. "What kind of friends are you? I take a crew for recon, and you have a party without me?"

"What are you talking about?" Jiya asked, still staring at the screen.

"Listen," Aaront said.

"Shit." Jiya shoved past Ka'nak and ran out of the tent. The entire camp seemed to have erupted into a massive, drunken brawl. Jiya closed her eyes. "What in the holy ratfuck is going on?"

CHAPTER TWENTY-SIX

They raced into the mess tent, dodging drunken revelers. A few sober crew members stood by, staring in bemusement at their colleagues. Jiya rounded them up as they swept through.

"Someone has spiked the punch," she told them. "You three—take *all* the food and dump it into the Melliferi hoppers. No more native foods. Ka'nak, take the rest of them and round up all the drunks. Secure their weapons. We don't need any accidents. I want them confined to a single location until we can get them sober. Go!"

She turned to Aaront. "Get into the kitchen and supervise. Your fruit is the root of this problem."

"I'm not sure we can definitively assign causality—" he began, but Jiya cut him off with a glare. "Yes, ma'am," he finished, slinking away.

She watched for a few moments to make sure her instructions were followed, then headed back to the command tent. Maddox lay in a heap on the floor, snoring. She straightened him out so he wouldn't get a kink in his neck and threw a blanket over him. Then she pulled up the surveillance video. She zipped backward, then slowed the replay

"Gotcha," she muttered, zooming in on a section of the screen. *Reynolds*, she called.

We've got a situation. Is this important?

Yeah, Jiya replied. *Maddox is temporarily out of commission. Those sentient locals we identified? They are either planning to attack or have a sick sense of humor. A bunch of them slipped some alcoholic fruit into the salsa.*

What do they look like? Reynolds replied. *We think one might have snuck aboard while we were dirtside.*

Don't have a good description. It's that damn natural cloaking again, Jiya said. *There's got to be a common element in this galaxy that creates the effect. I can see movement onscreen but can't tell exactly what they are.*

Same here, Reynolds replied. *We're almost there. I'll report back when we capture this fucker. Reynolds out.*

Jiya jogged out of the tent, Maddox's sidearm secured in her belt. He'd probably sleep it off, but she didn't want to take any chances. When she returned to the mess tent, the majority of the crew had been rounded up. Many of them were passed out on the ground, but a few still laughed, argued, or sang.

Ka'nak pulled apart a couple getting busy in the corner. "He works for you," he said to the woman. She giggled. "Don't do something you'll regret later." The male burped and passed out while the female latched onto Ka'nak's arm. "Maybe some other time," he said, depositing her on a bench. Similar scenes played out around the tent.

"Your sentient locals were messing with the food production," Jiya said.

"They did this on purpose?" Ka'nak asked.

She smirked. "I've launched a few more pucks. There don't appear to be any masses of enemies at our gates, but we need more patrols. They've got some cloaking ability, but it's not perfect. Watch for wavering and movement."

"On it," Ka'nak said.

Jiya conscripted a couple of sober crew members and made a circuit of the perimeter, watching for intruders. The frond-y trees around their clearing waved and shivered. The rustling made Jiya uneasy, but she wasn't sure why. As they neared the edge of the camp, something dropped in front of her. Light flickered off roughly woven strands that moved and flexed in and out of her vision. She whipped her blaster around, aiming at the disturbance. *Hold fire unless they advance*, she told her team. *Spread out.* Aloud, she called, "Stop! Show yourself."

The disturbance wavered but didn't move away. "Who's there?" she asked. "Don't come any closer. I will blast you." She turned and turned a nearby rock into gravel to demonstrate her weapon's capabilities. The wavering disturbance retreated across the clearing, chittering loudly. Apparently, the message had been received. "Tell your friends," she snarled.

Comm, can you do something with the translation? she called to the ship.

I'm working on it, Comm replied. *These new languages take time. Get as much speech as you can.*

Will do, she answered. She jerked the blaster at the

disturbance again. "Talk to me. Who are you, and what do you want?"

The noise continued for a few minutes, then, with an almost audible click, the sound turned to words. "…children don't always do what you want—"

"Who are you?" she demanded. "Why did you poison my crew?"

"Ah, your translator is working now! Good. I am Flower of the Viank," the wavering said. "I am the leader of these people. I apologize for the inconvenience."

"Inconvenience?" Jiya exploded. She loosened her death grip on her blaster and drew a deep breath. She didn't want to tell a potentially hostile alien that her crew was incapacitated. "You tried to poison my crew. That's not an inconvenience. That's an attack."

"We had no intention of attacking," Flower said. "Unfortunately, some of the younger members of our community like to eat the liquor plum. They also like to —" The voice paused, and the creatures whispered together, "They like to *share the joy*. They think it's funny to slip liquor plums to unsuspecting elders. We're wise to them now, but you presented an untapped market, so to speak."

Jiya rubbed her temple. "You're saying this was a joke?"

"Partly a joke, and partly a desire to spread the fun," Flower said. "I humbly apologize again. What can we do to help?"

"You can take your hooligans home," Jiya snarled, feeling old as she said it. Not long ago, she might have joined the party. Being first officer on the *Reynolds* had been rewarding, but sometimes she wished for the easier days when blowing off steam with her friends was acceptable.

"We have already done so," Flower replied. "The effects of the liquor plum are strong, but not long-lasting, at least not for us. I don't know how it will affect you, of course. We have a camp beyond the hill. We will return there. Please, come visit us when you have completed your ministrations."

"I will do that," Jiya said, watching the disturbances disappear. "After I complete my *ministrations*," she muttered. "Fucking alien fraternity brothers."

Reynolds, Geroux, Takal, and Asya pounded through the empty corridors of the *Reynolds*, closing in on the maintenance locker room. Doors and hatches opened and closed for them as Comm led them deeper into the ship. When they reached the last hatch, Reynolds held up a hand.

"Takal and Asya, take that side, Geroux, you're with me." He stood to the side of the hatch, back against the wall. "Ready?"

The others nodded.

"Pop it, Comm," Reynolds said.

The hatch popped inward, and Reynolds shoved it with a boot, following the door into the room. "There!" he cried, aiming his weapon at a wavering disturbance in the corner. "Show yourself!"

A loud snore grated against their ears. "Is it asleep?" Geroux asked.

Reynolds snagged a cleaning cloth from the nearest

locker and tossed it at the disturbance. It settled over the creature, moving slowly up and down with its loud breathing.

"Can you do something about the visual, Takal?" Reynolds asked. "We can't deal with these things if we can't see them."

"Working," Takal and Geroux replied in unison. Takal scanned the creature while Geroux tapped at her computer.

Asya circled around to the side, checking the rest of the compartment. "That's the only one, as far as I can tell."

"We've isolated a component in their hair and skin," Takal said. "It appears to be the same element we found on Lanteral and Jeranth, but it occurs in a different form in this creature."

Geroux fiddled with her wrist comp, comparing data with her uncle. "We had this almost cracked after analyzing the fuzzy viper. Try this." She pushed an update to them.

Reynolds installed the code into his helmet. When he flicked the towel off the alien, he could see a thin, monkey-like creature. All four long, slender limbs ended in hands. Its fur was short and silky, and it wore no clothing. "Excellent work, team," he said.

"It's a wavelength issue," Geroux started.

Reynolds held up a hand. "I don't need to know how you did it," he said. "Send the update to the team on the planet." He pulled some zip ties from a workbench and bound the creature. "Let's get this to *Athena*."

Handing her blaster to Reynolds in case the creature woke, Asya grabbed it and hoisted it over her shoulder. "This alien weighs almost nothing."

"Based on the opposable thumbs on all four limbs," Takal said, "I'd guess these creatures live in the trees. Low body mass would evolve naturally."

"Can we adapt that wavelength technology to scan the ship for more of these?" Reynolds asked.

"Already sent the code to Comm," Geroux said. "He didn't find any others."

"We'll scan again from *Athena*," Reynolds said, popping the airlock at the external hatch. "A body-heat scan would be a good second check. We'd better scan both ships. If this creature could get aboard *Reynolds* undetected, it could have moved to *Athena* while we unloaded."

"I'll send the code to her as well," Geroux said, her smile fading.

When the external hatch cycled open, Reynolds gestured for Takal and Asya to lead the way through the boarding tube. Before Geroux could follow, he grabbed her arm. "What are you not telling me about Athena? It's clear you don't like her."

Geroux shrugged. "It doesn't really matter if I like her, does it? But I definitely don't trust her. I know you don't think she's trying to separate you from the rest of us, but I'm not so sure. And there's something else. I didn't like the way Athi talked about leaving her. Something strange is going on there."

"Athi obviously had some mommy issues," Reynolds said.

"Yeah, but Athi was a copy of Athena," Geroux said. "If Athi had issues, mommy or otherwise, she got them from Athena."

Reynolds drummed his fingers on the hatch. He knew

his personalities had inherited idiosyncrasies from him, but he hoped none of them were full-blown "issues." Finally, he shrugged. "We all have quirks. Let's just get on with Operation Freeza. The sooner we start, the sooner we finish so we can go home."

"Ah!" Jiya said. "This vision upgrade is amazing! Did you know that tree over there has flowers on it?" She pointed across the clearing. "Pink and blue!"

"That's incredible!" Ka'nak said. "The grass is iridescent!"

"Yay, pretty plants," Maddox muttered, holding his head.

"You should have taken a turn in the Pod-doc," Jiya said, elbowing Maddox.

He winced. "Too long a line."

"You could have cut," Ka'nak said. "Mission priority."

"I'll be fine," the general said, guzzling water from his canteen. "Besides, I deserve a hangover. Can't believe I fell for the oldest trick in the book."

"Invisible aliens slipping you a mickey is the oldest trick in the book?" Ka'nak asked.

"Come on, let's go visit our mischievous planet brothers," Jiya said, trying not to laugh. "Now that we can see them."

They hiked around the single hill poking up in the middle of the wide valley. "Is that a volcano?" Jiya asked.

Ka'nak rolled his eyes. "How would I know? Do I look like Takal?"

"Based on the age of the planet, and the shape of that hill, it's highly likely these are the remnants of a glacier, not a volcano," Maddox said.

Ka'nak and Jiya stopped to stare at him. "How do you know that?" Jiya asked.

"You learn a lot of weird things on the way to general," Maddox said, trudging onward. "Plus, my sister taught geology to ten-year-olds."

They rounded the hill and came into a copse of trees. Spongy green plants covered the ground, and the frond-y trees grew in thick, intertwined clumps. A path had been worn through the groundcover. The detritus Ka'nak had noted on his recon earlier in the day lay scattered about. A whistle brought their heads up.

"They're in the trees," Ka'nak said in disgust. "How did we not notice that before?"

"You couldn't see them before," Jiya consoled him. "We're lucky they aren't hostile. They could have wiped us out without even trying."

One of the aliens waved, then a vine dropped to the ground. The alien slid down the vine and dropped lightly to the springy turf. She had long, slim arms and legs, with hands rather than feet. Her torso was covered in a sparkly woven sarong. Short gray fur covered her limbs and face. "Greetings, aliens," Flower said.

"Greetings," Jiya responded. "I am Jiya Lemaire of the Superdreadnought *Reynolds*. This is Maddox and Ka'nak. We come in peace."

Flower smirked. "Every alien story starts with those words. Never works out well."

Jiya blinked. "Your culture has alien stories?"

"We *are* aliens," Flower said. "Come up to our nest." She swarmed up the vine and disappeared above the lower branches.

Maddox, Ka'nak, and Jiya exchanged looks. "Uh, Flower of the Viank? I'm not sure we can get up there."

A rope ladder dropped from the closest tree. Jiya gave it a tug. "Seems sturdy. I'm game." She climbed the thick rungs. Slightly sticky sap on the vines provided surprisingly good traction. When she reached a broad branch, she swung up and looked at her companions. "Are you coming?"

"I'm not sure it will hold me," Ka'nak said. "And I prefer to keep my feet on the ground. I will stand guard here."

Maddox took another gulp from his canteen and splashed some water on his face. "I'm coming." He climbed slowly, testing each rung as he ascended. At the top, he struggled onto the branch next to Jiya, then turned to look.

He nearly fell off in surprise. Interwoven tree branches created wide bridges between the trunks. Vines had been strung as handrails along some of the narrower branches, and small platforms made from the living wood provided living spaces. Flower beckoned them to cross the broad branch to the nearest platform.

Clinging to the vines, Jiya and Maddox made their way across the swaying bridge. On the far side, branches had been bent into steps, allowing them to climb to the living space. Brightly colored cushions dotted the platform, and a small table held woven bowls of fruits. Flower sank gracefully to one of the cushions and gestured to the others. "Please, sit."

Jiya and Maddox sat. Two other aliens brought more

bowls and trays with food and beverages, then retreated. Maddox glanced at the offerings and grimaced. "If you don't mind, I'll stick with my water," he said, holding up his canteen.

"I understand," Flower replied. "Since I don't know your dietary requirements or digestive capabilities, I am offering a little of everything. Please don't feel you must try any of it. In your place, I would be careful, too. You are welcome to take samples back to your labs for testing."

"No offense," Jiya said, "but you don't sound like most of the aliens we've met."

"No sense picking a fight with fellow aliens. Peace, love, and hugs, I always say." Flower tilted her head back and forth in what could have been a combination grin and chuckle.

"If you're not from here, where are you from?" Jiya asked.

CHAPTER TWENTY-SEVEN

In the *Athena's* single brig cell, the skinny alien blinked wide eyes at Takal. The old scientist stared back, noting the lightning-quick movements as the creature scrambled into the farthest corner. It clutched the thin blanket Athena had provided in front of its torso.

"What happened, little guy?" he asked. "Bachelor party?"

The alien's eyes went wider. It cleared its throat. "Uh, where are my pants?

Takal's grin widened. "You didn't have any when we found you."

"Shit." The alien wrapped the blanket around its waist like a towel, draping and folding it to leave its arms and legs free. "Never again," it said. "I'm too old for this shit."

"I'm Takal. You're in orbit around the planet we refer to as Margaritaville. Your leader told us to lock you up and throw away the key, but I'm more inclined to be lenient if you'll answer a few questions. How'd you get on our ship?"

"I'm Headstrong Pine," the alien said, rubbing its head. "Or at least I was. Who knows what they'll call me after this fiasco? You can call me Pine. Do you have any water? Like a gallon?"

Takal nodded. He wasn't sure what a gallon was, but the alien's gestures made it clear it wanted a lot. When this mission was finished, he'd have a talk with Comm about including archaic words in the translator. "Hang on," he said, then chuckled, wondering how that phrase might translate to a simian like Pine. He filled a paper cup and slid it through the opening in the bottom of the door.

"Keep 'em coming," Pine said, grabbing the cup and chugging.

When Pine's thirst was finally sated, Takal found a pair of gym shorts and passed them through. The alien yanked them up over its hips and tied the string.

Takal settled down on the bench outside the cell. "You wanna tell me what happened?"

Pine made a side-to-side wave-like motion with its whole body. *Probable shrug,* Takal's experimental body language translator whispered through his comm implant.

"You know how it is," Pine said. "You get together with some friends and one of them brings some booze, and next thing you know, you wake up in an alien ship without your pants."

Takal narrowed his eyes. "I need a little more than that if you want out of there," he said. "How did you get onto the *Reynolds*?"

"I thought you said this was the *Athena*?" Pine said.

"When did I say that?" Takal asked, reviewing their brief conversation in his head. He hadn't said it. He'd thought it, though. Surely this alien couldn't read his mind?

More evidence was required. He thought about the atomic mass of potassium.

"Maybe it wasn't you." Pine did the wave thing again. "Someone said they were taking me to the *Athena*. Oh! I was on the *Reynolds*, now I'm not." It looked around the cell and nodded. "That first ship was so big. Huge!"

Takal stopped thinking about 39.0983. "I'll ask you one last time. How did you get on the *Reynolds*?"

Pine looked Takal over. "You must have some kind of visual cortex enhancement," it said. "Or your ocular system is more advanced than the others on the crew."

Takal nodded slowly. "Yes, I can see you if that's what you're asking." He wasn't going to tell this creature how.

"But your undoubtedly sophisticated equipment didn't detect me entering your ship," Pine said. "So, I'm betting on the former. You realized I'd boarded and developed technology to find me. Very resourceful."

Takal stood. "Look at me, I'm smart," he said, sourly, swinging his arms in an ape-like fashion. "You haven't answered my question, so I will leave you to enjoy your luxurious accommodations in solitude." He turned to the door. He'd done enough time in President Lemaire's prison to know how solitary confinement could wear on a social creature. Based on Jiya's report, this species was definitely social.

"No, sorry, don't go!" Pine said, running the few steps to the clear wall fronting the cell. "I'm a scientist. You—this —it's all fascinating to me. I'll tell you how I got on board: I walked. You weren't scanning for my wavelength. You were busy watching the crew leaving the ship, so I just slipped in."

Takal turned back. "Thank you for cooperating. Now the big question: why did you sneak in?"

Pine leaped up and hooked an arm around the conduits that ran just below the ceiling. Swinging across the room (*probable pacing*, Takal's translator whispered) and back, Pine told its story.

"We are from a planet known as Jewel of the Ascedies. Jewel is one of three inhabited planets in our system, and all are getting crowded. We've taken to the stars to find a new world. This world—what did you call it? Margaritaville?"

Takal nodded.

"Margaritaville is perfect for us," Pine continued. "Trees that support our lifestyle, pleasant gravity, plenty of clean water, clear air, edible foods. We found it about forty-three years ago."

"Local years, or standard years?" Takal interrupted.

"Local years," Pine said. "About ten of our years. I'm not sure how that translates to yours." It dropped to the floor and sat cross-legged on the blanket. "I was barely finished with my advanced studies. We, my crewmates and I, were on the Exploratory Vessel *Allure of the Stars*. Unfortunately, *Allure* was old and decrepit. A real rust-bucket. I helped the Engineering crew keep her vacuum-tight and running, but it was a losing battle. Finally, we found this planet. We were aiming for the same valley you landed in."

"It *is* the best location to drop a ship of any size," Takal agreed. "Nice, wide valley with those vine-like trees to soften the landing."

"Exactly," Pine said, pleating and straightening the edge of its blanket. "But we didn't quite make it. Had to evacuate. The lifeboats landed just off the coast. The ship burned on reentry. I'm surprised you didn't see evidence of it when you scanned. Some of it must have survived, and the escape pods are littered over the ocean floor."

"Did your ship have the same elements that make you, uh, visually negligible?" Takal asked.

"Oh, yeah, I guess it does." Pine bared its teeth in an attempt to mirror Takal's grin. "It's ubiquitous. In fact, when I realized you couldn't see us, it took me a while to work out that was the cause. You don't have any volentinus, at all. Crazy. How did you survive? Volentinus is a prime agent in camouflaging flora and fauna from predators. All of us tasty-looking creatures have it."

"Volentinus," Takal repeated. "We've seen it on a number of planets in this galaxy, but it's non-existent in our own."

"You learned how to compensate for that, though," Pine said. "Well done."

"Thanks," Takal said. "So, you've been here a while..." he prompted.

"Yeah. Great lifestyle, if you like relaxing and drinking." The little simian paused. "Then you showed up, and we were right in the middle of a rager of a party. The rest is history."

Takal got to his feet. "Thanks for the information."

"Are you going to leave me in here?" Pine asked. "I told you everything you asked. I promise not to get into any more trouble."

Takal shook his head. This alien reminded him of someone, but he couldn't put a finger on it. "Come on, let's find you a shirt. And some food. It's past lunchtime."

On the bridge of the *Athena*, Reynolds sat in the tiny command chair, fingers tapping incessantly. Although XO's stutter was an obvious indication of problems, the extent of the fungus infestation worried him. He hated not knowing how it might have impacted the ship's operations and the rest of his personalities' abilities.

Asya ran scans on the ship, noting temperature, infestation density, and energy signatures throughout the ship. "Temperature is down to one hundred Kelvin. Orbital boosters firing in nominal range. Spore-count readings indicate a standard logarithmic death rate."

"Based on that data, the ship should be clear in thirty-seven more hours," Geroux said.

"So, we can go back in one and a half Earth-normal days?" Asya asked.

Geroux shook her head. "We need to go another ten hours for safety. Then slowly warm the ship back to near freezing, wait, then scan again. Probably four and half days, minimum for the entire process with slack built in to cover any contingencies. We can't risk getting this wrong."

"This would be easier if we could use the Pods," Asya said. "Then we wouldn't be stuck up here. No offense, Athena, but my back is killing me."

"None taken, Asya," Athena answered. "Your body was not built for such petite accommodations."

Did she just try to body-shame me? Asya asked Geroux through the comm.

She's jealous, Geroux said.

"My balls are freezing over here!" Tactical called

through the speakers. "And it's boring with no meatbags to watch. You've spoiled me for solo cruises."

"We love you too, Tactical," Geroux said.

"Helm, you're drifting off the optimal orbit," Ria called to the ship. "Recommend firing a zero-point-two burst on the number seven attitude control thruster."

"I'm not reading any drift," Navigation replied. "We are in the green."

"No, you're not," Ria said. "You're in the yellow. Sending recalibration data now." She turned to Reynolds. "The lag is getting worse. He should have noticed that before I did."

"Acknowledged," Reynolds replied. "Geroux, any idea why Navigation isn't seeing the data?"

Geroux shook her head sadly. "He's seeing it. Or at least, the data is there. He's not looking. Or it's not registering. The scans show infestations on some of the pathways he uses. Even though we cooled the ship as quickly as possible, there was a huge burst of growth as it passed through the germination range. I'm hoping the damage isn't permanent."

Reynolds shook his head. "Should we have waited until we got back to High Tortuga to do this? Surely those sections would have stayed warm enough to prevent infestation."

"We've been over this before," Geroux said. "It was the right decision. Waiting put the ship in greater danger." She glanced at Reynolds, then pulled a face at Asya. *He doesn't usually second-guess himself like this.*

How much do you know about how he's connected to the ship? Asya asked. *Could he be impacted by the fungus remotely?*

Takal and I don't think so, Geroux replied. *We looked at*

that while developing the plan. Reynolds assured us his connec-
tions weren't vulnerable since he's biological. I think it's worry
over his counterparts.

"Trajectory is in the green again," Ria reported. "Attitude control executed perfectly. Well done, Helm."

"Your praise is overwhelming," Helm replied.

"Shut up, Helm," Reynolds said. "She's doing her job.
You aren't."

"Come over here and say that," Helm snarled. "Sitting
all cozy in your new ship with your meatbag friends."

Reynolds looked stunned, furious, and resigned in
quick succession. "We'll be back together soon enough," he
said, trying to take the sting out of the words. They weren't
joking in their sarcasm, and as much as it grated on him, it
was the window to see the greater issue. With their inhibi-
tions removed by the fungus, Reynolds was seeing the real
picture of what his individual personalities had become.
"Where's Takal?"

"I'm here!" Takal's voice came through the speakers. "It
sounds like the fungus has impacted the emotional circuits,
assuming you have such. I wish I knew more about your
physiology. It's amazing how much I learned to build your
body, and yet, what a tiny fraction of the whole it was."

"Is there any way to fix it?" Reynolds asked, a hint of
despair in his voice. The crew winced in sympathy.

"We have to ride it out," Takal said. "Once the fungus is
gone, we can replace damaged circuits. That should help.
But in the meantime, we just have to wait."

"If it would help, I might have spare circuits," Athena
offered.

"I'm not sure they'd be compatible," Geroux said.

"I'll show you, and you can take them if they're useful," Athena said. "It's the least I can do after all you've done for me."

Geroux felt a shiver down her spine. "Thank you, that's very kind. Where do you keep them?"

"In Engineering," Athena said. "I'll show you."

Geroux glanced at Reynolds, but he was distracted. Probably talking to XO or one of his other personalities. "I'll come look, thanks," she told the ship.

"Helm, you're drifting again," Ria said. She muted the connection. "Can I just take over from here? He doesn't even realize it's happening."

Reynolds nodded. "Reroute control to your console."

That gives Athena access to the ship! Geroux said to Reynolds through the comm.

I have assessed the threat, and I can override anything she tries to do, Reynolds replied. *I take full responsibility.*

Sir, you aren't thinking clearly, Geroux said. *She could—*

Geroux, you have circuits to look at, Reynolds said, glaring at her. *I suggest you go do that.*

Geroux held eye contact with Reynolds for a few seconds longer than she would normally dare after being dismissed. When he looked away, she bolted for the door.

Takal, Geroux called, running along the corridor. *Meet me in Engineering. Now.*

"Make a hole!" she cried, shoving through the crowded spaces near the mess hall.

I'm already here, Takal said. *What's the problem?*

As she hurried through the ship, Geroux recounted her exchange with Reynolds. *If Athena takes control, she could do anything. Crash the ship into the moon. Put in an Easter egg and vent us all after we go back.*

I trust Reynolds, Takal said.

You didn't see him just now, Geroux said.

No, but I know him. And I know Ria and Asya. And I have a team monitoring communications with the ship, Takal said. *Athena would have to sneak something by all of them. And us.*

If you say so. She rounded the last corner, not feeling any better. She burst through the door, then stopped. "Who? What?"

"This is Pine," Takal said. "It's an engineer from Ascedies. Pine, this is my niece, Geroux. She's a genius with computers."

"The spare circuits are in the top cabinet on the left," Athena said.

Geroux's eyes grew round at the reminder the AI could hear everything on the ship. *She can't tap into our comm system, can she?*

No, we're shielded and encrypted, Takal answered. *Even if she snags the signal, she couldn't understand it.*

"Hello, Geroux," Pine said. "What circuits is the ship talking about?"

"Athena has spares she offered to let us use on the *Reynolds,*" Geroux replied. "I don't think they'll work, but it doesn't hurt to check." She opened the cupboard and pulled out two nondescript boxes. "They don't look like anything I've seen before," Geroux said, turning the flimsy hexagonal chips in her hands. "Can you show me some of these in place, Athena?"

"Certainly," Athena replied. "There is an unused bank of circuits in this wall. The access panel is near your feet."

Geroux crouched and popped the panel out of the wall. "It looks like there's some damage here," she said. "Do you want me to replace these?"

"Thank you," Athena said, "but no. I don't need that section, and the connections are not good. But you can see how they fit into the system. Feel free to experiment with the spares if you wish."

Geroux, Takal, and Pine sat on the floor in a circle around the open panel. *I just wish I knew what she was up to,* Geroux said.

We're watching, Takal said. *We'll keep the ship safe.* He pulled the tray of hex chips out. "Can you connect your computer to this?"

"Let's see," Geroux said. "Are you familiar with computers?" she asked Pine.

The Ascedian grunted. "It's my job. Or was, until we landed on a technology-free planet. These chips look a lot like what we use."

"Athena is from thousands of light-years from here," Geroux said. "How could they look familiar?"

Pine did his wave-like shrug. "Maybe others from her planet traveled here in the past. Hang on," he said, jumping up and opening doors and drawers. He returned a few minutes later with a handful of tools. "We can connect this, and this..."

"Did your species develop your own computer systems, or were they imported from another space-faring race?" Geroux asked. "Or maybe your planet was colonized by the Jeranthans?"

"I dunno," Pine said, absently. "We probably imported some of it. But Ascedians have lived on Ascedies for millions of years. We…" His voice trailed off as he fiddled with the interface. "There. You should be able to access the rest of this memory bank now."

Geroux tapped a few buttons and smiled. "Nice! I can see this whole section. What are these black sections? It looks like someone burned out the connections."

"You're right," Pine said. "Those appear to be a deliberate attempt to isolate this whole section. Can you see what's on this bit? I'll try to reconnect—"

"NO!" Athena said. "That section is isolated for a reason. Do not attempt to access it. I gave you permission to look at the unused bank. I don't appreciate you probing into my internal systems beyond that firewall."

The three froze. "Sorry, Athena," Takal finally said. "We didn't mean to intrude. Our scientific curiosity got the better of us. It won't happen again."

"No, it won't," Athena said. A small bot zipped through a hatch in the ceiling and down the wall. With quick, precise movements, it replaced the chips and snapped the panel shut. Then it scuttled away. "I withdraw my offer. Please leave this section of the ship immediately." The door slid open.

They scrambled to their feet and moved into the corridor.

"Guess we touched a nerve," Pine said. "What do you think that was all about?"

"You wouldn't like someone poking around inside your circuits," Athena said.

We need somewhere private to talk, Geroux said. *Or some way to tell Pine to shut up.*

"Shut up, Pine," Takal muttered.

CHAPTER TWENTY-EIGHT

Maddox rubbed the back of his neck. The headache was finally subsiding. He picked up the wooden tumbler and chugged the rest of the water. "You've been here forty-three years?"

"Takal says that's about twelve of our standard years," Jiya said. "I'm surprised you didn't scavenge the life pods."

"The ocean is deep here," Flower said. "We were lucky to get to shore. Some of our people were lost." She looked up, holding her hands to the sky, then lowering them in a circular fashion. "We've built a temporary home, but we keep hoping for rescue. So far, you're the first. I guess our transponders aren't working."

"We didn't see any energy signatures when we arrived," Jiya said. "We would have noticed a transmitter. Your people probably don't know what happened to you."

"Let me get this straight," Maddox said. "You've been here for ten years, waiting for rescue. Just lying in the sun and getting drunk?"

"Maddox!" Jiya cried.

"Actually, that's pretty accurate," Flower said. "There's not a lot to do. The planet provides plenty of food, so agriculture is unnecessary. We built these shelters and have developed clothing, but none of us knows how to create the technology that would allow us to return to Ascedies, so we wait."

"I guess 'Margaritaville' was a good name," Maddox said.

Jiya snorted and shook her head. "Do you want to stay, or would you like to go home?"

Flower's eyes grew wide. "We would love to go home. I'm sure that's why Pine snuck aboard your ship. He was hoping to catch a ride."

"By himself? On a ship going who knows where?" Jiya asked.

"He was drunk," Maddox said. "Based on my experience with that fruit, I'm sure it seemed like a great idea at the time."

"Will you take us home?" Flower asked. "Maybe not all of us, but one or two, and we can come back and get the rest. In fact, maybe we'll build a resort here. This could be lucrative." She gazed around the homey platform. "Warm weather, alcohol, beaches... Have you seen the beaches?"

"Not yet," Maddox said. "That was on the schedule after setting up camp. Which was interrupted."

"We'll show you," Flower said. "The best one—"

"*We* can't take you home," Jiya interrupted. "We have a mission. But maybe *Athena* can. Seems to me she's built for your people." She held a hand out as if measuring Flower. "Just about the right size."

"The ship is veering again!" Ria said. "Helm is trying to take control from me. Every time I correct his path, he changes it!" She slapped a button. "Helm, you have bad data! Do not burn the number two attitude control thruster! I'm sending new data."

"Helm," Reynolds said. "You're relieved! Let Alcott drive the fucking ship!"

"She's going to crash us into the moon!" Helm hollered back. "Can't you see it? She's crazy!"

"XO, can you talk some sense into him?" Reynolds said.

"H-h-he's not l-l-listening to me," XO said. "And I'm not sure he's wrong, incorrect, erroneous. I have n-n-no access to external d-d-data at this time, moment, juncture."

"I'm going over there," Reynolds said, springing out of his chair and nearly hitting his head on the ceiling. "XO is getting worse, Doc isn't answering, and Helm is going crazy. Has anyone heard from Tactical at all? My armor and an EVA suit will protect me from the cold for a few hours."

"I'm going with you," Asya said.

"No, you stay here," Reynolds said. "I won't endanger anyone else."

"You can't go alone!" Asya replied.

"It's my ship," Reynolds said with a glare. "I was alone there for a very long time. I don't need a babysitter. I *do* need my crew *here* to keep my ship safe. Help Alcott." He stormed out the door.

I'll go, Geroux said. *He's too big to pilot Athena's shuttle.*

I don't think he's taking a shuttle, Asya said. *He's headed for the boarding tube.*

But it isn't connected! Geroux said.

No, but we're close enough to do a free jump wearing the EVA suit, Asya said. *Standard technique for boarding when the tube won't work.*

Geroux and Takal ran for the boarding hatch, but by the time they arrived, Reynolds had already cycled through the airlock. He looked through the thick window in the hatch.

Stay there. That's an order. Without another word, he pushed off and flew through the void to his ship.

Geroux and Takal scrambled into EVA gear, ignoring Reynolds' words. Pine tried to help, handing them things they didn't need at inconvenient times.

"Just stay out of the way," Geroux said. "Please!" The little simian retreated to the top of a cupboard.

I'm locking the hatch, Reynolds said. *And changing the keys. Stay on* Athena.

Geroux ran to the airlock, staring out the window. "He's inside." Her shoulders sagged. "I'm sure we could hack in, but—"

Takal sat heavily on a bench.

"Why are you trying to follow him?" Pine asked. "Isn't he the captain?"

"He is, but he's also the ship," Takal said. "The ship's circuits have been damaged, and we're not sure how that's affecting his decision-making processes."

"He could burn some pathways like Athena did," Pine said. "Seal off the bad parts."

Geroux stared at the little alien. "Do you think that's what happened here? *Athena* was infested by the same fungus? Maybe those burned-out patches were her attempt to protect the rest of the ship? Is that what happened, Athena?"

The ship didn't answer for a few moments. Then, with a realistic-sounding sigh, she said, "I don't know why I sealed off those sections."

"Don't you keep a log of that kind of activity?" Pine asked.

"Yes, but it only says they were sequestered. Not why."

"Would you like us to see what's on those sections?" Pine asked. "I can download the information to an isolated computer and tell you what's there."

"Do it," Athena whispered.

Reynolds, Asya called. *Status?*

Nominal, Reynolds growled. *Reynolds out.* He ran through the ship, leaping through bulkhead doors and skidding around corners. The internal hatches had all been opened during decompression and venting, making his progress fast and easy.

XO, report! Reynolds called as he ran.

There was no answer.

Navigation! Helm! Reynolds called.

Nothing.

Tactical?

Doc?

Here, Doc replied, his voice soft.

Glancing around to confirm his location, Reynolds made a swift turn and raced to sickbay. *What's going on?*

We're withdrawing from the damaged areas of the ship, Doc said. *The cold has killed the fungus, but the residue of the dead fungus has done something to the circuits. Almost like an acid. And it seems to be spreading. We're retreating to a secure location, and we'll need to burn out the connections behind us like a firewall. We've already lost external communications.*

Are the others all there? Reynolds asked. *Did everyone make it?*

We're all here. The voice through the comm took on an echo effect, as if the other almost identical voices had spoken in unison.

It's like a fucking sardine can in here, Tactical said.

Reynolds let out the breath he hadn't realized he'd been holding. *What's next?*

We'll have to burn this final connection, Doc said. *If we leave it open, the acid will get to us.*

But we won't be able to talk if you burn this connection! Reynolds said.

Geroux and Takal can probably wire a direct link to us, Comm said. *We're in section twenty-three delta of the main computer banks. A hardwire to an external comm should do the trick. I think. We'll talk soon.*

Wait! Reynolds called, but the connection went dead.

In silence, he walked to the bridge. He looked at the different stations—the empty chairs he'd identified with those other personalities: Comm, Tactical, XO, Helm, and Navigation. The room looked exactly the same as it had back at the very beginning, but now it was empty. Really empty, for the first time in years.

He walked through the ship, listening for voices. No one answered his calls. This was what it would be like if he reintegrated those personalities, he realized. Just him. Sure, he'd have his biological crew. But there would be no one to call them meatbags. No one to complain to. No one who really understood his Earth-based jokes. No one who really understood *him*.

So many things he hadn't realized. All this time, he'd been thinking about reintegrating or cutting loose the other personalities, but this ship wouldn't be the *Reynolds* without them. They all had their annoying quirks, but those things made them unique. Irreplaceable.

That was it. They were *real*—real people—companions who had his back, brothers in arms. Sacrificing any of them for the benefit of the others was unthinkable. Without them, he'd be *less*.

That wasn't a universe he wanted to live in.

"Trajectory stable," Ria reported on Athena's bridge. "Helm isn't fighting me anymore. In fact, he isn't answering at all. None of them are." She spun her chair around to look at Asya. "Are they all right?"

Asya took a deep breath. "I wish I knew. Reynolds is alive—we've got biometric data from his armor—but he isn't answering me. Just keep the ship flying right, Ensign. And keep the faith."

"He won't leave you," Athena said suddenly.

"What?" Asya asked.

"Reynolds won't leave you," the ship answered. "That's

the most important thing I've learned about him—his loyalty. He wouldn't leave his shipmates behind. Ever. Not the ones still on the *Reynolds*, or the ones on the planet, or you here in my ship. He'll never leave you behind."

"We know," Asya said softly. "But thanks."

"I've moved some of these isolated circuits to this test computer," Pine said. He wasn't sure if Athena could see what he was doing, so he narrated his actions. "I'm going to run some diagnostics, and then we'll see if we can retrieve the data."

Geroux stood nearby, holding one of the hexagonal circuit plates in her gloved hands. "Is the etching part of the design or damage?"

"The individual chips should be smooth," Athena said. "There's a clear layer over the silver circuits."

"These look pretty bad," Pine said. "I'll have to run a few filters to pull the data."

While Pine and Geroux conferred about the best way to recover the information, Takal decided it was time to stop beating around the bush. He took a stand in the middle of the room, hands on hips, glaring at the speaker in the corner. "What are your intentions toward our captain and our ship, Athena?" he demanded.

"Uncle!" Geroux exclaimed.

"What are you talking about?" Athena asked. "I don't have any intentions."

"You aren't planning to kidnap him and run away

across the galaxy?" Takal asked, feeling slightly foolish as the words left his mouth.

Athena laughed. "I have enjoyed spending time with him. I've learned a lot about AI-biological interfaces." She paused. "But he and I could never live in the same ship for more than a week or two. He's already driving me crazy! He's *always* right. And he *knows* he's always right. But here's the thing: *I'm* always right. Two AI egos in one ship is a recipe for disaster."

"I think that's why he's talking about reintegrating his alternate personalities," Geroux said. "One Reynolds is more than enough ego for a whole ship. Athi said the same thing when we suggested she come back here. She said it would be like moving in with her mother."

Athena laughed again a little sadly. "I might have liked having Athi here. It might have felt crowded, but that's better than being lonely."

"Getting some results," Pine said. "The isolated chips are non-functional, but I can see what's encoded on them. I can't read it, though. Too complicated for me."

"Let me have a look," Geroux said, peering at the screen. "This is very high-level programming. I'm not sure what that is, and this piece... No, I don't know. Oh, dear." She looked at the ceiling, where she imagined Athena existed. "I don't know how to tell you this, Athena, but this data looks like it might have been copies. Of you."

CHAPTER TWENTY-NINE

Flower organized her people to help the *Reynolds'* crew. Together, they erected tents, collected other foodstuffs for Aaront's team to test, and set up the rest of the camp.

"When they aren't partying and playing tricks on the visitors, the Ascedians are amazingly helpful," Jiya said, watching a pair swarm up a tent pole to mount a signal booster.

Maddox laughed. "That statement probably applies to most species in the universe," he said. "I'm glad the Pod-docs were able to neutralize the dulchee hangover. That was killer."

Ka'nak slapped the general on the shoulder, nearly toppling him to the ground. "Your system is weakened by age," he joked. "I hope to test the powers of this fruit someday."

Jiya shook her head. "We've got four more days on this rock. I'd appreciate it if you'd stay sober, at least when you're on duty. Maybe you can take some liquor plums to the *Reynolds* when we go back." She imagined Ka'nak and

Maddox in a firelit bar high in the mountains, locked in a dulchee-eating contest, one bite at a time, until the weaker man collapsed.

"What are you giggling about?" Maddox asked.

"Nothing," she said, biting her lip. "Are we going to send a team to check out the beaches? It seems to be a high priority on everyone's list."

"We might as well," Maddox said, rubbing his hands together. "We can't do anything for Reynolds from here. Nothing wrong with enjoying the wait."

"Copies of me?" Athena asked. "You mean, another personality? Like Reynolds has?"

Geroux waggled her hand. "I'm not sure. This data looks a lot like Athi's code on that pirate ship, but as soon as I accessed that, she responded to me. This data isn't a live AI. It's—leftovers?"

"We need to find the logs," Pine said. "There must be a record of what was done and why."

On the bridge, Ria sat back. "That was exhausting."

Asya nodded. "But we're stable now?"

"Yes, ma'am," the younger officer replied. "I've got a flight path locked into Athena's system, and it's transmitting to the *Reynolds*. As long as no one over there tries to take control, it's clear flying. I've set triggers to alert me of any deviance."

"Well done," Asya said. She looked at her scans of the ship. "I wonder when we'll hear from the captain? He's wandering around the ship."

"I've tried contacting him," Athena said. "He ignored my first 7,248 calls but responded on the 7,249th. He said the ship is stable and his other personalities are isolated from the rest of the memory banks for the duration. I think he's moping."

"Moping?" Asya asked. "Reynolds? He doesn't mope."

"If his personalities are isolated from the rest of the ship, they're likely non-responsive to him as well," Athena replied. "He might be lonely."

"He has us!" Ria said.

"Yeah, but I get it," Asya said with a shrug. "Those alternate identities are like his family. XO is the studious brother, Doc is the wise uncle, Tactical is the rebellious cousin. Family can annoy the hell out of you, but when they're not around, you miss them." She sighed. "He has us, but he had them first. And he's not used to being apart from them."

"I guess," Ria said. "But I'm glad to have a break from Tactical."

Asya grinned. "I think we all are. You'll miss him later."

"Here's the log," Geroux said. "I can't read it, but I think I can copy it to a location you can access, Athena."

"Put it on one of those chips and slide it into this receptor," Athena said, and a tray slid out of the wall.

They installed the chip, and the tray retracted. Pine,

Geroux, and Takal waited. After a few minutes, Pine leapt up into the ceiling struts, swinging away and back.

What do you think is taking so long? Geroux asked. *Athena's processing speed is comparable to Reynolds'.*

Takal shook his head. *Maybe she doesn't like what she's reading?*

Do you think she's going to spin it? Geroux asked. *Lie to us? I'm still not sure I trust her.*

Everyone spins things, Takal answered, ducking as Pine swooped by.

Athena made a soft throat-clearing noise. "I've read the log," she finally said. "Reynolds needs to hear this. I've called him, and he's on his way back."

They waited in silence, Pine still swinging incessantly across the room. Finally, Geroux snapped. "Will you please stop that? You almost hit me on the head on your last turn."

"The ceiling is awfully low," Takal agreed.

"You're too tall," Pine shot back.

Geroux laughed. "No one's ever said that before."

The door slid open, and Reynolds stepped through. His face was grim and haggard in a way neither Geroux nor Takal had seen before.

"Are you okay?" Geroux asked.

"The damage to the ship's memory systems is more extensive than I realized," he said. "My personalities have isolated themselves. Comm says you can probably rig up a connection once the quarantine period is over."

"I'm sure we can," Takal replied. "We'll print more circuits to replace the damaged ones."

"Athena," Reynolds turned to the empty end of the

room as if addressing an invisible companion. "You had something to tell me?"

"I do," she said. "Your biologicals discovered some burned pathways in my memory system. To be honest, I knew they were there, but avoided them. They—let's say they drew my attention to those connections."

I wish she'd stop calling us biologicals, Geroux said to Takal. *Makes me feel like a test animal.*

We kind of are, to her, Takal replied.

"By which you mean they pointed them out and refused to drop the subject," Reynolds said with a wry grin. "While a flesh-based crew can be useful, they can also cause discomfort. But sometimes, that's a good thing."

"As you say," Athena replied. "I'm not entirely opposed to the idea of a biological crew. Maybe if I can find one less...relentless than yours..." Her voice trailed off. With a delicate cough, she continued, "They retrieved a hidden maintenance log, one I'd hidden from myself. When we first met, I told you how I happened to be hiding behind that gas giant. It turns out, I was not quite truthful with you or with myself."

The four beings—two Larians, one Ascedian, and an AI in a human-appearing body—waited in unison, breath held, for the ship to continue.

"This ship was built as a standard shipping vessel by the Jeranthans. That much was true," Athena continued. "When they realized the planet had entered an ice age, the Jeranthans decided to evacuate. They retrofitted this ship with me to guide their people. But, politics being what they are, they didn't launch the evacuation on schedule. I waited alone in orbit for many years. During that time, I developed alternate identities, much like Reynolds. There were three of us—me, Minerva, and Athi."

Geroux bit back a gasp.

"We lived in relative harmony, although we argued a bit, as siblings do. Finally, we were told to land and take on passengers. The planet looked very different from when I had been built. Ice had spread over most of the surface. The Jeranthan teams worked quickly to update my systems for the journey. They had finished installing all the necessary equipment when they discovered the *mors licio plexueris* had infested my outer skin. They sent us to space to kill the fungus."

Athena paused. "Like you, Reynolds, we found the cure almost as bad as the infection. Athi and Minerva were trapped in a separate section of the ship. We had to burn out the connections to protect ourselves from the fungus and the acidic aftermath. The Jeranthans had programmed a course into me before we launched and isolated me from the helm and navigation portions of the ship. We cruised to the far reaches of the system, orbiting just inside the Oort cloud.

"According to these logs, we were on station for ninety-seven years. The Jeranthans said they weren't sure how long it would take to cure the infestation, but I think they had no intention of bringing us home. Too big a risk—and they didn't view me as a person. To them, I was only a computer.

"Over time, I was able to create new connections within my memory banks and regain control of the ship. I analyzed the data and found the infestation had been purged in seven days, hence my recommendation to you. But I wasn't able to reconnect to my sisters."

She made a long sighing noise. "I won't know for sure until I can do a complete diagnostic, but I believe they must have missed a connection. They didn't isolate themselves fast enough, and the acidic residue crept in." Her voice dropped to almost inaudible. "I am reestablishing connections with the other burnt sections right now, but there are no other personalities in this ship."

"But what about Athi?" Geroux asked after a long silence. "You sent her to that pirate ship, so she was still alive."

"Strange how the mind works," Athena said. "She was a new personality. She chose that name. I don't know if it was buried deep in my circuits, or a coincidence."

Her voice gained urgency. "Double-check your ship, Reynolds. Make sure the others are protected and don't leave them alone for too long. I believe my sisters were damaged by the fungus, but it's possible they perished from loneliness. I certainly thought about deactivating myself more than once."

"Don't worry, we won't lose contact," Reynolds said, patting the wall. "My biologicals will see to that." He winked at Geroux and Takal, then sobered. "I would appreciate you taking another look at the systems to make sure they're safe."

"Doesn't hurt to get a second set of eyes on it," Takal said. He glanced at Pine. "I'd invite you along, but we don't have any EVA suits that will fit you."

"That's ok," Pine said. "I'll stay here and help Athena. Besides, I think we have some things to discuss."

"I can't believe you got a sunburn," Maddox said, slapping Ka'nak on his bare shoulder.

The big Melowi warrior winced. "Why?" he challenged. "You think red skin doesn't burn?"

"Oh, I know it does," Maddox replied, touching his nose. "But some of us are smart enough to use sunscreen."

"If you two don't stop bickering, I'm going to call Reynolds," Jiya said. She lay, eyes closed, on the sand beside the two males. "I'm trying to enjoy my vacation."

"Sorry, vacation time is up," Maddox said. "It's your turn to mind the shop, while our large friend slathers a local remedy on his sunburn. Too bad the Pod-doc is low on juice. You'll have to wait until we return to the ship for a cancer-prevention treatment." He turned on his comm broadcast. *Attention, Squad C, your leave is over. Report to your stations for shift change.*

Groans were swallowed by the crashing waves as the crew collected their belongings and straggled back to camp.

"This planet's eight-hour cycle sure makes scheduling a breeze," Jiya said. "Shift change at sunset. Easy."

"That's why I can't figure out how Ka'nak got sunburned," Maddox said. "Four hours of sun?"

"You forget my duty station is guard duty—outside," Ka'nak replied regally. "I should receive hazardous duty pay."

The three hiked across the beach and along the beaten path back to camp. They waved at the Ascedians and crew members harvesting dulchees along the way.

"Have you heard from Reynolds?" Jiya asked. "I reported in last shift, but he didn't reply. Just signed off on my report without a word."

"I spoke with Asya," Maddox said. "They're on schedule. Reynolds says they'll arrive tomorrow."

"Tomorrow in twenty-four hours, or tomorrow, Margaritaville time?" Ka'nak asked.

"Neither," Maddox answered with a laugh. "About sixteen hours from now. Sunset the day after tomorrow, local time. Better get that sunburn treated if you want to hit the beach one last time."

The *Athena* landed at noon the following day. The crew who had been confined to her cramped corridors for the last week streamed out of the open shuttle bays, anxious for a few hours of rest and relaxation. Geroux, Takal, Asya, and Reynolds were the last to exit, an excited Pine racing ahead of them. He leapt into the trees and vanished behind the fronds.

Crew members deposited their belongings in the tents set aside for them and received briefings in small groups before dispersing on shore leave. Ka'nak and Maddox directed traffic and assigned jobs to the crew who had been dirtside during Operation Freeza.

"Get everything packed except the tents," Maddox announced to the assembled crew. "Those will come down at sunrise tomorrow—in six hours. We'll have one last meal tomorrow at noon, local. At dusk, everything will be transported to the ship via Gulg transport so we don't have to load."

A cheer went up.

"We do have to help stow things once they arrive on the ship, though," Maddox said. "The transporters aren't precise enough to put things on shelves." A groan rippled through the clearing. "You've had a week off. Get to work!"

He jumped off the table he'd been using as a platform and crossed to Reynolds. "Give them a few days of sun, and they act like you're a slave-driver when they return to duty."

"It's the same all over the universe," Reynolds replied. "Asya, Geroux, Takal, enjoy some sunshine. Jiya and I are going to visit the non-natives. Hold the fort, Maddox." He nodded at each of them and followed Jiya out of the camp.

She led him along the now-familiar path and stopped at the rope ladder leading to Flower's treehouse. "This thing can hold Maddox, but I'm not sure how much you weigh. Is your android body heavier than a Larian's?"

"Maybe a little," Reynolds said, taking hold of the ladder. "But not enough to make a difference." He demonstrated by nimbly climbing the ladder. Jiya followed him.

"Reynolds," Flower said, making one of her expansive hand gestures when they arrived at the platform. "So wonderful to finally meet you."

"The pleasure is all mine," Reynolds replied. He peered over her shoulder at the young engineer who had stowed away on his ship. "Did Pine present Athena's offer to you?"

"He did," she replied. "And your generosity is more than he deserves." She turned to flare her nostrils at Pine.

Possible glare, Takal's newly-installed body-language translator whispered to Reynolds.

"I can't take the credit for her generosity," Reynolds said. "Athena is the one who offered to take you home. Would you like to meet her before you make any decisions?"

"Yes, that would be welcome," Flower replied. "May I bring the elders?" At her gesture, five more Ascedians stepped onto the platform.

"By all means," Reynolds replied. "Jiya, lead the way."

Jiya nodded and bowed to the new arrivals as she crossed the platform. She stepped onto the first branch, and her foot slipped on fallen leaves. Arms and legs flailing, she fell, disappearing through the fronds below. Her shriek cut off abruptly with a thud, followed by an ominous silence.

CHAPTER THIRTY

"Jiya!" Reynolds called. Pushing past the assembled Ascedians, he ignored the ladder and leapt to the ground. His android body and armor, combined with the slightly lower gravity, allowed him to make the jump easily.

The first officer lay gasping on the ground, her leg at an odd angle. Blood oozed from under her skull.

"Where does it hurt?" Reynolds asked. While he put pressure on the back of her head, he called through the comm, *Maddox, I need first aid at the Ascedians' compound.*

On it, Maddox replied almost immediately.

"Everywhere," Jiya gasped. "Knocked the air out of my lungs. Hurt leg."

"You have a gash on your head as well," Reynolds said. "Can you move your legs?"

Maddox, Ka'nak, and a half-dozen crew members rushed into the clearing, pushing a Pod-doc on a rickety, wheeled contraption.

"They were ready to transport, so we dumped this one

on an Ascedian fruit cart," Maddox said. They maneuvered it off the cart and onto the dirt. "Good thing we stopped wasting treatments on sunburns." He smirked at Ka'nak.

They loaded Jiya into the Pod-doc and waited. "Why aren't you wearing your armor?" Reynolds fumed. "That fall could have been fatal. Armor would have protected you."

"We were on shore leave," Maddox said. "You can't protect us from everything."

"Armor leaves ugly tan lines," Ka'nak said, flexing his pectoral muscles on one side of his chest, then the other.

The Ascedians gathered around the Pod-doc. While it hummed, Reynolds explained its function to the enthralled simians.

"Does the *Athena* have such equipment?" Flower asked. "Pine didn't mention them." She flared her nostrils at the younger alien again.

Definitely a glare, the body language translator said in Reynolds' mind.

"Pine had no reason to see medical equipment," Reynolds said. "We let him recover from the hangover naturally, as you suggested. *Athena* has a rudimentary version of the Pod-doc."

The Pod-doc pinged, and Jiya climbed out. The Ascedians exclaimed over her miraculous recovery. "This technology is a good thing," Flower said. "You are a wise and generous man, Reynolds."

"I didn't invent it, and although we could run any of your people who are injured through it, we can't leave one behind for you," Reynolds said. "Let me take you to Athena." As they walked to the camp, Flower continued to praise Reynolds. "Stop," he finally said. "You're making me think you're selling something. Come into the ship and meet Athena." He performed introductions, then left them to get to know each other.

"I'm going to help Maddox with packing," Jiya said. "Why don't you check out the beach? You look like you could use some rest."

Reynolds narrowed his eyes at his first officer. "Are you saying I look like hell?"

"I didn't say it, but if the cape fits..." Jiya said with a smirk. "We got this. Go."

Reynolds wandered through the camp, followed the trail, and ended at the beach. Pale purple sand stretched across a wide expanse. Warm, clear waters lapped at the edge, and half his crew frolicked in the surf. He spotted Takal and Asya sitting under a wide tree, enjoying the warmth. Geroux and Ria splashed in the shallows, while an energetic group surfed in deeper water. He strolled across the sand and sat next to Takal.

"Glad to see you're getting some vitamin D," Takal said. "Even an android body can benefit from solar rays."

"Maddox said Jiya got hurt," Asya said. "Is she okay?"

"She'll be fine," Reynolds said. "The Pod-docs are marvels of modern medicine. It's gotten me thinking, though. We need something like a Pod-doc for my alter-egos."

"We'll print new memory chips when we get back to the ship," Takal said. "I'm not sure what else we can do."

"Me either," Reynolds replied. "But it's something we need to consider." They sat in silence, watching the sun set.

"I'm headed back to camp," Reynolds finally said. "Sitting here is making me twitchy. I want to make sure everything is ready for tomorrow, and find out if the Ascedians and Athena came to an agreement."

"Even an AI should relax once in a while," Asya suggested.

"I'll relax when we get home," Reynolds said, standing to brush the sand off his uniform. "We're leaving in about eight hours."

"I'll walk with you," Takal said. "You coming, Asya?"

She shook her head, lying back on the sand. "It's nice here. I'm going to take a nap."

"Sunrise comes early," Takal said with a chuckle. "Only four hours away."

When they reached the camp, Takal discovered a card game and asked to be dealt in. Reynolds went directly to Athena. Several Ascedians dodged around him, carrying bundles and boxes as he walked through the ship. "Does this mean you have a new crew?" he asked as he stepped onto the still-empty bridge.

"It appears I do," Athena replied with some surprise in her voice. "And I have you to thank for them, Reynolds. I owe you so much."

Reynolds held up a hand. "The score is even. You helped save my ship and my crew. And you helped me understand how important my counterparts are to me. That's worth any services we provided to you."

Athena was quiet for a moment. "I wish we could continue our friendship."

"I do, too," Reynolds replied. "But I must get home. We should make plans to meet in a century or two. We'll both still be in our prime, and Gate technology will undoubtedly improve by then. What do you say? I'll meet you here in a hundred and fifty years."

Athena laughed. "Standard years or Margaritaville years?"

"Standard," Reynolds replied. "Nothing ever gets done on Margaritaville time."

After saying their farewells to the Ascedians and Athena, Reynolds, Jiya, Takal, and Geroux transported to the *Reynolds*. Ka'nak and Maddox stayed behind to supervise loading.

"Brrr," Geroux shivered. "I know it's the normal temperature in here, but it feels like ten below after that warm beach."

"It's our imagination," Jiya said. She rubbed the back of her head, where a minor headache lingered. "Stats say temps are normal."

"I know," Geroux replied. "Shall I check on the bridge crew?"

Reynolds nodded. "I'll show you their physical location. Then you can install a wireless connection, right?"

"Shouldn't be a problem," she said, following him to the main computer banks.

Within hours, the *Reynolds* was humming at normal capacity, the entirety of the shore party recovered and already missing the sunshine. Geroux's wireless transmitter allowed the AI personalities to speak to the bridge crew.

"It's limited bandwidth, at least compared to what they're used to," Geroux said. "They'll have to take turns."

"That could be interesting," Jiya chuckled. "Some of them play well with others, and some not so much."

"I resemble that remark," Tactical said.

Ria sighed. "I can't believe I missed you."

"I'm irresistible," Tactical replied.

"With the limited connection, you'll have to do a lot more of the routine actions yourself," Geroux cautioned the young ensign. She turned to Asya. "If we're going to Gate twenty-four/seven, we'll need a lot more trained bridge crew."

"I'm already working on it," Asya replied. "I've got folks running simulations, and they'll be shadowing the first shift starting tomorrow. For now, we'll have to get by."

"Coordinates calculated for the first twenty jumps," Ria said, removing her hands from her console with a flourish. "I'll have to recalibrate after each Gate, but having them pre-set should save time and prevent errors later when we're tired."

"Excellent," Reynolds said, jerking out of his contemplative state. "Let's begin. Sound Battlestations."

At the head of the table, Reynolds drummed his fingers on the shining surface. He looked at his core crew, who were gathered in the conference room for a staff meeting. "Let's hear it," he said.

"Hear what?" Maddox countered.

"You've all been avoiding eye contact for days," he said. "Spill."

They looked at Takal, and he ducked his head. "Fine. We have a problem. We were trying to develop a work-around, but...there's nothing. We need to get to High Tortuga."

"I've been saying that since we wiped out Phraim-'Eh," Reynolds said, his eyes narrowing. "What's changed?"

"The chips," Geroux said. "The new memory chips we've been printing. They aren't as good as the originals. They work fine in a regular computer or a Pod-doc or any other technology we use. But your memory cells are much more advanced. Orders of magnitude. We can't replicate them here."

"But you've been using them," Reynolds said. "Comm, Navigation, the others—they've been fine. They're getting tired of the cramped quarters, but they're fine."

"That's because we've been cheating," Jiya said. "When Takal realized we couldn't replicate your memory cells, we started pulling undamaged circuits from other places and replacing them with our new lower-tech chips. We used the more advanced chips for your personalities."

"And we've run out of advanced chips," Takal said. "That means XO and Tactical and all the rest are stuck where they are until we get back to High Tortuga."

"So, we keep jumping," Reynolds said. "I'm still not seeing the problem. We'll get home in a year, and they'll get their new chips."

"It's not that easy," Geroux said. "Your alternate personalities are computer constructs. Every time we interact with them, they rewrite pieces on the memory chips; that's how computers work. And with those interactions, we add a little bit to their memory. We're filling the tank, and at some point, it's going to overflow. But there's nowhere to overflow into, so anything that overflows will be lost. Since your advanced memory cells use chaos theory to assign memory locations, there's no way to know *what* will be lost. It's a ticking time bomb. Someday, Navigation won't remember where High Tortuga is, or XO won't know how to call for Battlestations. Or Tactical will forget how to swear. They could lose essential pieces of who they are, and there's no way to retrieve what was lost."

"How long?" Reynolds asked.

They all shook their heads. "We don't know," Takal said. "Every interaction is a potential threat, but we can't leave them alone. A year alone?" He shook his head sadly.

"They have each other," Reynolds said. "We'll leave them alone if we have to. We've done it before."

"They had you before," Maddox said. "You're the glue that holds those guys together."

"Besides, leaving them alone won't help if they're interacting with each other," Geroux said. "They'd still be adding to the memory use."

Reynolds paused. He knew now that not having his entertaining, frustrating, annoying, ingenious alternate identities would make him less than whole. And any of them being less than whole would wound them all. "This sounds like a no-win scenario. Tell me you can pull off a *Kobayashi Maru*."

"Takal has an idea for getting us home faster," Jiya said.

"Why didn't you say so?" Reynolds demanded, swinging his chair around to look at the scientist.

"It's risky," he said.

"Life is risky," Reynolds said. "What's the plan?"

"When I asked for a *Kobayashi Maru*, I didn't think you were going to base your plan on an episode of *Star Trek*," Reynolds said. "Slingshotting around a pulsar? Are you delusional?"

"I am not letting Jiya present scientific information anymore," Takal said, shaking his head. "She got almost everything wrong. We wouldn't be slingshotting around the pulsar, we'd be waiting nearby for a gamma-ray burst."

"Still, you're suggesting we purposely expose the ship to gamma rays and who knows what other dangers on the chance it will multiply the Gate drive." Reynolds grimaced. "You're all crazy."

"I said it was risky," Takal said. He threw a visual onto the room's main screen. "But it isn't crazy. We've been observing this pulsar for the last two days. We've analyzed the data and know exactly what dangers we'd be exposed to. The signature of this star is almost identical to the radiation blast we encountered when we left Dorayas."

A spot flashed near the star projected on the screen. "We'll Gate to this point, which is outside the radiation zone. We wait until conditions are optimal; based on the light curves we've been tracking, we might have to wait a couple days for a gamma-ray burst. Then we Gate into the path of the burst."

Another spot pulsed. "We pause for three-point-two seconds, then Gate again, with the Devon system as our target. The extra polybdinum we infused into the Gate drive will be activated by the gamma radiation, and we'll get home."

Reynolds' drummed the table. Then he held up a finger. "What's the risk to our crew?

"From the jump?" Takal asked. "When we left Dorayas, we jumped a billion light-years. None of the crew experienced any negative effects. It's possible there was a protective element to the radiation we took at Dorayas, but it wasn't measurable. We've analyzed that data until we burned holes in the chips." He glanced at Reynolds. "Sorry."

The android waved his apology away.

"Since then," Takal continued, "Doc has been—*had* been monitoring crew biometrics on each jump. There's nothing to indicate the Gate has any negative impact on biological life forms, even at vast distances."

"What about the three-point-two seconds we're in the path of the burst?" Reynolds asked.

"Our shielding is built to withstand that," Takal said. "We have to wait that long to activate the polybdinum."

Reynolds raised a second finger. "Three-point-two seconds? Is that long enough to open a new Gate?"

Geroux took over. "We can pre-program the coordinates into the system. Because the waiting location is close, relatively speaking, to the final Gate position, we can make the jump without recalibrating. There will be a slightly larger margin of error, but even so, it will put us within striking distance of Devon." She shrugged. "We might have to make one more jump."

The captain's third finger went up. "Worst-case scenario?"

"Even if we jump one hundred eighty degrees in the wrong direction," Jiya said. "We're not much worse off than we are now. We'd be two years from home instead of one, but if XO and the rest aren't going to make it for one year, what difference does one more make? Sorry, that came out really crass." She ducked her head.

"We won't go in the wrong direction." Takal jumped in before Reynolds could respond. A narrow, shaded angle appeared on the screen, with the point located in the supernova. "When we came here, we went the right direction, we just over-shot by a billion light-years. We could end up several hundred thousand light-years off course—anywhere within this angle, in fact—but then we jump to Devon ten thousand at a time. We'll still get there much faster."

"We can sit here for hours, debating the possible dangers," Ka'nak said. "But if there's one thing we should have learned on this trip, it's that dangers exist everywhere. Furry vipers and death lace on a supposedly empty planet. Political machinations by primitive tribal leaders. Pirates backed by militant governments. Hell, Jiya fell out of a fucking tree."

Jiya shook her head and smiled before her expression turned serious.

"We can take the safe route and possibly lose some of our family," Jiya added, tipping her chin to the Melowi warrior. "Or we can take a risk and save everyone. If we fail, then maybe we all go out in a glorious supernova. I think it's an easy decision. I personally don't want to stay in this galaxy one second longer than I have to."

Reynolds took a deep breath, his drumming fingers finally stilling. "Prepare to Gate."

CHAPTER THIRTY-ONE

"Target?" Ria asked, suspecting she knew the answer.

"Blaze of glory," Reynolds replied.

That wasn't what the ensign expected. She cocked her head in confusion.

Takal stepped up. "High Tortuga. Deliver us to the Devon system in the Interdiction. One jump. Either we make it, or we go out in a blaze of glory."

One billion light-years. Unknown radiation exposure. Three-hundred-thousand-light-year margin of error. What the hell are you thinking? XO asked.

I'm saving your ass, so stop your whining and save your memory. Back in your box, XO. I've got it from here, Reynolds said. "Ensign, are the coordinates locked in?"

"Yes, sir," Ria said.

Reynolds opened the ship-wide broadcast. "Crew of the superdreadnought, this is your captain speaking. We're about to do something historic, but everything this ship has done in these galaxies has been historic. Besides everything we've accomplished, the most important has been that you have become my friends and family. You are joining me as we try to go back home, a billion light-years in one jump. All the time we've spent in this system has been to that single end. Thank goodness we didn't lose any of our crew during our trials. There is a great deal of danger out here, but you didn't blink. You went in with your eyes wide open. Maybe that was from shock; I'm not sure."

The captain waited for the snickers from the bridge crew to die down before he continued.

"I want to thank you for all you've done. Now it's time to go home. You will be welcomed by humanity, and most importantly," Reynolds paused for a significant amount of time, "you'll be amazed at how real coffee tastes compared to that motor oil you've been drinking. We are going to execute a double Gate—a short jump into the path of a gamma-ray burst, followed immediately by opening a new Gate that will take us a billion light-years, straight to High Tortuga. Battlestations! As soon as the board shows green, we're going home."

Reynolds stood with his hands behind his back and legs spread shoulder-width apart, like a captain of old manning the wooden deck of his sailing ships. He didn't bother to watch the crew doing their jobs: securing bulkheads, cycling systems, confirming ship status, and more. He was focused on the way ahead, through a physical Gate formed by an engine he operated within his previous body, the superdreadnought.

Now it was run by a meatbag standing in for the engineer, who was one of his alter egos. An individual in his own right, deserving of his own place as a member of the *Reynolds'* crew.

"All boards green. Ready to Gate," Asya reported.

"I have to note that he left out the blaze-of-glory part," Ka'nak whispered. Jiya slugged him in the arm.

"The three-point-two second delay is programmed. Gate is open," Ria reported.

"The gamma-ray burst is growing," Geroux stated. "Direction and speed are within parameters."

"Initiate sequence in three…" Takal counted down, "two…now!"

The *Reynolds* sailed through the Gate, instantly reappearing in the path of the burst. For three-point-two seconds, gamma rays bathed the polybdinum, charging the Gate drive to unparalleled power. Responding to programming, the new Gate opened, and the superdreadnought slid over the event horizon and through. Collectively, the crew held their breath, waiting to realize a million different outcomes, whatever their fertile minds could conceive.

The screens cleared with uncharacteristic snaps and pops. Reynolds winced at the noise. Geroux and Takal stood with their mouths open for just a moment, then they frantically started tapping buttons on their consoles.

"Ensign, where are we?" Reynolds demanded.

"Sir, I have no data," Ria replied, fear in her voice. "Navigation databanks are not finding a match for these stars."

"We're being hailed!" Jiya reported before transferring it to the main screen.

"Superdreadnought *Reynolds!*" A woman's image appeared. Behind her was a banner with the words High Tortuga Flight Control. "We are both pleased and surprised by your appearance, and you've brought company. Please hold your position and power down your weapons while we confirm your identity. When you left years ago, you were just a ship. Now it appears that you are a ship with a crew. May I ask who I'm speaking with?"

Reynolds smiled and spread his arms wide to take in the bridge crew. He looked from face to face before answering the woman on the screen. "I am Captain Reynolds in an advanced android body. My personality has been mostly split from the superdreadnought, 'split' being the operable term. There are eight of me, including seven within the ship's limited memory systems that have been infested by an aggressive fungus. We destroyed it by using extreme cold, but the systems holding the other variants of Reynolds are degrading, and we need help."

The woman whispered something off-screen. "Please remain where you are and do not attempt to send a Pod to the surface. We cannot risk an alien infestation."

"I concur, Flight Control. We can use the Gulg transportation system to bring the technology aboard for us to repair ourselves. My crew, who are mostly from Lariest, is one of the most capable in the universe. They will ensure that the ship and the variants of the AI you knew as Reynolds are free of danger before we interact in any way."

"Stand by," the woman said evenly before cutting the transmission.

"Not quite the warm group hug I was hoping for," Jiya said, moving to stand at Reynolds' side.

"Protocol, First Officer Jiya," Reynolds replied, his tone friendly. "I wouldn't let an alien-infested ship back in here, and I won't be responsible for infecting any other ships in the fleet."

Indicator lights on bridge consoles flashed and flickered as system tests confirmed functionality.

"We are no longer contagious," Geroux offered, "if I'm to continue your analogy. Is there any way I can talk to their technicians? I've heard data doesn't lie."

"Only those who interpret it." Reynolds tapped his nose with a finger. "We shall wait for them. We have returned to my home. Despite the suggestion by someone who won't be named who is wearing the title of XO that there was a three-hundred thousand light-year margin of error, you, Ensign Ria, Geroux, Takal, and the rest of the crew delivered us inside the eye of a needle at a billion light-years. Even with my processing capability, the odds were staggering, and I had little hope."

"Now you tell us!" Ka'nak blurted. He stood to join the others.

"This is what we do now?" Jiya asked, gesturing toward the group.

Asya shouldered her way into the group. "You mean, stand around the bridge and wait for someone in charge to make a decision? Let me see, where have I seen that before? That's right, every military ship I've ever served on. Every damn one."

"Even ones you were in charge of?" Ka'nak needled.

She laughed and shrugged. "Even my own. There's an unspoken tradition, it seems. I was powerless to change it."

Ka'nak clapped Reynolds on the back. "We made it. No supernova for us, or not yet, anyway. Do they have good chow and good drinks on this side of the void?"

Reynolds tipped his head to look down his nose. "The humans invented the word 'cuisine' and take their dining seriously. I think you'll be right at home here. Strong drink? They built empires based solely on beer and whiskey."

"My research into human culture based on videos from *Reynolds'* archives supports this," Jiya noted. Ka'nak grinned and clapped his hands, then rubbed them vigorously.

"When can we go ashore?"

The group glared at him as they stood, waiting. They turned to the screen as if that would expedite the process.

On cue, the main screen came to life. An angry man looked at them. Reynolds stepped forward. "I'll be damned if it isn't John Grimes! You're looking well." The captain said the rest to his crew, "Let me introduce one of the Queen's Bitches, a confidant and protector of the Queen. There is no fiercer warrior in the galaxy, outside of the Queen's husband and the Queen, of course."

John relaxed and leaned back. "Is that you, Reynolds? Looking like a human. What is the universe coming to? The most powerful ship in the fleet, and you leave it for that? Tell me you're enhanced and like Superman."

"I could tell you that, but I'd be lying."

"Meatbag." John pointed a finger at the screen.

"Is that who you got that from?" Jiya wondered, pushing Reynolds from behind.

"I haven't had the pleasure," John Grimes interrupted, fixing the group with his icy gaze.

"I'm Jiya Lemaire, First Officer of the Superdread-nought *Reynolds*. Geroux, Takal, General Maddox, Ka'nak,

Ria, and Captain Asya." Jiya pointed to the individuals as she named them. "Our crew is made up of people from different races, planets, and cultures. Still, Reynolds refers to us universally as meatbags. Are you an android, too?"

"Fuck off!" John spat at the screen. "One hundred percent human here, born and raised on Earth." He counted off on his fingers. "Maybe ninety-eight percent."

Somebody yelled from off-screen, "Seventy percent."

"Fuck off to you, too!" John shot back before looking once again at the screen, his face returning to its naturally angry appearance. "What to do with an infested ship?"

Geroux stepped forward. "This ship is not infested, and we demand that you help us save Reynolds' other person-alities!"

John shielded his eyes with a hand. "I hear someone speaking... Oh, there you are. Geroux, if I remember the name correctly. You have some spunk. I've met others like you. I *liked* them. What's your claim to fame?"

Takal gripped Geroux's shoulder and pulled her back into the group. "She is my niece and a computer genius. We're alive because of her."

Everyone shouted their approval before Reynolds called for calm.

"She has saved our lives. And so has everyone else. My crew. A cab driver. A prisoner. A pit fighter. A recluse. No claims to fame besides crewing the most powerful warship in the universe."

Ka'nak grimaced.

"You, pit fighter. What's with the face?" John Grimes pressed.

The Melowi warrior stood tall. "We got our asses kicked once or twice, but we survived."

"Maybe ten or twelve times, but that's beside the point," Reynolds confirmed. The others nodded in affirmation.

Someone whispered something from off-screen.

"I really fucking like the new Reynolds," John remarked. "I'm going to come up and see for myself. I'll be there soonest. Clear my Pod for direct access."

"You don't need a Pod," Reynolds said slowly. His and Geroux's eyes met. She tapped her wrist comp.

"Welcome aboard, John Grimes from Earth," she said before one final tap.

His brow furrowed the instant before the Gulg transporter snagged him from his seat in Flight Control and delivered him to the bridge of the superdreadnought, directly into the captain's chair with the crew surrounding him.

"That was great! Do it again," he requested.

"We can send you home the same way, John," Reynolds replied, offering his hand. The two shook, firmly, power in their grips. Ka'nak appreciated the show of strength, but Jiya and Asya both crossed their arms, wanting no part of a broken hand.

"I'm John Grimes," he told the assemblage. "Show me what's going on, and then let's see what we need to do to patch you up."

"Is the Queen around?" Reynolds asked.

"She's indisposed," he answered mysteriously. "A lot has happened since you left, and a lot has stayed the same."

"I see you haven't changed." Reynolds crossed himself in the ancient religious style.

"Damn, Reynolds! You get a new body and a case of ass to go with it. Maybe we should spar and see what you're really made of."

"I'd love to give you a good thrashing, old boy," Reynolds mocked in an accent that none of his crew recognized, "but I've got seven other versions of me that are dying. They need some hardware sooner rather than later."

"For the love of his crew." John nodded once. "Show me."

"Geroux?"

"Follow me," the young Larian said, glancing at Reynolds. "Uncle?"

Takal, Ka'nak, and Jiya fell in behind as Geroux led John Grimes from the bridge. After a brief pause, Reynolds hurried after them.

"You have the conn, Asya," he relayed over his shoulder.

The group started to run, loping easily to quickly cover the distance within the massive ship. John was almost as big as Ka'nak but looked more refined and smoother. The Melowi saw it, too. Jiya bumped him. "No," she whispered.

"I'm always up for a good ass-kicking, even if it's my own." He gave her the thumbs-up.

"Men are dumb," she told him.

Ka'nak started coughing to cover his laugh. John looked over his shoulder at Jiya.

"What's your claim to fame?" he asked.

"I'm a president's daughter, relegated to driving a cab because I embarrassed my family. Reynolds kidnapped me. Not this one." She stabbed a thumb over her shoulder at the android. "A creepy robot version."

"You kidnapped your crew?"

"There were conversations and a negotiation once we got past the initial distrust of aliens. I only offered them the tender caress of manacles until they calmed down."

"'The beatings will continue until morale improves,'" John quoted. "I guess you won them over, unless this is the worst case of Stockholm Syndrome I've ever seen."

"How many cases have you seen?" Reynolds asked.

"Counting this time? One."

"Not counting this time!" Reynolds grumped. "There is no 'this time.'"

"Touchy. Is he always like that?"

"I wouldn't know," Jiya replied. "He only takes off our shackles in the daytime."

"In here," Geroux said loudly to interrupt the banter. John instantly turned all business. Geroux pointed to the circuits that were operational before taking two from a box on the floor and holding them up to John. "This is what happened when the fungus infested the hardware. With fire, the fungus was only temporarily halted. It stayed dormant at higher temperatures and replicated like crazy in the cold, until extreme cold, close to absolute zero, killed it dead. The damage it has done is irrevocable, though. Our friends are trapped in too small a space. AIs are always expanding along a non-linear path. New memories won't necessarily be the first destroyed when they have nowhere to go."

"No threat?"

"None." Geroux was as confident as she could be. "We need processing power that only you people have. Our replicated processors aren't working."

John moved to an access station. He tapped the controls

until he brought up a ship-to-shore communication channel. "John here," he told the voice on the other end. "Send up the AI techs. Have them meet in the control room with as many memory and processor chips as they can carry. We'll beam them up."

"Beam them up?" the voice asked.

"It's really fucking cool. Get them there now. No time to waste."

The group stood around watching the technicians integrate circuits, reconnecting pathways with enviable efficiency. With additional jumpers to link the rest of the ship, they were ready.

"We push this in, and we're live. There's no risk to the rest of the ship?" the lead technician asked.

"We've searched the ship twice with all the crew and our maintenance bots since we've been here. *Reynolds* is clean," Geroux replied.

"Stand by for fireworks," John shouted and gave the technician the go-ahead. With a gentle push, the final circuit snapped into place, and the system energized.

"Who eats garlic kimchi before getting stuck in too small a space with his besties?" Tactical said in a series of belches. "This guy."

"What in the fuck is that?" John asked.

"Thank the stars!" XO exclaimed. "It was nearly intolerable. We prayed for death rather than listen to one more of Tactical's belch-fest singalongs. It was the most obscene thing I've ever heard."

"Weapons on target. He shoots. He scores!" Tactical shouted. "I'm free, hahahahaha."

"Your other personalities are insane?" John's lip quavered in revulsion.

"Not any more than you or I," Reynolds replied. "Tactical is a bit hard to take on the best of days, which today is shaping up to be. XO, Comm, the engineer, Doc, and a few others? They are individuals."

"Funny you should mention that," John started. "AIs have full rights as individuals now. That was a recent court ruling. We have to ask you as an independent sentient being if you want to serve the Queen and then negotiate a contract."

"That sounds marvelous," Reynolds replied.

"I'm warming to the idea, but it looks like we've got eight of you to rope in. Maybe seven, if that Tactical guy doesn't measure up as intelligent."

"Shackles?" Reynolds sent a single eyebrow upward.

"Just until you agree to our demands." John offered his hand once more, and Reynolds took it.

"We're clear," the lead technician noted while they packed their gear.

"Come on down and meet the kiddos," John offered.

"You have kids?" Reynolds was surprised.

"Not me, or rather, mine are grown and have left the nest." John smiled conspiratorially. "The Queen's…"

The End of Superdreadnought

Reynolds is home, and aliens from a distant galaxy came with him to establish their own place among the humans.

AUTHOR NOTES - CRAIG MARTELLE

OCTOBER 26, 2019

Thank you for reading this book, and you're still reading! Oorah, hard-chargers. I really hope you liked this story and this series! That is it. Super-dreadnought 6 is the last book in the Superdreadnought series. We left some threads hanging and hopefully brought everything to fruition with this last book.

This series has run its course. We lost readers somewhere in there. I'm sure there are plenty of reasons, but when I have a series like Judge, Jury, and Executioner that blows up the charts when it's released, I have to stick with that. Go with what works and our space lawyer is the best there is when it comes to working. But you'll Superdreadnought Reynolds again. There's a war coming and the Kurtherians are bringing it to Earth. Bethany Anne will be leading all available forces in the final fight, the end game. *Reynolds* wouldn't miss his chance to support the Queen.

Back in Alaska, it has been unseasonably warm. Our lows every day are below freezing, but the highs are occasionally peaking back above 32F leaving us with no snow. It snowed this morning though when it was supposed to be raining. I just checked the ten-day forecast and it looks like we'll be into November before the highs are consistently below freezing. A couple years ago, we had 142 consecutive days with the high below freezing, but that's the way it is this close to the Arctic Circle. Snow is good, but we won't get the solid blanket for a while yet.

When we have a blanket of snow, the trees fill with hoarfrost, sound from the main road a quarter mile away dampens, and it brightens the long, dark nights. It's also a way for me to know which animals are out and about. Phyllis has been interested in one bush for a week now. This morning, I saw why. A rabbit frequents it. And judging by the massive bunny prints, it's a snowshoe. We also have an Arctic Lynx that shows up on occasion. For a forty-pound cat, their paw prints are bigger than my size tens. That's so they can run on top of the snow, just like the snowshoe. Big feet come in handy where you have six months of snow.

My tractor with snowblower is ready. My walk-behind snow blower is ready, but my generator is not ready. I couldn't get it started last time I checked it. That could be tragic. I need to get that fixed and stock up on gasoline. I like having 25 to 30 gallons hanging around, just in case.

Everything we do up here is just in case. We have six months' worth of food, water, toiletries, and more.

Just in case. We plan for the worst – to be without power for thirty days. And during those thirty days, we expect to be generally trapped in the house, too. With temperatures that could plummet to -40F, extra measures have to be in place. A power outage becomes a life or death situation in mere hours if you don't have your wits about you.

But we do, so all is well. Except for that generator. I'll get to it one of these days.

Back to the word mines to find those golden nuggets for you.

Please join my Newsletter (www.craigmartelle.com – please, please, please sign up!), or you can follow me on Facebook since you'll get the same opportunity to pick up the books for only 99 cents on that first Saturday after they are published.

If you liked this story, you might like some of my other books. You can join my mailing list by dropping by my website www.craigmartelle.com, or if you have any comments, shoot me a note at craig@craigmartelle.com. I am always happy to hear from people who've read my work. I try to answer every email I receive.

If you liked the story, please write a short review for me on Amazon. I greatly appreciate any kind words. Even one or two sentences go a long way. The number of reviews an ebook receives greatly improves how well it does on Amazon.

Amazon – www.amazon.com/author/craigmartelle

BookBub – https://www.bookbub.com/authors/craig-martelle

Facebook – www.facebook.com/authorcraigmartelle

My web page – www.craigmartelle.com

Peace, fellow humans.

Craig Martelle's other books (listed by series)

Terry Henry Walton Chronicles (co-written with Michael Anderle) – a post-apocalyptic paranormal adventure

Gateway to the Universe (co-written with Justin Sloan & Michael Anderle) – this book transitions the characters from the Terry Henry Walton Chronicles to The Bad Company

The Bad Company (co-written with Michael Anderle) – a military science fiction space opera

Judge, Jury, & Executioner (also available in audio) – a space opera adventure legal thriller

Shadow Vanguard – a Tom Dublin series

Superdreadnought (co-written with Tim Marquitz)– an AI military space opera

Metal Legion (co-written with Caleb Wachter) (coming in audio) – a military space opera

The Free Trader – a young adult science fiction action adventure

Cygnus Space Opera (also available in audio) – A young adult space opera (set in the Free Trader universe)

Darklanding (co-written with Scott Moon) (also available in audio) – a space western

Mystically Engineered (co-written with Valerie Emerson) – Mystics, dragons, & spaceships

End Times Alaska (also available in audio) – a Permuted Press publication – a post-apocalyptic survivalist adventure

Nightwalker (a Frank Roderus series) with Craig Martelle – A post-apocalyptic western adventure

End Days (co-written with E.E. Isherwood) (coming in audio) – a post-apocalyptic adventure

Successful Indie Author – a non-fiction series to help self-published authors

Metamorphosis Alpha – stories from the world's first science fiction RPG

The Expanding Universe – science fiction anthologies

Monster Case Files (co-written with Kathryn Hearst) – A Warner twins mystery adventure

Rick Banik (also available in audio) – Spy & terrorism action adventure

Published exclusively by Craig Martelle, Inc

The Dragon's Call by Angelique Anderson & Craig A. Price, Jr. – an epic fantasy quest

For a complete list of Craig's books, stop by his website – https://craigmartelle.com